PENGUIN CLASSICS

MADAME BOVARY

GUSTAVE FLAUBERT, the younger son of a provincial doctor, was born in the town of Rouen in 1821. While still a schoolboy, full of romantic scorn for the bourgeois world, he professed himself 'disgusted with life'. At the age of eighteen he was sent to study law in Paris, but had no regrets when a mysterious nervous ailment interrupted this career after only three years. Flaubert retired to live with his widowed mother in the family home at Croisset, on the banks of the river Seine, near Rouen. Supported by a private income, he devoted himself to his writing.

In his early work, particularly *The Temptation of Saint Antony*, he gave free rein to his flamboyant imagination, but on the advice of his friends he subsequently disciplined this romantic exuberance in an effort to achieve artistic objectivity and a harmonious prose style. This perfectionism cost him enormous toil and brought him only limited success in his own lifetime. After the publication of *Madame Bovary* in 1857 he was prosecuted for offending public morals; his exotic novel, *Salammbô* (1862), was criticized for its encrustations of archaeological detail; *Sentimental Education* (1869), intended as the moral history of his generation, was largely misunderstood by the critics; and the political play *The Candidate* (1874) was a disastrous failure. Only *Three Tales* (1877) was an unqualified success, but it appeared when Flaubert's spirits, health and finances were at their lowest ebb.

After his death in 1880 Flaubert's fame and reputation grew steadily, strengthened by the publication of his unfinished comic masterpiece *Bouvard and Pécuchet* (1881) and the many remarkable volumes of his correspondence.

GEOFFREY WALL teaches French at the University of York. He also works as a literary biographer and a travel writer. His biography of Flaubert (2001) has been translated into four languages.

Half English and half French, MICHÈLE ROBERTS was born in 1949. She is the author of ten highly praised novels: *A Piece of the Night* (1978), *The Visitation* (1983), *The Wild Girl* (1984), *The Book of Mrs Noah* (1987), *In the Red Kitchen* (1990), *Daughters of the House* (1992), *Flesh & Blood* (1994), *Impossible Saints*

(1997), *Fair Exchange* (1999) and *The Looking Glass* (2000). She has also published collections of short stories, including *During Mother's Absence* (1993) and *Playing Sardines* (2001); three books of poetry, including *All the Selves I Was: Selected Poems 1986–1994* (1995); a book of essays, *On Food, Sex and God: On Inspiration and Writing* (1998); and co-authored four volumes of short stories. *Daughters of the House* was shortlisted for the 1992 Booker Prize and won the W. H. Smith Literary Award in 1993.

GUSTAVE FLAUBERT

Madame Bovary

PROVINCIAL LIVES

Translated with an Introduction and Notes by
GEOFFREY WALL
Preface by MICHÈLE ROBERTS

PENGUIN BOOKS

For Sara

PENGUIN BOOKS

Published by the Penguin Group
Penguin Books Ltd, 80 Strand, London WC2R ORL, England
Penguin Putnam Inc., 375 Hudson Street, New York, New York 10014, USA
Penguin Books Australia Ltd, 250 Camberwell Road, Camberwell, Victoria 3124, Australia
Penguin Books Canada Ltd, 10 Alcorn Avenue, Toronto, Ontario, Canada M4V 3B2
Penguin Books India (P) Ltd, 11 Community Centre, Panchsheel Park, New Delhi – 110 017, India
Penguin Books (NZ) Ltd, Private Bag 102902, NSMC, Auckland, New Zealand
Penguin Books (South Africa) (Pty) Ltd, 24 Sturdee Avenue, Rosebank 2196, South Africa

Penguin Books Ltd, Registered Offices: 80 Strand, London WC2R ORL, England

www.penguin.com

This translation first published 1992
Reissued with new Preface and Further Reading 2003

19

Copyright © Geoffrey Wall, 1992, 2003
Preface copyright © Michèle Roberts, 2003
All rights reserved

The moral right of the translator has been asserted

Set in 10.25/12.25 pt PostScript Adobe Sabon
Typeset by Rowland Phototypesetting Ltd, Bury St Edmunds, Suffolk
Printed in England by Clays Ltd, St Ives plc

ISBN-13: 978–0–140–44912–9

Contents

Preface

Wonderful Flaubert to pack so many different stories into one book, and to make all the parts and layers seem so perfectly fitted together.

Closing the novel, you might be crying your eyes out, as Flaubert himself was when he wrote the final, tragic scenes. Later on, you might start to wonder. You go back and reread. Like an aggressive child pulling a dead fly apart, you ask: what's this made of? We cannot, of course, respond exactly as Flaubert's contemporaries did to his masterpiece; great upheavals in our intellectual, political and sexual lives have subsequently intervened. We read differently. Yet this novel is a classic precisely because it goes on inviting generation after generation of readers into a passionate conversation about the dilemmas and conflicts it depicts.

Madame Bovary is utterly modern. It's the first sex-and-shopping novel, after all. Emma Bovary, desperately seeking satisfaction and fulfilment, employs retail therapy as an escape from an unhappy marriage, experiments with adultery, is obsessed with money and with material objects as substitutes for happiness. She's convinced it's men who've got it all: power and freedom and choice and ease of movement. She can't buy herself the male privileges she envies, so she spends money on blue glass vases and new curtains instead.

Madame Bovary is also modern in that it offers a take on that despised feminine genre, the romance, which is written off in our day as trash or as chick-lit. Emma's problems appear to stem from her belief that life should run sweetly as a romantic novel. Why do women read romances? Is it just because, as

Flaubert's narrator appears to suggest, women are weak and silly? What purpose do romances serve for Emma and her contemporaries? Some critics argue that, perhaps, in a culture that insists that women marry, that gives them little education or freedom, and which makes divorce unthinkable, their dramas allow a female reader to rehearse certain desperate questions. Does the figure of the villain conceal that of a hero? Will the hero turn out a villain? How do I know I've made the right choice? How do I know my husband will be good to me? The romances close off these important questions, even as they offer sentimental and reassuring answers. Emma depends on her reading, a consoling drug, because she is completely isolated, with no one to talk things over with. She is motherless. She has no women friends. She can't confide in her unsympathetic mother-in-law. Her maid can't help. The nuns at her school, and her local priest, offer only reactionary clichés. The Church denies to women any creative power other than that of mother-hood; and even that is proof of women's fallen nature. To want more is wicked. Emma is on her own, just like the heroine of a romance, and she has been brought up to require a male saviour.

If foolish women read fantasy, then wise men show the way things truly are. That's the set-up this novel proposes and sub-verts. It offers precise, sensual images of the material world, confident analyses of people's inner lives. Not necessarily objec-tive, though. Flaubert's famous doctrine of impersonality can't conceal his narrator's masculine point of view. His trousers peep out from under his skirts. *Madame Bovary* describes, sometimes mocks and sometimes accepts, a male-dominated society, a male-defined double standard of sexual morality. Emma is buried alive in this culture, which is why her story is necessarily buried inside that of her husband and Homais the pharmacist.

Flaubert is celebrated for his relish of grotesquerie, comedy, even cruelty. These energies help propel his story, as when, for example, Emma's final, desperate zigzag flight around Yonville ironically mirrors her earlier wild progress in the closed cab around Rouen. These abrupt rhythms co-exist with stiller gazes, with perspectives that are loving, tender and intimate. The

Norman landscape, the setting for the novel, is closely observed, vividly described. Emma can't appreciate the natural beauty surrounding her, because she's grown up in it and takes it for granted as the place where you live and work: the prison confining her. She can appreciate the charms of the forest only when she and Rodolphe have made love there for the first time; then sexual pleasure opens her eyes. Beauty for her resides elsewhere: in daydreams; in the tawdry ornaments and furnishings she brings in, bought on credit from the village draper. We glimpse her at her window, gazing longingly out. But Flaubert, looking in on her world from outside, paints exquisite still-lives of kitchens, workshops and dining rooms, with startling freshness and clarity. *Madame Bovary* is a supremely beautiful novel. Its world is always that of the everyday, but transfigured by Flaubert's vision. Sometimes he makes the reader feel like a mystic, appreciating the truth of material objects for what seems the first time. Sometimes he makes the reader feel like a voyeur, spying on Emma shaking down her long black hair, taking off her clothes.

But why does the woman have to die?

Women do, in nineteenth-century art. Look at opera, for example, and count the bodies.

In terms of this particular novel, on the plane of its apparent realism, we could say that Emma is simply desperate and ashamed; unable to face the ruin she has brought upon her family; anticipating the punishment the law and the Church would wish to inflict on her.

Mixed up with the moral transgression, however, is another.

In an early scene, in which, 'like a man', Emma wears a tortoiseshell lorgnon, we hear her speak for the first time when she asks Charles: 'Are you looking for something?' He has lost his riding-crop; Emma finds it for him; his desire is born. Later she plays with other masculine symbols, appropriating them to her own use: smoking cigarettes, drinking an entire tumbler of brandy, donning a waistcoat, wearing male fancy dress to a masked ball. She dominates her lover, Léon, both in bed and out of it. She escapes the traditional feminine enclosure of the house to roam the countryside and the city streets. Not content with working unpaid as a wife and mother running the house-hold, she steals the money which society decrees belongs to her husband.

Stealing masculine power and masculine privilege, Emma mixes up the categories of male and female. She becomes, in the terms of her world, less of a woman and more of a monster. She cannot be allowed to live.

Michèle Roberts

Acknowledgements

Thanks to all who generously gave advice, encouragement and inspiration: Emma Beddington, Jacques Berthoud, Andrew Boobier, Treva Broughton, Mike Brudenell, Fenella Clarke, Woof Clarke, Ruth Clayton, Jack Donovan, Richard Drain, Hugh Haughton, Peter Hulme, Angela Hurworth, Paul Keegan, David Moody, Mark Olsen, John Perren, Mary Perren, Sara Perren, Donna Poppy, Marcelle Saunders, Frank Wall, Gwyneth Wall and Nicole Ward-Jouve.

Chronology

1802 Achille-Cléophas Flaubert, Gustave's father, arrives in Paris to study medicine.

1810 Achille-Cléophas Flaubert moves to Rouen to work as deputy head of the hospital (known as the Hôtel-Dieu).

1812 Achille-Cléophas Flaubert marries the adopted daughter of the head of the Hôtel-Dieu.

1813 Birth of Achille Flaubert, Gustave's brother.

1819 Achille-Cléophas Flaubert appointed head of Hôtel-Dieu on the death of his superior. The family moves to the residential wing of the hospital.

1820 Achille-Cléophas Flaubert begins to buy parcels of land and property outside Rouen.

1821 December: birth of Gustave Flaubert.

1824 July: birth of Caroline Flaubert, Gustave's sister.

1825 The servant 'Julie' enters the service of the Flaubert family.

1830 First surviving letter by Flaubert.

1832 Enters Collège de Rouen as a boarder. Creation of *Le Garçon*, an anarchic Rabelaisian joker.

1835 Summer holidays on the coast, at Trouville. Meets the Collier family.

1836 First encounter with Elisa Schlésinger, on the beach at Trouville.

1839 Elder brother qualifies in medicine and marries.

1840 Passes final school examinations; voyage to Corsica with Jules Cloquet. Amour de voyage, in Marseille, with Eulalie Foucaud.

1841 November: registers as law student in Paris, though continues to live at home.

1842 July: moves to Paris. December: passes first-year law exams.

1843 February: writing first version of *L'Éducation sentimentale*. March: first meeting with Maxime Du Camp. August: fails second-year law exams.

1844 January: first nervous attack. April: father buys house at Croisset. June: Flaubert family moves to Croisset.

1845 March: sister marries Émile Hamard. April–June: family travelling in Italy. November: father falls ill.

1846 January: father dies; sister gives birth to a daughter. March: sister dies. July: first encounter with Louise Colet; marriage of Alfred Le Poittevin. August: begins friendship with Louis Bouilhet; first letter to Louise Colet.

1847 May–August: walking tour in Brittany with Maxime Du Camp.

1848 February: arrives in Paris, with Bouilhet, to see the street-fighting. April: death of Alfred Le Poittevin. May: begins work on first version of *La Tentation de saint Antoine*. August: break with Louise Colet. September: finishes first version of *Saint Antoine*. October: embarks with Du Camp on eighteen-month tour of the Orient.

1850 February: voyage up the Nile. May: crossing the desert by camel. August: death of Balzac; Flaubert and Du Camp arrive in Jerusalem. September: plan for journey to Persia abandoned; the travellers turn west. October: Rhodes. November: Constantinople. December: Athens.

1851 April: Flaubert in Rome; Du Camp returns to Paris. May: Flaubert arrives home in Croisset; resumes relations with Louise Colet. September: begins writing *Madame Bovary*.

1852 January: Du Camp awarded Légion d'honneur. September: Du Camp becomes editor of the *Revue de Paris*.

1853 September: death of père Parain, a favourite uncle.

1854 October: final break with Louise Colet.

1855 October: takes rooms in Paris.

1856 April: finishes *Madame Bovary*. May: rewriting *Saint Antoine*. October: first instalment of *Madame Bovary* published in *Revue de Paris*.

1857 January: Flaubert prosecuted for publishing an immoral book. February: Bovary trial ends in acquittal. April: *Madame Bovary* published in book form. October: begins work on *Salammbô*.

1858 April–June: visits Carthage and North Africa, site of *Salammbô*.

1862 February: finishes *Salammbô*. November: *Salammbô* published.

1863 January: first letter to George Sand. February: first meeting with Turgenev.

1864 January: niece Caroline engaged to Ernest Commainville. May: begins work on *L'Éducation sentimentale*. November: first visit to Compiègne as guest of the Emperor.

1866 August: nominated Chevalier de la Légion d'honneur. November: George Sand's first visit to Croisset.

1868 May: George Sand staying in Croisset.

1869 May: finishes *L'Éducation sentimentale*. July: death of Louis Bouilhet. November: publication of *L'Éducation sentimentale*. December: spends Christmas with George Sand in Nohant.

1870 August: beginning of Franco-Prussian war. December: victorious German troops arrive in Rouen.

1871 January: armistice signed with Prussia. May: insurrection in Paris. July: German troops leave Rouen.

1872 April: death of Flaubert's mother. June: finishes final version of *Saint Antoine*.

1874 March: *La Tentation de saint Antoine* published. August: begins writing *Bouvard et Pécuchet*.

1875 Bad health and financial problems. September: begins writing *La Légende de saint Julien*.

1876 March: death of Louise Colet. June: death of George Sand. August: finishes writing *Un Coeur simple*. November: begins work on *Hérodias*.

1877 April: publication of *Trois contes*.

1879 October: awarded official pension.

1880 February: Du Camp elected to the Académie française. May: death of Flaubert.

1881 House at Croisset is sold and subsequently demolished to make way for a distillery.

1882 January: death of brother, Achille Flaubert. Du Camp publishes his *Souvenirs littéraires*.

Introduction

THE AUTHOR

Born in 1821, Flaubert was the son of a highly successful provincial doctor, the director and chief surgeon of the municipal hospital in the town of Rouen. His family lived in the gloomy residential wing of the hospital, in the midst of blood and death, as Flaubert always remembered it. Just over the wall of the garden where he played as a child, there were corpses laid out in the dissecting-room. He and his sister would peep over the wall to observe their father, with his sleeves rolled up, probing and slicing, pausing to wave them angrily away from the forbidden spectacle.

Because he was merely the younger son, Gustave Flaubert was to be a lawyer. He began the training for his allotted profession with a heavy heart. But then in 1844, when he was twenty-three, the first of a series of disasters struck his family. On the very threshold of his adult career, he experienced the first of his so-called nervous attacks. Stricken by convulsions and hallucinations, he fell into a coma, followed by days of drowsiness and weeks of exhaustion. It was like an epileptic fit, though never conclusively diagnosed. But it was enough to keep him at home. He now had to abandon the legal studies he so detested. Henceforth he could enjoy the unmolested leisure of the convalescent. This was exactly what he wanted: time to write, time to savour the world.

In the following year, 1845, his sister Caroline, three years his junior and still an adored companion, was married. In Flaubert's opinion, the man of her choice was 'mediocrity incarnate', quite the stupidest of all his contemporaries.

In November 1845 Flaubert's father fell ill, with an abscess on his leg. He died of gangrene, after weeks of agony. Six days later, Caroline gave birth to a daughter, in that same house, where her father had just died. She caught puerperal fever and died six weeks later.

The premature deaths of his father and sister, along with the marriage of his elder brother, left Flaubert, aged twenty-five, at the head of a strange and sorrowful family. Mother and son, both of them twice bereft, set up house together, along with the motherless infant daughter of Caroline. The arrangement lasted for most of Flaubert's adult life. It was a family of sorts: a man and a woman and a child.

In 1849, after a decent interval had elapsed, Flaubert set off on an eighteen-month tour of the Near East. The letters he wrote from Egypt chronicle in exuberant detail the delights of temples and brothels. The grotesque conjunction of the sacred and the profane pleased him deeply. He spent a large part of his inheritance and he caught syphilis.

He returned to France in 1851. That autumn, in the month before his thirtieth birthday, he began work on *Madame Bovary*. He had promised himself and his friends that his first book would be a *thunderclap*. His début was indeed to be his masterpiece.

For his subject Flaubert took the unheroic, mediocre, provincial, everyday heart of *petit bourgeois* village life. He listened intently to the language of his class. He mimicked unerringly the pompous rhythms of paternal cliché as they sounded benignly from the lips of the doctor, the lawyer, the journalist and the priest. He had been listening since childhood, and he had a connoisseur's ear. He kept a scrap-book, entitled *The Dictionary of Received Ideas*, in which he collected and classified the choicest specimens. He marked the different voices, the public and the private, all the rival major dialects of medicine and science, romanticism and religion.

Gustave Flaubert, the contemporary of Baudelaire, Marx and George Eliot, never attempted any conspicuous escape from the constraints of his class. On the contrary, he stayed at home, most of his life, an awkward, disenchanted, mocking, loyal member of the bourgeoisie.

He saw that there was little point in attacking them openly. In 1851 only the quixotic revolutionary would have possessed such an infinite surplus of courage, hope and energy. As it seemed to Flaubert, there was quite obviously no better world, no other world than this. Consider the history of France over the preceding sixty years. Two revolutions, in 1789 and in 1848, had strengthened the power of the bourgeoisie and thereby proved, apparently, that there was no *real* alternative. For those seeking an escape there were only vivid enclosed worlds of fantasy. Baudelaire called them *artificial paradises*: wine, hashish, opium, prostitution, anarchism, occultism, dandyism, the Orient. Flaubert had tasted several of them and chosen to return home. The age of Byron was over. To Flaubert it made much better sense, and it would, he felt sure, be rather more agreeable, to attack his kind not by open rebellion, not in an embittered tirade, but by demoralizing his class from within.

To this end, he took first of all the stalest, the most predictable plot. It featured a man and a wife: he mediocre and contented, she bored and beautiful. She yearns for romance, takes a lover and eventually kills herself, in the midst of debt and despair. To quicken this commonplace stuff he invented a new style, weaving together the erotic, the sentimental and the ironic, in a perpetual tension, making it seem quite impersonal, and meticulously prosaic. Everyone talks in clichés, with not a word out of place, the rhythm holding it all together. He wanted to avoid, above all, the wretched flowing style, so soothing for the bourgeois reader whose taste in fiction had been formed by his great precursors, Walter Scott, Balzac, George Sand and Victor Hugo.

The style Flaubert invented for *Madame Bovary* was supremely influential. Though its origins are deeply idiosyncratic, it was to become the characteristic idiom of later realist fiction. It is now so pervasively familiar that it sounds like the true voice of modernity. Zola, Chekhov and Joyce, Kafka, Sartre and Camus: all take lessons from Flaubert.

What did he teach?

First of all, he cut dialogue down to a minimum. The characters have no long speeches. The unspoken comes into sharp
focus. There is no one obviously telling the story. There is simply
a voice coming from somewhere; it could almost be one of the
characters. The world of quite unremarkable everyday things is
described, in engagingly vivid detail: the dusty smell of a village
church, the stale warmth of a school class-room, the sound of a
family eating a meal together, the feel of dried mud flaking off
an elegant woman's boot.

Flaubert was naturally fluent and copious as a writer, but
it took him five years to write *Madame Bovary*. He worked
fastidiously, compulsively, often sixteen hours a day, revising
every sentence many times over, until it sounded exactly and
exquisitely as it should. In the new age of mass-production, in
a world of cheap crude fiction manufactured in quantity, every
sentence of this novel was to declare the enormity of the labour
that had gone into its making. It was to be a luxury item,
gratuitously crafted and minutely detailed. His mother
remarked, judiciously, that the pursuit of the perfect phrase had
desiccated his heart.

Madame Bovary carries as its subtitle *Moeurs de province*.
This might be translated as *Provincial Lives*. The phrase implies,
of course, the familiar indiscriminate contrast between Paris
and the rest of France. The Parisian, according to popular
belief, was a superior self-important creature: elegant, educated,
pretentious, superficial and cynical. The provincial, according
to the same mythology, was in every way inferior: uncouth,
narrow-minded, and avaricious, governed by petty jealousies
and engrossed in sanctimonious gossip. Before Flaubert, in the
1830s and the 1840s, the novelist Balzac had energetically contributed to these stereotypes; and Flaubert, not surprisingly, is
content to perpetuate them. The traditional contrast between
Paris and the provinces is an essential part of Flaubert's design.

The novel was written in the early 1850s. In France this was
the first decade of the railway. It was a time when the new
means of communication – the railway, the telegraph and the
newspaper – were accelerating the circulation of people, commodities and information. The country village was beginning to

feel the first shock of the new. The old small-scale local economy was changing. This was particularly evident in the northern region (Flanders, Normandy and Picardy), which had the most technically advanced agriculture, the best soils, the biggest farms and the richest farmers in France. Though Flaubert was writing *Madame Bovary* at a time and in a place of rapid social change, he contrived to locate it just outside this fast-encroaching modernity, in the last years of the old world. He emphasizes this by including fleeting references to present realities, little details and phrases which cumulatively frame the past-ness of the story. The so-called local colour, the Normandy idioms and the place-names both real and imaginary, add up to a code of deliberately *parochial* reference. They are silent gestures towards a fading common life of regional peculiarities.

THE HUSBAND

The story begins with a scene in a school class-room. A new boy arrives, wearing a remarkably ugly hat. He is not yet in uniform, which was always military-style for schoolboys in those days. He is, quite untranslatably, *en bourgeois*, Bourgeois: the word is present, discreetly, in the very opening sentence, simply the name of a code of dress. When he is asked to say his name, the new boy mumbles something quite inaudible. Then he bellows it out: *Charles Bovary!* It sounds like *Charbovari*. His awkwardness makes him the target of raucous collective mockery. There is uproar in the class-room. They all shout his name – *Charbovari! Charbovari!* – and stamp their feet to its sound.

We have begun with a *charivari*: ritualized anarchy. Originally the charivari was a serenade of rough music made by villagers banging under the newly-weds' window with kettles and pans, deriding an incongruous marriage. More generally, it came to mean the anarchic ritual mockery of an unpopular person. Latterly, the custom gave its name to a satirical magazine published in Paris, *Le Charivari*, the favourite reading matter of Flaubert's boyhood.

Charles's strange hat has been traced back to a cartoon in an issue of *Le Charivari* which appeared when Flaubert was twelve years old. But its meaning, in the novel, comes primarily from its context. It is a real monster of a hat. It breaks most of the rules for an object that then conveyed so economically the niceties of male social status. It is compounded bizarrely from real pieces of animal material (the bear, the beaver, the whale and the rabbit), from the shapes and the colours of edible things (prunes and sausages), and from an abstract geometry of circles and ovoids and polygons. It may recall, distantly, various descriptions in classical epic writing of the warrior-hero's helmet. Usually such objects are the naïvely superlative emblems of their wearer's valour. This inglorious bourgeois artefact announces an idiot.

The story is being told by one of Charles's classmates, remembering the scene in later life. There are clear traces of his schoolboy idiom. But we soon shift to a more spacious retrospect, looking further back in time. We hear of Charles Bovary's parents, the early days of their marriage, Charles's boyhood in the village, the priest who taught him to read, his mother's ambitions for him; then, jumping over his time at school, we learn about his days as a medical student and his mother's manoeuvres to marry him to a rich widow. By the end of the first chapter Charles is established as a young village doctor, firmly under the thumb of his new wife.

The opening chapter has the compactness and the quick tempo of a short-story. The sense of a life is deftly sketched out for us. But we are left, already, with questions unanswered. What about the remarkable hat? Why does it disappear, never to be mentioned again, when it has been so abundantly described? Is this Charles *genuinely* stupid? Does it matter if he is? Who is the novel going to be about? This young man seems far too dull to hold our interest.

Flaubert is exhibiting, by way of prelude, the drama of cultural formation. We follow, in the person of Charles, the making of average bourgeois man. We see the lengthy schooling it requires, at the hands of father and priest, schoolteacher and professor. We see how it takes a subjection to the disciplines of reading and writing, what sacrifices it exacts to the occult powers of the printed word. We know that Flaubert had suffered as a child, being supposed stupid because he was a slow reader, a dreamer with his mouth sagging open. And he had escaped from it all at the last possible moment, by taking refuge in illness. But Charles is not that clever. He is typically befuddled, indifferent, incompetent or just mechanically conscientious. He scrapes through, at each stage of his education, until he is perched, joylessly, in a job and a marriage and a house.

Only when this Charles meets Emma, the daughter of one of his patients, a rich farmer, is there another fully realized scene describing their first encounter. We see her through his eyes, at the farmhouse, in the kitchen, at the door or in the window. We notice her dress, hands, eyes, hair, lips. We hear her speak only one brief phrase.

There is so little dialogue, other than simple questions and answers. We notice that these characters do not speak their minds to each other. We are not certain of the value of what we are told. Everything seems to be, fictionally, normal. We know the who, the where, the when and the what. But the *why* escapes us. We may well overlook the real oddity of this as we move from the predominantly reported speech of the characters to the flowing voice of the story. There is an elusive but systematic ambiguity. These slightly peculiar features of the story are some- how connected: the paucity of the dialogue, the fleeting uncer- tainties of the narrative, the uncanny insistent authority of the writing itself.

It is also remarkable, in retrospect, that Emma's story should begin with these scenes from Charles's early life; remarkable too that it should end with the prolonged and inglorious tale of *his* descent into misery after her death. The husband's story clearly frames the story of his wife. Perhaps this is a form of subordination? A gesture of enclosure and control, whereby the feminine is put in its place, textually? It may conceivably be a sarcastic tribute to the social power of men. Or it may be only the heedless echo of that power. We are left with our suspicions.

We do know that Flaubert, a bachelor who lived with his mother, richly detested husbands and fatherhood and so-called conjugal love. The letters he wrote at the time of his elder brother's marriage are full of acid jokes about copulating newly-weds struck down by disaster. And he was evidently appalled, for deeper reasons, by his beloved sister's choice of husband. He deeply resented his best friend's marriage. 'Another person I love,' he lamented in a letter, 'is lost to me.' And he felt panic when his mistress, Louise Colet, tried to entangle him.

He saw husbands and fathers, in the main, as banal tyrants. But the women of his class appeared to be more spirited, less sluggishly conformist than their men. He had been entranced, one summer in his early adolescence, by Elisa Schlésinger, the stylish and seductive wife harnessed to a mediocre husband.

THE WIFE

At last we meet the heroine, the woman who gives the book its title. Though when we meet her she is not yet Madame Bovary. She is still Mademoiselle Emma Rouault. Charles's current wife is Madame Bovary; and so is his mother. Indeed there are three women in the book variously called Madame Bovary. The phrase, of course, refers to a social position: any woman who is the wife-of-Bovary can be called Madame Bovary. The heroine is ordinarily referred to as Emma. Her mother-in-law is apparently the veritable Madame Bovary.

The story is going to explore the space between those two names, between the intimate reality of Emma and the public masquerade of Madame Bovary. Emma has to live buried 'inside' Madame Bovary.

All through the courtship and the events of their wedding-day, we hear scarcely a word spoken. We follow the early days of their marriage, the house they live in, her face as he sees it on the pillow in the morning light, his myopic pleasure in her, and, for the very first time, a hint of her feelings towards him. He is kissing her arm, and she is holding him away: 'half laughing and half annoyed, just as one would with a clinging child'. When Emma finally comes into the foreground, she is already disappointed.

It is only when Flaubert has emphatically established that

disappointment, that he takes us back into Emma's early life. We now witness something of *her* cultural formation. Significantly, this making of the wife is more luxuriantly detailed, more closely rendered, than the parallel making of the husband.

We follow her education in conventional piety at a convent school. We are also offered a sustained evocation of her unofficial adolescent reading. This is a crucial point in the representation of Emma. The plausible imaginative immediacy of the writing masks a large unargued assumption that Emma's nascent feminine romanticism is only an inferior schoolgirl version of the real thing. Her romanticism is fashioned from the historical novels of Scott and the lyric poetry of Lamartine. All this is adulterated by the indiscriminate addition of quantities of anonymous sub-literary trash: oriental ballads, sentimental fiction, keepsake albums, picture-books and love-songs. Flaubert assumes that women are the perpetually credulous and eternally subordinate consumers of the most mediocre fantasy. It is not, he implies, a political problem of education and conditioning. It seems to be in the nature of the feminine itself.

Emma's reading exists in a radically disconnected form: as scenes, bits of stories, vivid fragments. In all of this there is no narrative, no sustained history, no refashioning of herself. As a reader she only wants what she can incorporate easily into the stereotyped repertoire of her fantasies. We are told that she reads Balzac and George Sand. But she evidently misses the point. The romantic feminism of George Sand and Balzac, their stories of the self-education and emancipation of the women of the 1830s, are mysteriously lost on Emma Rouault.

We look over her shoulder, and we are immersed along with her in these potent unrealities. We are drawn, with great skill, into a sustained imaginative contact with Emma. We feel that we are inside her head, under her skin, as we read. We seem to know her – thoughts and sensations, desires and fantasies and secret memories – inside out.

Much of the book's abiding power over its readers comes from this mirage of intimacy. There is an intensely pleasurable primary identification with Emma. As we read we undergo a chastely textual metamorphosis, a very delicate seduction.

Though quite disembodied, we are still drawn in. For it is a vital part of Flaubert's design to arouse his readers sexually. Not simply with a desire for Emma, though that is certainly a part of it. More gently, more subversively, with a desire to *be* Emma, to partake of her sensations and her feelings. Flaubert, we may speculate, found in the imagining and the writing of Emma Bovary a safe place to play at being a woman. The famous ironies have their origin and their energy in the powerful contrary need to disavow such a potentially contaminating femininity. Irony cleans away all those secret stains. Irony is the path that leads safely back to official realities.

The spell is constantly being broken, renewed and broken again and again, by small disconcerting touches, by details that work against Emma, against her vision and her desire and her sense of things. We always feel the ironic chill of disenchantment, like the dismaying banality that can blight any object of desire, undo its magic, destroy its power and leave us puzzling over a thing so diminished.

It is the tense alternation of feeling, of pathos and irony, of intimacy and estrangement, that makes up the sweet and sour pleasure of *Madame Bovary*. The final vindictive sourness comes with the taste of the white arsenic powder in her mouth (an inky taste, says Flaubert), the imagination of which caused the author to vomit repeatedly as he wrote the closing scenes.

Emma Bovary is the first in a procession of troubled and insubordinate young wives; she is the model for those adulterous bourgeois heroines who dominate seventy years of European fiction. Emma Bovary is the precursor of Thérèse Raquin, Anna Karenin, Hedda Gabler, Sue Bridehead, Ursula Brangwen and Molly Bloom. It can be no coincidence that most of the works in which these heroines appear were prosecuted for immorality when they were first published.

But among all of this scandalous company, Emma Bovary's punishment is the most terrible, the most lingering. She is poisoned by her own hand; she dies in a pain that is exactly adjusted to the intensity of our preceding identification. Even before her end, morality has been reasserted in its most conventional form. She is thwarted and betrayed by the commonplace egotistical prudence of those lovers who pose as her liberators. Her men are both content to play the grand passion, the romance of lawless desire, as long as they can return to the comforts of home when they've had their fill.

Emma's education and her early life, as depicted by Flaubert, have prepared her for silence and acquiescence. Characteristically, we see her at home, indoors, at the window. She is looking out for something, waiting for something to happen. She is stifling in a shabby little room cluttered with ordinary things, stifling in the everyday tedium of village life. When we see her out of doors, she is often anxious, exposed, afflicted, shivering in the wind, sweating with heat, stumbling across a ploughed field in the early dawn, or freezing cold, in a carriage on the way back from the town of Rouen.

It is a remarkable though inconspicuous fact that we only *hear* Emma, for the first time, some months after her marriage. She has walked out alone to the edge of the woods with her dog. She says simply, 'Oh, why, dear God, did I marry him?' Only the question is spoken aloud. And there is no dramatic scene of self-knowledge, recognition and resolve. There is only this meagre question, spoken aloud. It reaches no other human ear. Only her dog hears it. Yet it releases a sequence of memories and fantasies, set far away, in her school-days. Here, two generations before Freud's discovery of the unconscious, we find Flaubert already mapping the shadowy places of female inner space. Emma's imaginings are never marked, explicitly and negatively, as unreal. The scenes that she stages in the secret theatre of fantasy are told as though they were real. They are indistinguishable, textually, from real events. Grand passions are played out in her mind, with appropriately lavish costume, sumptuous décor, melodramatic script. Emma precociously invents the cinema while gazing on the pages of her keepsake album.

There are certain affinities between Flaubert and Freud. Both men begin from the enigma (so-called) of female sexuality. We know that Flaubert was fascinated by hysteria. He was writing in an age which had just invented the case-history. For his unpublished *The Temptation of Saint Antony* he had immersed himself in this new psychiatric literature, recognizing that hysteria was a buried treasure for any novelist. He savoured especially the implicit grotesquerie of the genre. The meticulously prosaic medical documentation of bizarrely abnormal human behaviour was greatly to his taste. Having been regarded in his early twenties as an epileptic, he saw himself – perhaps mischievously – as 'a case'. He was most impressed when a local doctor suggested to him that he was a hysterical old woman. And he gleefully announced that his excessive taste for herrings was 'hysterical' in origin.

For all that, *Madame Bovary* is conspicuously not a 'study in hysteria'. It does not centre on enabling the woman to tell her story. It does not trace out the broken and involuted form of the Freudian enigma. Nor does it attempt an archaeological reconstruction of forgotten experiences. Even the word *hysteria* is never used. Is this perhaps a deliberate silence? It is surely an interesting renunciation, in view of Flaubert's known engagement with the issue. He does not mention (nobody mentions) hysteria. The word is *nerves*. Emma, we are told several times, suffers from a nervous ailment.

In popular belief as well as in learned discourse, the nerves were the threads which join together the body and the mind. They were the unexplored source of mysterious disorders, the inexplicable nervous ailments which particularly afflicted young women. Artists were also conventionally nervous. For the nerves are the material basis of the emotions. Like the strings on a violin, they can quiver when touched, they can snap if wound too tight. Emma's nerves are described in these terms, and these terms recur precisely in various references to his own nerves contained in Flaubert's letters.

Emma's ailment, like that of her creator, marks out a limit, a boundary which is as much ideological as it is medical. She is full of secret riches of feeling which are hoarded from use, enjoyed only in solitude. Her wine turns all to vinegar. The unspoken words find utterance in bodily symptoms: the coughing, the loss of weight. As readers we know what it is that fills her silences. We follow the history of her emotions, the inner chronicle of her frustrations. We are granted immediate experience of the process of self-suppression which culminates in her being diagnosed as having a nervous ailment.

Not until nearly the end of the story does her self-imposed silence explode into words. She makes a very long, angry and eloquent speech against Rodolphe's refusal to give her the money she needs to pay her debts. She speaks out against the inequalities that have trapped her. She runs from Rodolphe's house and is struck down by hallucinations, when the earth begins to shake and 'everything in her head . . . poured out at once, in a single spasm, like a thousand fireworks exploding'.

Everything pours out, the unspoken bursts through in the form of 'fiery red globules . . . they clustered together, they penetrated her; everything disappeared'. It is a fiery sexual punishment. And her next action is to stuff her mouth with the powdery white arsenic that kills her. Her last, posthumous utterance is the 'black liquid' that 'streamed out, like vomit, from between her lips', staining the white satin wedding-dress in which she is to be buried.

THE NEIGHBOUR

Emma can never get enough: never enough money, enough love, enough pleasure. Homais, on the other hand, embodies a coarse and robust abundance. Emma and Homais – in French the two names suggest *femme* and *homme* – *woman* and *man*. Homais is the gross comic ballast to Emma's yearning but not-quite-tragic sublimities. Homais and Emma, masculine and feminine, they stand for the contrary energies that Flaubert himself awkwardly encompassed.

There may be more to Homais than is usually recognized, more of Flaubert in Homais than he acknowledged to himself, because his incontestable imaginative allegiance was to Emma. She is his first love, but Homais is evidently a close second.

Plainly Homais is the focus for Flaubert's satire on the bourgeois. He stands for that most potent discursive force in provincial life: the neighbour. He serves to expose the ideological decay of an erstwhile revolutionary class, though that is not quite how

Flaubert would have phrased it. Ever since early adolescence, Flaubert had regarded bourgeois existence as an immense, indistinct, unmitigated state of mindlessness. His *Dictionary of Received Ideas* was a monument to this precocious insight. For Flaubert, each bourgeois phrase, each bourgeois feeling, each bourgeois opinion, is touched by the hilarious dismaying suspicion of fakery. Solemnly and energetically proclaiming their clichés to each other, perhaps the bourgeois are indeed simply machines. They are stuck, like busy automata, in their perpetual false consciousness. There are hints of this sombre vision in *Madame Bovary*. Received ideas circulate unchallenged. But the suspicion is never allowed to take conclusive shape. The case remains teasingly unproven.

What does Homais do, the busiest of them all?

Most obviously, he talks a great deal. As soon as he comes on to the scene, at the beginning of Part Two, he takes over the conversation. He plays the part of a usurping comic narrator. He greets the newly arrived Charles and Emma. He tells them everything about the public life of Yonville. He is an invulnerably self-important know-all. The great torrent of Homais's talk splendidly fills up much of the space left empty by Flaubert's impersonal mode of story-telling. I suspect that Homais's omniscience, his cheerful journalistic mastery of the naïve formulae of narrative writing, his boundless opinions, are, in part, an affectionate parodic homage to the novelist Balzac. Balzac was Flaubert's immediate and immense literary precursor, and he had died only the year before *Madame Bovary* was begun. The initial problem for any débutant French novelist, in 1851, was how to avoid writing like a pale imitation of Balzac. How could Flaubert exorcize such a mighty ghost? In Homais he takes control of Balzac's paternal voice. He incorporates it, in comic form.

Truly abundant, though, Homais is even more than this incorporation of the Balzacian mode. He is clearly also a comic monomaniac: the crafty hypocrite, the medical charlatan, the quack, a figure out of Molière or Ben Jonson, with his plausible veneer of expert jargon. Yet Homais, unlike his forerunners, is *not* reassuringly exposed and humiliated at the end of the action.

In a sombre deviation from comic tradition, Homais survives, triumphantly uncorrected.

Beyond Balzac and Molière, Homais has his deepest roots in Rabelais. He is constantly associated with eating and drinking (though not with lechery, which is assigned to Rodolphe). Homais makes his first appearance at the height of epic scenes of cooking in the kitchen of the village inn. Thereafter he frequently invites himself to the Bovary dinner-table and offers copious expert advice on all aspects of cooking. We discover, on the day of the agricultural show (an idealizing official celebration of food) that Homais is the author of an academic treatise on cider. It clearly belongs to the Rabelaisian genre 'Praise of Boozing'. As a pharmacist Homais is the resourceful maker of all kinds of pills and potions. His magic foods promise to restore the eater's immortality. He is the pioneer of chocolate, the maker of jam, and the guardian of arsenic. In the midst of Emma's final crisis, as she begins her journey from Rouen to Yonville, we come across Homais, in the *Hirondelle*, bringing home as a special treat for his wife a parcel of special breakfast rolls, the *cheminots*. The cheminots are described in an unusual digressive paragraph which is explicitly Rabelaisian in its idiom. This is residual homage to an author Flaubert greatly admired. It is also a finely calculated opening-out on to a spacious and benign common reality, a world of breakfast rolls, of something nice to eat, just beyond the infernal circle inhabited by Emma. Finally, in the scene of the vigil over Emma's corpse, when Homais and the priest Bournisien engage in fierce and farcical debate over religion, their altercation ends with the great ideological antagonists eating and drinking together (whisky, cheese and brioche are specified) in an impulse of simple human complicity. Flaubert seems to have felt that this was possibly offensive or just too distractingly incongruous. He cut this particular paragraph from both the first edition of 1857 and from the final edition of 1874. He restored it in the editions of 1862, 1869 and 1873. It suggests that he couldn't make up his mind. Comedy and tragedy, food and corpses, were all simpler when kept further apart.

This grotesque and indestructible abundance, *à la Rabelais*,

is the foundation of Flaubert's satire on the bourgeois. It serves
to mitigate and to enrich the singular aggressiveness of satire. It
is worth emphasizing that Homais is historically a typical mid
nineteenth-century provincial intellectual: a *petit bourgeois*
polymath with predominantly scientific interests, a man engaged
in the kind of 'local' writing that was widely published under
the patronage of the regional academies. His type has now
almost disappeared, and this makes Homais seem more bizarre,
posthumously, than he was in his own day. We seize on the
superficially bizarre, and we miss how representative he is.

Homais embodies the progressive modernizing aspirations
of his class, as well as the historical contradictions that class
endures. Homais shows us the revolutionary 1790s as they
might be remembered from the prosperous 1840s. He is
vehemently anti-clerical. He maintains the republican anti-
clericalism of 1789, the radicalism of the heroic age. But he
stands for an anti-clericalism that has outlived its own best
energies. In Homais it has decayed and faded to a merely
mischievous, compulsive reflex.

To put it differently, he provides the focus of a satire on
anti-clericalism. If we take the final confrontation between
Homais and Bournisien, as they argue through the night, in the
room where Emma's dead body is laid out, we find only a banal
and farcical echo of the great debates of the late eighteenth
century between orthodoxy and enlightenment. This debate is
restaged over the corpse of a romantic heroine, for the maximum
of squalid incongruity, between two petty and inept village
antagonists. Characteristically for Flaubert, the argument has
been comically diminished to a brandishing of antithetical
phrases and texts. It is in no sense a real debate.

We could compare it with a parallel scene in the early pages
of Victor Hugo's novel *Les Misérables*. Hugo, born a generation
before Flaubert, was writing in the late 1840s. He stages exactly
the same argument as that between Homais and Bournisien. But
in Hugo's version the moral stature of each of the speakers is
potently idealized. The saintly liberal bishop is humbled by his
critic, an aged, eloquent, splendidly impenitent supporter of the
revolutionary *Convention*, a man who has remained stubbornly

loyal to the values of the most radical phase of the French Revolution.

The comparison between Flaubert and Hugo in their treatment of anti-clericalism reveals the immense ideological distance between two successive generations of writers who are both nominally bourgeois.

The adjunct to Homais's anti-clericalism is his faith in science. And here too Flaubert diminishes, to comic effect, the intellectual energies in play. In the age of Darwin, Pasteur, Helmholtz and James Clerk Maxwell, all of them near-contemporaries of Flaubert, Homais, the village pharmacist mixing potions in his so-called laboratory, is a puny specimen indeed. He is not, of course, a scientist in any real sense. He can't remember the three chemical components of methane, and this is offered as an early symptom of his wider ignorance. He is merely a man who talks a great deal about science, with naïve evangelical optimism.

Above all, Homais is a man of the printed word. Since the early 1830s the printed word had entered a new phase of its history. It was now pouring out, in disconcertingly crude abundance, from the new steam-powered printing presses. The socially efficacious printed word, propagated by these epic engines of discourse, is Homais's special province. His house is covered in gigantic lettering, advertising the pharmacy's wares. He is an avid reader and a conscientious collector of newspapers, as well as being an occasional contributor. He is rather unexpectedly like Emma in this respect. They share a passion for printed matter. Homais's taste is for the newspaper, the scientific journal and the learned treatise; Emma's is for romantic fiction, illustrated fashion magazines and sub-Gothic horror stories. Both are creatures of print.

Homais is a gifted *amateur* ideologue. We are given two extended samples of his writing: his newspaper articles on the agricultural show and on the operation to cure the club-foot. Their style is aptly lavish, hyperbolical, effusive, exaggerating. We are meant to enjoy seeing through them very easily. But his improvised performances are equally impressive. His predatory entrepreneurial skills hide themselves benignly behind altruistic phrases about progress and the general good.

His routine idealizations of marriage and family life scarcely sweeten his exercise of paternal power. His authority weighs heavily on those around him, the women, the children and the servants. In the public domain he is a servile opportunist. He enjoys an ingratiating facility with the various forms of official discourse.

Homais becomes ever more powerful in the final chapters, now that he has disposed of the Blind Man, and the wifeless Charles is fading away with grief. He is enthroned as 'the happiest of fathers, the most fortunate of men'. His public apotheosis comes in the book's closing sentence, as he is awarded the Legion of Honour. But his secret glory is played out a few pages before this, when he appears in bed wearing his Pulvermacher hydroelectric body-chain, before the eyes of his adoring wife. It is a most bizarre vision, pulling together conjugal eroticism (endlessly mocked by Flaubert), pseudo-medical gadgetry, and a bourgeois exoticism which is at once mythological–classical–oriental. It sets off a hilarious explosion of incongruities. This is followed by the account of Homais's part in devising a tomb for Emma: his chastely classical emblem and inscription merely cloak the miserable chaos of adultery, debt and suicide. By the end Homais controls everything, even sexuality itself. The Blind Man has been put away, Madame Homais has been erotically bedazzled, the adulteress has been inscribed as a loving wife (*amabilem conjugem*, in the words of her epitaph). All professional rivals have been put to flight. The last sentence in the book shifts ominously into the present tense, implying his perpetual dominion, beyond even the formal ending of the story.

THE LOVER

The only real criticism of Homais comes from Rodolphe. In conversation with Emma, on the day of the agricultural show, he makes various disparaging remarks about the pharmacist. But nothing comes of them, and Homais flourishes undiminished. It is curious that Rodolphe and Homais never appear together again. Rodolphe, uniquely, does not come within Homais's powerful reach. He alone is not subjected to his orthodoxies. Or so it appears. Why the segregation of these two men? Why can they not appear together, the neighbour and the lover?

If Homais is the public face of the bourgeois, paternalistic, public-spirited and progressive, then Rodolphe is the other side: the wild, virile, unfettered libertine, the rebellious, sub-Byronic man of the world. As such, he is merely the legitimate antithesis of Homais. He is only, disappointingly, the other side of the same thing. At heart Rodolphe and Homais are brothers. There is, in Flaubert's view of the matter, only one possible sexuality. The libertine is no freer, no more authentic in his desires, than the paterfamilias he scorns. His transgressions obey the same laws. The husband, away from home, reverts to the suppressed libertinism of his youth. This is clear from the fact that Homais, as soon as he escapes from his pharmacy in Yonville, picks up the Rodolphe ethos (or at least its idiom). In conversation with Léon, he affects a facile and cynical connoisseurship of all the varieties of female flesh.

This is the only scene in the novel which shows men talking openly about women. It offers the briefest comic glimpse into the social world of the nineteenth-century bourgeois male. The prevailing tone is ingeniously and aggressively prurient. It is a tone rarely heard in novels of the period, though it is the common currency of Flaubert's letters to his male friends. In this code of erotic innuendo, the symbolism of the phallic was, inevitably, the centrepiece. Pistols and swords, umbrellas and cigars all carry their charge of half-hidden meaning, their whispered intimations of desire.

The cigar, phallic symbol *par excellence*, is much in evidence. As Emma and Charles make their way home from the ball at La Vaubyessard, Charles happens upon the Viscount's green silk cigar-case, dropped by the roadside. He picks it up, and chokes ignominiously on the aristocrat's cigars; Emma takes possession of the cigar-case itself and weaves an elaborate aristocratic romance around this female symbol. Rodolphe's trite post-coital cigar and accompanying pen-knife are obvious enough. More curious than these 'official' symbols, though, are the variously veiled or distorted emblems which point to the heart of a peculiarly Flaubertian sexuality.

Consider all the jokes about Léon and his ever more melodramatic desire for Emma. First there is the cactus plant he
brings as a gift. Later, on the eve of their first adultery, only the
massive spire of Rouen cathedral itself will suffice to suggest the
dimensions of his desire. And the hotel room in Rouen, where
Emma and Léon meet to make love, is equipped with 'arrow-
headed curtain rods' and 'big balls on the fender' as well as a
pair of 'those big pink shells that sound like the sea when you
hold them to your ear'.

The gross obviousness of such symbols is most likely their
point. They allow for many an ingenious unofficial reference to
the physical realities of love, at a time when the printed word
and family conversation were both intricately inhibited in sexual
matters. Meanwhile, of course, there flourished that parallel
secret world of salacious masculine conversation. Its apparent
freedom was merely the legitimate antithesis of the social
repression of sexuality. The unspoken-but-obvious is a special
code for the initiated, an amusing and reassuring stratagem, a
happy complicity.

But there is another, darker vein of sexual reference in
Madame Bovary. It points towards a realm of anxious fantasy,
to the thought that the phallus may be lost or may attach itself
to the woman's body. There is a network of references to feet,
boots and shoes: at its most grotesquely explicit in the figure of
the ostler Hippolyte. His deformed foot, we recall, is operated
upon, most incompetently. It develops gangrene. It is then amputated and replaced by an elaborate artificial leg. (Flaubert's
father had died in 1846, after weeks of agony, from an unsuccessful operation for an abscess of his thigh, involving gangrene.)

Hippolyte has quite the ugliest foot. Emma has the most
remarkably elegant. The men all notice her feet. This was a
period of such all-concealing female costume that erotic interest
was characteristically displaced on to the ankle or the foot,
glimpsed briefly below a long and voluminous skirt. Charles
savours the sound of her clogs on the kitchen-floor in the farmhouse. Léon gazes at her for the first time, on the evening of her

arrival in Yonville, as she lifts her dress and holds out to the fire 'a foot clad in a small black boot'. Rodolphe, following her closely along the forest-path, 'glimpsed – just between that black hem and the black boot – the delicacy of her white stocking, like a snippet of her nakedness'. Justin, the adolescent boy who secretly adores Emma, delights in 'doing her boots', cleaning 'the mud of her assignations' from the fabric. And Léon, in the great days of their love, gives her 'pink satin slippers, edged with swansdown' and observes the effect very closely: 'When she sat on his knee, her leg, too short to reach the floor, would swing in the air; and the dainty shoe, which had no heel, would dangle from the toes of her bare foot.'

The four men who look at Emma (Charles, Léon, Rodolphe and Justin) fasten their eyes on her nails, her eyes, her teeth, hands, hair and feet. Just the edges of her body, just the little details. Their vision of Emma – and we are offered no other – is decidedly fetishistic. Her dresses, for instance, are always described with an emphatic connoisseur's precision. We know the fabric (merino, nankeen, cashmere) and the style (waistline, number of flounces, ribbons, fringes). Female *toilette* in general – the mysteries of knickers, petticoats and camisoles, the niceties of bandeau, chignon and corsage – all these are the focus of a perpetual excited interest.

But at the centre of these frills, where her body would be, there is a kind of blankness. There is much *imagined* nakedness, many clandestine erotic intimations of what might be there, beneath the coverings. This is one of Flaubert's 'specialities'. At such moments the writing slows down. The syntax is aptly involuted, the sentences are sensuously complicated. There is a special imaginative tempo, a place for reverie and delectation. But never the thing itself. Never the simple reality of a woman's unadorned flesh. There is always, interposed, some appendage or other, some accessory, something to draw the eye, to hold the imagination, to secure an image safely within the code of masculine desire.

READING AND WRITING

As a young man, Flaubert had surreptitiously refused to become a lawyer. The thought of being *useful* was quite odious to him. True to the defiant, mischievous ethos of its maker, there is not much evidence of socially productive labour in *Madame Bovary*. There is only the pharmacist Homais, secluded in the little room he calls the *Capharnaum*, his holy of holies, where he mixes and labels his medicines; only the village tax-collector Binet, working alone up in his attic, turning wooden serviette rings on his lathe. These two striking parallel images of passionate, solitary and gratuitous labour may also bring to mind a picture of Flaubert sitting at his desk, struggling with the rhythm of every phrase. Homais, Binet and Flaubert create around themselves a special enclosed space, a protected solitude. Each has a dignified alibi for his pursuit of the rapturous masculine fantasy of totally self-sufficient activity.

Flaubert worked at his writing, in his own terms. But his writing was not work, in social terms. While writing this book he was not yet the famous author of *Madame Bovary*. He was merely a man of modest private means in his early thirties who spent most of his time producing voluminous manuscripts of uncertain value. His first sustained composition, the work of his mid twenties, *The Temptation of Saint Antony*, had been abandoned, rather ominously, on the advice of his friends. The image of Binet at his lathe was perhaps a defensively joking self-caricature.

I have already mentioned Flaubert's idiosyncratic but exact sense of cultural formation. He demonstrated with poignant clarity the shaping social power of written language upon the inner lives of his main characters. But he had an even larger ambition than this. He grasped, ahead of his time, the pervasive quality of the modern. In the month before he began writing *Madame Bovary* he had visited the Crystal Palace Great Exhibition in London. There he would have seen displayed, in a ritual of world-historical self-congratulation, the global triumph of capitalism. It took the material form of a spectacular network of commodities.

Unobtrusively, Flaubert endeavoured to document in unprecedented detail the everyday cultural artefacts of his age. He attended with great imaginative precision not simply to the external contours of such objects, inert in themselves, but also to the vagaries of their actual use. He often evokes individual acts of reading, writing and looking. We behold, for example, a set of ancestral portraits, a fashion-plate, a map of Paris, a variety of legal documents, a medical journal, a women's magazine, an almanac, a list of medical lectures, the engravings in a keepsake album, a picture torn from a perfumier's catalogue, a daguerreotype portrait, a treatise on cider, an operatic performance, a work of medical pornography, a forged receipt for piano lessons, the ledger in a draper's shop, a bailiff's inventory of property for auction. The list is not at all systematic, but it confirms how habitually observant Flaubert was in such matters.

Such documentary exactness has a purpose that reaches beyond the satiric mimicry which inspired *The Dictionary of Received Ideas*. Flaubert's transcriptions are designed to foreground, comprehensively, the cultural processes of reading and writing. These transcriptions are a vital and neglected feature of his style. His narrative method, so disconcertingly impersonal, is not mere fastidiousness. Flaubert, ever the clandestine antibourgeois, judiciously abstains from the habitual forms of persuasion.

Writing such as this invites us, delectably, to reinvent our reading.

Further Reading

Julian Barnes, *Flaubert's Parrot* (London: Picador 1984). A sharp, entertaining fictional reinvention of Flaubert.

Victor Brombert, *The Novels of Flaubert: A Study of Themes and Techniques* (Princeton: Princeton University Press, 1966). Comprehensive, perceptive account of the major works.

Stephen Heath, *Gustave Flaubert: Madame Bovary*, Landmarks of World Literature series (Cambridge: Cambridge University Press, 1992). An elegant and richly polemical essay by a disciple of Roland Barthes focused on issues of language and sexuality.

Harry Levin, 'Flaubert', in *Gates of Horn: A Study of Five French Realists* (New York: Oxford University Press, 1963). Brilliantly condensed 80-page account of Flaubert's artistic programme.

Dacia Maraini, *Searching for Emma* (Chicago: Chicago University Press, 1993, 1998). Contemporary feminist meditation on Emma Bovary, relaxed and amusing, with a novelist's eye for detail.

Francis Steegmuller, *Flaubert and Madame Bovary: A Double Portrait* (London: Constable, 1993). First published in 1939; richly anecdotal, pleasingly written and unobtrusively intelligent, this remains the best account of the making of *Madame Bovary*.

T. Tanner, *Adultery in the Novel: Contract and Transgression* (London: Johns Hopkins University Press, 1999). Includes an excellent chapter on *Madame Bovary*.

Geoffrey Wall, *Flaubert: A Life* (London: Faber & Faber, 2001).

An intimate picaresque biography that places Flaubert in his own time and space, among his friends, relations and neighbours.

A Note on the Translation

Translating afresh the already translated classic text, the translator is drawn into dialogue with his or her precursors. Though I was working on different principles, and though I found that I eventually disagreed with some of their most cherished effects, I have profited from the posthumous conversation of three previous translators of *Madame Bovary*: Eleanor Marx, Alan Russell and Gerard Hopkins.

I have used Claudine Gothot-Mersch's edition of *Madame Bovary*, published by Garnier in 1971. I have preserved Flaubert's distinctive habits of punctuation, italicization and paragraphing. He persistently uses commas to segment his sentences in a way that is intended to be mildly disconcerting. Flaubert's italics are deployed to foreground certain phrases for our special scrutiny. We are invited to enjoy these phrases as prime specimens of cliché, pinned to the page. Flaubert used very short paragraphs to emphasize certain sentences, lifting them out of the visual flow of the printed page. It is a form of typographic slow-motion. These three devices fill some of the space left empty by the notorious elimination of the storyteller from the next called *Madame Bovary*.

Madame Bovary

Part One

We were at prep, when the Head came in, followed by a new boy not in uniform and a school-servant carrying a big desk. Those who had been asleep woke up, and every boy rose to his feet as though surprised in his labours.

The Head motioned us to sit down again; then, turning to the form master:

– Monsieur Roger, he said in a low voice, here is a pupil that I am entrusting to you, he can start off in the Fifth. If his work and his conduct are creditable, he will go up into the top class, appropriate to his age.

Standing in the corner, behind the door, so that we could hardly see him, the new boy was a country lad, about fifteen years old, and much taller than any of us. He had his hair cut square across his forehead, like a village choirboy, looking sensible and extremely embarrassed. Though he was not broad in the shoulders, his short green jacket with the black buttons must have been tight under the arms and revealed, at the cuffs, two red wrists more used to being bare. His legs, in their blue stockings, emerged from yellow-coloured trousers, hitched up very tight by his braces. He was wearing sturdy boots, ineptly polished, with hobnails.

We began reciting the lessons. He was all ears, like someone at a sermon, not even daring to cross his legs, or to lean on his elbows, and, at two o'clock, when the bell rang, the form master had to tell him to get into line with the rest of us.

We had a custom, on coming back into the class-room, of

throwing our caps on the ground, to leave our hands free; you had to fling them, all the way from the door, under the bench, so that they hit the wall and made lots of dust; it was *the thing to do*.

But, whether he had not noticed this manoeuvre or did not dare to attempt it, prayers were over and the new boy was still holding his cap on his knees. It was one of those hats of the Composite order,[1] in which we find features of the military bear-skin, the Polish chapska,[2] the bowler hat, the beaver and the cotton nightcap, one of those pathetic things, in fact, whose mute ugliness has a profundity of expression like the face of an imbecile. Ovoid and stiffened with whalebone, it began with three big circular sausages; then, separated by a red band, there alternated diamonds of velours and rabbit-fur; after that came a sort of bag terminating in a cardboard polygon, embroidered all over with complicated braid, and, hanging down at the end of a long cord that was too thin, a little cluster of gold threads, like a tassel. It looked new; the peak was gleaming.

– Stand up, said the teacher.

He stood up; his cap fell down. The whole class began to laugh.

He bent over to get it. A neighbour knocked it down with his elbow, he picked it up again.

– Disencumber yourself of your helmet, said the teacher, who was a man of some wit.

There was a roar of laughter from the class, which disconcerted the poor boy, and he didn't know whether he should hold on to his cap, leave it on the floor or put it on his head. He sat down and put it in his lap.

– Stand up, said the teacher, and tell me your name.

The new boy articulated, in a mumbling voice, a name that was inaudible.

– Again!

The same mumbled syllables were heard, submerged by the rumpus from the class.

– Louder! shouted the master. Louder!

The new boy, resolved to do his utmost, opened a gigantic

mouth and with all his might, as if he were calling somebody, hurled out one word: *Charbovari*.[3]

In one second all hell broke loose; rising to a crescendo with shrill rippling voices (they yelled, they barked, they stamped, they echoed: *Charbovari! Charbovari!*), rolling in isolated notes, subsiding most reluctantly, and abruptly starting off again along one bench from which there would erupt, like a squib still fizzing, bursts of stifled laughter.

However, under a deluge of penalties, order in the class was eventually restored, and the teacher, having managed to grasp the name of Charles Bovary, by having had it dictated, spelled out and read back to him, immediately ordered the poor devil to go and sit on the dunce's bench, right by the master's desk. He began to make a move, but, before he stood up, hesitated.

– What are you looking for? asked the teacher.

– My ca . . ., said the new boy timidly, looking anxiously around.

– Five hundred lines for the whole class! he exclaimed in a furious voice, suppressing, like *Quos ego*,[4] any fresh outburst.

– Now keep quiet! continued the teacher indignantly; and, wiping his forehead with the handkerchief he had just taken from under his cap: As for you, the new boy, you will write out for me twenty times the verb *ridiculus sum*.

Then, in a gentler voice:

– You will find it again, your cap; it hasn't been stolen.

All was calm again. Heads were bent over exercise-books, and the new boy stayed sitting there decorously for two whole hours, though there did come, now and again, the odd paper pellet flicked from the end of a quill that splattered over his face. But he wiped them off with his hand, and kept completely still, without looking up.

In the evening, at prep, he got his cuffs out of his desk, organized his belongings, ruled careful lines on his paper. We saw him working conscientiously, looking up every word in the dictionary and taking great pains. Thanks, no doubt, to this obvious willingness, he didn't have to go down into the lower class; for, though he just about knew his rules, his style was rather lacking in elegance. It was his village *curé* who had taught him Latin, his parents, for economy, having only sent him to college as late as possible.

His father, Monsieur Charles-Denis-Bartholomé Bovary, a former assistant army surgeon, implicated, around the year 1812, in a conscription scandal, and forced, about that time, to leave the service, had subsequently made the most of his personal talents to lay hold of a dowry of sixty thousand francs, in the person of the daughter of a textile merchant, seduced by his good looks. A handsome man, a big talker, always jingling about in his spurs, with whiskers that joined his moustache, fingers always decorated with rings and dressed in loud colours, he had the prowess of the soldier, with the easy enthusiasm of the commercial traveller. Once he was married, he lived for two or three years off his wife's fortune, dining well, rising late, smoking big pipes made of porcelain, never coming home until after the theatre, and always in and out of the cafés. The father-in-law died and left almost nothing; he was most indignant, *went in for textiles*, lost some money at it, then retired to the country, aiming to *make a bit*. However, since he knew no more about farming than he did about cottons, since he rode about on his horses instead of sending them to plough, drank his cider by the bottle instead of selling it by the barrel, ate the finest poultry in his yard and greased his hunting-boots with the lard from his pigs, it wasn't long before he realized he had better give up any idea of making a profit.

At a rent of two hundred francs a year, he eventually found somewhere in a village on the border between Caux and Picardy, a sort of place half farm, half private house; and there, chagrined, remorseful, cursing his fate, jealous of everybody, he shut himself away at the age of forty-five, disgusted with the world, he said, and determined to live in peace.

His wife had been mad about him originally; she had loved him with a servility that had turned him against her all the more. Once lively, expansive and affectionate, she became, with age (like an uncorked wine that turns to vinegar), a difficult whining neurotic. She had suffered so much, without complaint, at first, when she saw him chasing after every slut in the village and when a score of bawdy houses had sent him back to her late at night, worn out and smelling of drink. Then her pride had revolted. She fell silent, swallowing down her rage in a mute stoicism that she kept up until her death. She was constantly bustling about, busying here and there. She went to see the lawyers, to see the magistrate, remembered when the bills fell due, had them renewed; and, at home, did the ironing, the sewing, the washing, kept an eye on the workers, settled the accounts, while Monsieur, careless of everything, perpetually slumped in a drowsy churlishness from which he would only ever rouse himself in order to say something disagreeable to her, sat there by the fire, smoking, spitting into the cinders.

When she had a child, he had to be sent to a wet-nurse. Once he came home, the little lad was treated like a prince. His mother fed him on bread and jam; his father let him run about without any shoes, and, playing the philosopher, even declared that he could go stark naked, like young animals do. Contrary to maternal tenderness, he had in mind a certain manly idea of childhood, upon which he strove to form his own son, wanting him to be brought up harshly, in the spartan manner, to give him a strong constitution. He sent him to bed without a fire, taught him to take great swigs of rum and to shout insults at religious processions. But, being naturally peaceful, the boy responded poorly to his efforts. He was always trailing along with his mother; she would cut out little pictures for him, tell him stories, converse with him in endless monologues full of melancholy gaiety and delightful nonsense. Living in such isolation, she shifted on to this childish head all her scattered and broken vanities. She dreamed of high office, she already saw him, tall, handsome, talented, established, an engineer, or a magistrate. She taught him to read, and even taught him, on an old piano that she had, to sing two or three little ballads. But, invariably, Monsieur Bovary, unimpressed by such refinements, said that it *wasn't worth the bother*! Would they ever have enough to send him to a good school, buy him a practice or set him up in business? Anyway, *with a bit of grit, a man would always get on in the world*. Madame Bovary would bite her lip, and the child was left to wander about the village.

He used to follow the men ploughing, and, hurling clods of

earth, chase after the crows that flew off into the air. He ate up the blackberries that grew by the ditches, guarded the turkeys with stick in hand, helped with the harvesting, ran about in the woods, played hopscotch in the porch of the church on rainy days, and, on feast days, beseeched the sexton to let him ring the bells, so as to hang with his whole weight on the great rope and feel himself pulled aloft by its travel.

And so he grew up like an oak. He had strong hands, a good colour.

When he was twelve, his mother managed to have him begin his studies. They put the *curé* in charge. But the lessons were so brief and so disjointed that they never amounted to much. At any odd moment they used to happen, in the sacristy, standing up, in a rush, between a baptism and a burial; or else the *curé* would send for his pupil after the angelus, when he didn't have to go out. They went up to his room, they settled down: the gnats and the moths were fluttering round the candle. It was warm, the child went to sleep; and the old boy, dozing off with his hands on his stomach, was soon snoring away, mouth wide open. At other times, when Monsieur Le Curé, coming back from taking the viaticum to some sick parishioner, caught sight of Charles scampering across the fields, he would call him over, lecture him for a quarter of an hour and take the opportunity to have him conjugate his verbs at the foot of a tree. The rain would interrupt them, or a neighbour passing by. Nevertheless, he was usually pleased with him, even said that the young man had a good memory.

Charles could not carry on like this. Madame was emphatic. From shame, or rather fatigue, Monsieur surrendered quietly, and they waited another year for the lad to take his first communion.

Six more months went by; and, the following year, Charles was finally sent off to school in Rouen, whence his father conveyed him personally, towards the end of October, around the time of the Saint-Romain fair.

It would be impossible now for any of us to remember a thing about him. He was a boy of sober temperament, who played at play-time, worked in school hours, listened in class, slept well *never had anything given to him*

in the dormitory, ate well in the refectory. His guardian was a wholesale ironmonger on the Rue Ganterie, who took him out once a month, on Sunday, after he had shut his shop, sending him off for a walk round the harbour to look at the boats, then bringing him back to the school for seven o'clock, in time for supper. Every Thursday evening, he would write a long letter to his mother, in red ink with three wax seals; then he went through his history notes, or else read an old volume of *Anacharsis*[5] that was lying around in the prep-room. Out on walks, he talked to the servant, who came from the country just as he did.

By sheer hard work he always stayed at about the middle of the class; on one occasion, he nearly won a prize for natural history. But at the end of his third year, his parents took him away from the school and sent him to study medicine, convinced that he could pass the entrance exams under his own steam.

His mother found him a room, on the fourth floor, looking out over the Eau de Robec,[6] with a dyer that she knew. She made all the arrangements for his board, procured furniture, a table and two chairs, sent home for an old cherrywood bed, and bought as well a little cast-iron stove, along with the supply of wood that was to warm her poor child. Then she left at the end of the week, after a hundred exhortations to be on his best behaviour, now that he was to be left to himself.

The lecture list, when he read it on the noticeboard, made him feel dizzy: anatomy lectures, pathology lectures, physiology lectures, pharmacy lectures, chemistry and botany lectures, clinical practice and therapeutics, not to mention hygiene and *materia medica*, names with mysterious etymologies, like so many temple-doors guarding a sacred gloom within.

He didn't understand a thing; listen as best he might, he could not get hold of it. He worked even so, he had notebooks, he followed all the lectures, he never missed a visit. He carried out his little daily task just like the mill-horse, plodding his circle in the dark, grinding away in perfect ignorance.

To spare him some expense, his mother sent him every week, by the carrier, a piece of roast veal, which he had for his lunches, when he came in from his morning at the hospital, stomping his feet against the wall. Then he had to rush off to classes, to the

operating-theatre, to the hospice, and walk home again, from
the other end of town. In the evenings, after the meagre lodging-
house dinner, he went back up to his room and started work
again, still in his damp clothes that began to steam, in front of
the hot stove.

On fine summer evenings, at the hour when the warm streets
are empty, when servant-girls are playing shuttlecock in doorways, he would open his window and lean out. The river, which
makes this part of Rouen a kind of miserable little Venice,
flowed beneath, yellow, violet or blue, between its bridges and
its railings. Workmen, kneeling on the bank, were washing their
arms in the water. On poles jutting out from the attics, skeins
of cotton were drying off in the air. Facing him, away over the
roofs, there was the pure wide open sky, red from the setting
sun. It must be grand over there! So cool under the beeches!
And he opened his nostrils to breathe down the sweet smells of
the country, smells that never reached this far.

He lost weight, he looked taller, and his face acquired a sort
of doleful expression that made it almost interesting.

Inevitably, nonchalantly, he managed to release himself from
all the resolutions he had made. One day, he missed a visit, next
day his lecture, and, savouring indolence, eventually, he never
went back again.

He became a tavern-goer, a great domino-player. To closet
himself every evening in some scruffy public-room, so as to tap
on a marble table his little bits of sheep-bone marked with black
spots, this seemed to him a precious act of liberty, a deed that
raised him in his own estimation. It was like an initiation into
the great world, an access to forbidden pleasures; and, as he
went in, he would put his hand on the door-knob with an almost
sensual excitement. Henceforth, what had always been held in,
began to burst out; he memorized various ballads and sang them
to his lady-friends, enthused over Béranger,[7] learned to make
punch and had his first taste of love.

Thanks to these conscientious preparations, he totally failed
his Public Health Officer's exams. They were expecting him at
home that same evening to celebrate his success!

He set off on foot and stopped just outside the village, where he sent for his mother, and told her everything. She made excuses for him, blaming his failure on the injustice of the examiners, and reassured him, promising to sort it out. Only five years later did Monsieur Bovary know the truth; it was ancient history, he accepted it, unable in any case to imagine that any son of his could be a clot.

So Charles sat down to work again, and revised for his exams without stopping, learning all the questions off by heart. He got quite a decent pass. What a great day for his mother! They gave a fine big dinner.

Where should he go to practise his art? To Tostes. There was only one old doctor there. For ages and ages Madame Bovary had been watching out for his death, and the old chap hadn't even packed his bags before Charles was installed just across the road, as his successor.

But it wasn't quite enough to have brought up her son, have him taught medicine and discover Tostes for him to practise in: he had to have a wife. She found one for him: the widow of a bailiff from Dieppe, forty-five years old with twelve hundred francs a year.

Although she was ugly, thin as a rake, and splendidly be-pimpled, Madame Dubuc had no lack of suitors to choose from. To accomplish her plan, Mère Bovary had to trounce them all, and she even thwarted with great skill the machinations of a pork-butcher who had the backing of the priests.

Charles had pictured marriage as the advent of a better life, thinking he would be more free, and able to dispose of his own person and his own money. But his wife was master; in company he had to say this, not say that, eat fish every Friday, wear what she wanted him to, harass at her instigation the patients who didn't pay up. She opened his letters, watched over his comings and goings, and listened, through the partition wall, to his consultations, when there were women in his surgery.

She had to have her cup of chocolate every morning, she wanted endless attention. She complained incessantly about her nerves, about her chest, about her humours. The sound of footsteps made her ill; you left her alone, solitude was soon loathsome to her; you came back to her again, it was just to see her die, of course. In the evening, when Charles came home, she reached out from beneath the sheets with her long thin arms, put them round his neck, and, getting him to sit on the edge of the bed, began to tell him her troubles: he was neglecting her, he loved someone else! They had told her she would be unhappy; and she would end up asking him for a drop of medicine and a little bit more love.

2

One night, about eleven o'clock, they were awakened by the sound of a horse coming to a halt outside. The maid opened the attic window and parleyed for a while with a man below, in the street. He'd come for the doctor; he had a message. Nastasie came downstairs shivering, and went to unlock the door and draw the bolts, one by one. The man left his horse, and, following the maid, appeared in the room behind her. From inside his grey-tasselled woollen cap, he pulled out a letter wrapped in a scrap of cloth, and handed it ceremoniously to Charles, who lay with his elbows on the pillow to read it. Nastasie, by the bed, held the light. Madame, out of modesty, stayed facing the wall, her back turned.

This letter, sealed with a little seal of blue wax, begged Monsieur Bovary to come immediately to the farm known as Les Bertaux, to set a broken leg. Now, from Tostes to Les Bertaux it's a good eighteen miles across country, by way of Longueville and Saint-Victor. It was raining. It was a dark night. Madame Bovary the younger was worried that her husband might have an accident. So it was decided that the stable-boy should go on ahead. Charles would set off three hours later, once the moon came up. They would send a boy to meet him, to show him the way to the farm and open the gates for him.

At about four in the morning, Charles, well wrapped up in his cloak, set out for Les Bertaux. Still drowsy from his warm bed, he let himself be swayed by the soothing trot of his horse. When she stopped of her own accord at one of those holes fringed with thorns that they dig on the headland, Charles woke with a start, suddenly remembering about the broken leg, and he tried to bring to mind all the fractures that he knew. The rain had stopped; it was getting light, and, on the leafless branches of the apple-trees, birds were perching silently, ruffling up their little feathers against the chill wind of early morning. The flat landscape stretched out as far as the eye could see, and the clumps of trees around the farmhouses showed up, at wide intervals, as patches of deep violet on that vast grey surface, which blurred at the horizon into the dullness of the sky. Charles, now and again, opened his eyes; then, his mind clouding with fatigue, and sleep coming down upon him again, he soon entered a state of drowsiness in which, his recent sensations blending with his memories, he saw himself double, simultaneously student and husband, lying in bed as he had just been, walking through a hospital ward as he had done long ago. The warm smell of the poultices mingled in his head with the fresh smell of the dew; he could hear the iron rings running on the curtain rods around the beds and his wife sleeping ... As he passed through Vassonville, he saw, just by the ditch, a young boy sitting on the grass.

– Are you the doctor? asked the child.

And, when Charles said he was, he picked up his wooden shoes and started to run on ahead of him.

The Officer of Health, riding along,[8] gathered from what his guide was saying that Monsieur Rouault must be one of the more affluent farmers. He had broken his leg, the evening before, on his way home from Twelfth-Nighting, at a neighbour's house. His wife had died two years ago. With him there was only his young lady, who helped him with the housekeeping.

The ruts were getting deeper. They were nearly at Les Bertaux. The lad, slipping through a hole in the hedge, disappeared, and then re-emerged at the end of the yard and opened the gate. The horse slid on the wet grass; Charles stooped to pass beneath the branches. The watch-dogs in their kennels were barking and pulling on their chains. As he entered Les Bertaux, his horse took fright and went down.

It had the look of a substantial farm. You could see in the stables, over the tops of the open doors, great plough-horses

eating tranquilly from new racks. Stretching right along by the
outhouses there was a large dunghill, with steam rising from it,
and, in among the hens and the turkeys, five or six peacocks,
the ornament of every Caux farmyard, were pecking around up
on top. The sheepfold was long, the barn was high, with walls
as smooth as glass. In the shed there were two big carts and four
ploughs, with their whips, their collars, their full harness, with
blue fleeces soiled by the fine dust that drifted down from
the lofts above. The yard sloped upwards, planted with trees
symmetrically spaced, and there was a lively cackling from a
flock of geese near the pond.

A young woman, in a blue merino-wool dress with three
flounces, came to the door of the house to welcome Monsieur
Bovary, showing him into the kitchen, where a big fire was
blazing. Breakfast for the farm-people was cooking there, in
an assortment of little pots. Damp clothes were drying in the
fireplace. The shovel, the tongs and the snout of the bellows, all
of colossal proportions, were gleaming like polished steel, and
along the walls there hung a lavish array of pots and pans,
crudely mirroring the bright flames of the fire, together with the
early rays of the sun coming in through the windows.

Charles went upstairs, to see the patient. He found him in his
bed, sweating under his blankets, his cotton nightcap thrown
off into a far corner. He was a stocky little man of fifty, with
fair skin, and blue eyes, bald at the front, and wearing ear-rings.
At his side, on a chair, he had a large decanter of brandy, from
which he poured himself a drink every so often to keep up his
courage; but, as soon as he saw the doctor, his spirits sank, and,
instead of cursing as he had for the last twelve hours, he began
a feeble groaning.

The fracture was a simple one, with no complications of any
kind. Charles could not have hoped for anything easier. Then,
remembering the bedside manner of his professors, he comforted
the patient with all sorts of little phrases, surgical caresses, like
the oil they smear on the scalpel. To make some splints, they
went off to get from the cart-shed a bundle of laths. Charles
picked one out, cut it into sections, and smoothed it off with a
piece of broken glass, while the maid-servant tore up a sheet to

make bandages, and Mademoiselle Emma set about making some little pads. Because it took her a long time to find her sewing-box, her father became impatient; she said nothing; but, as she was sewing, she kept pricking her fingers, and then she put them to her lips to suck them.

Charles was surprised at the whiteness of her nails. They were lustrous, tapering, more highly polished than Dieppe ivories, and cut into an almond shape. Yet her hands were not beautiful, not white enough perhaps, and rather bony at the knuckles; they were also too long, with no softening curves. If she were beautiful, it was in her eyes; though they were brown, they seemed to be black because of the lashes, and they met your gaze openly, with an artless candour.

Once the bandaging was done, the doctor was invited by Monsieur Rouault himself, to *have a bite of something* before he left.

Charles went downstairs, into the parlour. Two places, with silver goblets, were set on a little table, at the foot of a big four-poster bed, its cotton canopy printed with pictures of Turks. There was an odour of orris-root and damp sheets, which came from the tall oakwood chest, facing the window. On the floor, in the corners, propped up, there were sacks of wheat. It was the overflow from the granary next door, just up the three stone steps. By way of decoration, hanging from a nail, in the middle of a wall with its green paint all flaking off from the saltpetre, there was a head of Minerva in black crayon, with a gold frame, inscribed below, in Gothic script: *To my dear Papa*.

First they talked about the patient, then the weather, the great frost, the wolves that roamed the fields, at night. Mademoiselle Rouault did not greatly enjoy living in the country, especially now that she was almost entirely responsible for the farm. As the room was slightly cold, she shivered as she ate, showing some of the fullness of her lips, which she had a habit of nibbling in moments of silence.

Round her neck was a white collar, turned down. Her black hair, brushed so smooth that each side seemed to be in one piece, was parted in a delicate central line that traced the curve of the skull; and, just revealing the tip of her ear, it coiled at the back into a thick chignon, with a rippling pattern at the temples, something that the country doctor now observed for the first time in his life. Her cheeks were touched with pink. She had, like a man, tucked into the front of her bodice, a tortoiseshell lorgnon.

After Charles had been upstairs to say farewell to Père Rouault, he came back into the parlour before he left, and found her standing at the window, her forehead against the glass, looking out into the garden, where the bean-poles had been blown down by the wind. She turned around.

– Are you looking for something? she asked.

– My riding-crop, please, he said.

And he began to hunt around on the bed, behind the doors, under the chairs; it had fallen to the ground, between the sacks and the wall. Mademoiselle Emma noticed it; she bent over the sacks of wheat. Charles, gallantly, sprang into action and, as he reached down over her, he felt his chest brush against the back of the girl bent beneath him. She straightened up, red-faced, and looked at him over her shoulder, handing him his riding-crop.

Instead of returning to Les Bertaux in three days' time, as he had promised, he was back the very next day, then regularly twice a week, not to mention unexpected visits now and again, as if in passing.

Everything, indeed, went well; the leg healed according to the book, and when, after forty-six days, Père Rouault was seen trying to walk all on his own around the yard, people began to consider Monsieur Bovary a man of great talent. Père Rouault said he wouldn't have had any better treatment from the top doctors in Yvetot or even in Rouen.

As for Charles, he scarcely bothered to ask himself why he enjoyed visiting Les Bertaux. Had he done so, he would no doubt have attributed his zeal to the gravity of the case, or perhaps to the fees he was expecting to receive. Though was that really why his visits to the farm were such a bright exception in the dull routine of his life? Those days he was up early, set off at a gallop, rode hard, got down to wipe his boots on the grass, and put on his black gloves before he went in. He liked to see himself riding into the yard, to feel the gate turning against his shoulder, to see the cock crowing on the wall, the boys running to meet him. He liked the barn and the stables; he liked Père Rouault, who gave him a fierce handshake and called him his saviour; he liked Mademoiselle Emma's little clogs on the clean-scrubbed kitchen flags; the high heels made her slightly taller, and, as she walked along in front of him, the wooden soles, springing back up again, clacked smartly on the leather boots she wore.

She always went with him as far as the doorstep. Waiting for them to bring his horse, she stood there by him. They had said goodbye, they had no more to say; the fresh air wrapped all about her, fondling the stray locks of hair at the nape of her neck, or tugging on the strings of the apron around her hips, fluttering them like streamers. One day, when it was thawing, the trees in the yard were oozing damp from their bark, the snow on top of the sheds was melting. She was at the door; she went to fetch her parasol, she opened it. The parasol, made of marbled silk, as the sun came shining through it, spread shifting colours over the whiteness of her face. There she was smiling in the moist warmth of its shade; and you could hear the drops of water, one by one, falling on the taut fabric.

When Charles first began going to Les Bertaux, the younger Madame Bovary never failed to ask about the patient, and, in the double-entry account-book that she kept, she had even chosen a nice clean page for Monsieur Rouault. But when she heard he had a daughter, she began to make inquiries; she discovered that Mademoiselle Rouault, brought up in a convent, with the Ursulines, had received, as they say, *a good education*, and that consequently she knew dancing, geography, drawing, embroidery and playing the piano. That was the end!

– So, she said to herself, that's the reason he looks so pleased when he's going to see her, and puts on his new waistcoat, at the risk of spoiling it in the rain? That woman! That woman! . . .

And she detested her, instinctively. At first, she vented her feelings in allusions, Charles did not pick them up; later, in casual remarks, that he let pass for fear of a row; finally, in remorseless diatribes to which he had no answer. – Why was he forever going back to Les Bertaux, now that Monsieur Rouault

was better and they still hadn't paid their bill? Ahah! Because
there was *a certain girl*, someone with plenty of small talk, who
did embroidery, and said clever things. That was what he was
after: he wanted young ladies! – And she went on:

– Père Rouault's daughter, a young lady! Fancy! Their grand-
father was a shepherd, and they've got a cousin who nearly had
to go to court for assault, in some quarrel. So much for all that
la-di-da of hers, showing off on Sundays in church in her silk
dress, like a countess. Anyway, without last year's rape-seed,
the old fellow would have been really stuck to pay his arrears
of rent!

From weariness, Charles ceased his visits to Les Bertaux.
Héloïse had made him swear he would never go again, with his
hand on the prayer-book, after much sobbing and kissing, in a
great explosion of love. He obeyed; but the audacity of his desire
protested against the servility of his conduct, and, with a kind
of innocent hypocrisy, he considered that this prohibition on
seeing her actually gave him a right to love her. And anyway,
the widow was skin and bones; she had long teeth; all year
round she wore a little black shawl with the point hanging down
between her scapulae; her lean frame she inserted into her
dresses like a thing sliding into a scabbard, dresses all too short,
that showed her ankles, and her great big shoes with the ribbons
criss-crossed over her grey stockings.

Charles's mother came to see them now and again; but, after
a few days, the daughter-in-law seemed to sharpen her to an
edge as keen as her own; and then, like a pair of knives, they
were into him with their scarifying remarks and their criticisms.
Unwise of him to eat so much! Why always be offering drinks
to everyone who drops in? What obstinacy, him not wearing
flannel!

It so happened early in the spring that a notary in Ingouville,
who managed widow Dubuc's capital, absconded, one fine day,
and took every penny with him. Héloïse, it was true, still owned,
as well as a share in a boat valued at six thousand francs, her
house in the Rue Saint-François; but even so, of all that fortune
that had been trumpeted so loud, not a thing, apart from a few
bits of furniture and some old clothes, had ever appeared in the

house. They had to find out where they stood. The house in
Dieppe was found to be riddled with mortgages right up to the
rafters; how much she had placed with the notary, God alone
knew, and the share in the boat came to no more than three
thousand francs. She had been telling lies, the little lady had! In
his exasperation, Monsieur Bovary senior, smashing a chair on
the floor, accused his wife of bringing misery on their son by
hitching him up to that harridan, whose harness wasn't worth
her hide. They came to Tostes. Questions were asked. There
were scenes. Héloïse, in tears, fell into her husband's arms,
beseeching him to protect her from his parents. Charles tried to
speak up for her. They were angry, and they left.

But *the damage was done.* A week later, as she was hanging
out the washing in the yard, she had a seizure and spat some
blood, and next day, as Charles turned his back to draw the
curtains, she said, 'Oh! My God!' heaved a sigh and passed out.
She was dead! How astonishing!

Once everything was finished at the cemetery, Charles went
home again. There was nobody downstairs; he went upstairs to
their room, saw her dress still hanging over the foot of the bed;
then, slumped across the escritoire, he stayed until it was night,
adrift in a troubled reverie. She had loved him, after all.

3

One morning, Père Rouault came to bring Charles the money
for setting his leg: seventy-five francs in forty-sou pieces, and a
turkey. He had heard about his misfortune, and consoled him
as best he could.

– I know what it's like, he said, clapping him on the shoulder;
I've been through it, just like you. The day I lost my dear wife I
went off into the fields so as to be all on my own; I dropped
down under a tree, I wept, I called to the good Lord, I ranted at
him; I just wanted to be like those moles I could see hanging up
there from the branches, with the worms crawling round their
insides, jiggered, you know. And when I thought as how other
folks, just that second, had their nice warm little wives in their

arms, I walloped the ground with my stick; I was out of my
mind very near, stopped eating, I did; thought of even going to
the café made me bad, you wouldn't believe it. Well now,
eventually, one day following another, spring on top of a winter
and autumn at the end of a summer, it just left off bit by bit,
inch by inch; went right away, and it was gone, gone down, I
mean, because there's always a bit of something left deep down,
like as if . . . a weight, just here, on your chest. Any road, since
it comes to us all in the end, you can't be letting yourself wither
away, wanting to be dead just because other folks has died. You
must pull yourself together, Monsieur Bovary; it'll pass. You
come over and see us; my daughter thinks about you, on and
off you know, and she says as how you're forgetting about her.
Here we are nearly spring; we'll fix you a bit of rabbit-shooting
in the warren, just to buck you up.

Charles followed his advice. He went back to Les Bertaux; he
found it all as he had last seen it, five months previously. The
pear-trees were already in blossom, and Père Rouault was up
and about again, coming and going, which made the farm seem
more cheerful.

Thinking it his duty to lavish every possible courtesy on the
doctor, because of his unhappy position, he begged him not to
take his hat off, spoke to him in an undertone, as if he had been
ill, and even pretended to be annoyed because they hadn't
cooked him something a bit lighter than for the others, such as
little pots of cream or some stewed pears. He told stories.
Charles found himself laughing; but the memory of his wife,
suddenly coming back, made him sad. Then coffee was served;
he thought of it no more.

He thought of it less and less, as he became used to living
alone. The novel pleasures of independence soon made his solitude more endurable. Now he could change his meal-times,
come and go without explanation, and, when he was really
tired, spread himself out, arms and legs, across the entire bed.
Hence, he coddled and pampered himself, and accepted any
consolations that were offered him. In point of fact, the death
of his wife had done him no harm at all in his profession, since
for weeks people had been saying: 'That poor young man! What

bad luck!' His name had spread, his practice had grown; and he could go to Les Bertaux just when he liked. He was oddly hopeful, obscurely happy; he thought himself better-looking as he brushed his whiskers in the mirror.

He arrived there one day about three o'clock; everybody was out in the fields; he went into the kitchen, but at first didn't notice Emma; the shutters were closed. Through the cracks in the wood, the sun cast long narrow stripes of brightness that broke across the angles of the furniture and trembled on the ceiling. Flies, on the table, were crawling up the glasses left there, and buzzing about in the bottom, drowning in the cider dregs. The daylight that came down the chimney, turning the soot on the fire-back to velvet, touched the cold cinders with blue. Between the window and the hearth, Emma was sewing; she wore no fichu, on her bare shoulders you could see little drops of sweat.

According to the country custom, she offered him something to drink. He refused, she insisted, and in the end asked him, laughingly, to have a glass of liqueur with her. So she went to the cupboard for a bottle of curaçao, reached down two little glasses, filled one right to the brim, poured only a drop into the other, and, after clinking glasses, raised it to her lips. As it was almost empty, she had to drink it from below; and, with her head right back, her lips pushed out, her neck stretching, she laughed at getting nothing, while the tip of her tongue, from between perfect teeth, licked delicately over the bottom of the glass.

She sat down again and she picked up her sewing, a white cotton stocking she was darning; she worked with her head bent; she said not a word, nor did Charles. The wind, coming under the door, rolled a bit of dust across the flagstones; he watched it drifting, and he heard only the pulse beating inside his head, and the cluck of a hen, far off, laying an egg in the farmyard. Emma, now and again, cooled her cheeks on the palms of her hands, chilling them again by touching the iron knob on the big fire-dogs.

She complained of having had, since the beginning of summer, spells of dizziness; she asked if sea-bathing would be good for her; she began to talk about the convent, Charles about his school, the phrases came to them. They went up to her room. She showed him her old music folder, the little books she had been given as prizes and the crowns made of oak-leaves, all forgotten at the bottom of the cupboard. And she told him about her mother, about the cemetery, and she even showed him the bed in the garden where she picked flowers, on the first Friday of every month, to lay upon her grave. But the gardener they had was hopeless; servants were such a problem! She would have dearly loved, if only during the winter, to live in town, though the very length of the fine days probably made the country even more boring in the summer; – and, according to what she was saying, her voice was clear, sharp or suddenly languid, with a trailing modulation that ended almost in a murmur, when she was talking to herself, – animated one moment, her eyes wide and innocent, then half closed, her gaze clouding with boredom, her thoughts drifting.

That night, on his way home, Charles went one by one through the things she had said, trying to remember them, to complete their meaning, so as to grasp something of her life before he had known her. But never could he imagine her, other than as he had first seen her, or exactly as he had just left her. He wondered what would become of her, whether she would marry, and whom? Père Rouault was, alas, decidedly rich, and she! . . . was lovely! But the image of Emma kept coming back to him, kept appearing before his eyes, and there was something monotonous like the noise of a humming-top droning in his ears: 'The doctor wants a wife, he does! The doctor wants a wife!' That night, he didn't sleep, his throat was dry, he was thirsty; he got up to take a drink from his water-jug and he opened the window; the sky was full of stars, there was a warm breeze, dogs were barking in the distance. His eyes turned towards Les Bertaux.

Thinking that after all he had nothing to lose, Charles promised himself he would ask for her when the opportunity arose; but, each time it did arise, the fear of not finding the appropriate words sealed up his lips.

Père Rouault would not have been vexed to have his daughter

taken off his hands, for she was hardly any use to him in the house. In his own mind he made excuses for her, thinking her too educated for farming, an accursed occupation, one that never made any man a millionaire. Far from making his fortune at it, the old chap was losing money every year; for, though he was an expert at driving a bargain, where he relished all the tricks of the trade, on the other hand the actual business of farming, with the internal management of the farm, suited him less than most. He really preferred not to take his hands out of his pockets, and he spared no expense where his own comfort was concerned, fond of good food, a big fire and a warm bed. He loved rough cider, a leg of lamb lightly cooked, coffee with brandy well mixed. He took his meals in the kitchen, on his own, in front of the fire, on a little table brought to him nicely set out, like at the theatre.

So once he noticed that Charles had the roses in his cheeks when he came near his daughter, which meant that one of these days he'd be asking for her in marriage, he chewed the whole thing over ahead of time. He did find him rather *weedy*, and this was not exactly the son-in-law he might have wished for; but he was said to be steady, careful with money, a clever chap, and most likely he wouldn't make too much fuss over the dowry. So, since Père Rouault was going to have to sell off twenty-two acres of *his property*, since he owed a lot to the mason, and to the harness-maker, since the cider-press needed a new shaft:

– If he asks me for her, he said to himself, he can have her.

At Michaelmas, Charles came to spend three days at Les Bertaux. The final day had slipped past like the rest, procrastinated away, a quarter of an hour at a time. Père Rouault went to see him off; they were walking down a deep lane, they were about to part; this was the moment. Charles gave himself just as far as the end of the hedge, and at last, when they had gone past it:

– Maître Rouault, he murmured, there is something I would like to say to you.

They came to a halt. Charles said not a word.

– Well, say your piece! I do have a fair idea what it's all about, said Père Rouault, laughing softly.

– Père Rouault . . . Père Rouault . . ., stammered Charles.

– Nothing as I'd like better, the farmer went on. I expect my little girl will go along with me, but we'd best ask her opinion. You be off, now; I'll get back home. If it's yes, do you follow me, there's no need for you to come back again, on account of the visitors, and, besides, it'd be too much for her. But so as you don't get yourself in a lather, I'll open the window-shutter wide against the wall: you'll be able to see it from the back, if you lean over the hedge.

And away he went.

Charles tethered his horse to a tree. He ran to the path; he waited. Half an hour went past, he counted nineteen minutes on his watch. Suddenly there was a banging noise against the wall; the shutter had jerked open, the catch was still quivering.

Next day, by nine o'clock, he was at the farm. Emma blushed when he came in, though she gave a forced little laugh, to keep herself in countenance. Père Rouault embraced his future son-in-law. All discussion of money matters was postponed; there was, after all, plenty of time, since the marriage could not decently take place before the end of Charles's period of mourning, that is to say, in the spring of the following year.

Winter went by them as they waited. Mademoiselle Rouault was busy with her trousseau. Part of it was ordered from Rouen, and she made the chemises and the nightcaps herself, from some fashion-plates that she borrowed. When Charles visited the farm, they talked about the preparations for the wedding, they wondered in which room to hold the dinner; they imagined the dishes they would need, and what should the entrées be?

Emma, however, yearned to be married at midnight, by torch-light;[9] but Père Rouault wouldn't hear of it. So there was a wedding-feast, with forty-three guests who sat eating for sixteen hours, which carried on the following day and into the next few days.

4

The guests arrived early, in their various vehicles, one-horse carts, two-wheeled wagons, old cabs with no hoods, furniture vans with leather curtains, and the young people from the nearest villages came standing, in farm-carts, in rows, holding on to the side-rails to stop themselves falling off, trotting along and thoroughly shaken about. People came from thirty miles away, from Goderville, from Normanville and from Cany. All the relatives on both sides had been invited, broken friendships had been mended, long-lost acquaintances had been written to.

Now and again, you could hear the crack of a whip behind the hedge; the gate would open: it was a cart coming in. Galloping right up to the bottom of the steps, it stopped abruptly, and emptied out its load; they got down from both sides, everyone rubbing their knees and stretching their arms. The ladies, in bonnets, wore dresses in the city style, gold watch-chains, pelerines tucked into their belts, or little coloured shawls pinned down behind, leaving the back of the neck bare. The boys, dressed just like their daddies, looked uncomfortable in their new clothes (that day indeed many were to step out in their very first pair of boots), and, standing there beside them, without a whisper, in her white communion dress let down for the occasion, you saw an adolescent girl, about fourteen or fifteen years old, probably their cousin or their elder sister, blushing, bewildered, her hair plastered with rose pomade, most anxious not to soil her gloves. As there were not nearly enough stable-boys to unharness all the carriages, the gentlemen rolled up their sleeves and went about it themselves. According to their different social positions, they wore tailcoats, overcoats, jackets or cutaway coats: – fine tailcoats, revered by an entire family, and taken from the wardrobe only for great occasions; overcoats with long skirts flapping in the wind, with cylindrical collars, with pockets the size of sacks; jackets of shoddy cloth, usually worn along with some kind of cap that had a brass hoop round the peak; very short cutaway coats, with a pair of buttons at the back set close together just like eyes, and tails that looked as though they'd been chopped out of a single plank, with a carpenter's axe. Others there were (but they, of course, would be sitting at the far end of the table) in their best smocks, smocks with the collar turned down, gathered in little pleats across the back, and fastened very low around the waist with an embroidered belt.

And the starched shirts were stiff as breastplates! Every head of hair was freshly clipped, ears were sticking out, cheeks were close-shaven; some there were who had left their beds before dawn, when there was scarcely enough light to be using a razor, and now had great diagonal gashes across their upper lip, or, along the jaw, flaps of detached skin as big as a three-franc piece, inflamed by the fresh air along the way, so that all those great white beaming faces were blotched with bits of pink.

Because the town hall was only a couple of miles from the farm, they went there on foot, and walked back, after the ceremony at the church. The procession held together at first, like a coloured scarf, winding across the fields, along the narrow twisting path through the green corn, soon it began to stretch out and split into little groups, dawdling along in conversation. The fiddler led the way, the scroll of his violin trimmed with ribbons; next came the bride and groom, the relatives, friends, in a crowd, and the children lingering behind, engrossed in stripping the seeds from the oat-grass, or playing their games, just out of sight. Emma's dress was so long that it dragged a little at the back; every so often, she stopped to pull it up, and then very delicately, with gloved fingers, she picked off the couch-grass and the thistle burrs, while Charles stood there, empty handed, waiting for her to be finished. Père Rouault, with a new silk hat on his head and cuffs on his black coat that hung down to the tips of his fingers, gave his arm to the elder Madame Bovary. Monsieur Bovary senior, who, thoroughly despising the lot of them, had simply come wearing a military-style coat with a single row of buttons, was spouting alehouse flatteries to a blonde peasant-girl. She curtsied, she blushed, quite lost for words. The other wedding-guests were talking business or playing sly tricks on each other, warming up for the party; and, whenever they stopped to listen, they could still hear the fiddler

squeaking away as he led them across the fields. When he noticed
that everyone was far behind him, he would stop to draw breath,
slowly rosin his bow, to give the strings a sharper sound, and
then he would set off again, wagging the neck of his violin
down-up-down-up, the better to mark out the rhythm for himself. From far away, the sound of the music scattered the little
birds.

It was in the wagon-shed that the table had been laid. There
were four sirloins, six dishes of chicken fricassee, a veal stew,
three legs of mutton, and, in the middle, a nice roast suckling
pig, flanked by four chitterlings with sorrel. At each corner,
stood jugs of brandy. Bottles of sweet cider had creamy froth
oozing out past their corks, and every glass had already been
filled to the brim with wine. Big dishes of yellow custard, shuddering whenever the table was jogged, displayed, on their
smooth surface, the initials of the newly-weds in arabesques of
sugared almonds. They had brought in a pastry-cook from
Yvetot for the tarts and the cakes. Because he was new to the
district, he had taken great pains; and at dessert he appeared in
person, carrying an elaborate confection that drew loud cries.
At the base, to begin with, there was a square of blue cardboard
representing a temple with porticoes, colonnades and stucco
statuettes all around, in little niches decorated with gold paper
stars; then on the second layer there was a castle made of Savoy
cake, encircled by tiny fortifications of angelica, almonds, raisins
and segments of orange; and finally, on the upper platform, a
green field with rocks and pools of jam and boats made out of
nutshells, there was arrayed a little Cupid, perched on a chocolate swing, its two poles finished off with two real rose-buds,
just like knobs, on the top.

It went on all day, the eating. When they were tired of sitting
down, they went out for a stroll around the farmyard or played
a game of corks in the barn; then it was back to the table. Some
of them, by the end, were asleep and snoring in their seats.
However, with the coffee, everything came back to life again;
they started singing, they did party tricks, they lifted weights,
they played *Under My Thumb*, they tried lifting the carts on to
their shoulders, they told bedroom jokes, they kissed the ladies.

At dark, when it was time to leave, the horses, stuffed to the ears with oats, could hardly be got back into the shafts again; they kicked, they reared, the harness broke, their masters were cursing or laughing; and throughout the night, by the light of the moon, on the country roads, there were carriages running away at full gallop, bouncing into the ditches, jumping over piles of stones, running up the bank, with women leaning right out to catch hold of the reins.

Those who were staying at Les Bertaux spent the night drinking in the kitchen. The children had fallen asleep beneath the benches.

The bride had pleaded with her father to be spared the traditional antics. However, a fishmonger cousin (who had even brought a pair of soles as a wedding-present) was about to squirt a mouthful of water through the keyhole, when Rouault arrived just in time to stop him, explaining that his son-in-law's social position did not permit such improprieties. The cousin, though with great reluctance, yielded to this argument. Inwardly, he accused Père Rouault of being proud, and he went off into a corner with four or five other guests who, having been unluckily served the scrag-end of the meat more than once, also felt that they had been badly treated, and were now all muttering about their host and quietly wishing his ruin.

The elder Madame Bovary had not opened her mouth all day. She had not been consulted about either the wedding-dress, or the organization of the banquet; she went to bed early. Her husband, instead of following her, sent to Saint-Victor for some cigars and smoked until daybreak, drinking kirsch grog, a mixture quite unheard of in those parts, and henceforth the source of his greatly enhanced local reputation.

Charles had no talent for the facetious, he had not shone at his wedding. He responded lamely to the quips, the puns, the word-play, the compliments and the ribaldries which were dutifully hurled in his direction as soon as the soup appeared.

Next morning, however, he seemed a different man. He was the one you would think had just lost his virginity, whereas the bride gave not the slightest sign of anything to anybody. Even the wittiest were lost for words, and they stared at her, as she went past, gravely inscrutable. But Charles was hiding nothing. He called her my wife, my dear, kept asking everyone where she was, went looking for her everywhere, and repeatedly he would take her off outside into the yard, where they caught sight of him, in among the trees, putting his arm around her waist, and walking along half leaning on her, as he nestled his face in the frills of her bodice.

Two days after the wedding, the couple departed: Charles, because of his patients, could not be away any longer. Père Rouault had them driven back in his cart and went with them himself as far as Vassonville. There he embraced his daughter one last time, stepped down and went upon his way. Once he had gone about a hundred yards, he stopped, and, as he watched the cart disappearing, with its wheels turning in the dust, he gave an immense sigh. Then he remembered his own wedding-day, his early life, his wife's first pregnancy; he was proper happy, he was, the day he'd fetched her from her father's, to the new house, mounted behind him trotting across the snow; for it was near Christmas and the fields were all white; she had one arm round him, her basket hanging on the other; the wind was lifting the long ribbons on her Caux head-dress, flapping the lace now and again across her mouth, and, when he turned round, there she was, close against his shoulder, her little pink face, smiling quietly, beneath the big gold brooch on her bonnet. To warm her fingers she slipped them, every so often, inside his shirt. So long ago, all of that! Their son, by now, he would have been thirty! He turned to look back, the road was empty. He felt as sad as an uninhabited house; and, as the sweet memories mingled with the sombre thoughts in his feast-fuddled head, he was quite tempted for a minute to go for a stroll round by the church. However, afraid that the sight of the place would only make him feel even sadder, he went straight back home.

Monsieur and Madame Charles arrived in Tostes, at about six o'clock. The neighbours were at their windows to see their doctor with his new wife.

The old servant introduced herself, paid her respects, apologized for not having dinner ready, and suggested that Madame, meanwhile, might look over her house.

5

The brick house-front was right in line with the street, or rather the road. Behind the door there hung a cloak with a little collar, a bridle, a black leather cap, and, in a corner, on the floor, a pair of leggings still caked with dry mud. To the right was the parlour, that is to say, a dining-room and a sitting-room combined. Canary-yellow wallpaper, lightened near the ceiling by a garland of pale flowers, was peeling away from its wrinkled canvas backing; white calico curtains, with a red fringe, hung at the windows, and on the narrow mantelpiece there gleamed a clock with a bust of Hippocrates, in between a pair of silver-plated candlesticks, under oval glass shades. On the other side of the passage was Charles's consulting-room, a small space about six yards across, with a table, three stools, and an office-chair. The volumes of the *Dictionnaire des sciences médicales*, uncut, but with their bindings damaged from being bought and sold so frequently, were the sole adornment of the six shelves of the pinewood bookcase. Cooking smells seeped through the wall, during consultations, and likewise anyone in the kitchen could hear the patients coughing next door as they recited their ailments. Next, opening directly on to the stable-yard, there was a large dilapidated room with a bread-oven, now used as a wood-shed, a cellar, a store-room, full of old ironmongery, empty barrels, disused garden implements, and a pile of other dusty objects whose purposes it was no longer possible to guess.

The garden, long and narrow, ran between clay walls with espaliered apricot-trees, down to a thorn-hedge that divided it from the fields. In the middle there was a slate sundial, on a stone pedestal; four flower-beds planted with skimpy dog-roses had been laid out symmetrically around the more useful square of kitchen-garden. At the far end, under the little fir-trees, a plaster *curé* stood reading his breviary.

Emma went upstairs. In the first room there was no furniture; but in the second room, the conjugal bedroom, there was a mahogany bed in an alcove with red hangings. A box covered in sea-shells adorned the chest of drawers; and, there, on the writing-desk, by the window, in a vase, was a bouquet of orange-blossom, tied up with white satin ribbons. It was a wedding-bouquet, the other bride's bouquet! She gazed at it. Charles realized, he picked it up and took it off to the attic, while Emma sat in an armchair (they were arranging her things around her), thinking about her own wedding-bouquet, packed in its bandbox, and wondering, vaguely, what would happen to it, if she should die one day.

She was busy, the first few days, pondering alterations to her house. She took the shades off the candlesticks, had the parlour repapered, the stairs repainted, and had benches put in the garden, around the sundial; and she even made inquiries about a pond with a fountain and some fish. Finally her husband, knowing how much she liked driving out, picked up a second-hand gig which, with new lamps and splash-boards in mottled leather, looked almost like a tilbury.

He was so happy and had not a single care in the world. A meal together, an evening walk along the road, the way she put her hand up to her hair, the sight of her straw hat hanging from a window-latch, along with all the other little things that Charles had never even dreamed of, now made up the circle of his happiness. In bed, in the morning, close together on the pillow, he gazed at the sunlight playing in the golden down on her cheeks, half hidden by the scalloped edges of her bonnet. So very close, her eyes seemed even bigger, especially when she first awoke and her eyelids fluttered into life. Black in the shadows, and deep blue in full daylight, as if the colours were floating layer upon layer, thickest in the depths, coming clear and bright towards the surface. His eye drifted away into the deep, and there he saw himself in miniature, head and shoulders, with his nightcap on his head and his shirt unbuttoned. He would get up. She would go to the window to watch him leaving; and she would lean on the sill, between the two pots of geraniums, in her dressing-gown, which was wrapped loose about her. Charles, down below, was buckling his spurs, one foot on the mounting-block; and she would carry on talking to him from up above, biting a piece from a flower or a leaf, blowing it down to him, and it glided, it floated, it turned half-circles in the air like a bird, catching, before it fell to earth, in the tangled mane of the old white mare, standing still at the door. Charles, from his horse, blew her a kiss; she waved to him, she closed the window, he was gone. And so he went, along the open road, unrolling in an endless dusty ribbon, down sunken lanes curtained over with trees, on footpaths where the corn grew knee-high, with the sun upon his shoulders and the morning air in his lungs, his heart filled with the night's enjoyments, tranquil the spirit and contented the flesh, he went along, ruminating over his happiness, like those who, after a meal, still relish the taste of the truffles.

When, until now, had he had any pleasure in life? Was it in his school-days, shut away behind those high walls, alone among his classmates, who had more money than he did or were better at their lessons, who laughed at his accent, who jeered at his clothes, whose mothers came to visit them with fancy cakes in their muffs? Or was it later, when he had been a medical student and had never had enough in his pocket to go dancing with some little factory-girl who would have become his mistress? Then he had lived fourteen months with the widow, whose feet, in bed, had been as cold as ice. Now, at last, he was the master of this lovely woman whom he adored. The universe, for him, did not extend beyond the silken round of her skirts; and he would reproach himself for not loving her, he needed to see her again; he hurried back home, climbed the stairs, his heart pounding. Emma, in the bedroom, was dressing; he came up on tiptoe, he kissed the back of her neck, she gave a cry.

He couldn't stop himself continually touching her comb, her rings, her scarf; sometimes he gave her big wet kisses on the cheek, sometimes a string of little kisses along her bare arm, from her fingertips to her shoulder; and she held him away, half laughing and half annoyed, just as one would with a clinging child.

Before her wedding-day, she had thought she was in love; but since she lacked the happiness that should have come from that love, she must have been mistaken, she fancied. And Emma sought to find out exactly what was meant in real life by the words *felicity*, *passion* and *rapture*, which had seemed so fine on the pages of the books.

6

She had read *Paul et Virginie*[10] and dreamed of the bamboo hut, Domingo the nigger, Faithful the dog, and especially of the sweet friendship of a dear little brother, who goes to fetch red fruit for you from great trees taller than steeples, or runs barefoot along the sand to bring you a bird's nest.

When she was thirteen, her father took her to the town, to put her in the convent. They stopped at an inn in the Saint-Gervais quarter, where supper was served to them on painted plates depicting the story of Mademoiselle de la Vallière.[11] The explanatory legends, half scratched away by the blades of many knives, glorified religion, the subtleties of the heart and the splendours of the court.

Far from being bored during her early days in the convent, she enjoyed the company of the good sisters, who, to entertain her, took her into the chapel, which you reached from the refectory by a long corridor. She played very little during recreation, had a good grasp of the catechism, and she was the one who always answered His Reverence's difficult questions. Never leaving the stale warmth of the class-room, living among those women with their white faces and their rosaries and copper crosses, slowly she was soothed by the mystic languor she inhaled from the perfumes of the altar, the chill of holy water and the glow of the candles. Instead of following the mass, she would gaze in her book at the pious vignettes with their azure borders, and she loved the sick lamb, the Sacred Heart pierced by sharp arrows, or poor Jesus, sinking beneath the weight of his cross. She attempted, as a mortification, to go a whole day without food. She tried to think of some vow or other to fulfil.

When she went to confession, she made up little sins so as to stay there longer, kneeling in the shadows, her hands joined, her face against the screen beneath the whispering of the priest. The metaphors of the betrothed, the spouse, the celestial lover and the eternal marriage, such as recur in sermons, excited a strange sweetness deep in her soul.

In the evening, before prayers, there was a reading in the schoolroom. During the week, it would be something taken from the Bible or from the *Lectures* of the Abbé Frayssinous,[12] and, on Sunday, passages from the *Génie du christianisme*,[13] as a treat. How she listened, the first time, to the sonorous lamentations of romantic melancholia echoing out across heaven and earth! If her childhood had been spent in the dark back-room of a shop in some town, she would now perhaps have been kindled by the lyric surgings of nature which only normally reach us as through the interpretation of a writer. But she knew the country only too well; she knew the lowing of cattle, the milking, the ploughing. Familiar with the tranquil, she inclined, instead, towards the tumultuous. She loved the sea only for the sake of tempests, the meadow only as a background for some ruined pile. From everything she had to extract some kind of personal profit; and she discarded as useless anything that did not lend itself to her heart's immediate satisfaction – endowed with a temperament more sentimental than artistic, preferring emotions rather than landscapes.

There was an old maid who used to come to the convent every month, for a week, to mend the linen. Protected by the archbishop as belonging to an ancient family of gentlefolk ruined during the Revolution, she ate in the refectory with the nuns, and spent a moment, after the meal, having a little chat with them before she went back to work. The girls would often slip out of the schoolroom to go and see her. She knew by heart the love-songs of the last century, singing them to herself, as she plied her needle. She would tell stories, bring you the news, do your errands in town, and lend the big girls, clandestinely, one of the novels she always kept in the pocket of her apron, from which the good lady herself devoured long chapters, in the intervals of her task. They were about love, lovers, loving, martyred maidens swooning in secluded lodges, postilions slain every other mile, horses ridden to death on every page, dark forests, aching hearts, promising, sobbing, kisses and tears, little boats by moonlight, nightingales in the grove, *gentlemen* brave as lions, tender as lambs, virtuous as a dream, always well dressed, and weeping pints. For six months, at the age of fifteen, Emma dabbled in the remains of old lending libraries. From Walter Scott, subsequently, she conceived a passion for things historical, dreamed about coffers, guard-rooms and minstrels. She would have liked to live in some old manor-house, like those chatelaines in their long corsages, under their trefoiled Gothic arches, spending their days, elbows on the parapet and chin in hand, looking out far across the fields for the white-plumed rider galloping towards her on his black horse. In those months she made a cult of Mary Stuart, and had an enthusiastic veneration for illustrious or ill-fated women. Joan of Arc, Héloïse, Agnès Sorel, La Belle Ferronière, and Clémence Isaure,[14] for her, they shone out like comets against the black immensity of history, whence there emerged as well, but further lost in shadow, and quite disconnected, Saint Louis under his oak-tree, the dying Bayard, a few ferocious crimes done by Louis XI, Saint Bartholomew's something or other,[15] the white plume of Henri IV, and always the memory of the painted plates exalting Louis XIV.

In the music lesson, in the ballads that she sang, there were nothing but little angels with golden wings, madonnas, lagoons, gondoliers, placid creations that allowed her a glimpse, for all the banality of the words and the clumsiness of the music, a glimpse of the seductive phantasmagoria of sentimental realities. Some of her companions brought back to the convent keepsakes received as New Year presents. They had to be kept hidden, it was quite a business; they used to read them in the dormitory. Delicately handling their fine satin bindings, Emma's dazzled eyes were drawn by the names of the unknown writers, most of them counts or viscounts, at the end of each piece.

She shivered as her breath lifted the tissue paper over the engravings, and it curved and half folded and then fell back, softly unfurling. And there, on a balustraded balcony, was a young man in a short cloak embracing a young girl in a milk-white gown, with a purse at her belt; or there were nameless portraits of blonde English ladies looking out at you, from under round straw hats, with their big bright eyes. You saw them lounging in carriages, gliding along through the park, with a greyhound bounding ahead of the equipage driven at a trot by two little postilions in white breeches. Others, dreaming on couches, an unsealed letter at their side, were gazing up at the moon, through the open window, half-draped with a dark curtain. The simple virgins, shedding a single tear, were blowing little kisses to doves through the bars of a Gothic cage, or, smiling pensively, they were plucking the petals from a daisy with their tapering fingers that curved just like long spike-tipped shoes. And the sultans with long pipes were there too, swooning in arbours, in the arms of dancing-girls, the djiaours, the Turkish sabres, the Greek fezzes, and, especially, the monochrome land-scapes of Dithyrambia, which often blend in a single image palm-trees and pine-trees, tigers to the right, a lion on the left, Tartar minarets on the horizon, Roman ruins in the foreground, then some camels kneeling; – the whole thing framed by a nicely hygienic virgin forest, with a great perpendicular sunbeam trembling on the water, steel grey, with white-etched signs, here and there, for floating swans.

And the shaded oil-lamp, fixed to the wall just above Emma's head, lit up all these pictures of the world, which flowed by one after another, in the silence of the dormitory, to the distant sound of a late cab somewhere still rolling along the boulevards.

When her mother died, she wept a great deal the first few days. She had a memorial card made from the dead woman's hair, and, in a letter she sent to Les Bertaux, full of sad reflections on life, she asked to be buried eventually in the same grave. The old man thought she was ill and came to see her. Emma was inwardly satisfied to feel she had reached at her first attempt that ideal exquisite pale existence, never attained by vulgar souls. So she drifted with the meanderings of Lamartine,[16] listened to harps on lakes, the songs of dying swans, the falling of leaves, the virgin hearts rising to heaven, and the voice of the Eternal speaking softly in the valleys. She grew bored, would not admit it, continued out of habit, out of vanity, and was eventually surprised to feel so calm, with no more sadness in her heart than she had wrinkles on her brow.

The good sisters, who had been so confident of her vocation, realized in great astonishment that Mademoiselle Rouault seemed to be slipping from their grasp. They had, indeed, lavished upon her so many prayers, retreats, novenas and sermons, had preached so thoroughly the reverence she owed to the saints and martyrs, and given so much good advice concerning the modesty of the body and the salvation of the soul, that she did just what horses do when the rein is too tight: she stopped short and the bit slipped from her mouth. With a mind that was practical, even in the midst of her enthusiasms, she had loved the Church for the sake of the flowers, music for the words of the ballads, and literature for its power to kindle her passions; this mind rebelled against the mysteries of faith, as she became ever more irritated by the discipline, which was a thing alien to her temperament. When her father took her away from the school, no one was sorry to see her go. The Mother Superior even found that she had, of late, displayed little reverence towards their community.

Emma, home once again, at first enjoyed managing the servants, then began to loathe the countryside and to long for her convent. The first time Charles came to Les Bertaux, she considered herself utterly disillusioned, with nothing more to learn, nothing more to feel.

But the anxieties of her new situation, or perhaps the agitation caused by the presence of this man, had sufficed to make her believe that she at last possessed that marvellous passion which had hitherto been like a gorgeous pink-feathered bird floating high above in a splendid poetical heaven; – and it seemed quite inconceivable that this calm life of hers could really be the happiness of which she used to dream.

7

Sometimes she thought that these were after all the best days of her life, the honeymoon, so-called. To savour their sweetness you would probably have to set off for those places with marvellous names where wedding-nights beget a more delicious lethargy. In a post-chaise, with blue silk blinds, slowly you climb the steep roads, and the postilion's song is echoing across the mountains with the sound of the goat-bells and the murmuring waterfall. As the sun is going down, on the shore of the bay you breathe the scent of lemon-trees; that night, on the terrace of a villa, hand in hand together, you gaze at the stars and you talk of the future. To her it seemed that certain places on earth must produce happiness, like the plants that thrive in a certain soil and are stunted everywhere else. Why could she not be leaning out on the balcony of a Swiss chalet, or hiding her sadness in a cottage in Scotland, with a husband wearing a long-tailed black velvet coat, and soft boots, a pointed hat and frills on his shirt!

It may well have been that she wanted somehow to confide these secrets of hers. But how could she give voice to an elusive malaise, that melts like a cloud, that swirls like the wind? She didn't have the words, the opportunity, the courage.

If Charles had only wished it, if he had but guessed it, if his eye had once greeted her thoughts, she knew that a sudden abundance would have dropped from her heart, as the ripe fruit will fall from the tree at a touch. But, as the intimacy of their daily life began to bind them closer, so there grew up an inward detachment which freed her from him.

Charles's conversation was as flat as any pavement, everyone's ideas trudging along it in their weekday clothes, rousing no emotion, no laughter, no reverie. When he was living in Rouen, he said, he had never ventured to the theatre to see the company from Paris. He couldn't swim, or fence or shoot, and he wasn't able to explain, one day, a riding term which she had come across in a novel.

A man, surely, ought to know everything, ought to excel in a host of activities, ought to initiate you into the energies of passion, the refinements of life, all its mysteries. But this man knew nothing, taught nothing, desired nothing. He thought her happy; and she resented his so-solid calm, his ponderous serenity, the very happiness that she brought him.

Sometimes she would be sketching; and for Charles it was hugely entertaining to stand there, bolt upright, watching her bent over the drawing-block, with her eyes half closed to see her work more clearly, or rolling up, between finger and thumb, little breadcrumb pellets.[17] And on the piano, the faster her fingers went, the more amazed he was. She struck the notes firmly, and ran all the way down from the top of the keyboard without stopping. Brought back to life again by her playing, the old instrument, with its buzzing strings, could be heard right at the other end of the village if the window was open, and often the bailiff's clerk, on his way down the street, hatless and beslippered, would stop and listen, with a sheet of paper in his hand.

Emma, what was more, knew how to run her house. She sent out the doctor's bills to the patients, in nicely phrased letters that scarcely mentioned money. When, on Sundays, they had one of the neighbours to dinner, she would contrive something rather special; she had the knack of arranging the plums in a pyramid on top of a few vine-leaves, she served pots of fruit preserve turned out on to a plate, and even talked of buying finger-bowls for use at dessert. From all this there redounded considerable acclaim for Bovary.

Charles began to feel rather pleased with himself for possessing such a fine wife. In the sitting-room he proudly showed off two little sketches of hers, done in pencil, which he had had mounted in very large frames and hung on the wall with long green cords. Coming out of mass, you saw him standing at his door in a pair of splendidly embroidered slippers.

He used to come back late, at ten o'clock, sometimes at midnight. He would ask for something to eat, and, since the maid had gone to bed, it would be Emma who saw to him. He took off his coat to be more at ease as he ate. One after another he recited the names of all the people he had met, the villages he had been to, the prescriptions he had written, and, well pleased with himself, he ate up the rest of the stew, cut the rind from his cheese, munched an apple, finished off the wine, then went up to bed, lay down on his back and began to snore.

Having long been used to a cotton nightcap, he found his silk handkerchief was always slipping off; and so his hair, in the morning, would be hanging down over his face, white with feathers from the pillow, which used to come undone in the course of the night. He always wore thick boots, with two great creases at the instep slanting towards the ankle, with the rest of the upper smooth and straight, as tight as on a shoe-tree. He said *they were plenty good enough for the country*.

His mother approved of such economies; for she still came to see him, whenever there was some rather violent outburst at home; and yet the elder Madame Bovary seemed to be prejudiced against her daughter-in-law. She found her *style too grand for her situation*; firewood, sugar and candles were *disappearing at a famous rate*, and the amount of coal that was used in the kitchen would have done dinners for twenty-five! She organized her linen-cupboards and taught her to keep an eye on the butcher when he delivered the meat. Emma accepted these instructions; Madame Bovary showered them upon her; and the words *mother* and *daughter* went back and forth all day long, accompanied by a little quiver of the lip, each woman uttering sweet words in a voice trembling with anger.

Back in the days of Madame Dubuc, the old woman felt she was still the favourite; but now, in Charles's love for Emma she saw a betrayal of her tenderness, an encroachment on what was her property; and she observed her son's happiness in dejected silence, like a ruined man gazing in, through the window, at the people dining in his old house. She reminded him, in the guise of reminiscence, of her troubles and her sacrifices, and, comparing these with Emma's carelessness, concluded that it was scarcely reasonable to adore her so exclusively.

Charles did not know what to say; he respected his mother, and he loved his wife immensely; the judgement of the one he considered infallible, and yet he found the other irreproachable. Once Madame Bovary had gone, he ventured timidly (and in the same terms) one or two of the more anodyne observations

he had heard from his mother; Emma, exposing his blunder
with a single word, sent him off to his patients.

However, according to the theories she believed, she did try
to rouse herself to love. By moonlight, in the garden, she would
recite all the passionate verses that she knew and sing to him
with a sigh many a melancholy adagio; but she found herself
just as calm afterwards as she had been before, and Charles
seemed neither more amorous nor more excited.

Once she had tried striking the flint upon her heart without
getting any spark from it at all, and, being moreover unable to
understand what she did not experience, just as she did not
believe in anything that came in unconventional form, she easily
convinced herself that there was nothing startling about
Charles's passion. His eagerness had turned into a routine; he
embraced her at the same time every day. It was a habit like any
other, a favourite pudding after the monotony of dinner.

A gamekeeper, cured by Monsieur of an inflammation of the
lungs, had given Madame a little Italian greyhound; she used to
take it with her when she went out for a walk, which she
sometimes did so as to be alone for a moment, and not to have
to look at the eternal garden and the dusty road.

She used to go as far as the beech-wood at Banneville, near
the derelict summer-house that stands on the edge of the fields,
at an angle to the wall. Down in the deep ditch, among the
grasses, there are slender reeds with keen-edged leaves.

She would begin by looking around her, to see if anything
had changed since the last time she was here. She found fox-
gloves and wallflowers in the same places, clumps of nettles
growing round the big stones, and patches of lichen along the
three windows, with their locked shutters rotting away, on their
rusty iron hinges. At first her thoughts, just drifting, strayed
randomly about, like her greyhound, running in circles across
the field, yapping at the yellow butterflies, hunting field-mice,
or nibbling at the poppies on the edge of a corn-field. Then her
ideas gradually came together, and, sitting on the grass, poking
at it with the point of her sunshade, Emma kept saying to herself:

– Oh, why, dear God, did I marry him?

She wondered whether, if her chances had been different, she might have met a different man; and she tried to imagine what it would have been like, the things that hadn't happened, the different life, the husband she hadn't met. They were certainly not all like this one of hers. He could have been handsome, witty, distinguished, attractive, as they were no doubt, the men her old schoolfriends had married. What were they doing now? In the city, amid the noise of the streets, the buzzing theatres and the bright lights of the ballroom, theirs was the kind of life that opens up the heart, that brings the senses into bloom. But this, this life of hers was as cold as an attic that looks north; and boredom, quiet as the spider, was spinning its web in the shadowy places of her heart. She remembered the prize-giving days at the convent, when she went up on to the platform to receive her little crowns. With her hair in plaits, her white dress and her prunella shoes showing, she did look pretty, and the gentlemen, as she made her way back to her seat, would lean over to pay her compliments; the yard was full of carriages, people were saying goodbye to her from their windows, the music-master was waving as he passed by, carrying his violin case. How far away it was! So very far away!

She called Djali,[18] held her between her knees, stroked her long delicate head and told her:

– Come on, kiss missy. Not a care in the world, have you?

Then, gazing at the elegant creature's melancholy expression as it slowly gave a yawn, she was moved; and, comparing it to herself, she spoke aloud to it, as if consoling one of the afflicted.

Now and again there came gusts of wind, sea-breezes sweeping right across the flat lands of Caux, bringing to inland fields the distant salt freshness. There was a whistling down among the rushes, a rustling and a fluttering in the beech-leaves; and the tree-tops, swaying to and fro, kept up their immense murmuring. Emma drew her shawl around her shoulders and got to her feet.

In the avenue, a dim green light filtered down through the leaves on to the smooth moss that crackled softly beneath her feet. The sun was setting; the sky was red between the branches, and the row of tree-trunks looked just like a brown colonnade against a golden background; seized with fear, she called Djali, hurried back to Tostes along the main road, slumped into an armchair, and spoke not a word all evening.

But, near the end of September, something extraordinary happened to her: she was invited to La Vaubyessard, home of the Marquis d'Andervilliers.

Secretary of State under the Restoration, the Marquis, in his attempt to re-enter political life, was just beginning his campaign as a candidate for the Chamber of Deputies. In the winter he made great distributions of firewood, and, in General Council, made enthusiastic demands for more new roads in his constituency. In the middle of summer, he had had an abscess in his mouth, which Charles had cured quite miraculously, with a nice touch of the lancet. The steward, sent to Tostes to pay for the operation, reported, that evening, how he had seen some superb cherries in the doctor's little garden. Now, the cherry-trees were doing badly at La Vaubyessard; Monsieur le Marquis asked Bovary for a few cuttings, made a point of thanking him in person, noticed Emma, thought she had a nice figure and didn't curtsy to him like a milkmaid; consequently it was not felt at the château that it would be overstepping the bounds of condescension, or on the other hand be committing an impropriety, to send the young couple an invitation.

One Wednesday, at three o'clock, Monsieur and Madame Bovary, in their gig, set off for La Vaubyessard, with a great big trunk strapped on behind and a hat-box on the platform. Charles had, in addition, a parcel down by his feet.

They arrived at nightfall, just as they were lighting the lamps in the park, to guide the carriages.

8

The château, recently built, in the Italian-style, with two salient wings and three flights of steps, lay at the far end of an enormous park, where a few cows grazed in among clusters of tall trees, while groups of shrubs, rhododendrons, syringa and guelder-rose spilled over the curve of the gravel drive with their unkempt clustering greenery. A stream ran under a bridge; through the mist you could make out thatched buildings, scattered across the park, which was bounded to left and right by thickly wooded hillside, and behind the house, among the trees, there stood, in parallel, the coach-houses and the stables, the only remains of the earlier château that had been demolished.

Charles's gig stopped at the middle flight of steps; servants appeared; the Marquis stepped forward, and, offering his arm to the doctor's wife, led her into the hall.

It was lofty, paved with marble, and the sound of footsteps, with the sound of voices, went echoing about like in a church. Opposite the entrance there was a straight staircase, and on the left overlooking the garden a gallery that led to the billiard-room, from whence came the click-click of ivory balls. As she passed through on her way to the drawing-room, Emma saw a group of grave-looking men, their chins resting on high cravats, each bemedalled, and smiling silently, as they made their strokes. On those dark-panelled walls, great gilded frames each displayed a black-lettered inscription. She read: 'Jean-Antoine d'Andervilliers d'Yverbonville, Comte de la Vaubyessard and Baron de la Fresnaye, killed at the Battle of Coutras, 20 October 1587.' And on another: 'Jean-Antoine-Henry-Guy d'Andervilliers de la Vaubyessard, Admiral of France and Knight of the Order of Saint Michael, wounded at the Battle of Hougue-Saint-Vaast, 29 May 1692, died at La Vaubyessard on 23 January 1693.' The rest of the sequence was scarcely visible, because the lamplight, directed down on to the green baize of the billiard-table, sent shadows floating about the room. Burnishing the canvases, the light scattered in delicate patterns, along the cracks in the varnish; and from each of those great dark rectangles edged with gold there appeared, here and there, a lighter section of painting, a pale brow, a pair of eyes gazing out at you, perukes curling over the powder-speckled shoulders of scarlet coats, or a garter-buckle above a shapely calf.

The Marquis opened the door into the drawing-room; one of the ladies stood up (the Marquise herself), came over to greet Emma, had her sit close by, on a little sofa, and began to talk to her amiably, as if she had known her for ages. She was a woman of about forty, with splendid shoulders, a hook-nose, a drawling voice, and wearing, that evening, over her auburn hair, a simple piece of lace that hung down at the back, in a triangle. A fair-haired young woman sat near her, in a high-backed chair; and the gentlemen, each with a little flower in his buttonhole, were talking to the ladies, grouped around the fireplace.

At seven o'clock, dinner was served. The men, the greater number, sat at the first table, in the hall, and the ladies at the second table, in the dining-room, with the Marquis and the Marquise.

Emma, as she entered the room, felt herself immersed in warmth, a mixture of the scent of flowers and fine linen, the smell of roast meat and the odour of truffles. The candle-flames were mirrored from the curves of silver dishes; the cut glass, blurred under a dull film of moisture, glistened faintly; there were posies in a line along the table; and, on the large-bordered plates, the serviettes, made into the shape of a bishop's mitre, each held a little oval loaf down between their folds. Purple-red lobster-claws straddled the plates; fresh fruit was piled in shallow baskets lined with moss; the quails were unplucked, the steam was rising; and, in silk stockings, knee-breeches, white cravat and frilled shirt, solemn as a judge, the butler, handing the dishes, each already carved, between the shoulders of the guests, would drop on to your plate with a sweep of his spoon the very morsel of your choice. On the great copper-railed porcelain stove, the statue of a woman, swathed up to her chin, gazed steadily down upon the crowded room.

Madame Bovary noticed that several of the ladies had not put their gloves inside their glasses.[19]

There, at the top of the table, alone among all these women, stooped over his ample plateful, with his napkin tied around his neck like a child, an old man sat eating, drops of gravy dribbling from his lips. His eyes were bloodshot and he had a little pigtail tied up with a black ribbon. This was the Marquis's father-in-law, the old Duc de Laverdière, once the favourite of the Comte d'Artois, in the days of the Marquis de Conflans's hunting-parties at Vaudreuil, and he, so they said, had been the lover of Marie Antoinette, in between Monsieurs de Coigny and de Lauzun. He had led a tumultuous life of debauchery and duelling, of wagers made and women abducted, had squandered his fortune and terrified his whole family. A servant, standing behind his chair, announced loudly, in his ear, the dishes which he pointed to with a mumble; again and again Emma's eyes kept coming back to this old man with the sagging lips, as though to something wonderfully majestic. He had lived at court and slept in the bed of a queen!

Iced champagne was served. Emma shivered from head to foot when she felt the cold taste in her mouth. She had never seen pomegranates before, never eaten a pineapple. Even the powdered sugar looked whiter and finer than elsewhere.

The ladies, at this point, went up to their rooms to make ready for the ball.

Emma arrayed herself with the meticulous care of an actress making her début. She did her hair in the style the hairdresser recommended, and she put on her muslin dress, laid out on the bed. Charles's trousers were too tight in the waist.

– These ankle straps are going to be awkward for dancing, he said.

– Dancing? said Emma.

– Yes.

– You must be out of your mind! They'd laugh at you. You stay sitting down. Anyway, it's more appropriate for a doctor, she added.

Charles said nothing. He paced up and down, waiting for Emma to finish dressing.

He saw her in the mirror, from behind, between two candles. Her dark eyes seemed even darker. Her hair, billowing smoothly around her ears, had a blue sheen; the rose in her chignon was quivering on its fragile stem, with artificial dew-drops on the tips of the leaves. She wore a dress of pale saffron yellow, trimmed with three bouquets of pompon roses mixed with green.

Charles went to kiss her shoulder.

– Leave me alone! she said, you're creasing my dress.

They heard a ritornello on the violin and the sound of a horn. She went down the stairs, controlling the urge to run.

The quadrilles had begun. People were arriving. There was a crush. She sat down near the door, on a little sofa.

When the quadrille was over, the floor was left to the men, standing about talking in groups, and the servants in livery bringing large trays. Along the rows of seated women, painted fans were rippling, bouquets of flowers were screening smiling faces, and gold-capped scent-bottles were tilting in unclasped hands with white gloves that revealed the shape of the fingernails and marked the skin at the wrist. The lace frills, the diamond brooches, the medallion bracelets were quivering on every corsage, gleaming on every breast, chiming out from each bare arm. In their hair, nicely smoothed across the forehead and coiled at the back, they had, in crowns, in bunches or in sprays, forget-me-nots, jasmine, pomegranate-blossom, wheat-ears or corn-flowers. Sitting there placidly, mothers with frowning faces sported scarlet turbans.

Emma's heart beat faster when, her partner holding her with just his fingertips, she stepped into the line, and waited for the first note to sound. But soon the feeling left her; and, swaying to the rhythm of the orchestra, she glided away, nodding her head gently. A smile rose to her lips at various subtleties from the violin, playing the solo, now and then, while the other instruments were silent; you could hear the clink of gold coins changing hands in the next room, across the card-tables; then they all came in together, the cornet gave a resounding blast, feet picked up the rhythm again, skirts billowed out and brushed together, hands were joined, hands were parted; the same eyes that had turned away came back again, to meet your gaze.

Various men, a dozen or more, between the years of twenty-five and forty, scattered among the dancers or talking in doorways, stood out from the crowd by a family likeness, despite the differences of age, dress or appearance.

Their coats looked better cut, of smoother cloth, and their hair, combed forward to curl at the temple, seemed to glisten with a superior pomade. They had the complexion that comes with money, the clear complexion that looks well against the whiteness of porcelain, the lustre of satin, the bloom on expensive furniture, and is best preserved by a moderate diet of exquisite foodstuffs. Their necks turned gracefully in their low cravats; their long whiskers flowed down over their collars;

they wiped their lips on handkerchiefs embroidered with large
initials, and deliciously scented. Those who were past their
prime looked youthful, and even the faces of the young wore a
certain maturity. In their coolly glancing eyes lingered the calm
of passions habitually appeased; and, from beneath their
polished ways, they exuded that peculiar brutality which comes
from a too-casual supremacy in everything that demands
strength and amuses one's vanity, the handling of race-horses
and the company of fallen women.

A few steps from Emma, a gentleman in a blue coat was
talking about Italy to a pale young lady arrayed in pearls.
They were extolling the size of the pillars in St Peter's, Tivoli,
Vesuvius, Castellamare and Cascina, the roses in Genoa, the
Coliseum by moonlight. With her other ear Emma was listening
to a conversation full of words she didn't understand. They
were grouped around a very young man who, the week before,
had beaten Miss Arabella and Romulus, and won two thousand
guineas jumping a ditch, in England. One was complaining
about his racers gaining weight; another, about the printing
errors that had mangled his horse's name.

The ballroom was stifling; the lamps gave a dull light. People
drifted into the billiard-room. A servant climbed on to a chair
and broke two windows; at the sound of breaking glass,
Madame Bovary turned her head and glimpsed outside, close to
the panes, peasant faces gazing in. And memories of Les Bertaux
came back to her. She saw the farmhouse, the muddy pond, her
father in his smock under the apple-trees, and an image of
herself, in the old days, skimming her finger over the cream
on the milk-churns in the dairy. But, in the great dazzlement
of this hour, her past life, always so vivid, was vanishing without
trace, and she almost doubted that it had been hers. There she
was at the ball; beyond it, only a great blur of shadows. Here
she was eating a maraschino ice, holding the silver cockle-shell
in her left hand, her eyes half closing, the spoon between her
lips.

A lady, close by, dropped her fan. A man was passing.

– Would you be so kind, sir, said the lady, as to pick up my
fan from behind this sofa?

The man made a bow, and, as he was reaching out his arm, Emma saw the young lady's hand drop something white, folded in a triangle, into his hat. The gentleman, retrieving the fan, presented it to the lady, ceremoniously; she thanked him with a nod of her head and made a show of inhaling the scent from her bouquet.

After supper – with quantities of Spanish and German wines, with shell-fish soup and almond milk soup, Trafalgar puddings and every sort of cold meat set in aspic that quivered on the plate – the carriages, one after the other, began to move off. Lifting the corner of the muslin curtain, you could see their lantern-flames sailing off through the shadows. The seats were clearing; a few card-players lingered on; the musicians were moistening their fingertips on their tongues; Charles was half asleep, leaning against a door.

At three in the morning, the cotillion began. Emma had never learned to waltz. Everyone was waltzing, Mademoiselle d'Andervilliers herself and the Marquise; there remained only the château guests, about a dozen people.

However, one of the dancers, familiarly addressed as *Viscount*, with a low-cut waistcoat that seemed to be moulded to his chest, came back a second time to invite Madame Bovary to dance, promising that he would guide her and that she would manage splendidly.

They began slowly, and went faster. They were turning: everything was turning around them, the lamps, the furniture, the panelling, the parquet floor, like a disc on a spindle. Passing near the doors, Emma's dress, at the hem, caught on his trousers; their legs entwined; he looked down at her, she looked up at him; a lethargy came over her, she stopped. They set off again; and, quickening the pace, the Viscount, pulling her along, disappeared with her to the end of the gallery, where, panting for breath, she almost fell, and, for a moment, rested her head upon his chest. And then, still spinning round, but more slowly, he conducted her back to her seat; she slumped against the wall and put her hand over her eyes.

When she opened them again, in the middle of the room, there was a lady sitting on a stool with three gentlemen kneeling before her. She chose the Viscount, and the violin began to play.

Every eye was on them. Round and round the room they went, she holding herself erect with head down, and he in his fixed pose, shoulders back, arm curved, chin held high. She could certainly waltz, that woman! They carried on for ages and exhausted everyone else.

Conversation lasted a few minutes longer, and then, after saying good night, or rather good morning, the guests retired to bed.

Charles dragged himself upstairs, his legs *felt like lead*. He had spent five long hours, standing by the card-tables, watching them play whist without understanding a thing. He gave a great sigh of pleasure once he had pulled off his boots.

Emma put a shawl around her shoulders, opened the window and leaned out.

The night was dark. A few drops of rain were falling. She inhaled the damp air that felt so cool upon her eyelids. The music from the ball was still buzzing in her ears, and she made an effort to keep herself awake, so as to prolong the illusion of this world of luxury which she was so soon to relinquish.

The first light was in the sky. She gazed at the windows of the château, avidly, trying to guess which were the rooms of the people she had noticed that evening. She yearned to know their lives, to penetrate, to merge with them.

But she was shivering with cold. She took off her clothes and she curled up in between the sheets, next to a slumbering Charles.

There were many people down at breakfast. The meal lasted ten minutes; no liqueurs were served, to the doctor's astonishment. Then Mademoiselle d'Andervilliers gathered up scraps of brioche in a basket, to take for the swans on the lake, and they went for a walk around the hothouse, where exotic plants, covered in spines, rose up in pyramids beneath hanging vases from which there spilled out long green clustering tendrils, like an overflowing nest of serpents. The orangery, at the far end, led by a covered way to the outbuildings. The Marquis, to entertain the young woman, took her to see the stables. Above the basket-shaped racks, there were porcelain plaques with the names of the horses in black letters. Each of the animals would tramp in its stall, as you went past it, and clicked your tongue. The woodwork in the tack-room shone like an elegant parquet floor. The carriage-harness was arranged in the middle on two revolving posts, and bits, whips, stirrups and curbs stood in a row along the wall.

Charles, meanwhile, went to ask one of the servants to harness his gig. It was brought round to the front step, and, once the parcels were crammed in, the Bovarys said their farewells to the Marquis and the Marquise, and set off for Tostes.

Emma, in silence, was watching the wheels go round. Charles, perched on the very edge of the seat, was driving with his arms held wide, and the little horse was ambling along between the shafts, which were rather too big for him. The loose reins were slapping on his rump, sopping in a frothy sweat, and the box tied on behind kept banging about.

They were on the heights at Thibourville, when suddenly, from in front of them, several horsemen rode by, laughing, with cigars in their mouths. Emma thought she recognized the Viscount: she looked back, and saw only the silhouettes of heads rising and falling, according to the different tempo of the trot or the gallop.

A mile further on, they had to stop to mend one of the traces that had broken.

But Charles, giving the harness a final glance, saw something on the ground, between the horse's feet; and he picked up a cigar-case edged in green silk with a coat of arms at the centre like on the door of a carriage.

– There's even a couple of cigars in it, he said; just right for tonight, after dinner.

– You smoke, do you? she asked.

– Sometimes, when I have the opportunity.

He put his find in his pocket and whipped up the nag.

When they arrived home, the dinner was not ready. Madame lost her temper. Nastasie responded insolently.

– Leave this room! said Emma. The impudence . . . you are finished.

For dinner there was onion soup, and a piece of veal cooked

with sorrel. Charles, sitting opposite Emma, rubbed his hands together cheerfully and said,

– How nice it is to be back home again!

They could hear Nastasie crying. He was fond of the poor girl. She had, previously, kept him company through many a long evening, in the time of his widowhood. She was his first patient, his oldest acquaintance in the area.

– Have you really given her notice? he said at last.

– Yes. And what of it? she asked.

They warmed themselves in the kitchen, while their bedroom was made ready. Charles lit a cigar. He smoked it thrusting his lips forward, spitting repeatedly, flinching at every puff.

– You'll make yourself ill, she said scornfully.

He put his cigar down and ran to the pump for a glass of cold water. Emma, snatching the cigar-case, threw it forcibly to the back of the cupboard.

Time went so slowly, the next day! She went for a walk in her little garden, up and down the same paths, stopping by the flower-beds, by the espalier, by the plaster *curé*, stupefied by the sight of all these old things she knew so well. How far away it seemed already, the ball! What force was it that sundered thus the morning of the day before yesterday from this evening? Her journey to La Vaubyessard had made a hole in her life, just like those great crevasses that a mountain storm will sometimes open up in a single night. She made no protest though; piously she folded away in the chest of drawers her lovely ballgown and even her satin slippers, with their soles yellowed from the beeswax on the dance-floor. Her heart was just like that: contact with the rich had left it smeared with something that would never fade away.

So it filled the time for Emma, remembering the ball. Every time Wednesday came around again, she said to herself when she woke: 'A week ago . . . two weeks ago . . . three weeks ago, I was there!' Slowly, slowly, the faces blurred in her memory, she forgot the tune of the quadrille; no longer did she see so clearly the liveries and the apartments; certain details disappeared, but the regret remained.

9

Often, while Charles was away, she used to go to the cupboard and take out, from between the folded linen where she had left it, the green silk cigar-case.

She would look at it, open it, and then breathe the scent of its lining, a mixture of tobacco and verbena. Whose could it be? . . . The Viscount's. Perhaps it was a present from his mistress. It had been embroidered on a rosewood frame, a delicate thing kept hidden from all eyes; the labour of many hours, over it had hung the flowing curls of the pensive embroiderer. A sigh of love had passed into the fabric of the work; every touch of the needle had stitched fast a vision or a memory, and each one of those entwining threads of silk was the elaboration of the same speechless passion. And the Viscount, one morning, had taken it with him. What had they spoken of, as it lay upon the broad mantelpiece, between the vases of flowers and the Pompadour clocks? She was in Tostes. And he . . . he was in Paris, now. Far away! What was it like, in Paris? What an immense name! She said it softly to herself again, for the pleasure of the sound; it rang in her ears like a great cathedral-bell, it flamed before her eyes, even on the labels of her pots of ointment.

At night, when the carriers in their carts went by under her windows, singing 'La Marjolaine',[20] she would wake up; and, as she listened to the sound of their iron-hooped wheels, soon muffled by the soft earth when they left the village, she would say to herself:

– Tomorrow they'll be there!

And she followed them in her mind, up and down the hills, through the villages, rolling along the main road by the light of the stars. But after a certain distance, she always came to a blur and her dream gave out.

She bought herself a street-map of Paris, and, with the tip of her finger, she went shopping in the capital. She walked up the boulevards, stopping at every turning, between the lines of the streets, passing the white squares that stood for houses.

Eventually she would close her tired eyes, and in the darkness she would see the gas-jets writhing in the wind, the folding carriage-steps that were let down with a great clatter outside the main door of the theatre.

She took out a subscription to *La Corbeille* (a paper for women) and to *Le Sylphe des Salons*. She devoured every single word of all the reviews of first nights, race-meetings and dinner-parties, took an interest in the début of a singer, the opening of a shop. She knew the latest fashions, the addresses of the best tailors, the days for the Bois or the Opera. She studied, in Eugène Sue,[21] descriptions of furniture; she read Balzac and George Sand, seeking to gratify in fantasy her secret cravings. Even at the table, she had her book with her, and she would be turning the pages, while Charles was eating and talking to her. The memory of the Viscount haunted her reading. Between him and the fictional characters, she would forge connections. But gradually the circle of which he was the centre widened around him, and the halo that he wore, as it floated free of him, spread its radiance ever further, illuminating other dreams.

It was Paris, rippling like the ocean, gleaming in Emma's mind under a warm golden haze. The swarming tumultuous life of the place was divided into several parts, classified into distinct tableaux. Emma grasped only two or three of these, and they hid all the rest from her, apparently representing the whole of humanity. The diplomats walked on polished floors, in drawing-rooms panelled with mirrors, around oval tables covered in velvet cloths with gold fringes. This was the world of trailing gowns, of high mystery, of anguish cloaked under a smile. Next came the realm of the duchesses; they were pale; they got up at four o'clock; the women, poor angels, wore petticoats trimmed with English lace, and the men, superfluously talented beneath the mask of frivolity, would ride their horses half to death in an afternoon, spend the summer season in Baden, and, when they eventually reached forty, marry heiresses. From the backrooms of restaurants where people eat after midnight, by candlelight, there came the laughter of the motley crowd of writers and actresses. Extravagant as kings, they were, full of idealistic ambitions and wild enthusiasms. They lived on a higher plane,

between heaven and earth, among storm-clouds, so sublimely.
As for the rest of the world, it was nothing, it was nowhere,
it scarcely seemed to exist. Indeed the nearer things were,
the more her thoughts turned away from them. Everything
in her immediate surroundings, the boring countryside, the imbecile petits bourgeois, the general mediocrity of life, seemed
to be a kind of anomaly, a unique accident that had befallen
her alone, while beyond, as far as the eye could see, there
unfurled the immense kingdom of pleasure and passion. She
confused, in her desire, sensual luxury with true joy, elegance
of manners with delicacy of sentiment. Like some tropical plant,
did love not require the correct soil and a special tempera-
ture? The sighing in the moonlight, the long embracing, the
tears flowing down on to the hands of the one forsaken, all the
fevers of the flesh and the tender anguish of loving – none of
these could be had without a balcony in some great tranquil
château, without a silk-curtained deep-carpeted boudoir, with
lavish vases of flowers and a bed on a little platform, without
the sparkle of precious stones and the glitter of gold-braided
livery.

The lad from the post-house who came every morning, to
groom the mare, went along the passage in his great big clogs;
his smock was full of holes, he wore no stockings inside his
shabby slippers. That was the groom in knee-breeches that she
had to make do with! Once he had done his job, he didn't come
back again until next day; for Charles, when he got in, would
put his own horse in the stable, unsaddle and tether her, while
the maid brought a bundle of hay and tossed it, as best she
could, on to the rack.

To replace Nastasie (who eventually left Tostes, shedding
floods of tears), Emma took on a girl of fourteen, an orphan
with a sweet face. She forbade her to wear cotton caps, taught
her that she had to address them using the third person, to bring
glasses of water on a plate, to knock before entering a room,
taught her how to iron, how to starch, how to dress her mistress,
tried to make a lady's maid of her. The new girl obeyed without
a murmur so as to keep her job; and, because Madame, usually,
left the key in the sideboard, Félicité would take a little supply

of sugar up to bed every night and eat it there in secret, after she had said her prayers.

Sometimes, in the afternoon, she would go across the road for a chat with the postilions. Madame would be upstairs, in her room.

She would be wearing her dressing-gown unbuttoned, revealing, between the copious folds of her corsage, a pleated chemisette with gold buttons. Round her waist she had a cord with big tassels, and her little wine-red slippers had large knots of ribbon, spreading down over the instep. She had bought herself a blotting-pad, a writing-case, a pen-holder and envelopes, though she had nobody to write to; she would dust her ornaments, look at herself in the mirror, pick up a book, then, dreaming between the lines, let it fall into her lap. She yearned to travel or to go back to living in the convent. She wanted equally to die and to live in Paris.

Charles, in rain and snow, rode along the country lanes. He ate omelettes at farmhouse tables, thrust his hand down into damp beds, had his face splashed with warm-spurting blood, listened to many a death-rattle, examined the contents of chamber-pots, unbuttoned plenty of grubby under-linen; but he found his way, every evening, to a blazing fire, a meal, a comfortable chair, and an elegant woman, delectable and fragrant, with a quite mysterious perfume, from her skin perhaps, scenting her skirts.

She had him enthralled with her various refinements: one moment it was a new way of making paper sconces for the candles, or a flounce that she altered on her gown, or an impressive name for some rather ordinary dish, one that the cook had spoiled, but that Charles devoured to the very last morsel. In Rouen she saw ladies wearing bunches of trinkets on their watch-chains; she bought some trinkets. For her mantelpiece she wanted a pair of large blue glass vases, and, a little later, an ivory workbox, with a silver-gilt thimble. The less Charles understood of these niceties, the more they beguiled him. They added to the number of his pleasures and the comforts of his fireside. It was like a sprinkling of gold-dust along the narrow track of his life.

He was in fine shape, he looked on top form; his reputation was firmly established. The country people were very fond of him because he was not conceited. He treasured their children, never went inside a tavern, and, what was more, he inspired confidence by his integrity. He was particularly successful with catarrhs and chest complaints. Very wary of killing his patients, Charles, indeed, seldom prescribed anything but sedatives, an emetic now and then, a foot-bath or leeches. Not that he was afraid of surgery; he would bleed people quite prolifically, as if they were horses, and for pulling teeth he had *a devil of a grip*.

Eventually, *to stay in the swim*, he took out a subscription to *La Ruche médicale*, a new journal that had sent him its prospectus. He would read a little bit of it after dinner; but the warmth of the room, added to the labours of digestion, used to send him to sleep after five minutes; and there he stayed, with his chin on his hands, and his hair like a dishevelled mane hanging down to the foot of the lamp. Emma looked at him with a shrug of her shoulders. Oh, why, at least, didn't she have for a husband one of those ardent taciturn men who work at their books all night, and finally, at sixty, when the rheumatism comes on, wear a string of medals, on their dress coats, so badly cut. She would have liked this name of Bovary, the name that was hers, to be famous, to see it displayed in the book-shops, quoted in the newspapers, known all over France. But Charles hadn't an ounce of ambition! A doctor from Yvetot, with whom he had recently happened to confer, had humiliated him somewhat, right at the patient's bedside, in front of the assembled relatives. When Charles told her, that evening, about the incident, Emma raged loud and long against his colleague. Charles was touched at this. He kissed her forehead with a tear in his eye. But she was boiling with shame, she wanted to hit him, she went out to the passage to open the window, and breathe the fresh air to calm herself.

– What a pathetic man! What a pathetic man! she said in a whisper, biting her lip.

She was, indeed, finding him increasingly irritating. As he got older, he seemed to be getting coarser in his ways; during dessert, he used to cut bits off the corks from the empty bottles; after meals, he used to suck his teeth; eating his soup, he made a gurgling noise with every mouthful, and, as he put on weight, his eyes, already tiny, seemed to be pushed up towards his forehead by the swelling of his cheeks.

Emma, sometimes, would tuck the red border of his jumper under his waistcoat, or arrange his cravat, or throw away the shabby pair of gloves he intended to put on; and it was not, as he imagined, for his sake, it was for herself, in a burst of egotism, of nervous vexation. And sometimes she told him about what she had been reading, a passage from a novel, a new play, or some little tale about *the upper crust* she had come across in her paper; for, after all, Charles was somebody to talk to, an ever-open ear, an ever-ready approbation. She confided a great deal in her greyhound! She would have confided in the logs in the fireplace and the pendulum on the clock.

Down in her soul, the while, she was waiting for something to happen. Like a shipwrecked sailor, she perused her solitary world with hopeless eyes, searching for some white sail far away where the horizon turns to mist. She didn't know what her luck might bring, what wind would blow it her way, what shore it would take her to, whether it was a sloop or a three-masted schooner, laden with anguish or crammed to the portholes with happiness. But, every morning, when she awoke, she hoped it would happen that day, and she listened to every sound, jumping to her feet, surprised when nothing came; then, as day came to its end, with an ever greater sadness, she was longing for the morrow.

Spring came round again. She felt quite breathless in the first of the warm weather, when the pear-trees were in blossom.

From the beginning of July, she was counting on her fingers how many weeks were left until the beginning of October, thinking that the Marquis d'Andervilliers, perhaps, would be giving another ball at La Vaubyessard. But September went by with neither letter nor visit.

After the annoyance of this disappointment, a blankness once more filled her heart, and now the days began their same old procession again.

One after another, along they came, always the same, never-ending, bringing nothing. Other people's lives, however drab they might be, were at least subject to chance. A single incident could bring about endless twists of fate, and the scene would shift. But, in her life, nothing was going to happen. Such was the will of God! The future was a dark corridor, and at the far end the door was bolted.

She gave up the piano. What was the point? Who would be listening? Since she could never play at a concert, in a short-sleeved velvet gown, on an Érard piano, running her fingers over the ivory keys, and feel, like a breeze, murmurs of ecstasy circling around about her, it was not worth the boredom of practising. She left her sketch-books and her embroidery in the cupboard. Completely pointless! Sewing annoyed her.

– I've read everything, she said to herself.

And she sat there playing with the fire-irons, or watching the rain falling.

How sad she felt on Sunday, when they rang the bell for vespers! She listened, blankly engrossed, to the clang-clang-clang of the cracked church-bell. A cat up on the roof, stepping out slowly, arched his back in the faint sunlight. Along the main road, the wind was puffing little clouds of dust. Far away, now and again, a dog was howling: and the bell, in a steady rhythm, kept on tolling out the monotonous notes that drifted away across the fields.

Now they were coming out of church. The women in polished clogs, the peasants in new smocks, in front of them the little children skipping along bareheaded, they were on their way home. And, until dark, five or six men, always the same few, stayed playing *bouchon*, just outside the main door of the inn.

It was a hard winter. Every morning the window-panes were thick with frost, blurring the light, like clouded glass, to a dim whiteness that often scarcely varied in the course of the day. By four in the afternoon, it was time to light the lamp.

On fine days she went down into the garden. The dew had left a silvery lace over the cabbages and hung long shining threads between them. There were no birds singing, everything seemed to be asleep, the straw-covered espalier and the vine like a great diseased serpent under the coping of the wall, where you could see, close up, the wood-lice crawling on their tiny legs. Under the spruce-trees, near the hedge, the breviary-reading *curé* in the three-cornered hat had lost his right foot, and even the plaster, crumbling away in the frost, had left mangy white patches on his face.

Then she went upstairs again, locked her door, put coal on the fire, and, swooning from the heat, felt the boredom pressing down heavier upon her. She would have gone downstairs to talk to the maid, but decorum would not allow.

Every day, at the same time, the schoolmaster, in his black silk cap, would open his shutters, the village policeman would go past, wearing his sabre over his tunic. Morning and evening, the post-horses, three by three, crossed the street to drink from the pond. Now and again, the bell on a tavern door would clink, and, when it was windy, you could hear the creaking of the set of little copper basins hanging from their rods, which did duty as the sign of the wig-maker's shop. By way of decoration, it had an ancient fashion-plate stuck on one of the window-panes and a wax bust of a woman, which had yellow hair. The wig-maker, like her, grieved for his blighted vocation, for his hopeless prospects, and, dreaming of a shop in some great city, in Rouen, for instance, on the quayside, near the theatre, he would spend the whole day walking up and down, between the town hall and the church, gloomily waiting for customers. Whenever Madame Bovary looked up, she would see him still there, like a man on sentry-duty, with his cap down over one ear and his shoddy jacket.

Sometimes, in the afternoon, a man's face would appear at the parlour window, a swarthy face with black whiskers, and a slow broad gentle smile that showed his white teeth. Immediately a waltz started up, and, on top of the organ, in a little salon, dancers the size of your finger, women in pink turbans, Tyrolean peasants in their jackets, monkeys in frock-coats, gentlemen in knee-breeches, they went round and round, in among the armchairs, the sofas, the console tables, mirrored in bits of glass held together at their edges by a strip of gold paper. The man turned the handle, gazing right and left and up towards the windows. Every so often, squirting a long jet of green saliva

down at the kerbstone, he would lift the instrument with his
knee, to ease the hard strap from his shoulder; and so, whining
and lingering, or brisk and cheerful, the music would flow
whirring from the box through a pink taffeta curtain, set behind
an arabesque copper grill. They were the tunes being played far
away in the theatres, sung in the salons, danced to in the evenings
by the light of chandeliers, echoes from another world that
carried as far as Emma. A never-ending saraband was unwinding
in her head, and, like an Indian dancing-girl on a flower-
patterned carpet, her thoughts were leaping to the music, swinging from dream to dream, from sorrow to sorrow. Once the
man had got a few coins in his cap, he would pull down an old
blue woollen cover, hitch his organ on to his back and trudge
off down the road. She used to watch him going.

But it was particularly at meal-times that she could not stand
it any more, in that little room on the ground floor, with its
smoking stove, its creaking door, its sweating walls, its damp
flagstones; it seemed as though all the bitterness of life was being
served up on to her plate, and, with the steam off the stew, there
came swirling up from the depths of her soul a kind of rancid
staleness. Charles was a slow eater; she nibbled a few nuts, or
else, leaning on one elbow, spent the time sketching lines on the
oilcloth with the tip of her knife.

Now she let everything go in the house, and the elder Madame
Bovary, when she came to spend a few days in Tostes over Lent,
was much surprised by the change. She who had always been
so fastidious and so elegant, now spent entire days without
getting dressed, wore grey cotton stockings, and used cheap
tallow candles. She kept saying that, since they were not rich,
they had to economize, adding that she was very contented, very
happy, liked Tostes very much indeed, along with other novel
declarations that left the mother-in-law quite lost for words.
Anyway, Emma no longer seemed inclined to follow her advice;
on one occasion, when Madame Bovary took it upon herself to
announce that masters ought to keep watch over their servants'
religion, she had given her such an angry look and such a cold
smile, that the good woman never touched on the subject again.

Emma was becoming difficult, capricious. She would order

different food for herself, and leave it untouched; one day drink only fresh milk, and, next day, cups of tea by the dozen. Often she refused to go out of the house, then she felt stifled, opened the windows, put on a flimsy dress. When she had thoroughly scolded her maid, she would give her presents or send her off to see the neighbours, just as she would sometimes throw all the silver in her purse to a beggar, though she was not in the least kind-hearted, nor readily aware of the feelings of others, typical of the offspring of most country-people, whose souls, like the callused hands of their fathers, have grown a hard skin.

Towards the end of February, Père Rouault, to commemorate his cure, came over in person with a splendid turkey for his son-in-law, and he spent three days in Tostes. Since Charles was with his patients, Emma kept him company. He smoked in the bedroom, spat into the grate, talked farming, calves and cows, poultry and parish council; such that when she finally shut the door behind him, she felt a kind of pleasure that surprised her. Besides, she no longer hid her scorn for anything or anyone; and sometimes she would come out with peculiar opinions, condemning whatever was generally accepted, and praising perversion and immorality: which left her husband open-mouthed.

Would this misery last for ever? Would she never escape? She was every bit as good as all the women who lived happy lives! At La Vaubyessard she had seen duchesses with thicker waists and inferior manners, and she cursed God for his injustice; she used to lean her head against the wall and weep; she envied the riotous life, the nights of dancing, the insolence of pleasure and the wildness she had never known, things that were surely to be had.

She grew pale and had palpitations. Charles administered valerian and camphor baths. Everything that they tried seemed to exacerbate her condition.

On certain days, she chattered away in a febrile torrent; these moods of exaltation were followed by states of torpor in which she lay there without speech or motion. What would revive her was sprinkling a bottle of eau-de-Cologne on her arms.

Since she complained perpetually about Tostes, Charles supposed that her illness must be caused by something in the locality, and, fixing on this idea, he seriously considered setting up somewhere else.

Now she began drinking vinegar to make herself thinner, contracted a little dry cough and lost her appetite completely.

It was a blow for Charles to leave Tostes after four years there and just when *he was beginning to get on*. Still, if it had to be! He took her to Rouen to see his old professor. It was a nervous ailment: she needed a change of air.

After fishing about here and there, Charles heard of a place in the Neufchâtel area, a sizeable market-town called Yonville-l'Abbaye, where the doctor, a Polish refugee, had decamped the week before. He wrote next to the local pharmacist to find out the size of the population, the distance from the nearest doctor, how much his predecessor had earned in a year, and so on; and, once he was satisfied with the answers, he decided to move some time in the spring, if Emma's health had not improved.

One day, as she was tidying a drawer in readiness to leave, she pricked her finger on something. It was the wire in her wedding-bouquet. The orange-blossom was yellow with dust, and the silver-fringed satin ribbons were fraying at the edges. She threw it on to the fire. It burst into flame quicker than dry straw. Then it was like a red bush on the cinders, being gradually eaten away. She watched it burning. The little imitation berries crackled, the wires twisted, the braid melted; and the paper petals, withering away, hovering in the fireplace like black butterflies, finally vanished up the chimney.

When they set out from Tostes, one day in March, Madame Bovary was pregnant.

Part Two

Yonville-l'Abbaye,[1] so-called from an old Capuchin abbey of which not even a stone now remains, is a market-town about twenty miles from Rouen, between the Abbeville and the Beauvais roads, down in a valley washed by the Rieule, a small stream that flows into the Andelle, after turning three water-mills near its mouth, and here you find a few trout, which schoolboys, on Sundays, delight to hunt with rod and line.

You leave the main road at La Boissière and you carry on along the slope as far as the top of the Côte des Leux, where you can see the whole valley. The river divides it into two regions quite distinct in character: everything to the left is pasture, everything to the right is cultivated. The meadows extend beneath a cluster of low hills and eventually join up with the pastures of Bray, while, on the eastern side, the plain, rising gently, widens as it goes and unfurls its fields of golden corn as far as the eye can see. The water that flows beside the grass marks out a crooked white seam between the colour of the meadow and that of the plough lands, and the landscape looks like a great spreading cloak with a collar of green velvet, edged in silver braid.

On the far horizon, as you approach, you have the oak-trees of the forest of Argueil, with the escarpment of the Côte Saint-Jean, streaked from top to bottom with long jagged red lines; these are the rain gullies, and those brick-red tints, tiny threads of colour against the grey of the mountains, come from the large number of ferruginous springs that flow near by, in this region.

Here you are on the borders of Normandy, Picardy and the Ile-de-France, a bastard region where the language is without accentuation, as the landscape is without character. This is where they make the worst Neufchâtel cheeses in the whole district, and, what is more, the farming is expensive, because it takes so much manure to enrich this crumbly soil full of sand and pebbles.

Until 1835, there was no passable road into Yonville; but at about this time there was built a *local highway* which links the road to Abbeville with the one to Amiens, and is sometimes used by the wagoners going from Rouen into Flanders. However, Yonville-l'Abbaye has stood still, in spite of its *new outlets*. Instead of improving the soil, they are clinging to pasture, however impoverished, and the sleepy market-town, standing aloof from the plain, has continued naturally to grow towards the river. You see it from afar, sprawled along the bank, like a cowherd snoozing by the water.

At the foot of the hill, after the bridge, begins a road planted with young aspens, which leads you directly to the first houses. They are enclosed with hedges, in the midst of yards full of straggling outhouses, wine-presses, cart-sheds and whisky-stills, scattered in among the thick bushy trees festooned with ladders, poles or scythes hooked up in their branches. The roof-thatch, like a fur cap pulled over the eyes, hangs about a third of the way down the low windows, their thick bulging panes adorned with a centre-knot, rather like the bottom of a bottle. Up against the plaster walls with their black diagonal beams there leans the occasional sickly pear-tree, and the doorway has a little swing-gate to keep out the chicks, when they come pecking around, on the step, for crumbs of brown bread dipped in cider. Eventually, the yards get smaller, the houses are closer together, the hedges disappear; a bundle of fern swings under a window on the end of a broomstick; there is a blacksmith's forge and then a wheelwright's with two or three new carts, standing outside, blocking the road. Then, through the railings, you see a white house across its circle of lawn embellished with a Cupid, his finger on his lips; two urns in cast-iron stand at either side of the front-steps; the brass plates gleam on the door; this is the notary's house and the finest in the district.

The church is on the other side of the street, twenty paces further on, as you go into the square. The little graveyard which surrounds it, enclosed by a low wall, is so full of graves that the old slabs flat on the ground make an unbroken pavement, where the grass has sketched out neat green squares. The church was completely rebuilt in the final years of the reign of Charles X.[2] The wooden roof is beginning to rot at the top, and, here and there, the blue paintwork is pitted with black. Above the door, where the organ would be, there is a gallery for the men, with a spiral staircase that echoes under their clogs.

The daylight, coming in through the plain glass windows, falls obliquely over the benches set at right angles to the wall, with here and there a straw mat on a nail, and just below in big letters the words: *Monsieur So-and-so's Bench*. Further on, where the nave narrows, the confession-box faces a statuette of the Virgin, dressed in a satin robe, her tulle veil sprinkled with silver stars, and her cheeks becrimsoned like an idol from the Sandwich Islands; at the far end a painting of *The Holy Family, Presented by the Minister of the Interior*, high over the main altar between four candlesticks, closes off the view. The choir-stalls, made of pinewood, have been left unpainted.

The market (in other words, a tiled roof on twenty or so posts) takes up almost half of the main square in Yonville. The town hall, built *to the design of a Paris architect*, is a kind of Greek temple on the street corner, next door to the pharmacist's shop. It has, on the ground floor, three Ionic columns and, on the first floor, a semi-circular gallery, while the tympanum which crowns it displays a Gallic cockerel, resting one foot on the Charter[3] and holding in the other the scales of justice.

But what particularly catches the eye, just across from the Golden Lion, is the pharmacy of Monsieur Homais! In the evening, particularly, when his oil-lamp is lit and the red and green jars that adorn his window cast forth, on the street, their two coloured beams; then, behind them, as though in Bengal lights, you get a glimpse of the pharmacist's shadow, bent at his desk. His house, from top to bottom, is plastered with inscriptions written in longhand, in copperplate, in block capitals: VICHY, SELTZER & BARÈGES WATERS, PURGATIVE SYRUPS,

RASPAIL'S ELIXIR, ARABIAN SWEETMEATS, DARCET'S PASTILLES, REGNAULT'S OINTMENT, BANDAGES, BATHS, MEDICINAL CHOCOLATE . . . And the sign, taking up the whole width of the shop, says in gold letters: HOMAIS, PHARMACIST. There, at the back of the shop, behind the big scales screwed down on the counter, the word *Laboratory* unfurls above a glass door, which, halfway up, announces once again HOMAIS, in letters of gold, on a black ground.

There is nothing further to see in Yonville. The street, the only one, about a gunshot in length, with a few shops on each side, stops short at the bend in the road. If you turn right and follow the foot of the Côte Saint-Jean, you soon reach the cemetery.

During the cholera, to make it bigger, they knocked down a section of wall and bought three acres of adjoining ground; but this whole new section is almost uninhabited, the graves, as ever, are piling up around the gate. The sexton, who is also the grave-digger and the church-beadle (reaping thus a double benefice from the corpses in his parish), has availed himself of the empty ground to plant out some potatoes. Year by year, though, his little plot is dwindling away, and, when an epidemic strikes, he doesn't know whether to rejoice in the number of the deceased or whether to bewail their burial.

– You feed off the dead, Lestiboudois! the *curé* eventually said to him, one day.

This sombre phrase set him thinking; it checked him for a time; but, to this day, he is still cultivating his tubers, and even maintains quite calmly that they grow naturally.

Since the events we are about to describe, nothing, indeed, has changed in Yonville. The tricolour flag made of tin-plate is still turning on top of the church-steeple; the fancy-goods shop still flutters its two calico streamers in the wind; the foetuses in the pharmacist's, like pale giant fungi, are rotting softly in their cloudy alcohol, and, above the main door of the inn, the old golden lion, faded by the weather, still displays to those below its frizzy poodle's mane.

On the evening the Bovarys were due in Yonville, the widowed Madame Lefrançois, mistress of this inn, was in such a great fluster that the sweat was pouring off her as she saw to her pots and pans. It was market-day tomorrow. The meat had to be carved ready, the chickens dressed, the soup and the coffee made. And she also had the meal to do for her regulars, for the doctor, for his wife and their maid; the billiard room was echoing with roars of laughter; three millers, in the bar parlour, were calling for someone to bring them brandy; logs were blazing, coals were singing, and, on the long table in the kitchen, amid the joints of raw mutton, stood piles of plates that trembled to the jumping of the block where the spinach was being chopped. You could hear, in the backyard, a squawking of chickens as the servant-girl chased after them to cut their throats.

A man in green leather slippers, with a slightly pock-marked face, and a gold-tasselled velvet cap on his head, was warming his back by the fire. His face expressed nothing but self-satisfaction, and he seemed just as contented with life as the goldfinch hanging above his head, in a wicker cage: it was the pharmacist.

– Artémise! cried the landlady, chop some sticks, fill the jugs, get some brandy, hurry up! If only I knew what dessert to give these folks you've got coming! Dear to goodness! The furniture-moving men are starting up their racket in the billiard-room again! And that cart of theirs is still in the main gate! The *Hirondelle* could come and smash into it. Shout for Polyte and tell him to shift it! . . . Just fancy, since this morning, Monsieur Homais, they must have played fifteen games and drunk eight jars of cider. They'll be tearing my cloth for me, she added, keeping an eye on them, her skimmer in her hand.

– No great harm in that, replied Monsieur Homais, you'd buy another one.

– A new billiard-table! exclaimed the widow.

– Since that one is falling to pieces, Madame Lefrançois; I'm telling you again, you do yourself no good, no good whatever. And anyway the players these days, they want narrow pockets and heavy cues. People don't play marbles any more; everything's changing! You have to move with the times! Look at Tellier, now . . .

The landlady went red with vexation. The pharmacist added:

– His billiard-table, say what you like, it's nicer than yours; and suppose somebody thought of getting up a patriotic tournament for Poland or the flood victims in Lyon . . .[4]

– It won't be riff-raff like him that frightens us! interrupted the landlady, shrugging her fat shoulders. Off with you! Be off with you! Monsieur Homais, as long as the Golden Lion keeps going, folk'll keep on coming. We've a tidy bit put by, we have. One fine morning you'll see the Café Français closed, and a nice *For Sale* on the shutters! . . . Get a new billiard-table, she went on, talking to herself, when that one's so handy for folding my washing, and, in the shooting season, I've slept half a dozen on it! . . . Where's that dawdler Hivert got to!

– Will you wait on him for your gentlemen's dinners? asked the pharmacist.

– Wait for him? And what about Monsieur Binet? When it strikes six you'll see him come in; nobody in the world like that one for punctuality. Always wants his own chair in the little room! He'd rather be dead than have to eat anywhere else! And the fuss he makes! And so particular about his cider! Not like Monsieur Léon; that one, he turns up sometimes at seven o'clock, even half seven; never so much as looks at what he's eating. What a nice young man! Never have a cross word from him.

– Because there's a big difference, you see, between someone who's had an education and an old soldier turned tax-collector.

The clock struck six. Enter Binet.

He was wearing a blue frock-coat, drooping limply from his spindly form, and his leather cap, its ear-flaps tied up with strings over the top of his head, revealed, under the cocked peak, a bald forehead flattened by the years of wearing a helmet. He had on a black waistcoat, a horsehair collar, grey trousers, and, winter and summer, a pair of well-polished boots with two symmetrical swellings, where his big toes bulged up. There was not a hair out of place in his blond beard, which, circling the jaw, made a frame like a flower-bed around his long sallow face, with its little eyes and hooked nose. Expert at all card-games, keen on hunting, with lovely handwriting, he had at home a lathe,[5] at which he spent his time turning serviette-rings to

clutter up his house, with the jealousy of an artist and the egoism
of a bourgeois.

He made for the little parlour; but first they had to get the
three millers out of there; and, while his table was being laid,
Binet stayed silently in his chair, near the stove; then he closed
the door and took off his cap, as always.

– Not exactly one to fatigue the ear with polite conversation,
is he! said the pharmacist, once he was alone with the landlady.

– Never get any more out of him, she replied; we had here,
last week, two cloth-salesmen, a bright pair of lads they were,
told such a pack of tall stories, that night, I was laughing till I
cried; well that one, he sat there, like a snail, without a word.

– Oh, yes, said the pharmacist, no imagination, no dazzle,
none of the little social graces.

– They do say he's talented, though, protested the landlady.

– Talented? replied Monsieur Homais. That! Talented? In his
own line, it is possible, he added in a calmer voice.

And he went on:

– Now, if a businessman, one with influential connections, if
a magistrate, a doctor, or a pharmacist should be so engrossed
that they become eccentric and even rather abrupt, I can understand that; the history books are full of such stuff! But, at least,
they do have something to be thinking about. Me, for example,
how many times have I searched for my pen on the desk to write
a label, only to find, ultimately, that I'd put it behind my ear!

Madame Lefrançois, meanwhile, went to the door to see if
the *Hirondelle* were coming. She gave a start. A man dressed in
black stepped suddenly into the kitchen. You could make out,
in the last glow of the fading light, his ruddy face and his athletic
frame.

– What can we do for you, Monsieur Le Curé? asked the
mistress of the inn, as she reached up on the mantelpiece for
one of the brass candlesticks that stood there in a row with
their candles. What will you have? A drop of cassis, a glass of
wine?

The churchman refused most tactfully. He had come for his
umbrella, which he had forgotten the other day at the convent
of Ernemont, and, after begging Madame Lefrançois to have it

sent round to him at the presbytery during the evening, he went off to the church, where the angelus was ringing.

Once the pharmacist could no longer hear his footsteps from the square, he declared such behaviour most unbecoming. This refusal to take any refreshment seemed to him a piece of the most odious hypocrisy; priests did their tippling on the sly, and they were all set to bring back the days of the tithe.

The landlady went to the defence of her *curé*:

– Anyway, he could lay four of your sort across his knee! Last year it was, he helped our people get the straw in; he could carry six bales at once he could, he's that strong!

– Bravo! said the pharmacist. So send your daughters to confess to such well-endowed lads! Personally, if I were the government, I'd have the priests bled once a month. Yes, Madame Lefrançois, every month, a good phlebotomy, in the interests of public safety!

– You hold your tongue now, Monsieur Homais! You godless man! You have no religion!

The pharmacist answered:

– I do have a religion, my religion, and I have rather more than that lot with their jiggery-pokery. I'm the one who worships God! I believe in the Supreme Being, in a Creator, whoever he may be, I care not, who has put us on this earth to do our duty as citizens and fathers; but I don't need to go into a church and kiss a lot of silver plate, paying out for a bunch of clowns who eat better than we do! You can honour him just as well in the woods, in a field, or even contemplating the ethereal vault, like the ancients. My God is the God of Socrates, of Franklin, Voltaire and Béranger! I'm one for the creed of the *Savoyard Curate*[6] and the immortal principles of '89! I cannot, therefore, abide an old fogey of a God who walks round his garden with a stick in his hand, lodges his friends in the bellies of whales, dies with a loud cry and comes back to life three days later: things absurd in themselves and completely opposed, what is more, to every law of physics; it all shows, incidentally, that the priests have always wallowed in squalid ignorance, doing their utmost to engulf the population along with them.

He paused, looking around him for an audience, for, in his

effervescence, the pharmacist had briefly fancied himself at a full meeting of the municipal council. But the landlady had stopped listening to him; her ear was straining after a distant rumbling. There came the sound of a carriage, mixed in with a clatter of loose chains striking the ground, and the *Hirondelle* at last halted outside the door.

It was a yellow box stuck on two large wheels which, coming right up to the roof-line, blocked the passengers' view of the road and spattered their shoulders. Its narrow little windows rattled in their frames when the coach doors were closed, and they had fresh dry mud splashes, here and there, on the old coating of dust, which even the heavy rain storms had not quite washed away. It was drawn by three horses, with one leading, and, when you went downhill, it scraped the road with a jolt.

Some of Yonville's bourgeois appeared on the square; they were all talking at once, asking for news, for explanations and hampers; Hivert couldn't get a word in. He was the one that did the village's errands in town. He went round the shops, bringing back rolls of leather for the cobbler, bits of iron for the farrier, a barrel of herring for the inn, bonnets from the milliner's, wigs from the hairdresser's; and, along the road, on his way back, he dealt out his parcels, throwing them over the farmhouse gates, standing up on his seat, and shouting at the top of his voice, while his horses ambled along on their own.

An accident had held him up: Madame Bovary's greyhound had escaped across the fields. They had whistled him for a good fifteen minutes. Hivert had even gone back a couple of miles, thinking he would see him any minute; but they had to press on in the end. Emma had wept, lost her temper; she had blamed Charles for the mishap. Monsieur Lheureux, the draper, who happened to be in the coach as well, had tried to console her with various examples of lost dogs who recognized their masters after many years. He had heard of one, he said, that found its way from Constantinople to Paris. Another one had gone two hundred miles in a straight line and swum across four rivers; and his own father had had a poodle which, after twelve years away, suddenly jumped up on his back, one evening, in the street, as he was going out to dinner.

2

Emma got out first, then Félicité, Monsieur Lheureux and a nurse, and they had to wake Charles in his corner, where he had fallen fast asleep as soon as it went dark.

Homais introduced himself; he offered his compliments to Madame, his respects to Monsieur, said he was delighted to have been able to do them some service, and added cheerfully that he had made bold to invite himself to dinner, his wife being away.

Madame Bovary, once she was in the kitchen, made for the fireplace. With the tips of her fingers, she took hold of her dress at the knee, and, lifting it just to her ankle, held out to the fire, above the leg of mutton on the spit, a foot clad in a small black boot. The flames lit every inch of her, a harsh brilliance penetrating the weave of her dress, the fine pores of her white skin and even her eyelids that she blinked repeatedly. Vivid reds washed over her, driven by the wind that blew in through the open door.

From the other side of the fireplace, a young man with blond hair was watching her in silence.

Because he was so very bored in Yonville, where he worked as a clerk in Guillaumin's office, Monsieur Léon Dupuis (it was he, the second of the regulars at the Golden Lion) tended to dine late, hoping there might come to the inn some traveller with whom to have an evening's conversation. On the days his work was over early, for want of anything better to do, he had little choice but to arrive right on time, and to endure a tête-à-tête with Binet from the soup all the way through to the cheese. So it was a great pleasure for him to accept the landlady's suggestion that he join the party of new arrivals for dinner, and they moved into the big parlour, where Madame Lefrançois, for the occasion, had had four places laid.

Homais asked permission to keep on his skull-cap, for fear of coryza.

Then, turning to his neighbour:

– Madame is doubtless a little weary? One is so frightfully shaken about in our *Hirondelle*!

– Very true, replied Emma; but I always relish the upheaval; I do love being on the move.

– Such a dreary business, sighed the clerk, being stuck in the same old place!

– Now, if you were like me, said Charles, endlessly having to be on my horse . . .

– Surely, Léon continued, addressing himself to Madame Bovary, nothing is more pleasant, to my mind; when one has the chance, he added.

– Indeed, said the apothecary, a medical practice is not all that arduous in this part of the world; for the state of our roads permits the use of a cabriolet, and, in general, the fees are quite good, the farmers being well off. You get, medically speaking, apart from the usual cases of enteritis, bronchitis, bilious attacks, etc., a few cases of marsh fever at harvest time, but, on the whole, nothing very serious, nothing of special note, except for sundry cases of scrofula, due no doubt to the deplorably unhygienic conditions in the dwellings of our peasantry. Ah! You will find every sort of prejudice to be combated, Monsieur Bovary; plenty of obstinate habits, and every day they will clash with your scientific efforts; for they still have recourse to novenas, to relics, to priests, rather than coming naturally to see the doctor or the pharmacist. The climate, however, is actually not too bad, and we even include in the vicinity a few nonagenarians. The thermometer (I have made my own observations) drops as low as four degrees in the winter, and, in high summer, touches twenty-five, thirty centigrade at the very most, which gives us a maximum of twenty-four, or else fifty-four Fahrenheit (English scale), no more! And, as it happens, we are sheltered from the north wind by the Forest of Argueil on one side, from the west wind by the Côte Saint-Jean on the other; and this heat, you see, which on account of the water vapour given off by the river and the considerable presence of cattle in the meadows, which exhale, as you know, a good deal of ammonia, that's to say nitrogen, hydrogen and oxygen (no, just nitrogen and hydrogen), and which, sucking up the humus from the soil, mingling these several emanations, doing them up in a bundle, so to speak, and combining spontaneously with the electricity

circulating in the atmosphere, whenever there is any, it could in
the long run, as happens in the tropics, engender insalubrious
miasmas; this heat, I tell you, is tempered precisely in the quarter
from whence it comes, or rather from whence it would be
coming, which is to say from the south, by the south-easterly
winds, which, having cooled themselves off in crossing the Seine,
sometimes lash down upon us, like breezes from Russia!

– Do you at least have any walks in the neighbourhood? said
Madame Bovary, talking to the young man.

– Oh, hardly any, he answered. There is a spot they call the
Pasture, at the top of the hill, just at the edge of the forest.
Sometimes, on Sunday, I go, and stay there with a book, to
watch the setting of the sun.

– I do think there is nothing in the world so splendid as a
sunset, she went on, but especially by the sea.

– Oh, I adore the sea, said Monsieur Léon.

– And do you not feel, replied Madame Bovary, that the mind
drifts unfettered upon that immensity, whose contemplation
raises up the soul and feeds a feeling of infinity, of the fabulous?

– It's just the same with mountain scenery, Léon went on. I
have a cousin who went to Switzerland last year, and he told
me one cannot imagine the poetry of lakes, the magic of water-
falls, the gigantic sight of glaciers. You see pine-trees of an
incredible size, spanning the torrent, cabins suspended over
precipices, and, a thousand feet below you, whole valleys, when
the clouds separate. Such sights as these must be an inspiration,
an incitement to prayer, to ecstasy! I'm not a bit surprised at
that famous musician who, to excite his imagination the more,
used to go and play the piano by some imposing scene.

– Are you a musician? she asked.

– No, but I do love music, he answered.

– Ah, don't you listen to him, Madame Bovary, interrupted
Homais, stooping over his plate, it's sheer modesty. Why, my
boy! Mmm! The other day, up in your room, you were singing
'L'Ange gardien'[7] so charmingly. I heard you from the laboratory; you delivered it like an actor.

Léon actually lodged at the pharmacist's, where he had a little
room on the second floor, overlooking the square. He blushed

at this compliment from his landlord, who had already turned to the doctor and was enumerating for him, one after the other, the principal inhabitants of Yonville. He kept telling anecdotes, giving information; nobody really knew how rich the lawyer was, *and there was the Tuvache lot* who gave themselves great airs.

Emma continued.

– And what music do you prefer?

– Oh! German music, the kind that sets you dreaming.

– Do you know the Italians?

– Not yet, but I shall see them next year, when I go to live in Paris, to finish my law.

– As I had the honour of informing your good husband, said the pharmacist, with regard to that poor Yanoda who disappeared; you will find yourselves, thanks to his recklessness, in possession of one of the most comfortable houses in Yonville. What makes it especially convenient for a doctor is a door on to the Lane, which makes it possible to come and go without being seen. In fact, it's equipped with every domestic amenity: wash-house, kitchen with scullery, sitting-room, fruit-loft. He was quite a rogue. Quite a chap for splashing out, he was! He had built for himself, at the end of the garden, by the river, an arbour just for drinking beer in the summer, and if Madame is fond of gardening, she'll be able . . .

– My wife doesn't care much for it, said Charles; she'd rather, even though she's been recommended to take exercise, stay in her room the whole time, reading.

– That's like me, remarked Léon; what could be better, really, than an evening by the fire with a book, with the wind beating on the panes, the lamp burning? . . .

– I do so agree, she said, fixing on him her great black eyes open wide.

– Your head is empty, he continued, the hours slip away. From your chair you wander through the countries of your mind, and your thoughts, threading themselves into the fiction, play about with the details or rush along the track of the plot. You melt into the characters; it seems as if your own heart is beating under their skin.

– Oh, yes, that is true! she said.

– Has it ever happened to you, Léon went on, in a book you come across some vague idea you once had, some blurred image from deep down, something that just spells out your finest feelings?

– I have had that, she answered.

– That, he said, is why I particularly love the poets. I find verse more tender than prose, and it brings more tears to the eye.

– Though rather exhausting after a while, Emma went on; and at the moment, you see, I adore stories that push on inexorably, frightening stories. I detest common heroes and temperate feelings, the way they are in life.

– Indeed, observed the clerk, since such books do not touch the heart, they stray, it seems to me, from the true end of Art. So lovely, amid life's disappointments, to be able to dwell in fancy on nobility of character, pure affections and pictures of happiness. As for me, living here, far from the world, it's my only distraction; but Yonville has so very little to offer!

– Like Tostes, I expect, said Emma; so I always had a subscription to a library.

– If Madame would do me the honour of using it, said the pharmacist, who had just caught these last words, I have at her disposal a library comprising the best authors: Voltaire, Rousseau, Delille, Walter Scott, *L'Echo des feuilletons*, and so forth, what is more, I take various periodicals, among them *Le Fanal de Rouen*,[8] every day, for which I have the privilege of being correspondent for the districts of Buchy, Forges, Neufchâtel, Yonville and environs.

Two and a half hours now, they had been at the table; Artémise, the maid, dragging her carpet-slippers nonchalantly over the flagstones, brought the plates in one at a time, forgot everything, understood nothing and always left the door of the billiard-room-half open, so that it kept tapping against the wall with its latch.

Without realizing, while he was talking, Léon had put his foot on one of the bars of the chair in which Madame Bovary was sitting. She was wearing a little cravat made of blue silk, that made her tube-pleated batiste collar stick up like a ruff; and, whenever she moved her head, half her face was screened by the fabric or else was pleasingly revealed. So it was, side by side, while Charles and the pharmacist were chatting, they embarked on one of those vague conversations in which every random phrase always brings you back to the fixed centre of a mutual sympathy. Paris theatres, titles of novels, new quadrilles, and the society they knew nothing of, Tostes where she had lived, Yonville where they were, they went through it all, talked it over until the end of dinner.

When the coffee had been served, Félicité went off to arrange the bedroom in the new house, and the diners soon rose from the table. Madame Lefrançois was asleep by the fire, and the ostler, with a lantern in his hand, was waiting for Monsieur and Madame Bovary to show them the way home. In his red hair were tangled wisps of straw, and he limped with his left leg. Once he had the priest's umbrella in his free hand, off they went.

The village was asleep. The market-hall pillars cast great shadows. Everything was grey, like on summer nights.

But, as the doctor's house was only fifty yards from the inn, they had to say good night almost at once, and the party dispersed.

Emma, even in the hall, felt on her shoulders, like damp linen, the descending chill of the plaster. The walls were freshly done, and the wooden stairs creaked. In the bedroom, upstairs, a dull pale light came in through the uncurtained windows. You could just see the tops of trees, and the meadows beyond, half drowned in the mist, that smoked in the moonlight, along the line of the river. In the middle of the room, topsy-turvy, there were commode drawers, bottles, curtain-rods, gilt poles with mat-tresses on chairs and basins on the floor – the two men who had brought the furniture had just dropped everything, carelessly.

This was the fourth time she had slept in a strange place. The first had been the day she went to the convent, the second when she arrived at Tostes, the third at La Vaubyessard, this was the fourth; and each time it had turned out to have been the inauguration of a new phase in her life. She didn't believe that things could look the same in a different place, and, since her portion of experience had thus far been nasty, no doubt that which yet remained on her plate would taste better.

3

Next morning, when she got up, she noticed the clerk in the square. She was in her dressing-gown. He looked up and greeted her. She gave a brief nod and closed the window.

All day long Léon was waiting for six o'clock to come; but, when he got to the inn, the only person he found was Monsieur Binet, at the table.

That dinner-party the previous evening had been a major event for him; never, until now, had he talked for two whole hours to a *lady*. So how had he been able to expound to her, and in such a flow of words, dozens of things he could never have put so nicely before? He was usually timid, with the kind of bashfulness that is one part modesty and one part dissimulation. People in Yonville considered his manners *very genteel*. He listened to the opinions of his elders, and seemed by no means extreme in his politics, a remarkable thing in a young man. And he was talented, he painted in water-colours, read music, and happily talked literature after dinner, when he wasn't playing cards. Monsieur Homais respected his education, Madame Homais was fond of him for his good nature, for he often went out into the garden with the Homais children, a perpetually grubby little lot, very spoiled and rather languid, like their mother. As well as the maid looking after them, they had Justin, the pharmacy apprentice, a distant cousin to Monsieur Homais who had been taken into the house out of charity, and who also worked as a domestic servant.

The apothecary showed himself the best of neighbours. He advised Madame Bovary about the tradesmen, sent specially for his own cider-merchant, tasted the stuff himself, and down in the cellar kept an eye on the proper placing of the cask; he revealed how to go about getting a supply of cheap butter, and made an arrangement with Lestiboudois, the sexton, who, as

well as his sacerdotal and mortuary functions, looked after the
main gardens in Yonville, by the hour or by the year, according
to people's preferences.

It was not altruism alone that prompted the pharmacist to
such obsequious cordiality, there was a purpose behind it.

He had infringed the law of 19th Ventôse, Year XI, Article
I,[9] which forbids any person not holding a diploma to practise
medicine; consequently, after having been furtively denounced,
Homais had been summoned to Rouen, before the Procurator
Royal, in his private chambers. The magistrate had received him
standing, in his robes, ermine at the shoulder and a flat cap on
his head. This was in the morning, before the court session.
You could hear the stout boots of gendarmes going along the
corridor, and a distant sound as of great locks being shut. The
pharmacist's ears were ringing so loudly that he fancied he
was going to have a stroke; he imagined dungeons, his family
weeping, the pharmacy sold off, the display jars scattered; and
he had to go to a café for a glass of rum and soda to calm his
mind.

Gradually, the memory of this admonition faded, and he
continued, as before, to give innocuous consultations in his
back-room. But the mayor had it in for him, his colleagues were
jealous, he had to be very wary; winning over Monsieur Bovary
with courtesies, it was to put him under an obligation, and to
hinder him from speaking out later, should he notice anything.
And so, every morning, Homais brought him *the paper*, and
often, in the afternoon, left the pharmacy for a moment to pay
a social call on the medical officer.

Charles was dispirited: the patients were not coming. He
would stay sitting hour after hour, in silence, would go for a
sleep in his consulting-room or watch his wife sewing. To pass
the time, he worked on odd jobs about the house, and he even
tried painting the attic with some spare paint the decorators had
left. But he was preoccupied with money matters. He had spent
so much on repairs at Tôstes, on Madame's wardrobe and on
moving house, that the whole dowry, more than three thousand
écus, had trickled away in two years. And the various things
damaged or lost in the move from Tostes to Yonville, not to

mention the plaster *curé*, falling from the cart after a violent jolt, and shattered into a thousand pieces on the street in Quincampoix!

A more agreeable matter came to beguile him, namely his wife's pregnancy. As her time drew nearer, so he began to dote on her the more. It made a new flesh-bond between them and was like a covenant of their more intricate union. Whenever he watched her indolent stride and her uncorseted body moving softly from the hips, whenever they were face to face and he gazed easily upon her as she sat weary in her chair, his happiness brimmed over; he would get up, embrace her, stroke her face, call her little mummy, try to make her dance, and murmur, with tears and smiles together, the various fond absurdities that came into his head. The thought of having impregnated her was delectable to him. Now he lacked nothing. He knew human life from end to end, and he sat with both elbows on the table, imperturbable.

Emma at first felt a great astonishment, then she was eager to be delivered, to know what it was like to be a mother. But, unable to spend as much as she would have liked, on a swing-boat cradle with pink silk curtains and embroidered baby-bonnets, she gave up the layette in an outburst of bitterness, and ordered it in one go from a village dressmaker, without choosing or discussing anything. So it was she missed that delight in the preparations that rouse maternal tenderness, and her affection was perhaps, from the very start, somehow impaired.

However, since Charles, at every meal, talked about baby, she was soon daydreaming quite incessantly about it.

She wanted a son; he would be strong and dark, she would call him George; and this idea of having a male child was like an anticipated revenge for the powerlessness of her past. A man, at least, is free; he can explore each passion and every kingdom, conquer obstacles, feast upon the most exotic pleasures. But a woman is continually thwarted. Both inert and yielding, against her are ranged the weakness of the flesh and the inequity of the law. Her will, like the veil strung to her bonnet, flutters in every breeze; always there is the desire urging, always the convention restraining.

She gave birth one Sunday, at about six, as the sun came up.
– It's a girl! said Charles.
She turned aside and passed out.

Almost immediately, Madame Homais rushed in and embraced her, as did Mère Lefrançois, from the Golden Lion. The pharmacist, a man of discretion, offered her only a few provisional felicitations, through the half-open door. He asked to see the baby, and pronounced it well formed.

During her convalescence, she spent a long time looking for a name for her daughter. First, she went through various names with Italian endings, such as Clara, Louisa, Amanda, Atala; she rather liked Galsuinde, better still Yseult or Léocadie. Charles wanted to call the child after her mother; Emma was against it. They went through the church calendar from end to end, and they consulted outsiders.

– Monsieur Léon, said the pharmacist, when I was talking about it to him the other day, is amazed that you haven't chosen Madeleine, which is excessively fashionable nowadays.

But old Madame Bovary made a great fuss about it being the name of an evil woman. Monsieur Homais, for his part, had a predilection for names that commemorated great men, illustrious deeds or noble ideas, and it was upon this system that he had christened his four children. Thus, Napoléon stood for glory and Franklin was for liberty; Irma, perhaps, was a concession to romanticism; but Athalie[10] was in homage to the most immortal masterpiece of the French stage. Because his philosophical convictions did not interfere with his artistic tastes, the thinker never stifled in him the man of feeling; he was discriminating, allowing for imagination and for fanaticism. In this tragedy, for example, he condemned the ideas, but he admired the style; he deplored the doctrine, but he applauded every detail, and his exasperation against the characters went with an enthusiasm for their speeches. Whenever he read the great passages he was enraptured; but, when he considered how the clerics used them for peddling their wares, he felt wretched, and in this confusion of feeling that weighed upon him he would have liked first to put the crown personally on Racine's head and then have a good half hour arguing with him.

At last, Emma remembered how at the Château de la Vaubyessard she had heard the Marquise address a young woman as
Berthe; from that moment it was the only name, and, since
Père Rouault couldn't be there, they asked Homais to be the
godfather. His christening presents were all items from his shop,
namely: six tins of jujubes, a whole jar of sweetmeats, three little
tins of marshmallow paste, and, what was more, half a dozen
sugar-candy sticks he'd found in a cupboard. In the evening
after the ceremony, there was a big dinner-party; the *curé* was
there; it was lively. Monsieur Homais, over the liqueurs, began
singing 'Le Dieu des bonnes gens',[11] Monsieur Léon sang a
barcarole, and the elder Madame Bovary, who was the god-
mother, a ballad from the days of the Empire; finally, Monsieur
Bovary senior insisted they bring down the baby, and he pro-
ceeded to baptize her with a glass of champagne poured over
her head. This mockery of the first of the sacraments enraged
the Abbé Bournisien; Old Bovary replied with a quotation from
'La Guerre des dieux',[12] the *curé* rose to leave; the ladies
implored; Homais intervened; and they managed to get the cleric
back in his seat, who then quite tranquilly picked up his saucer
and finished the rest of his cup of coffee.

Monsieur Bovary senior stayed on in Yonville for a month,
dazzling the population with a superb silver-braided army-cap,
which he wore in the morning, while out smoking his pipe in
the square. With his habit of drinking a good deal of brandy, he
was always sending the maid to the Golden Lion to buy him a
bottle, on his son's account; and he used up, for perfuming his
silk cravats, every drop of eau-de-Cologne in Emma's stock.

His daughter-in-law was by no means unhappy in his company. He had seen a bit of the world: he used to talk about
Berlin, Vienna, Strasbourg, about his days as an officer, the
mistresses he'd had, the big lunches he'd been at; he became
flirtatious, and sometimes even, on the stairs or in the garden,
would seize her round the waist, calling:

– Watch yourself, Charles!

Madame Bovary senior began to fear for her son's happiness,
and, worrying that her husband might, in the long run, have
an immoral influence on the young woman's mind, she now

hastened their departure. Perhaps she had even graver anxieties. Monsieur Bovary was no respecter of persons.

One day, Emma was quite suddenly taken with a desire to see her little girl, who had been put out to nurse with the carpenter's wife; and, without looking in the almanac to see if the six weeks of the Virgin had elapsed, she set off for the Rolets' dwelling, situated at the far end of the village, at the bottom of the hill, between the main road and the meadows.

It was midday; the houses had their shutters closed, and the roof-slates, glistening in the harsh light of a clear blue sky, seemed to be showering out sparks near the gable-crest. The wind sweltered. Emma was feeling faint as she walked along; the stones on the path hurt her feet. She wondered whether to turn back, or whether to go in somewhere and sit down.

At that moment, Monsieur Léon emerged from a nearby door with a parcel of documents under his arm. He came up to greet her and stood in the shade outside Lheureux's shop, under the grey awning that stuck out.

Madame Bovary said that she was on her way to see her baby, but that she was getting tired.

– If . . ., said Léon, not daring to go on.

– Are you heading anywhere? she asked. And, when the clerk said he was not, she implored him to accompany her. By the evening it was all over Yonville, and Madame Tuvache, the mayor's wife, declared in the presence of her maid that *Madame Bovary was compromising herself*.

To reach the nurse's house, they had to turn left at the end of the road, as though going to the cemetery, and follow, between small houses and backyards, a little path bordered with privet. It was in flower, and so were the veronica, the eglantines, the nettles and the young brambles that sprang out of the bushes. Through the hole in the hedge, they could see, around the hovels, a pig asleep in the sun on a dunghill, or cows with their wooden collars, rubbing their horns against the tree-trunks. Together, side by side, they strolled along, she leaning on his arm and he slowing his stride to the measure of hers; ahead of them, a swarm of flies drifted along, humming in the warm air.

They knew the house by an old walnut-tree that gave it shade.

Squat, with a brown tile roof, outside it had, just under the attic window, a braided string of onions dangling. Some kindling was propped up in the thorn fence, around a bed of lettuces, a few head of lavender and some sweet-peas trained up on sticks. A trickle of dirty water was oozing over the grass, and there were various ragged garments scattered about, woollen stockings, a red calico nightdress, and a big coarse linen sheet spread out on top of the hedge. At the sound of the gate, the nurse appeared, holding on one arm the baby she was feeding. With her other hand she pulled along a poor sickly tot, his face covered in scabs, the son of a Rouen draper. His parents, too taken up with their business, had left him in the country.

– Come in, she said; your little girl is over there asleep.

The room, on the ground floor, the only one there was, had on the far wall a large bed with no curtains, while the kneading-tub took up the wall with the window, which had one pane patched with a star of blue paper. In the corner, behind the door, gleaming hobnailed boots were arranged under the washing-slab, near a bottle full of oil with a feather in its mouth; a *Mathieu Laensberg*[13] lay on the dusty mantelpiece, among the gun-flints, the candle-stumps and the bits of tinder. The most recent superfluity in this room was *Fame Blowing Her Trumpet*, a picture no doubt cut out from some perfumier's catalogue, and nailed up on the wall with half a dozen cobbler's pegs.

Emma's baby was asleep on the floor, in a wickerwork cradle. She picked her up wrapped in her blanket, and began singing gently as she rocked her.

Léon walked around the room; he thought it strange to see this beautiful woman in her cream cotton dress, in the midst of such misery. Madame Bovary blushed; he turned away, fancying that his look might have been somewhat impertinent. She laid the little girl down again, just as she vomited over the collar of her dress. The nurse hurried over to wipe it off, protesting that it wouldn't show.

– All sorts she does down me, she said. I'm forever rinsing her off! If you was to be so obliging as to leave word with Camus the grocer, that he might let me take a bit of soap when I need some? It'd be a bit more convenient for you, with me not bothering you again.

– All right, all right! said Emma. Good day, Mère Rolet.

And out she went, wiping her shoes at the door.

The woman followed her to the end of the yard, saying how hard it was for her getting up in the night.

– I'm that jiggered with it sometimes, I fall asleep in the chair; now then, you might just let me have a little bit of ground coffee which would do me for a month and I'd have it in the morning with milk.

After enduring her thanks, Madame Bovary set off again; and she was only a little way down the path, when the sound of clogs made her turn round: it was the nurse!

– What is it?

The peasant-woman, drawing her aside, behind an elm, started telling her about her husband, who, with his job and the six francs a year that the captain . . .

– Come to the point, said Emma.

– Well, the nurse went on, heaving a sigh between each word, I'm afeard as he'll be vexed to see me drinking coffee on my own, you know, men . . .

– But you will get some, repeated Emma, I'm giving you some! You tiresome thing!

– Alas! My poor dear lady, it's his wounds, they give him terrible cramps in his chest. He even says as how cider weakens him.

– Do hurry up, Mère Rolet!

– Well, she went on, with a curtsy, if it wasn't too much to ask of you . . . – another curtsy – if you would – and her eyes were pleading – a little jug of brandy, she said at last, and I'll rub your little girl's feet with it, as tender as your tongue they are.

Once rid of the nurse, Emma took Monsieur Léon's arm again. She walked along quickly for some time; she slowed down, and her gaze came around from the path ahead and happened upon the shoulder of the young man, whose frock-coat had a black velvet collar. His auburn hair tumbled down over it, smooth and well combed. She noticed his fingernails, which were longer than was usual in Yonville. It was one of the clerk's main occupations, looking after them; and he kept, for this purpose, a special pocket-knife in his desk.

They returned to Yonville, walking along by the water. In the summer heat, more of the bank was above water, exposing the garden walls to their base, with their little flights of steps going down to the river. It was flowing silently, swift and cold to the eye; tall clustering grasses arched over it, bending to the current, and, like cast-off green hair, uncoiled their fronds in the limpid depths. Now and then, on the tips of the reeds or the leaves of the water lilies, some slender-legged insect crawled or came to rest. Sunbeams pierced the tiny blue bubbles in the waves as they rippled and died away; the old lopped willows gazed in the water at their grey bark; out beyond, all around, the meadows looked empty. It was dinner-time in the farmhouses, and the young woman and her companion heard as they walked only the fall of their steps on the earth, the words they spoke to each other, and the whisper of Emma's dress as it swished about.

The garden walls, their copings adorned with great splinters of glass, were as hot as conservatory windows. In the brickwork, wallflowers had pushed their way up; and, with the edge of her open sunshade, Madame Bovary, as she passed, scattered a few of their faded petals into yellow dust; or else a trailing spray of honeysuckle and clematis would scratch on the silk, getting caught up in the fringes.

They were talking about a troupe of Spanish dancers, expected soon at the theatre in Rouen.

– Will you be going? she asked.

– If I can, he answered.

Had they nothing else to say to one another? Their eyes indeed were full of a more serious conversation; and, while they were struggling in search of banal phrases, each felt assailed by the same languor; it was like a murmur from the soul, profound, unbroken, eclipsing the sound of their voices. Seized with wonder at this fresh sweetness, they had no thought of telling it aloud or seeking out its cause. Pleasures yet to come, like the shores of tropical islands, cast out across the sea's immensity their melting influence, on scented breezes; and in this enchantment they lie swooning, with no thought for whatever may lie in wait below the horizon.

The ground, in one spot, had been trampled by cattle; they had to step across on big green stones, spaced in the mud. She often stopped for a second to see where to tread, and, balancing on the wobbling stone, her elbows in the air, bending forward, doubt in her eye, she was laughing, in her fear of falling into a puddle.

When they reached her garden, Madame Bovary pushed open the little gate, went running up the steps and disappeared.

Léon went back to his office. The boss was out; he cast an eye over some documents, then cut himself a quill, and in the end got his hat and left.

He went to the Pasture, high up on the Côte d'Argueil, at the edge of the forest; he lay down on the ground beneath the pines, and looked at the sky through his fingers.

– I am so very bored! he said to himself. So very bored!

He was sorry for himself, living in this village, with Homais for a friend and Guillaumin for a master. The latter, immersed in his work, with his gold-rimmed spectacles and his red whiskers over his white cravat, was quite insensible to all mental refinement, even though he affected a stiff English manner which had impressed the clerk in the early days. As for the pharmacist's wife, she was the best wife in Normandy, gentle as a lamb, cherishing her children, her father, her mother, her cousins, weeping over others' misfortunes, cheerfully indulgent in her house, and a detester of corsets; but so slow-moving, so boring to listen to, so common in appearance and so limited in her conversation, that though she was thirty and he was twenty, though they slept in adjacent rooms, and though he spoke to her every day, he had never once imagined that she could be a woman to anyone, nor that she possessed any attribute of her sex other than the skirts.

And after her, who else was there? Binet, a few shopkeepers, two or three publicans, the *curé*, and finally Monsieur Tuvache, the mayor, with his two sons, prosperous churlish dullards who farmed their own land, gobbled up huge Sunday dinners, always went to church, and were quite insufferable company.

But, against the dull background of all these human faces, the image of Emma stood out distinctly, yet at a greater distance; for he sensed between himself and her a kind of dark abyss.

In the beginning, he had called on her several times accompanied by the pharmacist. Charles had not seemed particularly enthusiastic in his welcome; and Léon was abashed, between the fear of being indiscreet and the desire for an intimacy that he judged almost impossible.

4

Once it turned cold, Emma quitted her bedroom for the parlour, a long room with a low ceiling and, on the mantelpiece, a clustering coral-stem displayed in front of the mirror. Sitting in her armchair, near the window, she watched the village people going past along the pavement.

Léon, twice a day, went from his office to the Golden Lion. Emma, from afar, heard him coming; she would lean forward to listen; and the young man would slip behind the curtain, dressed always the same and never turning his head. But in the dusk, when, with her chin in her left hand, she had abandoned her unfinished embroidery on her knee, she often shuddered at the sight of that quick-gliding shadow. She got up and ordered the table to be laid.

Monsieur Homais would arrive during dinner. Skull-cap in hand, he came tiptoeing in to avoid disturbing anyone, always repeating the same phrase: 'Evening everyone.' Then, once he had taken his place, at the table, between husband and wife, he would ask the doctor for the latest news of his patients, and the latter would consult him in the matter of prospective emoluments. Next they would discuss what was *in the paper*. Homais, by this stage of the day, almost knew it off by heart; and he would reproduce it in full, with the editorial comments and all the stories of individual catastrophe from home and abroad. But, once this topic was played out, he was not slow to venture a few observations on the foodstuffs before him. Sometimes

even, rising from his chair, he would delicately indicate to
Madame the most tender morsel, or, turning to the maid, he
would offer her advice on the compounding of stews and the
dietetics of seasonings; he talked aroma, osmazome, pulps and
gelatine in a dazzling display. With more recipes in his head
than there were jars in his pharmacy, Homais excelled in the
making of various preserves, vinegars and sweet cordials, and
he also knew about the latest patent calefactory inventions,
along with the art of preserving cheeses and of nursing sickly
wines.

At eight o'clock, Justin came to fetch him to lock the pharmacy. Homais would give him a shrewd look, especially if
Félicité were there, having noticed his apprentice's fondness for
the doctor's house.

– That rascal of mine, he said, is starting to get ideas, and I
do believe, devil take me, he's in love with your maid.

But a worse misdeed, one for which he was rebuked, was his
continually listening to their conversation. On Sundays, for
example, they couldn't get him out of the parlour, after Madame
Homais had called him to take the children, who were falling
asleep in the armchairs, crumpling the baggy calico covers.

Not many people came to these gatherings at the pharmacist's,
his malicious tongue and his political opinions having estranged
him from a succession of respectable people. The clerk never
failed to turn up. As soon as he heard the door-bell, he would
run to greet Madame Bovary, take her shawl, and put away,
under the pharmacy desk, the big slippers made of felt which
she wore over her shoes, when it was snowing.

First they had a few rounds of *trente-et-un*; then Monsieur
Homais would play *écarté* with Emma; Léon, standing behind
her, gave his advice. Standing with his hands on the back of her
chair, he gazed at the teeth of the comb thrust into the coils of
her hair. Every time she reached out to play a card, it lifted her
dress on the right side. From the coiled mass of her hair, shades
of brown flowed down her back, until, fading away gradually,
little by little, they ended in shadow. Her dress, as she sat back
again, spilled over both sides of her chair, in ample swelling folds, that reached right down to the floor. When Léon

sometimes felt it under the sole of his boot, he stepped backwards, as if he had trodden on something living.

Once the game of cards was over, the apothecary and the doctor played dominoes, and Emma, changing places, her elbows on the table, leafed through *L'Illustration*. She had brought along her fashion magazine. Léon sat beside her and they looked at the engraved plates together and waited for each other at the bottom of the page. Often she would ask him to read her some poetry; Léon would declaim the lines lingeringly, dwindling to a whisper in the amorous passages. But the noise of the dominoes vexed him; Monsieur Homais was an expert, he beat Charles by a full double six. Once they had finished the third hundred, they would both stretch out in front of the fire and fall asleep in no time. The flames were dying down among the cinders; the teapot was empty; Léon was still reading. Emma listened to him, as she automatically twirled round the shade of the lamp, its gauze painted with pierrots driving carts and tightrope-walkers, with their poles. Léon would stop, with a gesture in the direction of his sleeping audience; they would talk to each other with voices lowered, and the conversation they were having seemed the sweeter, for not being overheard.

And so between them there arose a kind of alliance, a continual commerce in books and ballads; Monsieur Bovary, not a jealous man, was unsurprised.

On his birthday he received a handsome phrenological bust, decorated down to the thorax with numbers and painted blue. This was one of the clerk's little attentions. There were many more, even running errands, for him, in Rouen; and when a certain novel started a fashion for cactuses, Léon bought some plants for Madame, which he carried on his knee, in the *Hirondelle*, pricking his fingers on their spines.

She had fixed up, at her window-sill, a little shelf with a rail for her flowerpots. The clerk also had his own little hanging-garden; they would observe each other at the window, tending their flowers.

Among the windows in the village, there was one even more often occupied; for, on Sundays, from morning until night, and every afternoon, if the weather was bright, you could see at the window of his attic the lean profile of Monsieur Binet bent at his lathe, making the monotonous snoring droning noise that was audible even in the Golden Lion.

One evening, on his return, Léon found in his room a wool and velour rug with a leaf-pattern on a pale background. He called Madame Homais, Justin, the children, the cook. He told his employer about it; everyone wanted a glimpse of this rug; why should the doctor's wife be sending the clerk *favours*? It looked odd, and they made up their minds that she must be his *sweetheart*.

Anyone would have thought so, the way he was forever expounding her charm and her wit, until one day Binet answered him quite brutally with:

– What does it matter to me, when I have nothing to do with her!

He was in agony thinking out ways to *declare his feelings*; and, hesitating endlessly between the fear of displeasing her and the shame of being so pusillanimous, he wept his tears of dejection and desire. He made emphatic decisions; he wrote letters and tore them up, gave himself ultimatums which he subsequently ignored. He often set out, intending to risk everything; but this resolution deserted him in Emma's presence, and, when Charles, reappearing, invited him out in his gig to go and see one of his local patients, he accepted immediately, bowed to Madame and went along. Her husband, was he not something of hers?

As for Emma, she never once questioned herself to see if she loved him. Love, she believed, had to come, suddenly, with a great clap of thunder and a lightning flash, a tempest from heaven that falls upon your life, like a devastation, scatters your ideals like leaves and hurls your very soul into the abyss. Little did she know that up on the roof of the house, the rain will form a pool if the gutters are blocked, and there she would have stayed feeling safe inside, until one day she suddenly discovered the crack right down the wall.

5

It was a Sunday in February, an afternoon of snow.

The party, Monsieur and Madame Bovary, Homais and Monsieur Léon, had gone to see, a couple of miles from Yonville, in the valley, a flax-mill that was being built. The apothecary had brought along Napoléon and Athalie, for the sake of giving them some exercise, and Justin accompanied them, carrying the umbrellas on his shoulder. Nothing could have been less curious than this curiosity. On a large patch of waste land, littered, among the piles of sand and gravel, with various cog-wheels already rusting, there was a long rectangular building perforated with small windows. They had not finished it off yet, and you could see the sky through the timbers in the roof. Tied to the gable-end beam, a bouquet of straw and wheat-ears was fluttering its tricolour ribbons.

Homais was speaking. He was explaining to *the company* the future importance of this establishment, calculating the strength of the floors, the thickness of the walls, and bewailing the fact that he didn't have a metric rod, like the one belonging to Monsieur Binet for his own special use.

Emma, after giving him her arm, was leaning just against his shoulder, and she gazed at the disc of the sun radiating far and wide, through the haze, its pale splendour; but she turned her head: there was Charles. He had his cap pulled down to his eyebrows, and his thick lips were trembling, adding a touch of stupidity to his face; even his back, his tranquil back, was irritating to behold, and in the very look of his coat she found all the banality of the man.

While she was scrutinizing him, savouring in her irritation a kind of voluptuous depravity, Léon stepped forward. The cold that turned him pale seemed to leave upon his face a gentler weariness; between his cravat and the loose collar of his shirt there showed the whiteness of his neck; the lobe of his ear peeped from beneath a lock of hair, and his big blue eyes, raised to the clouds above, seemed to Emma more limpid and more beautiful than the mountain lakes that mirror the sky.

– Little wretch! suddenly shouted the apothecary.

And he ran to his son, who had just jumped into a pile of lime to turn his shoes white. Crushingly scolded, Napoléon began to howl, while Justin was wiping his shoes with a handful of straw. But a knife was needed; Charles offered his.

– Ah! she said to herself, he carries a knife in his pocket, like a peasant.

Hoar-frost was falling, and they turned back to Yonville.

Madame Bovary, that evening, didn't go to see her neighbours, and, once Charles had gone, and she felt herself alone, the contrast recurred to her with the acuity of a sensation almost immediate and with that lengthening of perspective that memory bestows upon its objects. Watching from her bed the bright burning fire, she could still see it, still the same, Léon over there, holding his cane with one hand and with the other holding Athalie, who was tranquilly sucking on a piece of ice. She found him charming; she couldn't shake him off; she remembered his other gestures from other days, phrases he had used, the sound of his voice, everything about him; and she repeated, pouting her lips as for a kiss:

– Yes, charming! Charming! ... And in love? she asked herself. In love with? ... With me!

The evidence was instantly obvious to her, her heart leaped. The flame in the hearth cast on the ceiling a trembling joyful glow. She turned on to her back and spread wide her arms.

Then began the eternal lamentation:

– Oh! If only heaven had willed it! And why not? What prevented it? ...

When Charles, at midnight, came in, she pretended to wake up, and, when he made a noise undressing, she complained of migraine, asking nonchalantly what had happened during the evening.

– Monsieur Léon, he said, went to bed early.

She couldn't hold back her smile, and she fell asleep with a new enchantment filling her soul.

Next day, at dusk, she received a visit from Monsieur Lheureux, the draper. A clever man he was, this shopkeeper.

Born in Gascony, but a Norman by adoption, he married a

southerner's verbosity to the cunning of the Cauchois. His plump, flaccid, beardless face looked as though it might have been steeped in a decoction of liquorice, and his white hair brought out the sharp glint in his little black eyes. Nobody knew what he had been before: a pedlar, some said, a banker in Routot, according to others. One thing was certain, he could do calculations, in his head, complicated enough to frighten Binet himself. Polite to the point of obsequiousness, he always stood with his back half bent, in the posture of a greeting or an invitation.

Leaving at the door his hat with the black silk band, he put a green box on the table, and began by lamenting to Madame, most ceremoniously, that he had not won her confidence before. A little shop like his was not one to attract a lady of *fashion*; he stressed the word. But she had only to give her order, and he would undertake to supply her with whatever she wanted, be it haberdashery or linen, hosiery or fancy goods; for he went into town four times a month, regularly. He did business with the leading houses. Mention him at the Trois Frères, at the Barbe d'or or at the Grand Sauvage; all the gentlemen there knew him like an old friend! For today, he had come to show Madame, in passing, various articles he happened to have, thanks to a very rare stroke of luck. And from the box he took out half a dozen embroidered collars.

Madame Bovary examined them.

– There is nothing I require, she said.

Next Monsieur Lheureux delicately exhibited three Algerian scarves, several packets of English needles, a pair of straw slippers, and, finally, four egg-cups delicately carved by convicts from coconut-shells. Then, his hands on the table, his neck outstretched, his back bent, his mouth gaping wide, he followed Emma's gaze, wandering undecided among his wares. Every so often, as though to get rid of the dust, he flicked a finger along the silk scarves, unfolded for display; and they rustled faintly, their woven flecks of gold gleaming out, in the green evening light, like little stars.

– How much do they cost?

– The merest trifle, he answered, but there's no hurry; whenever you please; we're not Jews!

She thought for a few moments, and in the end she declined again. Quite unmoved, Monsieur Lheureux replied:

– Very well, we'll see about it another day; I've always been able to get on with the ladies, except my own, anyway!

Emma smiled.

– What I mean is, he said amiably after his little joke, I'm not worried about the money . . . I could let you have some, if need be.

She made a gesture of surprise.

– Aha! he said quickly in a low tone, I wouldn't have to look very far to get some for you; definitely.

And he began to ask after Père Tellier, the proprietor of the Café Français, whom Monsieur Bovary was then attending.

– What's the matter with him, Père Tellier? He coughs fit to shake the whole house, and I'm a bit worried that before too long it'll be a wooden overcoat he needs, not a flannel vest. Too much carousing in his younger days. That sort, Madame, they had no discipline at all! He burned himself up with brandy! But it vexes me, you know, to see an acquaintance give up the ghost.

And, while he was fastening up his box, he chattered on about the doctor's patients.

– It must be the weather, I suppose, he said scowling at the window, as causes this illness. I feel a bit down in the mouth myself; one of these days I shall just have to come and consult the doctor, for the pain in my back. Anyway, good evening, Madame Bovary; at your service; your very humble servant!

And he shut the door gently.

Emma had her dinner served in her room, by the fire, on a tray; she took her time eating; she was pleased with things.

– How sensible I've been! she said to herself when she thought about the scarves.

She heard footsteps on the stair: it was Léon. She got up, and took from the chest of drawers, piled with dusters to hem, the one on top. She was looking very busy when he appeared.

The conversation languished, Madame Bovary falling silent again and again, while he seemed most embarrassed. Sitting on a low chair, near the hearth, he was twirling her ivory needle-case in his fingers; she was stitching away, or, occasionally, with her fingernail, turning down the hem of the cloth. She said nothing; he kept quiet, captivated by her silence, as he would have been by the sound of her voice.

– Poor boy! she was thinking.

– How have I offended her? he was wondering.

Léon, eventually, said that he had to go, one of these days, to Rouen, on office business.

– Your music subscription has expired, shall I renew it?

– No, she replied.

– Why?

– Because . . .

And, pursing her lips, slowly she drew out a long stitch of grey thread.

This work of hers irritated Léon; Emma's fingertips seemed to be sore from it; a gallant phrase came into his head, but he didn't risk it.

– Are you going to give it up?

– What? she said quickly. Music? Good heavens, yes I am! Don't I have my house to run, my husband to look after, a hundred and one things to do, a whole string of duties that must come first!

She looked at the clock. Charles was late. She played the anxious wife. Two or three times she even said,

– He's so kind!

The clerk was fond of Monsieur Bovary. But Emma's tenderness on his account was rather an unpleasant surprise; nevertheless he continued with his praises, which he heard from everyone, he said, and particularly the pharmacist.

– He is a fine man, Emma went on.

– Indeed, said the clerk.

And he began to talk about Madame Homais, whose slovenly appearance was usually a source of laughter with them.

– What does it matter? interrupted Emma. A good mother doesn't care how she looks.

And she relapsed into her former silence.

It was the same over the next few days; her talk, her manner, everything changed. She was obviously putting her heart and soul into the housework, attending church regularly and keeping her maid under stricter control.

She fetched Berthe home from the nurse. Félicité brought her in whenever visitors called, and Madame Bovary would undress her to show off her limbs. She declared that she adored children; it was her consolation, her joy, her passion, and she accompanied her caresses with lyrical effusions, which, to anyone other than the people of Yonville, would have recalled Sachette in *Notre-Dame de Paris*.[14]

When Charles came home, he found his slippers warming by the fire. Now there were always linings in his waistcoats, and buttons on his shirts, and there was a certain pleasure in looking at all the cotton nightcaps piled neatly in the cupboard. She no longer scowled, as she used to, at going for walks round the garden; what he proposed was always consented to, though she never anticipated the desires to which she yielded without a murmur; – and when Léon saw him by the fire, after dinner, both hands on his stomach, both feet on the fender, his cheeks pink from eating, his eyes moist with contentment, the child crawling on the carpet, and that slender woman leaning over the back of his chair to kiss his forehead:

– This is madness! he said to himself, how could I ever touch her?

To him she looked so virtuous and inaccessible, that all hopes, even the vaguest, were abandoned.

But, by this renunciation, he set her upon an extraordinary pinnacle. She was disentangled, in his mind, from the carnal qualities that were not his to enjoy; and, in his heart, she soared aloft, ever higher and ever further, as in some magnificent apotheosis, enraptured. It was one of those pure sentiments that do not interfere with daily life, that we cultivate for their very rarity, and whose loss is more distressing than their possession is delightful.

Emma grew thinner, her cheeks turned pale, her face looked longer. With her black hair, her large eyes, her straight nose, her gliding step, always silent now, did it not seem as if she passed through life almost without touching it, bearing on her brow the pale mark of a sublime destiny? She was so sad and so

calm, so gentle and yet so shy, that by her side you felt under
the spell of a frosty charm, just as you shiver in church at the
scent of the flowers mingling with the feel of cold marble. Even
other people were not safe from this seduction. The pharmacist
said:

– She is a woman of great talent who would not be out of
place as the wife of a sub-prefect.

The housewives admired her thrift, the patients her manners,
the poor her charity.

But she was filled with lust, with rage, with hatred. That
elegantly pleated dress concealed a heart in turmoil, and those
lips so chaste told nothing of her torment. She was in love with
Léon, and she sought solitude, the better to take her pleasure,
undistracted, in images of him. The actual sight of him upset
these voluptuous meditations. Emma trembled at the sound of
his footsteps; and, in his presence, the emotion subsided, leaving
her with only an immense astonishment that finished in sadness.

Léon never knew, as he forlornly left her house, that she
had just stood up to gaze after him through the window. She
followed his comings and goings; she kept a close eye on his
countenance; she made up an elaborate story to give colour to
her visiting his room. The pharmacist's wife she thought so
lucky to be sleeping under the same roof; and her thoughts were
continually settling on that house; like the pigeons from the
Golden Lion who came to dabble there, in its gutters, their pink
feet and their white wings. But the more Emma became aware
of her love, the more she suppressed it, to keep it from showing
and to diminish it. She would have liked Léon to guess at it; and
she imagined various coincidences and catastrophes that might
have hastened discovery. Doubtless it was inertia or terror that
held her back, and modesty as well. She fancied that she had
pushed him too far away, that the moment was gone, that all
was lost. But the pride, the joy of saying to herself 'I am virtuous',
and of looking at herself in the mirror striking poses of resignation, consoled her somewhat for the sacrifice she believed she
was making.

Now the cravings of the flesh, the yearning for money and
the melancholia of passion, all were confounded in a simple

sorrow; – and, instead of averting her thoughts from him, she enthralled herself the more, inflaming her hurt, and giving it every possible encouragement. She was annoyed by a meal clumsily served or a door half open; she bemoaned the velvet she didn't have, the happiness that might have been, her dreams that were too high, her house that was too cramped.

What exasperated her was that Charles seemed to have no notion of her torment. His conviction that he was making her happy struck her as impudent imbecility, his uxorious complacency as ingratitude. Who was it all for, her being so good? Was it not he who was the obstacle to felicity, the cause of misery, just like the spike on the buckle of the complicated set of straps that cramped her every step?

And so she directed solely at him all the manifold hatred that sprang from her ennui, and every effort to curtail it served but to augment it; for those vain efforts only added to the other reasons for despair and contributed even further to their estrangement. Even his gentleness pushed her into rebellion. Domestic mediocrity drove her to sumptuous fantasies, marital caresses to adulterous desires. She would have liked Charles to beat her, so that she might, with some justice, detest him and take her revenge. Sometimes she was startled by atrocious schemes that came into her head; and she had to carry on smiling, had to hear herself always saying she was happy, had to try to look happy, let them think her happy!

There were, however, moments of disgust at her own hypocrisy. The temptation would seize her to elope with Léon, somewhere, far away, to build a new destiny; but straight away inside her soul there opened up a great black gulf.

– Besides, his love for me has gone, she thought; what am I to do? What help will come? What consolation? What comfort?

She was left broken, panting, inert, sobbing in a low voice as her tears flowed.

– Why ever don't you tell Monsieur? asked the maid, when she came in during one of these crises.

– It's nerves, answered Emma; there's no cure, so don't mention it to him, he'd worry.

– Oh, yes, Félicité went on, you're just like la Guérine, Père

Guérin's daughter, the fisherman at Pollet, the one I knew in
Dieppe, before I came here. She was so sad, so sad, just to see
her standing on her front-step, she looked for all the world like
a white shroud spread out by the door. Her trouble, from what
they say, was a kind of fog she had in her head, and the doctors
couldn't do a thing, nor the *curé*. Whenever it took her really
bad, she'd go off on her own along the beach, and the customs
officer, on his rounds, often found her lying there flat on her
face and crying into the pebbles. And after she was married, it
went off, so they say.

– But with me, said Emma, it was after I married that it came on.

6

One evening as she was sitting by the open window, watching
Lestiboudois, the sexton, trimming the box-hedge, she suddenly
heard the angelus ringing.

It was early April, when the primroses are in flower; a warm
breeze rolls over the newly turned flower-beds, and the gardens,
just like women, seem to be making ready for the great days of
summer. Through the arbour trellis and away beyond, you can
see the river sketch out its winding curves all across the hay
meadows. Evening mists were drifting among the leafless
poplars, mellowing their line with a tinge of violet, paler and
more transparent than a delicate web tangled in their branches.
Far away, the cattle were on the move; their tramping and their
lowing quite inaudible; and the bell, still ringing out, kept up its
placid lamentation.

Swayed by the steady chime, the young woman's mind strayed
far away among her memories of childhood and school. She
remembered the tall candlesticks on the altar, towering over
the vases full of flowers and the tabernacle with its miniature
columns. She wanted, once again, to be merged still into the
long line of white veils, touched with black here and there by
the stiff hoods of the good sisters kneeling at their prie-dieu; on
Sundays, at mass, when she looked up, she had seen the sweet
face of the Virgin through the swirling blue-grey clouds of

incense. And now a great tenderness took hold of her; she felt soft and all forlorn, like a little feather spinning in a great storm; and it was quite obliviously that she went towards the church, eager for any act of devotion, if it would absorb her soul and erase her whole existence.

She met, on the square, Lestiboudois, on his way back; for, to avoid curtailing his work-time, he preferred to break off and start again, thus ringing the angelus whenever it suited him. Besides, ringing it earlier called the children to their catechism class.

Some of them, having arrived early, were playing marbles on the flagstones in the cemetery. Others, astride the wall, were swinging their legs, hacking with their clogs at the tall nettles that grew between the garden wall and the most recent graves. It was the only patch of green; the rest was just stone, continually covered in dust, despite the sacristy broom.

The children ran around in their canvas shoes as though it had been a playground, and you could hear the clamour of their voices above the clanging of the bell. It diminished with the oscillations of the great rope, hanging down from the high belfry, which trailed its end on the floor below. The swallows were gliding, squeaking, slicing the air with their wings, and hurrying back to their yellow nests, beneath the tiles on the coping. At the far end of the church, a lamp was burning, a night-light wick inside a glass hanging up. From a distance, it looked like a white blotch flickering above the oil. A long ray of sunlight cut right across the nave, making it even darker in the aisles and the niches.

– Where is the *curé*? Madame Bovary asked a little boy who was playing at waggling the turnstile in its over-large socket.

– He's coming, said the boy.

Just then, the presbytery door creaked, Abbé Bournisien appeared; the children, pell-mell, fled into the church.

– Little rascals! muttered the priest. Always the same!

And, picking up a battered catechism which he had just stepped on:

– No respect for anything!

But, once he noticed Madame Bovary:

– Excuse me, he said, I did not recognize you.

He stuffed the catechism into his pocket and stood there, still swinging the heavy vestry key on two fingers.

The rays of the setting sun fell directly on his face, fading the colour from his woollen cassock, shiny at the elbows, frayed at the hem. Stains from grease and tobacco followed the line of little buttons down his broad chest, growing more plentiful away from his neck-band, where the copious folds of red flesh reposed. He had just had his dinner and was breathing heavily.

– How are you keeping? he added.

– It's dreadful! replied Emma. I'm in misery.

– Well now, so am I, said the cleric. The start of the hot weather, don't you think, it's remarkably debilitating? But there you are! We are born to suffer, as Saint Paul says. But, Monsieur Bovary, what does he think about it?

– Him? she said with a disdainful gesture.

– What? said the simple man in astonishment, he doesn't prescribe you anything?

– Aah! said Emma, earthly remedies are not what I need.

But the *curé*, every so often, glanced into the church, where the kneeling youngsters were shouldering each other, and tumbling over like a pack of cards.

– I wanted to know . . . she went on.

– Just you wait, Riboudet, shouted the priest in an angry voice, I'll come and box your ears for you, you little monkey!

Then, turning to Emma,

– That's the son of Boudet the carpenter; his parents are well-off and let him do whatever he likes. Though he'd learn fast, if he wanted to, for he's a bright lad. You know sometimes, for a joke, I call him *Ri*boudet (like the hill on the way to Maromme) and I even say: *mon* Riboudet. Ha! Ha! Mont-Riboudet! The other day, I told that one to His Grace, who laughed, he deigned to laugh. And Monsieur Bovary, how is he?

She didn't seem to hear. He went on:

– Busy as ever, most likely? For we are certainly, he and I, the two people in the parish who have the most to do. But he's the one who heals the body, he added with a heavy laugh, and I'm the one who does the souls!

Beseechingly, she fixed her eyes upon the priest.

– Yes, she said, you ease all sorrows.

– Oh, I don't know about that, Madame Bovary! Only this morning, I had to go over to Bas-Diauville about a cow that was bloated; they thought it was bewitched. Every cow they have, I don't know how it is . . . Excuse me! Longuemarre and Boudet! Goodness gracious me! Will you both stop it!

And, with a leap, he flew into the church.

At that moment, the youngsters were bunched around the great lectern, clambering on to the cantor's stool, opening the missal; and some of them, on tiptoe, were just about to venture right inside the confessional. But the *curé*, in a trice, dispensed a hail of blows. Taking hold of the collars of their jackets, he lifted them up off the ground and put them down again on their knees on the flagstones in the choir, rather firmly, as if he meant to wedge them there.

– Indeed, said he, returning to Emma, and unfolding his big cotton handkerchief, holding one corner between his teeth, the farmers do have a very hard time!

– And so do others, she replied.

– Absolutely! The workers in the towns, for instance.

– That's not really . . .

– Pardon me! I have known poor young mothers there, virtuous women, of course, veritable saints, who didn't even have enough bread.

– But what of all those, replied Emma (and the corners of her mouth were twitching as she spoke), those, Monsieur Le Curé, who have bread, and don't have any . . .

– Fire in the winter, said the priest.

– Oh! Does that matter?

– What? Does it matter? It rather seems, at least to me, that once you have a good fire, good food . . . after all it . . .

– My God! My God! she sighed.

– Is there anything the matter? he said, approaching anxiously. It's indigestion, I expect? You ought to be at home, Madame Bovary, with a nice cup of tea; it'll pick you up, or a glass of cold water with some brown sugar.

– Why?

And she looked like someone waking from a dream.

– Because you were rubbing your hand across your forehead. I thought you must have been feeling faint.

Then it occurred to him:

– But you were asking me about something? What was it now? I forget.

– Me? Nothing . . . nothing . . . repeated Emma.

And her gaze, wandering about, settled eventually on the old man in the cassock. Each now contemplating the other, face to face, in silence.

– Well, Madame Bovary, he said at last, you must excuse me, but duty calls, you know; I must dispatch these rascals of mine. Here we are with First Communion almost upon us. We shall be caught out again, I rather fear! So, after Ascension Day, I shall keep them in every Wednesday on the dot for an extra hour. Poor little things! It's never too soon to set their feet on the pathways of the Lord, as, indeed, He himself has advised us through the mouth of his divine Son . . . Felicitations, madame; my respects to your good husband!

And he went into the church, making his genuflection at the door.

Emma watched him disappearing between the double line of pews, moving ponderously, his head bent a little to one side, his hands unclasped.

She turned on her heel, abruptly, like a statue on a pivot, and set off home. But the gruff voice of the priest, the clear voices of the children, still reached her ears and continued at her back:

– Are you a Christian?

– Yes, I am a Christian.

– What is a Christian?

– One who, being baptized . . . baptized . . . baptized.

She climbed up the stairs holding on to the banisters, and, once she was in her room, dropped into an armchair.

In through the window a soft white light was gently rippling down. The furniture seemed to be more solidly in place, lost among the shadows as if upon a darkening ocean. The fire was dead, the clock was ticking still, and Emma was slightly stupefied by the calm that was in things, for within her was such turmoil.

But there, between the window and the work-table, was little Berthe, tottering along in her knitted boots, trying to reach her mother, to grab hold of the ends of her apron strings.

– Leave me alone! said Emma, pushing her away.

The little girl soon came back again, even closer, up against her mother's knees; and, leaning to steady herself, she gazed up at her with big blue eyes, as a thread of clear saliva dribbled from her lips on to the silk of the apron.

– Leave me alone! repeated the young woman sharply.

The look on her face frightened the child, who began to cry.

– Can't you leave me alone! she said, elbowing her away.

Berthe fell over by the chest of drawers, against the brass fitting; she cut her cheek on it, blood trickled down. Madame Bovary rushed over to pick her up, broke the rope on the bell, called for the maid at the top of her voice, and was about to start cursing herself, when Charles appeared. It was dinner-time, he was home.

– Look, my dear, Emma said to him in a tranquil voice: here's the little one, who has just had a fall while playing.

Charles reassured her, it was nothing serious, and he went off to get some sticking-plaster.

Madame Bovary did not go down for dinner; she wanted to stay upstairs alone to look after her child. Watching her sleep, the remains of her anxiety gradually ebbed away, and she thought herself rather silly and rather fine to have worried like that over such a little thing. Berthe, certainly, had stopped sobbing. Her breathing scarcely lifted the cotton coverlet. Big tears had gathered at the corners of her half-closed eyelids, and between her lashes there showed a pair of pale eyes, quite sunken; the plaster, stuck on her cheek, stretched the skin crookedly.

– A strange thing it is, thought Emma, this child is so ugly!

When Charles came home at eleven o'clock from the pharmacy (where he had gone, after dinner, to return the rest of the sticking-plaster), he found his wife standing by the cradle.

– I do assure you it's nothing, he said, kissing her on the forehead; don't torment yourself, poor darling, you'll make yourself ill!

He had stayed a long time at the apothecary's. Though he had not obviously seemed very upset. Monsieur Homais, nevertheless, had made an effort to steady him, to *buck him up*. They had talked about the various dangers that beset childhood and about the carelessness of servants. Madame Homais knew about that, still bearing the scars on her chest from a bowlful of hot soup that a cook, long ago, had spilt down her pinafore. Accordingly, these good parents took every sort of precaution. The knives were never sharpened, the floors never waxed. There were iron bars on the windows and strong guards on the fireplaces. The Homais children, for all their independence, couldn't make a move without somebody there watching them; at the slightest sign of a cold, their father crammed cough syrups into them; and even beyond the age of four they had to wear, implacably, great big quilted bonnets. This, indeed, was Madame Homais's obsession; her husband was in silent agonies over it, fearing the possible effects of such compression upon the intellectual organs, and he even went so far as to say to her:

– Do you really want to turn them into Caribs or Botocudos?

Charles, meanwhile, had tried several times to interrupt the conversation.

– I need to have a word with you, he had whispered in the clerk's ear, and the latter had led the way upstairs.

– Does he suspect something? wondered Léon. His heart was racing and he was lost in speculation.

Charles at last, having shut the door, asked him to have a look in Rouen at the price of a fine daguerreotype; it was a sentimental surprise devised for his wife, a delicate gesture, a portrait of himself in his black frock-coat. But he did want to *know what he was letting himself in for*; this errand should be no trouble for Monsieur Léon, since he went into town every week, more or less.

Why did he? Homais suspected some *little adventure*, some liaison behind it. But he was mistaken; Léon had no sweetheart. He was sadder than ever, as Madame Lefrançois observed from the amount of food he left these days on his plate. To get to the bottom of it, she questioned the tax-collector; Binet replied, disdainfully, that he had never been *put on the police pay-roll*.

His companion, though, seemed very peculiar, for Léon would often throw himself back in his chair and stretch out his arms, complaining vaguely about life in general.

– It's because you haven't got any hobbies, said the tax-collector.

– Such as?

– If I were you, I'd have a lathe!

– But I don't know anything about lathes, replied the clerk.

– That is true! said the other man, stroking his chin, with a look that mingled disdain and satisfaction.

Léon was tired of loving for nothing; and he was beginning to feel the weary burden of repetition in a life with no interests to guide and no hopes to sustain it. He was so bored with Yonville and with the people there, that the sight of certain faces, of certain houses would irritate him beyond endurance; and the pharmacist, great fellow though he was, now seemed completely intolerable. Even so, the prospect of a new situation was almost as alarming as it was seductive.

This anxiety soon turned into impatience, and Paris now began to flaunt, in the distance, the fanfare of masked balls and the laughter of girls. Since he had to finish his law there, why didn't he go now? Who was stopping him? And he began to make inward preparations: he planned in advance how he might spend his day. He furnished, in his head, a set of rooms. He would lead the life of an artist! He would have guitar lessons! He would have a dressing-gown, a beret, a pair of blue velvet slippers! And already he was admiring a pair of crossed foils over his mantelpiece, with a death's head and the guitar up above them.

The difficult thing was his mother's consent; though nothing could have looked more reasonable. Even his employer was advising him to try another office, where he could get on more quickly. Taking a middle course, then, Léon looked for a position as second clerk in Rouen, didn't find one, and finally wrote a long detailed letter to his mother, expounding the case for going to live in Paris immediately. She gave her consent.

He was certainly in no hurry. Every day, for a whole month, Hivert was carting for him, from Yonville to Rouen, from Rouen to Yonville, boxes, valises, parcels; and, once Léon had mended his wardrobe, had his three armchairs restuffed, had bought a supply of silk scarves, made rather more preparations than are required for a voyage around the world, he delayed from week to week, until there came a second letter from his mother urging him to be gone, since be wanted to pass his exam before the holidays.

When the moment came for embracing, Madame Homais wept; Justin was sobbing; Homais, in manly fashion, concealed his feelings; he wanted to carry his friend's overcoat as far as the gate of the notary, who was taking Léon to Rouen in his carriage. The young man had just enough time to say his farewells to Monsieur Bovary.

When he reached the top of the stairs, he stopped, he felt so out of breath. When he came in, Madame Bovary started to her feet.

– Here I am, once again! said Léon.

– I knew you would!

She bit her lip, and a rush of blood beneath the skin turned her face quite pink, from the roots of her hair right to the edge of her collar. She just stood there, her shoulder leaning against the panelling.

– The doctor isn't here?

– He's gone out.

She repeated:

– He's gone out.

There was a silence. They gazed at each other; and their thoughts, confounded in one common anguish, met in an intimate embrace, like two tremulously naked lovers.

– I would like to kiss Berthe goodbye, said Léon.

Emma came down a few steps, and she called Félicité.

Quickly he glanced around the room, taking in the walls, the shelves, the fireplace, as though to penetrate it all, to carry it all away with him.

But she came back, and the maid brought in Berthe, who was dangling a little windmill upside down on a string.

Léon kissed her on the neck several times over.

– Goodbye, poor little thing! Goodbye, little love, goodbye!

And he gave her back to her mother.

– Take her, she said to the maid.

They were alone.

Madame Bovary, with her back to him, had her face pressed to the window-pane; Léon was holding on to his hat and tapping it gently on his thigh.

– It's going to rain, said Emma.

– I have a coat, he replied.

– Ah!

She turned towards him, her chin lowered and her forehead prominent. The light flowed over her brow as over polished marble, down to the curve of the eyebrows, disclosing neither what she saw in the distance nor what she was thinking deep down inside.

– Well, this is goodbye! he sighed.

Abruptly she looked up again.

– Yes, goodbye . . . now go!

They moved towards each other; he held out his hand, she hesitated.

– English fashion, then, she said, allowing him to take her hand as she forced out a laugh.

Léon could feel it between his fingers, and the very substance of his being seemed to be flowing down into that moist palm.

He opened his hand; their eyes met once again, and he disappeared.

Once he reached the market-place, he stopped, and hid behind a pillar, to take his last look at that white house with its four green shutters. He thought he saw a shadow at the window of her room; but the curtain, magically unhooking itself, slowly stirred its long oblique folds, which spread out suddenly, and hung down straight, as rigid as a wall of plaster. Léon began to run.

From a distance, in the road, he saw his employer's carriage, and beside it a man in a rough apron, holding the horse. Homais and Maître Guillaumin were chatting together. They were waiting for him.

– A last embrace, said the apothecary with tears in his eyes.

Here is your overcoat, dear friend; don't catch cold! Take care! Look after yourself!

– Come on, Léon, jump in! said the notary.

Homais leaned over the splash-board, and, in a voice broken by sobbing, uttered these two sad words:

– Safe journey!

– Good night, answered Maître Guillaumin. Let her go! Off they went, and Homais turned for home.

Madame Bovary had opened her window on to the garden, and she was watching the clouds.

They were massing in the western sky towards Rouen, a fast-uncoiling blackness, its edges trimmed with great strands of sunlight, like golden arrows on a display trophy, while the rest of the empty sky was white as porcelain. But a gust of wind curved the poplars, and now the rain was falling; it spluttered over the green leaves. Then the sun came out, the hens clucked, sparrows shook out their wings in the damp bushes, and as the pools of rain on the gravel ebbed away they took the pink flowers fallen from an acacia.

– He must be so far away already! she thought.

Monsieur Homais, as usual, came at half past six, during dinner.

– Well now, he said as he sat down, we have embarked our young man.

– So it seems! replied the doctor.

Then, turning in his chair:

– And what's the news with you?

– My wife, though, this afternoon, she was a little upset. You know women, anything flusters them! Especially mine! And it would be quite wrong for us to make any fuss, since their nervous system is very much more receptive than ours.

– Poor Léon, said Charles, how will he get on in Paris? Will he get used to it?

Madame Bovary sighed.

– Oh, come on now! said the pharmacist clicking his tongue, the little restaurant parties! The masked balls! The champagne! He'll be in his element, I promise you.

– I don't think he'll go wrong, protested Bovary.

– Nor do I! Homais answered emphatically, though he will have to go along with the others, if he doesn't want to be taken for a Jesuit. And you have no idea what they get up to, those jokers, in the Latin Quarter, with the actresses! Anyway, students are very well thought of in Paris. As long as they have a few of the social graces, they are received in the best circles, and there are even ladies in the Faubourg Saint-Germain who fall in love with them, which gives them, eventually, the chance of making an excellent marriage.

– Even so, said the doctor, I worry that he may ... you know ...

– Quite right, interrupted the apothecary, it's the other side of the coin! You do always have to keep one hand on your wallet. Now, just suppose you're in the park; somebody or other comes up to you, well dressed, medal perhaps, and you could take him for a diplomat; he accosts you, you chat; he makes an impression, offers you a pinch of snuff or picks up your hat for you. So you get on famously; he takes you to a café, invites you to his place in the country, introduces you over drinks to all and sundry, and, nine times out of ten, because he wants to filch your purse or lead you into pernicious habits.

– That is true, said Charles; but I was thinking mainly of the illnesses, like typhoid fever, for instance, that attack students from the provinces.

Emma shuddered.

– Because of the change of diet, continued the pharmacist, and the resulting perturbation in the general economy. And the water in Paris, you know! The restaurant cooking, that spicy food overheats your blood eventually, and, whatever they say, it doesn't come up to a good stew. Personally, I've always preferred home cooking; it's healthier! So, when I was studying pharmacy in Rouen, I lived in a boarding-house; I had my meals with the professors.

And on he went, expounding his general opinions and his personal tastes, until the moment Justin came to get him to make an egg-flip that someone had ordered.

– Never a moment's respite! he cried. Always on the go! I

can't be away for one minute! Like an old cart-horse, forever sweating blood! What a life of drudgery!

– By the way, he said, have you heard the latest?

– What?

– It seems rather likely, said Homais raising his eyebrows and making his most serious face, that the Seine-Inférieure Agricultural Show will take place this year in Yonville-l'Abbaye. The rumour, anyway, is in the air. This morning the newspaper had something about it. It would be of the utmost importance for this area. But we can talk about it some other time. I can see my way, thank you both. Justin has the lantern.

7

The next day, for Emma, was one of mourning. Everything seemed to be wrapped in a confusion of shadows drifting over their surfaces, and sorrow plunged into her soul with a muffled howling, like the sound of the winter wind in some abandoned château. It was the kind of reverie that comes when something vanishes for ever, the lassitude we feel when some habitual movement is interrupted, when any prolonged vibration comes to a sudden stop.

Just as after La Vaubyessard, when the quadrilles had been swirling in her head, she felt a dull melancholy, a lethargic despair. Léon reappeared, taller, more beautiful, more charming, less distinct; though far away from her, he had not left her, he was there, and the walls of the house seemed to carry his shadow. And she could not take her eyes from that carpet where he had walked, from those empty chairs where he had sat. The river was still flowing, and sending slow ripples along the smooth banks. They had walked along there many many times, by the same murmuring waves, over the moss-covered stones. What sunny days they had had! What fine afternoons, alone, in the shade, at the end of the garden! He would be reading aloud, bare-headed, sitting on a pile of firewood; the cool meadow breezes would flutter in the pages of his book and among the nasturtiums in the arbour . . . He was gone, the only light of her life, her only hope of happiness! Why had she not seized that joy when it came to her? Why had she not held it fast, knelt to it, when it tried to escape? And she cursed herself for not having loved Léon; she thirsted for his lips. She felt an impulse to run after him, to throw herself into his arms, to say: 'Here I am, I'm yours!' But Emma was quite confounded by the prospective difficulty of the enterprise, and her desires, inflated by regret, only became ever more intense.

Henceforth, her memory of Léon formed the core of her ennui; it crackled away brightly, just like, on the Russian steppe, a travellers' fire left burning on the snow. She rushed towards it, she huddled up to it, delicately rousing the greying embers, she went searching for anything to keep it alight; her most distant reminiscences as well as the most recent events, her feelings and her imaginings, her voluptuous cravings that were melting away, her plans for future happiness that creaked like dead branches in the wind, her sterile virtue, her fallen hopes, her domestic drudgery, these she collected up and used to rekindle her sadness.

But the flames were subsiding, either because the fuel was running low or because it was piled too high. Love was gradually dimmed by absence, regrets were smothered by habit; and the glare of the fires that had crimsoned her pale sky now thickened and faded slowly into shadow. In the stagnation of her consciousness, she even mistook disgust with her husband for an aspiration towards her lover, the scorch of hatred for the warmth of tenderness; but, since the storm was still blowing, and passion burned to ashes, no help came, no sun appeared, black night was all about her, and she was quite lost in a bitter cold that travelled through her.

Now the bad days of Tostes came back again. This time she thought herself far more unhappy: for she was experienced in sorrow, with the certainty that it would never end.

Any woman who had imposed such great sacrifices on herself could well be permitted a few fancies. She bought a Gothic prie-dieu, and in one month she spent fourteen francs on lemons for cleaning her nails; she wrote off to Rouen, to order a blue cashmere dress; she chose the very best scarf from Lheureux;

she tied it round her waist over her dressing-gown; then, with the shutters closed, and a book in her hand, she would recline on a sofa in her accoutrements.

Often, she changed her coiffure: she did her hair *à la chinoise*, in loose curls, in plaits; she parted her hair at the side and rolled it under, like a man.

She decided to learn Italian: she bought dictionaries, a grammar, a supply of paper. She began some serious reading, in history and philosophy. At night, sometimes, Charles woke with a start, thinking they had come to fetch him to a patient.

– Coming, he mumbled.

And it was the sound of Emma striking a match to relight the lamp. But her reading went the same way as her needlework, cluttering the cupboard, half finished; she picked it up, put it down, went on to something else.

She had moods, when she was easily enticed into extravagance. She swore one day, to contradict her husband, that she could drink down a big tumbler of brandy, and, as Charles was foolish enough to dare her to it, she swallowed the brandy every drop.

In spite of her giddy airs (the phrase used by the bourgeois wives of Yonville), Emma still had a joyless look, and, habitually, at the corners of her mouth, she had that tightness that crumples the faces of old maids and bankrupts. She was pale all over, as white as a sheet; pinched about the nostrils, with a vague look in her eye. After discovering three grey hairs at her temples, she talked a great deal about getting old.

Often there were fainting fits. One day, she spat blood, and, as Charles was fussing about, very obviously anxious:

– Bah! she said, what does it matter?

Charles went off to take refuge in his study; and he wept, both elbows on the table, sitting in his office chair, under the phrenological bust.

Then he wrote to his mother, asking her to come, and they had long discussions together on the subject of Emma.

What should they do? What could they do, since she refused to have any kind of treatment?

– Do you know what your wife needs? said Madame Bovary

senior. She needs some hard work, some manual labour. If she were like nearly everyone else, forced to earn a living, she wouldn't have these vapours of hers, which all come from stuffing her head with nonsense and leading a life of idleness.

– But she is always busy, said Charles.

– Ah! Busy indeed! And with what? Busy reading novels, wicked books, things written against religion where priests are made a mockery with speeches taken from Voltaire. It all leads to no good, my poor boy, and anyone with no religion always comes to a bad end.

Therefore, it was decided to prevent Emma from reading novels. This was by no means an easy matter. The old lady took it upon herself: on her way through Rouen she was to call in person at the lending library and notify them that Emma was cancelling her subscription. Would they not have the right to tell the police, if the librarian still persisted in his poisonous trade?

The farewells between mother and daughter were cool. In the three weeks they had spent together, they hadn't exchanged half a dozen words, apart from the usual inquiries and compliments when they met at the table, and in the evenings before bed.

Madame Bovary left on a Wednesday, market-day in Yonville.

The square, since early morning, had been cluttered with a line of carts, tipped on end with their shafts in the air, stretching out along by the houses all the way from the church to the inn. On the other side, there were canvas stalls selling cotton goods, blankets and woollen stockings, with bridles for horses and packets of blue ribbons, their ends fluttering about in the wind. Great big pots and pans were stacked on the ground, between pyramids of eggs and hampers of cheeses, with bits of straw sticking out; just by the threshing machines, hens clucking in little cages were stretching out their necks through the bars. The people, crowding together in one place and refusing to move away, were in danger of breaking down the front of the pharmacy. On Wednesdays, the shop was never empty and you had to push your way in, less to buy medicines than for the sake of a consultation, so vast was the fame of the great Homais in the local villages. His robust aplomb fascinated the country people. They regarded him as a greater doctor than any of the doctors.

Emma was stationed at her window (she was often there: the window, in the provinces, replaces theatres and promenading), and she was amusing herself observing the throng of rustics, when she noticed a gentleman in a frock-coat of green velvet. He was wearing yellow gloves, though shod in heavy gaiters; and he was heading towards the doctor's house, followed by a peasant walking with head bent and a rather thoughtful look.

– Can I see the doctor? he asked Justin, who was on the doorstep, talking to Félicité.

And, taking him for the doctor's servant:

– Tell him that Monsieur Rodolphe Boulanger de la Huchette is here.[15]

It was not out of any territorial vanity that the newcomer had added *de la Huchette* to his name, but merely to make himself known. La Huchette was an estate near Yonville, where he had just bought the château, along with two farms he was working himself, though without putting himself to any great trouble. He was a bachelor, and said to have at least *fifteen thousand a year*.

Charles came into the room. Monsieur Boulanger introduced his man, who wanted to be bled because he had *pins and needles everywhere*.

– Purge me, it will, he said to every argument.

So Bovary sent for a bandage and a basin, and asked Justin to hold it. Turning to the villager who was already going white:

– Don't be afraid, my lad.

– No, no, he said. Go ahead!

And, with a touch of bravado, he held out his large arm. At the prick of the lancet, blood spurted out and splashed down the mirror.

– Bring the basin nearer! exclaimed Charles.

– Mind! said the peasant. Comes out like a little fountain! Really red is my blood! That must be a good sign, don't you think?

– Sometimes, the medical officer remarked, they feel nothing at first, then the syncope occurs, especially with well-built chaps, like this one here.

The peasant, when he heard this, dropped the lancet-case he had been twiddling. The jerk of his shoulders made the back of the chair creak. His hat fell off.

– I knew it, said Bovary, pressing one finger on the vein.

The bowl was beginning to shake in Justin's hands; his knees were trembling, he turned pale.

– Emma! Emma! called Charles.

In one bound, she was down the stairs.

– Vinegar! he shouted. Oh! Good God, two at once!

And, in his agitation, he fumbled with the compress.

– It's nothing, said Monsieur Boulanger in a tranquil tone, as he took Justin in his arms.

And he sat him on the table, leaning his back against the wall.

Madame Bovary began to undo his cravat. There was a knot in the strings of his shirt; she spent a few minutes working with her slender fingers at the young man's neck; then she poured some vinegar on his temples and blew upon it, delicately.

The ploughman revived; but Justin's syncope persisted, his pupils disappearing into their pale sclerotic, just like blue flowers in milk.

– We must, said Charles, hide this from him.

Madame Bovary took the bowl. To put it under the table, in the movement of her bending down, her dress (it was a summer dress with four flounces, in yellow, low-waisted, with a full skirt), her dress spread out wide all about her on the tiled floor; and, when Emma, crouching down, swayed a little as she put out her arms, the swelling fabric subsided, along the contours of her bodice. She went to get a jug of water, and she was melting lumps of sugar in it when the pharmacist arrived. The maid had been to fetch him in the midst of the hubbub; seeing that his apprentice had his eyes open, he breathed again. Then, stepping around him, he looked him up and down.

– Fool! he said; little fool, really! F-double-O-L! A serious business, isn't it, a phlebotomy! And from a lad who's afraid of nothing! He's like a squirrel, this one is, climb up to any height he will, to scrump a few nuts. Oh, yes, say something, have a

little boast. What splendid propensities for any future pharmacist; you could find yourself called upon in the gravest circumstances, before a court of law, to enlighten the conscience of the
judiciary; and you still have to keep your head, put your case,
show them you're a man, or else be taken for an imbecile!

Justin made no answer. The apothecary went on:

– Who asked you to come here? You're always pestering
Monsieur and Madame. On Wednesdays, anyway, your presence is quite indispensable to me. At this moment there are a
score of people in the shop. I have left everything just for your
sake. Come on, off with you. Quick, march! Wait for me there,
and keep an eye on the jars.

Once Justin, doing up his cravat, had left, they talked about
fainting fits. Madame Bovary had never had one.

– That is extraordinary for a woman! said Monsieur Boulanger. But some people are very delicate. Indeed I have seen one
of the seconds, at a duel, lose consciousness merely at the sound
of the pistols being loaded. She looked up at him, her eyes full
of admiration.[16]

– With me, said the apothecary, the sight of other people's
blood has no effect at all; but the very idea of my own flowing
would be enough to make me faint, if I thought about it too
much.

Meanwhile Monsieur Boulanger sent his man back, urging
him to compose himself, now that his whim was over.

– It has procured to me the advantage of your acquaintance,
he added.

And he was looking at Emma as he said it.

He deposited three francs on the corner of the table, gave a
casual bow and off he went.

He was soon on the other side of the river (this was his way
back to La Huchette); and Emma could see him in the meadow,
walking along beneath the poplars, pausing every so often, like
someone lost in thought.

– She is rather nice! he was saying to himself; she is very nice,
that doctor's wife. Lovely teeth, dark eyes, a dainty little foot,
and the style of a Parisienne. Where the devil did she come
from? Where did he find her, that great oaf?

Monsieur Rodolphe Boulanger was thirty-four years old; his temperament was brutal and his intelligence shrewd; having been with a large number of women, he was something of an expert. This one he had found pleasing; so he was dreaming about her, and her husband.

– I think he's very stupid. She is certainly tired of him. What a lout! With his dirty nails and his three days of beard. While he trots off after his patients, she sits darning socks. And we are bored. We want to live in town, dance the polka every night. Poor little thing! Gasping for love, just like a carp on the kitchen-table wants to be in water. Three words of gallantry and she'd adore you, I'm sure of it. She would be tender, charming ... Yes, but how do we get rid of her afterwards?

All of pleasure's little encumbrances, merely glimpsed in prospect, made him, by contrast, think about his mistress. She was an actress in Rouen, kept by him; and, when he pondered this image, which was cloying even to remember:

– Ah, Madame Bovary, he thought, is much prettier, and somewhat fresher. Virginie, really, is getting rather fat. She's so fastidious in her pleasures. And anyway, what a mania for pink prawns!

The countryside was deserted, and around him Rodolphe heard only the regular swishing sound of his boots across the grass, with the noise of the grasshoppers hidden far away in the oats; he could see Emma there in the room, dressed just as he remembered, and in his head he stripped her clothes off.

– Oh! I shall have her! he shouted as he crushed, with one swing of his stick, a clod of earth in his path.

And immediately he explored the tactical side of the enterprise. He asked himself:

– Where could we meet? And how? There'll be the brat forever pestering us, and the maid, the neighbours, the husband, every sort of endless botheration. Damn it! he said. Far too much trouble!

Then he started again:

– It's those eyes of hers, they go right into your heart. And that pale skin ... and I who simply adore pale women!

At the top of the Côte d'Argueil, his decision was made.

– All I have to do is make the opportunity. All right, I'll call
in now and again, send them some game, some poultry; I'll have
myself bled, if necessary; we'll be friends, I'll invite them over
to visit me . . . Hah! By Jove! he added. There's the show coming
up soon; she'll be there, I shall see her. We shall make a start, a
bold start, it's always best.

8

It had actually come, the day of the great show! From early on
that solemn morning, all the inhabitants, at their doors, were
discussing the preparations; garlands of ivy had been hung
above the main door of the town hall; a tent, in a meadow, had
been put up for the banquet, and, in the middle of the square,
in front of the church, a kind of bombard was to mark the
arrival of the Prefect and the naming of the prizewinners. The
National Guard from Buchy (there was none at Yonville) had
come to augment the fire-brigade, who had Binet as their captain. He was wearing, that day, a collar even higher than usual;
and, buttoned tight into his tunic, he was so stiff and rigid above
the waist that all the vital energy in his body seemed to have
descended into his two legs, which were tramping away, crisply,
rhythmically. As there was some rivalry between the tax-
collector and the colonel, each of them, to show their talents,
drilled their men separately. Red epaulettes and black breastplates passed alternately to and fro. It was never-ending, over
and over again! Never had there been such a splendid display.
Several bourgeois, the previous evening, had washed their
houses; tricolour flags were hanging from open windows; the
wine-shops were full; and, with the fine weather, the starched
bonnets, the gold crosses and the coloured shawls looked
brighter than snow, sparkled in the strong sun, scattered their
swirling streaky pattern over the sombre monotone of the
frock-coat and the blue smock. The local farmers' wives, getting down from their horses, unfastened the thick pins that
had held their dresses tucked up high out of the dirt; the husbands, for their part, anxious for their hats, kept them covered

under pocket-handkerchiefs, holding one corner between their teeth.

The crowd came into the main street from both ends of the village. They poured out of the lanes, out of the alley-ways, out of the houses, and from time to time there came the bang of a door-knocker falling, behind ladies in thread gloves, on their way out to see the festivities. One thing was especially admired, that was the pair of long frames covered in fairy lights which flanked the platform where the officials were to sit; and what was more, up against the four columns of the town hall, there was a kind of pole, each one carrying a little banner in greenish fabric, richly inscribed in letters of gold. One read COMMERCE; another AGRICULTURE; the third INDUSTRY; and on the fourth THE ARTS.

But the jubilation that shone in every face seemed to cast a cloud on Madame Lefrançois, the innkeeper. Standing on her kitchen-steps, she was muttering to herself:

– Stupid things! So stupid with their great canvas shed! Do they think the Prefect is going to enjoy dining over there, in a tent, like a circus clown? They call that nonsense doing the place good. It really wasn't worth it, getting a cook-shop man from Neufchâtel! For what? For cowherds! For ragamuffins!

The apothecary came past. He had on a frock-coat, yellow nankeen trousers, beaver-skin shoes and, amazingly, a hat – a squat little hat.

– Your servant! he said; excuse me, I am in a hurry.

And as the plump widow asked where he was going:

– Seems funny to you, doesn't it? I who am always immured in my laboratory like the rat inside his cheese.

What cheese? said the innkeeper.

– Oh, nothing, nothing! Homais went on. I was merely trying to convey to you, Madame Lefrançois, that I am usually rather a recluse. Today, however, in the circumstances, I really must . . .

– Oh, you're off over there are you? she said disdainfully.

– Yes, I am, replied the apothecary in astonishment. Am I not a member of the Advisory Committee?

Mère Lefrançois gazed at him a few moments, and eventually answered with a smile:

– That's a different thing! But what's farming got to do with you? You're an expert, are you?

– I certainly am, since I'm a pharmacist, indeed a chemist! And chemistry, Madame Lefrançois, being the pursuit of the knowledge of the reciprocal and molecular action of natural bodies, it follows that agriculture is found to be comprised within its domain! And, in effect, composition of manure, fermentation of liquid, analysis of gas and influence of miasmas, what is this, I ask you, if not chemistry pure and simple?

The innkeeper said nothing. Homais went on:

– Do you think it necessary, to be an agronomist, to have actually tilled the soil or fattened poultry, oneself? What you need is knowledge of the composition of the substances concerned, geological strata, atmospheric conditions, properties of the soil, of minerals and rain-water, density of the different bodies and their capillarity. And so on. And you need a thorough grasp of the principles of hygiene, to supervise and criticize the construction of buildings, the feeding of animals, the alimentary needs of servants. And what is more, Madame Lefrançois, you have to know your botany; be able to identify plants. Do you follow me? Which are salutary and which are deleterious; which are unproductive and which are nutritious; whether it's worth rooting them out here and resetting them over there; propagating some, destroying others; in short, you have to keep up with science in pamphlets and published papers, always be on the alert, to point out improvements . . .

The innkeeper never took her eyes off the door of the Café Français, and the pharmacist kept going.

– Would to God our farmers were chemists, or at least would they might pay more heed to the wisdom of science! Look, I have recently written a weighty opuscule, a memorandum of more than seventy-two pages, entitled: *Du cidre, de sa fabrication et de ses effets; suivi de quelques réflexions nouvelles à ce sujet*,[17] which I sent in to the Agronomical Society of Rouen; it even won me the honour of being received among its members, Agricultural Section, Pomological Division. Now! If my work had found its way into print . . .

But the apothecary stopped, for Madame Lefrançois looked so very preoccupied.

– Just look at them! she was saying. Would you credit it! Such a swill-house!

And, with a shrugging of the shoulders that stretched the threads of her woollen jacket across her bosom, she pointed with both hands at the rival wine-shop, now loud with voices singing.

– Anyway, not much longer now, she added; another week, and that's it.

Flabbergasted, Homais stepped back. She came down her three steps, and, whispering in his ear:

– Surely! Haven't you heard? The bailiffs will have him this week. It's Lheureux who's selling him up. He's slain him with his bills.

– What an appalling catastrophe! exclaimed the apothecary, who always had the proper expressions for every conceivable situation.

So the innkeeper began to tell him the whole story, which she had heard from Théodore, Maître Guillaumin's servant, and, though she detested Tellier, she did condemn Lheureux. He was a wheedler, a crawler.

– There he is! she said, in the market; bowing to Madame Bovary, with her green hat on. And she's on Boulanger's arm.

– Madame Bovary! said Homais. I shall hasten over to offer her my compliments. Perhaps she'll enjoy having a seat in the enclosure, under the peristyle.

And, not listening to Mère Lefrançois, who was calling him back to tell him more of the story, the pharmacist went striding off, his lips smiling and his knees stiff, lavishing salutations left and right, and taking up a great deal of room with the long tails of his frock-coat, which fluttered in the wind behind him.

Rodolphe had noticed him from afar and quickened his pace; but Madame Bovary got out of breath; so he slowed down and said to her with a smile, in a brutal tone:

– I just want to avoid that oaf; you know, the apothecary.

She nudged him with her elbow.

– What does that mean? he asked himself.

And he watched her from the corner of his eye, as they walked on.

Her profile was so calm that it gave away nothing whatever. It stood out in the strong light, in the oval of her bonnet fastened with pale ribbons that looked like strands of river-weed. Her eyes, with their long curving lashes, were looking straight ahead, and, though wide open, they looked slightly constricted, because the blood in her cheeks was pulsing softly beneath the delicate skin. Between her nostrils the flesh glowed pink. She was leaning her head to one side, and you saw between her lips the pearly crowns of white teeth.

– Is she making fun of me? pondered Rodolphe.

However, that gesture of Emma's had been merely a warning, for Monsieur Lheureux was at their side, and he spoke to them now and again, as if to begin a conversation.

– What a superb day! Everyone's out! The wind's in the east.

Neither Madame Bovary, nor Rodolphe, spoke a single word in reply, yet their slightest movements drew him sidling up to them with a 'Beg your pardon?' and a hand raised to his hat.

When they reached the blacksmith's house, instead of following the road as far as the gate, Rodolphe, brusquely, took the footpath, pulling Madame Bovary along; he shouted:

– Good evening, Monsieur Lheureux! See you presently!

– You certainly shook him off! she said with a laugh.

– Why ever, he went on, let oneself be pestered? And, since, today, I have the pleasure of being with you . . .

Emma blushed. He left his sentence unfinished. He spoke of the fine weather and the satisfaction of walking in the open. A few daisies had pushed through.

– Such pretty Easter daisies, he said, and oracles aplenty for maids in love.

He added:

– If I were to pick some. What do you think?

– Are you in love? she said with a little cough.

– Mmmm! Who knows, answered Rodolphe.

The meadow was beginning to fill up, and housewives bumped into you with their big umbrellas, their baskets and

their youngsters. Often you had to move over for a long line of
countrywomen, servants with blue stockings, flat shoes, silver
rings, who smelled of milk as they went past. They were walking
along holding hands, and so they spread themselves across the
field, from the row of aspens right up to the banqueting tent.
But now it was time for the judging, and the farmers, one after
another, were entering a sort of arena marked out by a long
rope hung on some posts.

The animals were there, muzzles turned to the rope, rumps
great and small jostling in a crooked line. Sluggishly the pigs
dug their snouts into the earth; calves were bellowing; lambs
were bleating; the cows, one leg folded, sprawled their bellies
on the grass, and, chewing cud slowly, blinked their great eyelids
at the little flies buzzing around them. Wagoners, in their shirt-
sleeves, held in prancing stallions by the halter, as they whinnied
frantically after the mares. These were standing quiet, reaching
out necks and flowing manes, while their foals were lazing in
their shadows, or coming now and then to suck; and, above the
undulating line of these massed bodies, you saw rising in the
wind, like a wave, the whiteness of a mane, perhaps a sharp pair
of horns sticking up, or the heads of men running. Set apart,
outside the arena, a hundred yards away, there was a great black
muzzled bull, with an iron ring fixed in his nose, and he was
quite motionless, just like a thing made of bronze. A child in
ragged clothes had hold of him on a rope.

Meanwhile, between the two ranks, various gentlemen were
advancing earnestly, examining each animal, and conferring in
an undertone. One of them, who seemed more eminent, made a
few notes, as he went, in a book. It was the chairman of the
judges: Monsieur Derozerays from Panville. As soon as he recognized Rodolphe, he stepped up briskly, and said to him with a
smiling friendly look:

– Really, Monsieur Boulanger, are you deserting us?

Rodolphe protested that he was just coming over. But, when
the chairman had gone:

– Damn it, no, he said, I'm not going: your company rather
excels his.

And, though full of mockery for the show, Rodolphe, to get

about more freely, showed the gendarme his blue ticket, and
even stopped now and then in front of some fine specimen that
Madame Bovary scarcely appreciated. He realized this, and now
began to make jokes about the ladies of Yonville and their way
of dressing; he apologized for his own careless style. It was that
mingling of the everyday and the exotic, which the vulgar,
usually, take for the symptom of an eccentric existence, of
unruly feeling, of the tyranny of art, always with a certain scorn
for social conventions which they find seductive or exasperating.
Thus, his cambric shirt with the frilly cuffs that puffed out over
his grey linen waistcoat with the wind and his broad-striped
trousers that showed off his nankeen boots at the ankle, with
gaiters of patent leather. They were so well polished that they
reflected the grass. He trampled in them through the horse-dung,
one hand in the pocket of his jacket, and his straw hat at an
angle.

– Anyway, he added, when you live in the country . . .

– There's no point, said Emma.

– Very true! replied Rodolphe. To think that not one of these
good people is capable of appreciating so much as the style of a
coat.

And they talked about the mediocrity of all things provincial,
of the lives it stifled, the illusions that perished there.

– That's why, said Rodolphe, I'm sinking into a miserable . . .

– You! she said in astonishment. But I thought you were very
cheerful?

– Oh, yes, so I seem, because with other people I have learned
how to hide my face with a joker's mask; and yet, how many a
time, when I see a cemetery, in the moonlight, have I asked
myself if I'd not be better off side by side with those laid to
rest . . .

– Oh! And what of your friends? she said. You do not think
of them.

– My friends? What friends? Do I have any? Who is there that
cares for me?

And he accompanied these last words with a kind of sighing
whistling sound.

But they were pushed asunder by a great scaffolding of chairs

being carried by a man behind them. He was so over-laden that
you could see only the toes of his clogs, and the tips of his
fingers, stretching out. It was Lestiboudois, the grave-digger,
carting among the multitude the chairs from the church. Full of
ideas wherever his own interests were concerned, this was his
way of making something out of the show; and his scheme was
bringing him returns, for he had more trade than he could cope
with. In fact, the villagers, feeling the heat, were quarrelling
over these seats that had the smell of incense in their straw, and
against the thick chair-backs, bespattered with candle grease,
they were leaning with a certain veneration.

Madame Bovary took Rodolphe's arm again; he went on as
though talking to himself:

– Yes. So many things I have missed. Ever alone. Ah! If I had
had an aim in life, if I had met with tenderness, if I had found
someone . . . Oh! How I should have spent every ounce of energy
in my body, I'd have vanquished anything, crushed anything.

– It still seems to me, said Emma, you are scarcely one of the
wretched of this world.

– Oh! You think so? said Rodolphe.

– Because after all . . ., she went on, you are free.

She hesitated:

– Rich.

– Don't make fun of me, he replied.

And she swore that she was not making fun, when a cannon
boomed out; instantly everyone scurried back towards the
village.

It was a false alarm. The Prefect did not arrive; and the
judges were greatly perplexed, not knowing whether to open
the proceedings or whether to wait.

At last, from the far end of the square, there appeared a large
hired landau, drawn by two skinny horses, being vigorously
lashed by a coachman in a white hat. Binet only just had time
to shout 'Fall in!' and the colonel to do likewise. They ran to
the stack of rifles. There was a lot of pushing. Some of the men
even forgot to fasten their collars. But the prefectorial equipage
seemed to divine this predicament, and the pair of yoked nags,
dallying in their harness, trotted slowly up to the pillared front

of the town hall just as the National Guard and the firemen were deploying there, with drums beating, marking time.

– Steady! shouted Binet.

– Halt! shouted the colonel. Dressing by the left!

And, after a 'present arms' that clattered like a copper kettle rolling downstairs, all the rifles were lowered.

Now was seen, stepping down from the carriage, a gentleman dressed in a short jacket trimmed with silver braid, bald in front, with a great tuft of occipital hair, sallow in complexion and most benign in appearance. His two eyes, bulging and heavily lidded, were half closed to examine the multitude, while he lifted his sharp nose and fixed a smile on his sunken lips. He recognized the mayor by his sash and explained to him that the Prefect had not been able to come. He himself was a councillor at the Préfecture; then he added various apologies. Tuvache offered his civilities in return, the other confessed himself abashed; and there they were, face to face, with their foreheads almost touching, the members of the committee all around them, the municipal councillors, the dignitaries, the National Guard and the crowd. Pressing his little black tricorn hat to his breast, his Honour the Councillor reiterated his salutations, while Tuvache, bent like a bow, was smiling back, stammering, fumbling for words, protesting his loyalty to the monarchy, and the honour being done to Yonville.

Hippolyte, the ostler from the inn, came up to take the horses' reins from the coachman, and, limping along on his club-foot, he led them off through the gates of the Golden Lion, where a crowd of peasants gathered to look at the carriage. The drum rolled, the howitzer thundered, and one by one the gentlemen ascended the platform, sitting down in the armchairs of red Utrecht velvet lent by Madame Tuvache.

They all looked alike, these people. Their soft fair faces, lightly tanned by the sun, were the colour of sweet cider, and their bushy whiskers spilled over high stiff collars, held up by white cravats tied in large bows. All the waistcoats were velvet, double-breasted; all the watches sported long ribbons trimmed with oval seals made of cornelian; and every pair of hands rested on a pair of thighs, discreetly arranging the crotch of the trousers, made of a smooth glossy cloth that shone more brilliantly than the leather of their hefty boots.

The ladies in the party were at the back, under the porch, between the pillars, while the common herd were facing them, standing up, or sitting on the chairs. Lestiboudois had brought there all those he had moved from the meadow, and he even kept running back to fetch more from the church, creating such an encumbrance with his dealings that everyone had great difficulty reaching the little steps up to the platform.

– I do think, said Monsieur Lheureux (addressing the pharmacist, who was heading off to his seat), they ought to have stuck up a pair of Venetian masts there; with something rather severe and rich for ornament; it would have been a really pretty sight.

– Unquestionably, replied Homais. But what do you expect! The mayor runs the show on his own. He hasn't much taste, poor old Tuvache, and he's completely devoid of what is known as artistic genius.

Meanwhile Rodolphe, with Madame Bovary, had gone up to the first floor of the town hall, into the council chamber, and, as it was empty, he had declared that this would be just the place from which to enjoy the spectacle in peace and quiet. He took three stools from around the oval table, under the bust of the monarch, and, moving them to one of the windows, they sat down side by side.

There was a great commotion on the platform, long whisperings, negotiations. At last, the councillor stood up. They knew by now that his name was Lieuvain, and they were passing this name on to each other, in the crowd. Once he had collected a few papers together and held them close to his eye, to see the better, he began:

– Gentlemen, may I be permitted first of all (before addressing you upon the object of our gathering here today, and this sentiment will, I'm sure, be shared by all of you), may I be permitted, I say, to pay tribute to the administrative authorities, to the government, to the monarch, gentlemen, to our sovereign, that beloved king to whom no branch of prosperity public or private is a matter of indifference, and who guides with a hand at once so firm and so wise the chariot of state amid the ceaseless perils of a stormy sea, one who knows, moreover, how to compel respect for peace as well as war, industry, commerce, agriculture and the arts.

– I ought, said Rodolphe, to move back a little.

– Why? said Emma.

But, at this moment, the councillor's voice rose to an extra-ordinary pitch. He declaimed:

– The days are gone, gentlemen, when civil discord smeared our public places with blood, when the landowner, the mer-chant, the worker himself, as he lay down in the evening to peaceful slumbers, trembled lest he woke to the sudden clang of the seditious tocsin, when the most subversive slogans sapped audaciously the very foundations . . .

– Because someone, said Rodolphe, may see me from down below; then I'll be in for a fortnight of making excuses, and, with my bad reputation . . .

– Oh! You slander yourself, said Emma.

– No, no, it is execrable, I can assure you.

– However, gentlemen, the councillor continued, if, putting from my memory such sombre scenes, I turn my gaze again upon the present state of our fair land: what do I now see? Everywhere commerce and the arts are flourishing; everywhere new means of communication, like so many new arteries in the body politic, opening therein new relations; our great manufac-turing centres are busy once more; religion, reinvigorated, smiles in every heart; our ports are crowded, confidence is restored, and France at last draws breath!

– Even so, added Rodolphe, perhaps, as the world sees things, they may have a point?

– How is that? she asked.

– What! he said. Do you not realize that there are souls in endless torment? They are craving for dreams and action, the purest passions, the wildest pleasures, and thus they cast us into all kinds of fantasies, and foolishness.

Then she looked at him just as you gaze upon a traveller come from a far-away land.

– We don't even have that consolation, we poor women!

– Sad consolation, for it brings no happiness.

– But does anything ever? she asked.

– Yes, one day you find it, he said.

– And this is what you have realized, said the councillor. You, the farmers and the workers of the soil; you, the peaceful pioneers in an enterprise entirely civilized! You, the men of progress and morality! You have realized, I say, that the tempests of politics are truly even more terrible than the chaos of the elements . . .

– One day you find it, repeated Rodolphe; one day, quite suddenly, just when hope seems lost. And the horizon opens up, it's like a voice crying: 'Behold!' You feel you must tell this person the secrets of your life, give them everything, sacrifice everything for them. Nothing is actually said, you just know. You have seen each other in your dreams. (And he was looking at her.) There it is at last, the treasure you have sought so long, there, right in front of you; shining, sparkling. Though you still have doubts, you dare not believe it; you stand there dazed, just as if you stepped from shadow into sunlight.

And, as he finished his speech, Rodolphe added pantomime to phrase. He passed his hand across his face, just like a man stricken with vertigo; he let it fall down on Emma's. She withdrew hers. But the councillor was still reading:

– And who would be surprised at that, gentlemen? Only one so blind, so immersed (I do not flinch from saying it), so immersed in prejudices of another age as still to misconceive the spirit of our agricultural communities. Where, indeed, do we find greater patriotism than in the country, greater devotion to the common cause, in a word, greater intelligence? And I do not mean, gentlemen, that superficial intelligence, the vain ornament of idle minds, but rather that profound and judicious intelligence, which applies itself above all else to the pursuit of useful ends, contributing thus to the good of each, to the amelioration of the common life and to the buttressing of the state, fruit of respect for the law and the habit of duty . . .

– Not again! said Rodolphe. Always duty, I'm sick of the very word. They're a bunch of old fogies in flannel vests, bigoted old women in bed-socks saying their prayers, droning endlessly in our ears: 'Duty! Duty!' Damnation! To feel what is great, to cherish what is beautiful, that's what duty is! Not to accept every one of society's conventions, with all the ignominy they inflict upon us.

– All the same . . . all the same . . ., objected Madame Bovary.

– No! Why castigate the passions? Are they not the only beautiful thing there is on earth, the source of heroism, enthusiasm, poetry, music, art, of everything?

– But we must sometimes, said Emma, heed the opinions of other people and accept their morality.

– Oh, the thing is there are two moralities, he replied. The little conventional one that men have made up, one that's endlessly changing and that brays so fiercely, makes such a fuss down here in this world, like that mob of imbeciles you see there. But the other morality, the eternal one, is all about and above, like the fields around us and the blue sky that gives us light.

Monsieur Lieuvain had just wiped his mouth with his handkerchief. He continued:

– And what should I be doing here, gentlemen, demonstrating to you the usefulness of agriculture? Who is it that provides for our needs? Who is it that furnishes our sustenance? Is it not the farmer? The farmer, gentlemen, who, impregnating with unwearied hand the teeming furrows of our countryside, brings forth the corn, which, once crushed, is turned to powder by means of cunning engines, issues thence under the name of flour, and, from there, conveyed to the cities, is swiftly delivered to the baker, who confects from it a nourishment for rich and poor alike. Is it not likewise the farmer who fattens for our garments, his prolific flocks in the meadows? For how should we be clothed, how should we be nourished without the farmer? And is there, gentlemen, any real need to seek out examples so far afield? Who has not frequently pondered the various important things we collect from that modest animal, the ornament of our poultry-yards, who furnishes us with a soft pillow for our slumbers, succulent flesh for our tables, and eggs? But I should never finish if I were required to enumerate one after the other the diverse products that the well-tended earth, like a bounteous mother, lavishes upon her children. Here, the vine; there, the cider-apple trees; there, the rape-seed; further afield, cheese; and flax; gentlemen, let us not forget flax! Which has in recent years made great headway and to which I would most particularly draw your attention.

There was no need for him to do that: for every mouth in the crowd was hanging open, as if to drink up his words. Tuvache, next to him, was listening goggle-eyed; Monsieur Derozerays, occasionally, closed his eye-lids gently; and further on, the pharmacist, with his son Napoléon between his knees, had a hand cupped to his ear so as not to lose a single syllable. The other members of the committee slowly wagged their chins into their waistcoats, in token of their appreciation. The firemen, in front of the platform, were leaning on their bayonets; and Binet, motionless, had his elbow stuck out, with the tip of his sabre in the air. Perhaps he could hear, but he certainly couldn't see a thing because of the visor on his helmet that came down over his nose. His lieutenant, the youngest son of Tuvache Esquire, had overdone his own even more; for there he was wearing an enormous helmet that wobbled on his head, leaving one end of his cotton scarf hanging down. He was smiling underneath it with the sweetness of a young child, and his pale little face, streaming with sweat-drops, wore an expression mingling beatitude, affliction and a need for sleep.

The square was packed right up as far as the houses. There were people leaning out of every window, others were standing in every door, and Justin, in front of the window of the pharmacy, seemed quite transfixed in contemplation of what he was watching. In spite of the silence, Monsieur Lieuvain's voice was lost on the air. It reached the ear in disconnected phrases, interrupted here and there by chairs scraping among the crowd; and you heard, suddenly, erupting from somewhere behind, the drawn-out bellowing of a cow, or else the bleating of lambs calling to each other at street corners. The cowherds and the shepherds had driven their flocks all this way, and they were clamouring every so often, as their tongues plucked at various bits of foliage dangling near their muzzles.

Rodolphe had moved in closer to Emma, and he was talking in a low voice, speaking rapidly:

– Don't you find this social conspiracy revolting? Is there one single feeling they do not condemn? All the noblest instincts, all the purest sympathies are persecuted and maligned, and if ever two poor souls should meet, everything is organized so that they cannot be joined as one. Yet they will strive, they will beat their wings, they will call out each to each. Oh! Come what may, sooner or later, in six months, ten years, they will be together, will be lovers, because Fate ordains it, because they were born for each other.

He sat with his arms folded on his knees, and, now lifting his face towards Emma, he was gazing directly at her, fixedly. In his eyes she noticed little threads of gold, and she could even catch the scent of the pomade in his glossy hair. And then the swooning was upon her, she remembered the Viscount who had waltzed her at La Vaubyessard, whose beard, like this man's hair, gave off that scent of vanilla and lemon; and, mechanically, she half shut her eyes to breathe it deeper. But, as she did so, bracing herself upon her chair, she noticed in the distance, right on the far horizon, the old *Hirondelle*, the coach coming slowly down the Côte des Leux, trailing behind it a long plume of dust. It was in this yellow coach that Léon had, so many times, come back to her; and along that very road that he had gone away for ever. She thought she saw him over the way, at his window, then it was all a blur, clouds went past; it felt as if she was still turning in the waltz, under the bright chandeliers, on the Viscount's arm, as if Léon were not far away, was going to come ... and yet all this time she could smell Rodolphe's hair beside her. The sweetness of this sensation went down deep into her past desires, and just like grains of sand in a puff of wind, they were swirling about in the subtle breath of the odours that were spilling down into her soul. She opened wide her nostrils several times, eagerly, to breathe in the freshness of the ivy around the tops of the columns. She took off her gloves, she wiped her hands; then, with her handkerchief, she fanned her face, while through the pulsing of her temples she could hear the murmuring of the crowd and the voice of the councillor psalming out his phrases.

He was saying:

– Endurance! Perseverance! Heed neither the voice of habit,

nor the over-hasty teachings of rash empiricism! Dedicate yourselves above all else to the improvement of the soil, to good
manure, to the development of the various breeds, equine,
bovine, ovine and porcine. May such show-days be for you like
a peaceful arena where the victor, departing, will hold forth a
hand to the vanquished and fraternize with him, in the hope
of triumphs to come. And you, venerable attendants, humble
domestics, whose arduous labours no government until this
very day has ever taken into account, come forth to receive
recompense for your silent virtues, and be assured, henceforth,
that the state has you in its eye, that it encourages you, that it
protects you, that it will respect your just demands and lighten,
so far as in it lies, the aching burden of your sacrifice.

Monsieur Lieuvain now sat down; Monsieur Derozerays
stood up: another speech began. His was, perhaps, nothing so
flowery as the councillor's; but it was distinguished by more
positive qualities of style, that is to say, a knowledge more
precise and themes more exalted. Accordingly, praise of the
government played a lesser role; religion and agriculture were
rather more in evidence. They were shown the relation between
them, and how they had always contributed to civilization.
Rodolphe, with Madame Bovary, was talking dreams, prem-
onitions, magnetism. Reaching back to the birth of human
society, the orator depicted for us the barbaric era when men
lived on acorns, deep in the woods. They had shed their animal
skins, put on clothes, ploughed the earth, planted the vine.
Was this for the good? Monsieur Derozerays asked himself this
question. Beginning with magnetism, little by little, Rodolphe
had got as far as affinities, and, while the chairman cited Cin-
cinnatus at his plough, Diocletian planting his cabbages and
the emperors of China bringing in the New Year by planting
seeds, the young man was explaining to the young woman that
these irresistible attractions had their origin in some previous
existence.

– Look at us, for instance, he said, why did we meet? By what
decree of Fate? It must be because, across the void, like two
rivers irresistibly converging, our unique inclinations have been
pushing us towards one another.

And now he took her hand; she didn't take it back again.

– Prize for general farming! shouted the chairman.

– Just now, for instance, when I came to see you . . .

– To Monsieur Bizet of Quincampoix.

– Did I know that I would be escorting you?

– Seventy francs!

– A hundred times I wanted to leave, and I followed you, I stayed.

– Manures!

– As I shall stay this evening, tomorrow and the day after, all my life.

– To Monsieur Caron, from Argueil, a gold medal!

– For never before have I found anyone so entirely charming.

– To Monsieur Bain, from Givry-Saint-Martin!

– I shall carry with me the memory of you.

– For a merino ram . . .

– You will forget me, though, I will have faded like a shadow.

– To Monsieur Belot, from Notre-Dame . . .

– Oh! No, surely, I will be somewhere in your thoughts, in your life?

– Swine category, prize shared by Monsieur Lehérissé and Monsieur Cullembourg; sixty francs!

Rodolphe gripped her hand, and he felt it warm and trembling like a captive turtle dove that strives to take wing again; but, whether she was trying to disentangle it or whether she was responding to his pressure, her fingers moved; he exclaimed:

– Oh, thank you! You are not repulsing me! You are so sweet. You realize that I am yours. Permit me to see you, to gaze upon you!

A breeze that came in through the windows ruffled the cloth on the table, and, in the square, down below, it lifted the big bonnets of the peasant women, like the wings of white butterflies flitting about.

– Use of oilseed-cake, the chairman continued.

He was going faster.

– Flemish manure – cultivation of flax – drainage – long leases – domestic service.

Rodolphe was silent now. They were looking at one another.

A supreme desire set their parched lips trembling; and sooth-
ingly, easily, their fingers entwined.

– Catherine-Nicaise-Élisabeth Leroux, from Sassetot-la-
Guerrière, for fifty-four years' service on the same farm, a silver
medal – with a value of twenty-five francs!

– Where is she, Catherine Leroux? repeated the councillor.

She did not appear, and voices were heard whispering:

– Go on!

– No.

– Over on the left!

– Don't be shy!

– Oh, isn't she silly!

– Well, is she here or not? shouted Tuvache.

– Yes! . . . There she is!

– Let her come up here!

Then was seen stepping on to the platform a little old woman,
moving timidly, and apparently cringing deep into her shabby
clothes. On her feet she had great wooden clogs, and, around
her hips, a large blue apron. Her thin face, swathed in a simple
hood, was more creased and wrinkled than a withered russet
apple, and from the sleeves of her red camisole there dangled a
pair of long hands, with bony knuckles. The dust from the barn,
the soda for washing and the grease from the wool had made
them so crusted, cracked, calloused, that they looked grimy even
though they had been rinsed in fresh water; and, from long
service, they stayed half unclasped, almost as though to set
forth of themselves the simple testimony of so much affliction
endured. A hint of monastic rigidity intensified the look on her
face. No touch of sadness or affection softened that pale gaze.
Living close to the animals, she had assumed their wordless
placid state of being. It was the first time she had found herself
in the midst of such a large gathering; and, inwardly terrified by
the flags, by the drums, by the gentlemen in frock-coats and by
the councillor's Legion of Honour medal, she stood quite still,
not knowing whether to step forwards or to run away, nor why
the crowd were pushing her on and the judges smiling at her.
There she stood, before these flourishing bourgeois, this half-
century of servitude.

– Come along now, venerable Catherine-Nicaise-Élisabeth Leroux! said the councillor, who had taken the list of prize-winners from the chairman's hands.

And alternately scrutinizing first the sheet of paper, then the old woman, he repeated in a paternal tone:

– Come along now, come on.

– Are you deaf? said Tuvache, bouncing in his armchair.

And he shouted in her ear:

– Fifty-four years of service! A silver medal! Twenty-five francs! They're for you.

Once she had her medal, she gazed down at it. Now a beatific smile spread across her face and you could hear her muttering as she went off:

– I shall give it to our *curé*, to say some masses for me.

– What fanaticism! exclaimed the pharmacist, leaning across to the notary.

The meeting was over; the crowd dispersed; and, now that the speeches had been read out, everyone resumed their stations and everything went back to normal: the masters bullied the servants, and they beat the animals, lethargic champions heading back to the byre, a crown of green upon their horns.

Meanwhile the National Guard had climbed to the first floor of the town hall, with buns stuck on their bayonets, and the regimental drummer carrying a crate of bottles. Madame Bovary took Rodolphe's arm; he escorted her home; they parted at her door; he strolled alone around the meadow, waiting for the start of the banquet.

The feast was long, noisy, badly served; people were so packed in you could scarcely move your elbows, and the narrow planks being used for benches nearly broke beneath the weight of the guests. Everyone fed abundantly. Everyone grabbed their money's worth. The sweat was running down every brow; and a whitish vapour, like river-mist on an autumn morning, floated above the table, between the lamps hanging down. Rodolphe, leaning his back on the canvas of the tent, was thinking so intently of Emma that he didn't hear a thing. Behind him, on the grass, servants were stacking up the dirty plates; his neighbours were talking, he gave them no answer; they filled up his glass, and a silence settled in his thoughts, in spite of the growing noise around. He was dreaming about what she had said and about the shape of her lips; her face, as if in a magic mirror, flared in the militia's cap-badges; the folds of her dress hung down the walls, and long days of love rolled out to infinity across the landscape of the future.

He saw her again in the evening, during the fireworks; but she was with her husband, Madame Homais and the pharmacist, who was most anxious about the danger from stray rockets; and, every other minute, he would leave the party to go and give Binet advice.

The fireworks delivered to Tuvache had been stored, with excessive caution, down in his cellar, so now the damp powder was very difficult to ignite and the big set-piece, supposed to show a dragon biting its tail, was a complete flop. Now and again, a feeble roman candle went off; the gaping crowd let out a roar mingled with shrieks from the women who were being tickled in the ribs under cover of darkness. Emma, silently, nestled gently against Charles's shoulder; lifting her chin she followed across the night sky the rockets' fiery tracks. Rodolphe was watching her by the lanterns' flamy light.

They burned down slowly. The stars blazed out. A few drops of rain began to fall. She knotted her scarf over her bare head.

At that moment, the councillor's cab emerged from the yard of the inn. His coachman, who was drunk, slumped suddenly and you could see clearly, above the hood, between the two lanterns, his bulky form swaying to the right and left, with the pitching of the springs.

– Quite honestly, said the apothecary, we ought to chastise drunkenness! I'd like to see written up, every seven days, at the door of the town hall, on a special noticeboard, the names of all those who, in the last week, had been intoxicated with alcohol. Besides, from the statistical point of view, you would have a kind of public record which could be very . . . Excuse me . . .

And he ran over to the captain again.

The latter was on his way home. He was going back to his lathe.

– Perhaps it might not be a bad idea, Homais said to him, to send one of your men or to go yourself . . .

– Leave me in peace, will you, replied the tax-collector, there is nothing to worry about!

– No cause for alarm, said the apothecary, once he had rejoined his friends, Monsieur Binet has given me his guarantee that precautions have been taken. No sparks will fall. The pumps are full. Our beds await us.

– My goodness! Just what I need, said Madame Homais, who was yawning hugely; never mind now, we've had a really lovely day for our show.

Rodolphe repeated in a low voice and with a tender look:

– Ah! Yes, really lovely.

And, after their good nights, they went their separate ways.

Two days later, in *Le Fanal de Rouen*, there was a long article on the show. Homais had composed it, extempore, the very next morning.

Whence these festoons, these flowers, these garlands? Whither hastens this crowd, like the surges of an angry sea, beneath a torrential tropical sun pouring forth its heat upon our furrows?

Next, he mentioned the condition of the peasants. Certainly, the government was doing a great deal, but not enough! *Fear naught*, he cried to it; *a thousand reforms are indispensable, let us bring them to pass*. And dealing with the arrival of the councillor, he did not omit *the martial air of our militia*, nor *our sprightliest maidens*, nor *the old men with bald heads, latter-day patriarchs, some of whom, the remnants of our immortal phalanxes, felt their hearts beating once again to the manly sound of the drum*. He mentioned himself foremost among the members of the prize committee, and even recollected, in a footnote, that Monsieur Homais, the pharmacist, had sent in a memorandum on cider to the Agricultural Society. When he reached the prize-giving, he portrayed the joy of the winners in dithyrambic terms. *Fathers embracing their sons, brothers brothers, husbands their wives. Many a one showed his humble medal with pride, and no doubt, once home again, at his fair wife's side, will he hang it, weeping the while, upon the plain walls of his cottage.*

About six o'clock, a banquet, served in Monsieur Liégard's meadow, assembled the principal persons at the show. The utmost cordiality reigned there throughout. Divers toasts were proposed: Monsieur Lieuvain, to the King: Monsieur Tuvache, to the Prefect: Monsieur Derozerays, to Agriculture! Monsieur Homais, to Industry and the Arts, those twin sisters! Monsieur Leplichey, to Progress! In the evening, brilliant fireworks suddenly illumined the skies. 'Twas a veritable kaleidoscope, a true scene from the opera, and, for a moment, our little locality could have fancied itself transported into the midst of a scene from the Thousand and One Nights.

Let it be stated that no untoward incident occurred to disrupt this family occasion.

And he added:

Only the clergy were remarked to be absent. No doubt the sacramentals have a different idea of progress. As you wish, apostles of Loyola!

9

Six weeks went by. Rodolphe had not come back. Then, one evening, he appeared.

The day after the show, he had said to himself:

– Mustn't go back too soon; that would be a mistake.

And, at the end of the week, he had gone off for some hunting. After the hunting, he had thought it was too late, and he put it to himself like this:

– Well, if she loved me at first sight, by now she will be longing to see me again, and she ought to love me even more. Press on, in that case!

And he knew that his scheme had worked, when, as he came into the room, he noticed Emma turn pale.

She was alone. The day was fading. The short muslin curtains, over the window, darkened the evening shadows and the goldwork on the barometer, caught in a ray of sunlight, scattered fire across the mirror, among the convolutions of the coral frame.

Rodolphe did not sit down; and Emma scarcely replied to his polite opening phrases.

As for me, he said, I have been so busy. I've been ill.

– Seriously? she exclaimed.

– Well! said Rodolphe sitting beside her on a stool, no! . . . Actually I didn't want to come here again.

– Why?

– Can you not guess?

He looked at her once again, but with such violence in his manner that she turned away her head with a blush.

– Emma . . .

– Monsieur! she said, moving slightly away.

– Oh, yes! You see, he replied in a melancholy voice, I was right to want to stay away from you; the sound of your name replenishes my soul, it slipped from my lips, and you forbid it me! Madame Bovary! . . . So they all call you! . . . It's not your name, anyway; you borrowed it!

He repeated:

– Borrowed!

And he hid his face in his hands.

– Yes, I think continually of you! . . . Memories of you break my heart! . . . Oh, no! forgive me! . . . I shall leave . . . Farewell! . . . I shall go far away . . . so far that you will never hear tell of me again! . . . And yet . . . today . . . some peculiar force drove me to you! Oh, why struggle against Fate . . . why resist the angels smiling! Why not yield to what is beautiful and charming and adorable!

It was the first time that Emma had ever heard such things said to her; and her vanity, like a body unclenching in a steam-bath, melted open, softly and fully, at the warm touch of his words.

– But, he continued, though I haven't visited you, though I could not see you, oh! I have at least communed deeply with the things around you. In the night, every single night, I would leave my bed, make my way here, and gaze upon your house, the roof shining in the moonlight, the trees in the garden swaying under your window, and a little lamp, a light, shining through the windows, in the shadow. You never knew that out there, so near and so far, there was a poor wretch . . .

She turned to him with a sob.

– How good you are! she said.

– No, I love you, it's very simple. How could you doubt it? Tell me that you know; one word! Just one!

And Rodolphe, imperceptibly, let himself slide from the stool to the floor; but they heard a sound of clogs from the kitchen, and the parlour door, he noticed, was not shut.

– It would be a great kindness, he went on as he climbed to his feet, if you were to satisfy a whim of mine.

He wanted to look over her house; he yearned for this intimacy; and, as Madame Bovary saw no objection, they were both getting to their feet when Charles came in.

– Good evening, doctor, Rodolphe said to him.

The medical officer, flattered by this unexpected title, launched into obsequiousness, and the other man used the moment to gather his thoughts again.

– Your wife, he said, was telling me about her health . . .

Charles interrupted: he was, indeed, extremely worried for her; his wife's palpitations had recurred. Rodolphe asked if horse-riding might not be beneficial.

– Certainly! Excellent . . . perfect! . . . There's an idea! You should follow it up, my love.

And, when she pointed out that she had no horse, Monsieur Rodolphe offered her one of his; she refused his offer; he did not insist; and, to account for his visit, he explained how his carter, the one who had been bled, was still suffering from dizziness.

– I'll pay a call, said Bovary.

– No, no, I'll send him over to you; we'll come together; that'll be more convenient for you.

– So be it! I'm most obliged to you.

And, as soon as they were alone:

– Why don't you accept Monsieur Boulanger's proposition? It is most gracious.

She made a sulky face, gave every kind of excuse, and in the end declared that *it might look rather odd*.

– I really don't care how it looks! said Charles, turning on his heel. Health comes first! You're making a real mistake.

– And how am I supposed to go riding when I don't have a riding-habit?

– We must order you one, he replied.

The riding-habit decided her.

When the costume was ready, Charles wrote to Monsieur Boulanger that his wife was at his disposal and that they were counting on his kindness.

The next day, at noon, Rodolphe turned up at Charles's door with two saddle horses. One wore pink rosettes at the ears and a lady's saddle in doe-skin.

Rodolphe had chosen high boots of soft leather, telling himself that she had probably never seen anything like them; indeed, Emma found his attire charming, when he appeared on the landing in his full velvet coat and his white worsted breeches. She was ready, she was waiting for him.

Justin slipped out of the pharmacy to look at her, and even the apothecary stopped work. He was urging good advice on Monsieur Boulanger.

– Accidents happen so suddenly! Do take care now! Your horses may be skittish!

She heard a noise up above her head: it was Félicité drumming on the window-pane to amuse little Berthe. The child blew down a kiss; her mother responded with a wave of her riding-crop.

– Do have a pleasant ride! called Monsieur Homais. And don't take any risks! Stay on the straight and narrow!

And he waved his newspaper as he watched them disappear.

As soon as it felt the soft earth, Emma's horse broke into a gallop. Rodolphe galloped by her side. Now and then they exchanged a brief word. Her head slightly bowed, her bridle-hand held high and her right arm extended, she yielded to the rocking motion of the saddle.

At the bottom of the hill, Rodolphe let go the reins; they made off together in a single leap; at the top, the horses suddenly stopped, and her long blue veil fell limp again.

It was early in October. There was a mist upon the country-side. Vapours thronged to the horizon, along the line of the hills; and, peeling away, they ascended, vanishing. Now and again, as the clouds parted, in a ray of sunlight, there appeared in the distance the roofs of Yonville, with the gardens by the river, the courtyards, the walls and the church-steeple. Emma half closed her eyes to find her own house, and never had this dismal village where she lived seemed to her so small. From the height at which they stood, the whole valley seemed an immense pallid lake, evaporating into the air. Scattered clumps of trees stood out like black rocks; and the tall rows of poplars, their tops clear up above the fog, looked just like a wind-swept shoreline.

Beside them, across the turf, between the pine-trees, a brown light swirled in the damp air. The earth, reddish like powdered tobacco, absorbed the sound of their feet; and, with the tips of their shoes, as they walked on, the horses pushed fallen pine-cones in front of them.

Rodolphe and Emma followed the border of the wood. Now and again she turned aside, to avoid his gaze, and she saw only the rows of pine-trunks, an endless procession that stupefied her slightly. The horses were blowing. The saddle-leather was creaking.

Just as they entered the forest, the sun came out.

– God is with us! said Rodolphe.

– Do you think so! she said.

– Come on! Come on! he said.

He clicked his tongue. The two horses broke into a trot.

The tall bracken, beside the path, kept catching in Emma's stirrup. Rodolphe, as they went on, leaned over each time and pulled it loose. At other times, to push aside the branches, he passed close to her, and Emma felt his knee touching her leg. The sky had turned to blue. The leaves were motionless. There were great expanses full of heather in flower; and patches of violets alternated with the debris from the trees, grey, orange or gold, according to the different foliage. Every so often, in among the bushes, they heard a little glide and flutter of wings, or else the hoarse and soft cry of the rooks, as they flew off into the oaks.

They dismounted. Rodolphe tethered the horses. She went ahead, over the turf, between the wheel-ruts.

But her long skirts hindered her, even though she held them up at the back, and Rodolphe, walking behind her, glimpsed – just between that black hem and the black boot – the delicacy of her white stocking, like a snippet of her nakedness.

She stopped.

– I am tired, she said.

– Come on. Keep going! he said. Undaunted!

A hundred yards further on, she stopped again; and, through her veil, which hung obliquely from her man's hat to her hips, you could make out her face, in a slight blue haze, just as if she were swimming beneath the waves of the sea.

– So where are we going?

He made no answer. Her breathing was quick and broken. Rodolphe glanced about and nibbled at his moustache.

They reached a bigger clearing where the young trees had been felled. They sat down on a fallen tree-trunk, and Rodolphe began to tell her of his love.

He didn't frighten her off with compliments. He was calm, serious, melancholy.

Emma listened to him with her head bowed, while with the toe of her boot she kept pushing at the wood shavings on the ground.

But, when this phrase came out:

– Are not our destinies thus mingled?

– Ay no! she replied. You know very well. It's impossible.

She stood up to go. He seized her wrist. She stopped. She gazed steadily at him, love blurring her eyes, and she said emphatically,

– Oh! Enough . . . not another word about this . . . Where are the horses? Time to go back.

His gesture was angry and impatient. She asked again:

– Where are the horses? Where are the horses?

Smiling a strange smile, with a hard look in his eye, with his teeth clenched, he closed in upon her, opening his arms. She recoiled, trembling. She stammered:

– Oh! You're frightening me! You're hurting me! We must go!

– If we must . . ., he said, his face changing.

And immediately he became respectful, caressing, timid. She gave him her arm. They turned back. He said:

– What was the matter? Tell me. I don't understand. You're making a mistake. You must be. In my soul you are like a madonna on a pedestal, in a high place, secure and immaculate. But I need you to stay alive. I need your eyes, your voice, your thoughts. Be my friend, my sister, my angel!

And he reached out his arm and put it around her waist. Gently she tried to free herself. He held her like this, as they walked.

But they heard the two horses cropping the leaves.

– Oh! Not yet, said Rodolphe. We're not going yet! Stay!

He guided her further along, around a little pool, where the duckweed lay green on the surface. Rotting water lilies floated, stuck among the reeds. At the sound of their steps in the grass, frogs sprang away into hiding.

– I mustn't. I mustn't, she kept saying. I'm mad to listen to you.

– Why? . . . Emma! Emma!

– Oh! Rodolphe! . . . Slowly the woman spoke his name, leaning on his shoulder.

The woollen stuff of her dress caught on the velvet of his jacket, she stretched back her white neck, swelling with a sigh, and, swooning, blind with tears, with a deep shudder as she hid her face, she yielded.

The evening shadows were falling, the sun on the horizon, passing through the branches, dazzled her eyes. Here and there, all around her, among the leaves or on the earth, patches of light were trembling, just as if humming-birds, in flight, had scattered their feathers. Silence everywhere; strange tenderness coming from the trees; she felt her heart, as it began to beat again, and the blood flowing in her body like a river of milk. And she heard in the distance, beyond the wood, on the far hills, a vague and lingering cry, a murmuring voice, and she listened to it in silence, melting like music into the fading last vibrations of her tingling nerves. Rodolphe, a cigar between his teeth, was mending one of the two broken reins with his little knife.

They rode off back to Yonville, by the same road. They saw

in the mud the tracks of their horses, side by side, and the same bushes, the same stones in the grass. Nothing around them had changed; and yet, for her, now, something had come to pass more awesome than if the very mountains had shifted about. Rodolphe, from time to time, leaned across and put a kiss upon her hand.

How charming she was, on horseback! Her straight back, her slender waist, her knee crooked on the mane of her horse, her complexion bright from the fresh air, in the soft evening light.

Entering Yonville, she pranced her horse on the cobbled street. Eyes examined her from the windows.

At dinner, her husband said how well she was looking; but she pretended not to notice when he asked a question about her ride; and she sat there, with her elbow beside her plate, between the two burning candles.

– Emma! he said.

– What?

– Well, I called on Monsieur Alexandre this afternoon; he has an old mare, still nice looking, just a bit broken-winded, and I'm sure she could be had for about a hundred crowns.

He added:

– And thinking you would be pleased, I said we'd have her . . . I paid for her . . . was that a good idea? Do tell me.

She nodded her assent; and, a quarter of an hour later:

– Are you going out this evening? she asked.

– Yes. Why?

– Oh, nothing really, dear.

And, as soon as she was rid of Charles, she went upstairs and shut herself away in her room.

At first, it was like a swoon; she saw the trees, the roads, the ditches, Rodolphe, and she still felt his arms around her, as the leaves trembled and the reeds whispered.

But, when she looked in the mirror, she was startled by her own face. Never had she had eyes so large, so black, so mysterious. Something subtle, transfiguring, was surging through her.

She kept saying to herself: 'I have a lover! A lover!', savouring this idea just as if a second puberty had come upon her. At last, she was to know the pleasures of love, that fever of happiness which she had despaired of. She was entering something marvellous where everything would be passion, ecstasy, delirium; blue immensity was all about her; the great summits of sentiment glittered in her mind's eye, ordinary existence appeared far below in the distance, in shadow, in the gaps between these peaks.

She summoned the heroines from the books she had read, and the lyric host of these unchaste women began their chorus in her memory, sister-voices, enticing her. She merged into her own imaginings, playing a real part, realizing the long dream of her youth, seeing herself as one of those great lovers she had so long envied. Indeed, Emma felt the satisfaction of revenge. Had she not suffered enough? This was her moment of triumph, and love, so long sealed in, poured out in a copious fizzing rush. She savoured it without remorse, without anxiety, without worry.

The next day passed in strange sweet doings. Solemn promises were made. She told him the story of her sorrows; Rodolphe stopped her with his kisses; and, watching him with eyes half shut, she insisted that he speak her name again, that he repeat the words of love. It was in the forest, as on the day before, in a clog-makers' hut. The walls were made of thatch, and the roof came so low that they had to stoop. They were sitting close to each other on a bed of dry leaves.

From that day forward, they wrote to one another regularly every evening. Emma would take her letter to the end of the garden near the river, leaving it in a crack in the wall, Rodolphe would come to collect it, leaving a letter of his own, and always she complained that his were too short.

One morning, when Charles had gone off before dawn, she was taken with the notion that she must see Rodolphe immediately. She could reach La Huchette quickly, stay there an hour, and be back in Yonville again while everyone was still asleep. The thought of it left her gasping with desire; soon she found herself half-way across the meadow, walking rapidly, without a backward glance.

It was just the break of day. Emma, from far away, recognized her lover's house: two fan-tailed weathercocks were silhouetted black in the pale first light.

Beyond the farmyard, there was a big building which had to be the château. In she went, as if, at her approach, the walls had parted of themselves. A great staircase rose direct to the upper corridor. Emma lifted the latch of a door, and there, on the far side of the room, she sensed a man asleep. It was Rodolphe. She gave a shriek.

– You here! You here! he kept saying. How did you manage to do it? . . . But your dress is all wet!

– I do love you, she replied as she put her arms around his neck.

After the success of this first bold venture, every time that Charles went out early, Emma dressed quickly and tiptoed down the flight of steps to the edge of the water.

But when the plank-bridge for the cows had been lifted, she had to follow the garden walls fronting the river; the bank was slippery; to save herself from falling, her fingers gripped at the clusters of shrivelled wallflowers. Then she set off across fresh-ploughed fields, and went in up to her ankles, staggering along, her elegant boots clogged with mud. Her silk scarf, tied over her hair, rippled in the meadow breeze; she was scared of the cattle; she began to run; she arrived breathless, pink-cheeked, her whole body exhaling a sharp scent of sap and greenery and open air. Rodolphe, at this early hour, was still asleep. It was just like a spring morning filling his bedroom.

The long yellow curtains, over the windows, softened the light to a dense golden blur. Emma would grope her way, eyes blinking, and the drops of dew hanging in her hair were just like a topaz halo around her face. Rodolphe, with a laugh, would draw her to him and press her to his heart.

She would explore his room, opening the drawers, combing her hair with his comb and looking at herself in his shaving-mirror. Often she would even pick up the big pipe from the bedside-table, where it lay beside a carafe of water, among pieces of lemon and lumps of sugar. She put the stem between her teeth.

They needed a good quarter of an hour for their farewells.

Emma would weep; she wanted to stay with Rodolphe for ever.
Something stronger than she was pushing her towards him, so
much so that, one day, when he saw her appear unexpectedly,
he gave a frown, like someone vexed.

– What's the matter? she said. Aren't you well? Do tell me!

In the end he announced, in a serious voice, that her visits
were becoming reckless and that she was compromising
herself.

10

Little by little, these fears of Rodolphe's took hold of her. Love
had intoxicated her at first, she had had no thought of anything
beyond it. But, now that her life depended on him, she dreaded
losing the least part of his love, or even merely upsetting him.
On her way home from his house, she gazed anxiously around,
scrutinizing every figure that came into view, every cottage
window from which she might be noticed. She listened for
footsteps, for voices, for the sound of the plough; and she would
come to a stop, more pale and more trembling than the leaves
of the poplars swaying above her head.

One morning, coming back in this state, she suddenly thought
she saw the long barrel of a carbine which seemed to be aimed
at her. It was sticking out at an angle over the edge of a small
tub, half buried in the grass on the edge of a ditch. Emma,
almost fainting with terror, still walked on, and a man got up
out of the tub, just like something out of a jack-in-the-box. He
had gaiters buckled up to the knees, his cap pulled down to his
eyes, quivering lips and a red nose. It was Captain Binet, lying
in wait for wild duck.

– You ought to have called out sooner! he shouted. When you
see a gun, you must always give a warning!

This was the tax-collector's way of trying to hide the shock
he had just had; for a prefectorial decree had forbidden duck-
shooting except from a boat, and Monsieur Binet, in spite of his
respect for the law, was actually in the wrong. And so he kept
thinking he could hear the gamekeeper coming. But this worry

heightened his pleasure, and, all alone in his tub, he was relishing his luck and his cunning.

At the sight of Emma, he seemed mightily relieved, and immediately launched into a conversation:

– Not very warm, *rather chilly*!

Emma was silent. He went on:

– Well you must have been up rather early?

– Y ... y ... ess, she said falteringly; I've been to see the wet-nurse, where my baby is.

– Oh, yes! Of course! I've been out here myself, you know, ever since the crack of dawn; but the weather is so foul that unless the birds perch on the ...

– Good day, Monsieur Binet, she broke in, turning away from him.

– Your servant, madame, he replied impassively.

And he climbed back into his tub.

Emma regretted her brusque farewell to the tax-collector. He would, no doubt, jump to unfavourable conclusions. The story about the wet-nurse was the worst excuse; everyone in Yonville knew very well that the Bovary child had been back at home with her parents for a whole year now. Besides, nobody lived out over there; that road led only to La Huchette; so Binet had guessed where she'd been, and he would not be keeping quiet, he'd be gossiping, it was a certainty! She spent the whole day racking her brain for any conceivable story, haunted every second by the picture of that imbecile with the game-bag.

Charles, after their dinner, seeing her uneasy, suggested, for an amusement, taking her to the pharmacist's; and the first person she saw in the pharmacy was him, that tax-collector again! He was standing by the counter, in the glowing light of the big red jar, and he was saying:

– I'd like half an ounce of vitriol please.

– Justin, shouted the apothecary, bring us the sulphuric acid.

Then, to Emma, who was about to go up to Madame Homais's room:

– No, stay here, don't bother, she's coming down. Warm yourself at the stove while you wait ... Excuse me ... Good evening, doctor (for the pharmacist took great pleasure in saying the word *doctor* just as if, in using it on someone else, he could appropriate for himself some portion of the splendour it held for him) . . . But be careful not to knock the mortars over! Better get the chairs from the small parlour; you know very well we never move the armchairs from the drawing-room.

And Homais was rushing out from behind the counter, to put his armchair back in its place, when Binet asked him for half an ounce of sugar-acid.

– Sugar-acid? said the pharmacist disdainfully. Never heard of the stuff! Perhaps oxalic acid is what you want. It's oxalic, isn't it?

Binet explained that he wanted something abrasive to make up a copper solvent for getting the rust off some of his hunting-gear. Emma shuddered. The pharmacist began to say:

– Indeed the weather is not propitious, because of the humidity.

– Anyway, added the tax-collector with a sly look, there are some people who seem to like it.

She was choking.

– Give me another . . .

– He'll never go away! she was thinking.

– Half an ounce of colophony and some turpentine, four ounces of yellow wax, and an ounce and a half of animal black, please, to clean up the polished leather bits on my gear.

The apothecary was beginning to cut the wax, when Madame Homais appeared with Irma in her arms, Napoléon by her side and Athalie close behind her. She went to sit on the velvet-cushioned bench, under the window, and the little boy squatted on a stool, while his elder sister prowled around the jujube-box, next to her daddy. He was filling funnels and stoppering flagons, he was sticking labels, he was fashioning parcels. Everyone was silent; and the only sound was the occasional clink of weights on the scales, and the murmured words of the pharmacist as he gave his apprentice various instructions.

– How's your little lady? Madame Homais asked suddenly.

– Quiet! exclaimed her husband, as he wrote down the figures in his rough book.

– Why didn't you bring her? she went on in a loud whisper.

– Hush! Hush! said Emma, pointing her finger at the apothecary.

But Binet, engrossed in checking his bill, had not heard anything, most probably. At last, he left. And now Emma, unburdened, gave an enormous sigh.

– You are breathing heavily! said Madame Homais.

– Oh . . . it's because of this heat, she replied.

So they discussed, next day, how best to contrive their meetings; Emma wanted to bribe his servant with a gift; but it would be better to find some discreet house in Yonville. Rodolphe promised to look out for one.

Throughout the winter, three or four times a week, at the dead of night, he would appear in the garden. Emma, quite intentionally, had removed the key from the wicket-gate, and Charles thought it had been lost.

To warn her, Rodolphe would throw a handful of gravel against the shutters. She jumped to her feet; but sometimes she had to wait, because Charles had a passion for chattering by the fire, and he did go on interminably. She was wild with impatience; if looks could have done it, hers would have hurled him out of the window. In the end, she began to undress for the night; she took up a book and went on reading quite serenely, as if she were engrossed in the story. But Charles, who was in bed, would call her to him.

– Come on, Emma, he would say. Time for bed.

– I'm coming, she would always answer.

Because the candles dazzled him, he would turn to the wall and fall asleep. She would creep out, holding her breath, smiling, trembling, half-undressed.

Rodolphe had an enormous cloak; he wrapped her in it from head to foot, and, putting his arm about her waist, he would conduct her without a word to the far end of the garden.

To the arbour, on the same old crumbling wooden bench where long ago Léon had gazed at her so amorously, all the summer evening. She scarcely gave a thought to him these days.

The stars were shining through the branches of the leafless jasmin. Behind them they could hear the sound of the river flowing, and, every so often, the click-click of the withered reed-stalks. Immense shadow forms, here and there, billowed out across the gloom, and sometimes, fluttering with one great solid pulse, they stood aloft and curved over, great waves of darkness, speeding as though to engulf them. The cold of the night made their embraces the warmer; their sighs sounded more eloquent upon their lips; their eyes, scarce visible to each other, seemed bigger, and, amid such silence, there were whispered phrases which rang sharp and pure upon their hearts, echoing there with a quickening cadence.

On rainy nights, they took refuge in the consulting-room, between the cart-shed and the stable. She lit one of the big kitchen candles, one that she had hidden behind the books. Rodolphe would settle himself, quite at home. The sight of the bookshelves and the desk, of the whole room, roused his mirth; and he couldn't resist making various jokes about Charles which Emma found embarrassing. She would really have liked to see him more serious, rather more dramatic perhaps, sometimes, as when she thought she heard footsteps coming towards them along the garden path.

– Someone's coming! she said.

He blew out the light.

– Do you have your pistols?

– Why?

– Why . . . to defend yourself, Emma replied.

– Against your husband? Poor lad!

And Rodolphe finished off his phrase with a gesture which signified:

– I'd crush him with one finger.

She was in awe of his bravery, even though she sensed behind it a sort of indelicacy and a naïve coarseness that shocked her.

Rodolphe pondered long upon this business with the pistols. If she had spoken in earnest, it was utterly ridiculous, he thought, even rather odious, for he had no reason, himself, to hate the worthy Charles, not being devoured – as they say – by jealousy; – and, on the topic of Charles, Emma had sworn him a solemn oath that he thought in equally poor taste.

Besides, she was becoming rather sentimental. They had had to exchange miniatures; great handfuls of hair had been cut off;

and now she was insisting on a ring, an actual wedding-ring, as a symbol of eternal alliance. She often spoke to him about the bells at evening or the *voices of nature*; then she would talk about her mother, and about his mother too. (Rodolphe had lost his twenty years ago.) Emma, even so, comforted him in sweet baby-language, as if he had been a lost child, and sometimes she even said to him, as she gazed out at the moon:

– I am sure that up there, together, they approve of our love.

But she was so lovely! He had had few women so guileless. This undebauched love was something new to him, and, luring him from his comfortable habits, it soothed both his pride and his sensuality at once. Emma's raptures, which his bourgeois common sense disdained, seemed to him, in his heart of hearts, charming, since they were dedicated to his person. And now, sure of being loved, he took fewer pains, and imperceptibly his manner changed.

There were no more of those sweet words that made her weep, as in the early days, none of the fierce caresses that sent her wild; and now, their great love, in which she dwelt immersed, seemed to dwindle beneath her, like the waters that vanish into the bed of the river, and she could see the mud. She would not believe it; she redoubled her tenderness; and Rodolphe, increasingly, displayed his indifference.

She didn't know if she regretted having yielded to him or if, on the contrary, she really wanted to dote upon him the more. The humiliation of feeling her own weakness was turning into a rancour dulled by the pleasures of the flesh. It was not affection, it was like a perpetual seduction. He was subjugating her. She was almost afraid of him.

On the surface, though, things seemed calmer than ever, Rodolphe having managed to organize her adultery according to his whim; and, by the end of six months, when spring came round, they were, with each other, like a married couple tranquilly nourishing a domestic flame.

It was the time when old Rouault used to send his turkey in memory of the mended leg. The gift always came with a letter. Emma cut the string that fastened it to the hamper, and read the following lines.

My dear children

I hope this will find you in good health and that this year's will be as
good as the others; because it looks, I reckon, a bit more tender, and
bigger. But, next time, for a change, I'll give you a cock, unless you
prefer to stick to *peckers*, and send me back the hamper, if you wouldn't
mind, along with the two old ones. I've had an accident with the shed,
one night it was blowing hard and the roof flew off up into the trees.
The harvest has not been too good neither. So, I don't know when I'll
be over to see you. It's so difficult for me leaving the house, since there's
just been me, my poor Emma!

And here there was a gap between the lines, as if the old man
had dropped his pen to dream a while.

As for me, I'm pretty well in myself, apart from a cold I caught the
other day at the fair in Yvetot, where I'd gone over to hire a shepherd,
after I'd sacked the old one for being so particular about his food.
Really we do have such a hard time with that bunch of brigands! And
he was dishonest, into the bargain. I heard from a pedlar that had had
a tooth pulled when he was over your way this winter that Bovary was
working hard as ever. This comes as no surprise, and he showed me
his tooth: we had a coffee together, I asked him if he had seen you, he
said not, but he had seen a couple of horses in the stable, so it sounds
as if business is doing well. I'm glad for you, my dear children, and
may God send you every happiness imaginable. It grieves me that I still
have not seen my beloved little granddaughter Berthe Bovary. I have
planted her, in the garden, under your window, a wild plum-tree, and
I won't let anyone touch it, except to make some jam later on, and I'll
keep it in the cupboard for her when she comes. God bless, my dears.
Daughter, I send you a kiss, and you my son-in-law, and the little girl,
one on each cheek.

I am, most sincerely
Your loving father
Théodore Rouault

She sat for several minutes, holding the rough sheet of paper
between her fingers. The spelling mistakes were all tangled up
in each other, and Emma followed the kindly train of thought

that came through, clucking away like a hen stuck in a thorn-hedge. The writing must have been dried with the ash from the grate, for a little grey dust trickled off the letter on to her dress, and she almost thought she could see her father bending over the hearth to reach the tongs. What a long time it was now since she had sat with him, on the stool in the chimney-corner, burning the end of a stick in the big flames from the crackling reeds. She remembered summer evenings full of sunlight. The colts used to whinny when you went past, and they galloped, galloped . . . Under her window there was a beehive, and sometimes the bees, swirling about in the light, would bounce off the panes like soft balls of gold. What happiness in the old days! What freedom! What hope! What an abundance of illusions! Nothing left of them now! She had dissipated them in the exploits of her soul, in each successive phase: in virginity, in marriage, and in love; just like a traveller who leaves some portion of her wealth at every inn along the road.

But who was it that made her so unhappy? Where was the extraordinary catastrophe which had overwhelmed her? And she raised her head, looking around, as if to find the cause of what was making her suffer.

An April sunbeam sparkled over the porcelain on the dresser; the fire burned; she could feel through her slippers the softness of the rug; the day was bright, the air was warm, and she heard her child shrieking with laughter.

The little girl was rolling about on the lawn, in among the drying hay. She was lying on her stomach on top of one of the stacks. Her nurse held on to her by her skirt. Lestiboudois was raking up near by, and, every time he came near, she leaned out, waving both arms in the air.

– Bring her to me! said her mother, rushing up to embrace her. I do love you, my poor little thing! I do love you!

Noticing that the folds of her ears were slightly dirty, she rang there and then for some warm water, and washed her, changed her linen, her stockings, her shoes, asked her hundreds of questions about her health, just as if she had been away for weeks, and, finally, kissing her again and crying a few tears, she handed her back to the maid, who was standing quite amazed at such extravagant devotion.

Rodolphe, that evening, found her more serious than usual.

– It'll pass, he thought; it's only a mood.

And he missed three consecutive meetings. When he did come, her manner was cold and almost disdainful.

– Oh! You're wasting your time, my pretty one . . .

And he pretended not to notice her melancholy sighing, nor the handkerchief she kept taking out.

This was when Emma repented!

She even asked herself why it was she detested Charles, and whether it wouldn't be better to be able to love him. But there was little about him to nourish her revival of feeling, leaving her quite encumbered with her need for self-sacrifice, until the apothecary provided her with just the opportunity.

11

He had just lately read a panegyric on a new method for the cure of club-foot; and, as a partisan of progress, he now conceived the patriotic notion that Yonville, *to keep up with the times*, ought to have operations for talipes.

– Because, he said to Emma, what do we risk? Merely consider (and he counted off on his fingers the advantages of this experiment): success almost certain, alleviation and rehabilitation for the patient, rapid and easy fame for the surgeon. Your husband, for example, why should he not relieve poor old Hippolyte from the Golden Lion? Bear in mind that he would infallibly spread the story of his cure to everyone that passes through the inn, and (Homais lowered his voice and looked around) what is there to stop me sending off a little paragraph all about it to the newspapers? My goodness me! An article gets around . . . people talk about it . . . in the end it snowballs! And who knows then? Who knows?

In fact, Bovary could manage it; nothing suggested to Emma that he was not competent, and how satisfying for her to have coaxed him into taking a step that would enhance his reputation and increase his income. She only wanted to lean upon something rather more solid than love.

Charles, importuned both by the apothecary and by his wife, let himself be convinced. He sent to Rouen for Dr Duval's treatise,[18] and, every evening, with his head held between his hands, he plunged himself into his book.

While he was studying the *equinus*, the *varus* and the *valgus*, which is to say, catatalipes, endotalipes and exotalipes (or, rather, the various deviations of the foot, whether downwards, inwards or outwards), along with hypotalipes and anatalipes (in other words, downward torsion and upward stretching), Monsieur Homais, using every kind of argument, was exhorting the ostler to submit to the operation.

– The most you will feel is, perhaps, a slight pain; it's a simple prick, rather like being lightly bled, no worse than the excision of a corn might be.

Hippolyte, meditating, rolled his eyes, stupidly.

– Of course, the pharmacist went on, it's none of my business! It's for your sake! Purely from compassion! I'd love to see you, my lad, freed from your hideous claudication, and that rocking of the lumbar regions, which, whatever you say, must hinder you in the pursuit of your occupation.

Homais pictured to him how much more vigorous and more nimble he would feel afterwards, and he even insinuated that he would do better with the women, and the ostler's face broke out in a great crude grin. Next he went to work on his vanity.

– You call yourself a man do you? Just suppose that you had been called up, to go away and fight for the flag? . . . Ah, Hippolyte!

And Homais turned away, announcing that he was baffled by such obstinacy, such blindness in spurning the blessings of science.

The poor man gave in, for it was almost a conspiracy. Binet, who never meddled in other people's business, Madame Lefrançois, Artémise, the neighbours, and even the mayor, Monsieur Tuvache, everyone coaxed him, preached at him, humiliated him; but, what made up his mind was *the fact that it wouldn't cost him a thing.* Bovary even promised to provide the machine for the operation. Emma had thought of this generous touch; and Charles was in agreement, telling himself in his heart of hearts that his wife was an angel.

With the pharmacist's advice, and after three false starts, he had the carpenter, aided by the locksmith, fashion a kind of box weighing about eight pounds, a lavish apparatus of wood and iron, leather and sheet-metal, nuts and screws.

But now, to know which of Hippolyte's tendons to cut, it was essential first of all to find out what sort of club-foot he had.

He had a foot that almost made a straight line with the leg, though this did not prevent it from being turned inwards, so that it was an *equinus* with a touch of *varus*, or else a slight *varus* with a strong tendency to the *equinus*. But on this *equinus*, actually as large as a horse's hoof, with rough skin, stiff tendons, huge toes, and black nails just like the rivets on a horseshoe, on this foot the taliped, from morning till night, galloped about like a stag. He was regularly to be seen in the market-square, skipping all round the carts, with his odd foot out first. He actually seemed sturdier on this leg than on the other. After long service, it had acquired almost moral qualities of patience and energy, and when there was heavy work to be done, he propped himself on it, usually.

Now, since it was an *equinus*, the Achilles tendon would have to be cut, and then if need be he could deal later with the anterior tibial muscle in order to cure the *varus*: for the doctor did not dare to risk two operations at once; and he was in fact already trembling, for fear of injuring, ignorantly, some vital part.

Not Ambroise Paré,[19] applying for the first time since Celsus, after an interval of fifteen centuries, an immediate ligature to an artery; not Duputryen,[20] about to open up an abscess through a thick encephalic layer; not Gensoul, when he performed the first ablation of the upper maxillary, none of these had a heart so trembling, a hand so shaking, a mind so tautened as Monsieur Bovary when he approached Hippolyte with tenotome in hand. And, just like in a hospital, there lay on a sidetable, a pile of lint, some waxed threads, lots of bandages, a pyramid of bandages, every single bandage from the apothecary's shop.

It was Monsieur Homais who, ever since morning, had been organizing these preliminaries, as much to dazzle the multitude as to nourish his own illusions. Charles pierced the skin; they heard a sharp crack. The tendon was cut; the operation was finished. Hippolyte could not get over his surprise; he bent over Bovary's hands to cover them with kisses.

– Come on, calm down, the apothecary was saying, you can show your gratitude to your benefactor afterwards!

And he went down to announce the outcome to five or six of the curious who were waiting in the yard, thinking that Hippolyte was going to appear walking straight. Once he had buckled his patient into the machine, Charles went home, where Emma, in great anxiety, was waiting for him at the door. She flung her arms round his neck; they sat down to dine; he ate a great deal, and with dessert he even wanted a cup of coffee, a debauchery he only permitted himself on Sundays when they had guests.

The evening was delightful, full of talk, full of dreams to share. They spoke about the fortune they would make, about the improvements to be made in the house; he saw his reputation spreading, his prosperity increasing, his wife loving him perpetually; and she found herself happily revived in a new sentiment, healthier, better, happy to feel some tenderness for this poor boy who so adored her. The image of Rodolphe passed, fleetingly, through her mind; but her eyes came back to rest upon Charles; she even noticed to her surprise that his teeth were not too bad.

They were in bed when Monsieur Homais, defying the cook, burst into the room, holding up in his hand a sheet of paper freshly penned. It was his announcement destined for *Le Fanal de Rouen*. He was bringing it for them to read.

– You read it, said Bovary.

He read:

In spite of the prejudices that still cover part of the face of Europe like a veil, light is nevertheless beginning to penetrate our countryside. Thus it was that, on Tuesday, our little city of Yonville found itself the scene of a surgical experiment that is at the same time an act of high philanthropy. Monsieur Bovary, one of our most distinguished practitioners . . .

– Too much! Too much! said Charles, overcome with emotion.

– Oh, no, not at all. Nonsense, man! . . . *Operated for club-foot* . . . I haven't used any scientific terms, because, you know, in a newspaper, perhaps not everyone would understand; the masses must be . . .

– Of course, said Bovary. Go on.

– To continue, said the pharmacist. *Monsieur Bovary, one of our most distinguished practitioners, operated for club-foot on a man called Hippolyte Tautain, ostler for the past twenty-five years at the Golden Lion Hotel, kept by Madame Lefrançois, on the Place d'Armes. The novelty of the venture and the interest taken in the patient had drawn such a congregation of inhabitants that there was a veritable encumbrance on the threshold of the establishment. The operation, furthermore, was effected almost miraculously, with only some few drops of blood appearing on the skin, as though to announce that the obstinate tendon had at last yielded to the endeavours of art. The patient, strange to tell (we affirm this* de visu*), registered no pain whatever. His condition thus far leaves nothing to be desired. Everything indicates that the convalescence will be brief, and who knows but that we shall, at the next village fête, see our valiant Hippolyte conspicuous in the bacchic dances, at the centre of a chorus of revellers, proclaiming thus to every eye, by his pranks and his capers, a complete recovery. Glory to the noble men of science! Glory to those unwearied spirits who consecrate their nights to the amelioration or indeed the solace of their fellow creatures. Glorious! Thrice glorious! Shall we not cry aloud that the blind shall see, the deaf shall hear, and the lame shall walk again? But everything that fanaticism once pledged to the chosen few, science now accomplishes for the whole of mankind! We shall keep our readers regularly informed of the progress of this remarkable cure.*

Just five days later, this did not stop Mère Lefrançois from turning up scared to death and shouting:

– Help! He's dying! It's driving me mad!

Charles rushed over to the Golden Lion, and the pharmacist, who noticed him crossing the square, hatless, abandoned the shop. He arrived, out of breath, red-faced, anxious, and asking everyone on their way up the stairs:

– What can have happened to our fascinating taliped?

He was writhing, the taliped, in atrocious convulsions, such that the contraption boxed round his leg was knocking against the wall hard enough to bash it down.

Taking a great many precautions, so as not to disturb the position of the limb, the box was duly removed, and they saw a horrible sight. The shape of the foot was disappearing into a swelling, so gross that the entire skin seemed ready to burst open, and it was covered with patches of bruising inflicted by the famous machine. Hippolyte had already complained that it hurt; nobody had listened; they had to admit that he had not been completely wrong and they let him free for a few hours. But hardly had the oedema gone down a little, than the two men of science thought fit to reinstall the limb in the apparatus, clamping it on even tighter, to hasten the whole process. At last, three days later, when Hippolyte could bear it no more, they removed the machine yet again, and were quite astonished at the results confronting them. A livid tumefaction was spreading up the leg, and there were blistering patches, with a black liquid seeping out. Things were taking a serious turn. Hippolyte was beginning to get bored, and Mère Lefrançois had him moved into the little parlour, near to the kitchen, so that he might at least have some entertainment.

But the tax-collector, who dined there every day, complained bitterly about this forced companionship. And so they carried Hippolyte across into the billiard-room.

There he lay, groaning under his rough blankets, pale, unshaven, hollow-eyed, and, from time to time, he would move his sweating head over the dirty pillow where the flies were playing. Madame Bovary would come to see him. She brought him linen for his poultices, and consoled him, encouraged him. Not that he lacked for company, especially on market-days, with the peasants around him, playing billiards, fencing with their cues, smoking, drinking, singing, braying.

– How are things? they'd say, clapping him on the shoulder.

Not up to much, by the look of you! Completely your own fault.
Now you ought to do such and such . . .

And they told him stories about people who had been cured
by remedies quite different from his; and, by way of consolation,
they would add:

– Thing is, you're pampering yourself! You get yourself out
of there now! Coddled like a lord! Anyhow, you old bugger,
you don't smell too sweet.

The gangrene was spreading higher and higher. Bovary himself felt ill from it. He called in every hour, every few minutes.
Hippolyte gazed at him, his eyes filled with terror, and stammered out, sobbing:

– When will I be better? . . . Save me! . . . I'm badly, I am! I'm
badly.

And the doctor always left with advice that he diet.

– Don't you listen to him, my lad, said Mère Lefrançois;
they've martyred you quite enough already. You'll just be
weaker than ever. Here you are, swallow this!

And she offered him some rich broth, a slice of mutton, a
rasher of bacon, and sometimes little tumblers of brandy, which
he didn't have the strength to lift to his lips.

Abbé Bournisien, hearing that he was worse, insisted on seeing
him. He began by pitying him for his sufferings, while exhorting
him to rejoice in them, since it was the will of the Lord, and to
grasp this opportunity to reconcile himself with heaven.

– You see, said the cleric in a paternal tone, you were rather
neglecting your duties; we scarcely ever saw you at divine service; how many years can it be since you last came near the Holy
Table? I do realize that your labours, that the great bustle of
this world may have kept you from any thought for your salvation. But this very instant is the hour for reflection. Don't
despair, though; I have known great sinners begging for His
mercy just as they were about to appear before God (you have
scarcely come to that yet, I know), and they did surely die in a
state of grace. Let us hope that you, like them, will give us a
good example. Now, as a precaution, what could there be to
stop you reciting morning and evening a 'Hail Mary, full of

grace' and an 'Our Father which art in heaven'! Yes, do this for me, to please me. What can it cost you? Will you promise me?

The poor devil promised. The *curé* came back again day after day. He chatted with the innkeeper and even told anecdotes mixed with jokes, and puns that Hippolyte could not understand. As soon as an opportunity came up, he went back to matters religious, putting on an appropriate face.

His zeal seemed to work; and before long the taliped expressed the desire to make a pilgrimage to Bon-Secours, if he were cured: Monsieur Bournisien said that he could see no objection to this; two precautions were better than one. *It couldn't do any harm.*

The apothecary sounded off against what he called *priestly manoeuvres*; they were interfering, he claimed, with Hippolyte's convalescence, and he kept saying to Madame Lefrançois:

– Leave him alone! Leave him alone! You're damaging his morale with your mysticism!

But the good woman wouldn't listen to another word from him. It was *his fault*. In a spirit of perversity, she hung a stoup full of holy water, and a sprig of boxwood, right on the patient's bed.

However, religion seemed no better for him than surgery, and the inexorable putrefaction was still spreading upwards from the extremities towards the stomach. Though they varied the medicines and they changed the poultices, the muscles, day by day, slackened ever more, and in the end Charles answered with a consenting nod of his head when Madame Lefrançois asked him if, as a last resort, she could send for Monsieur Canivet of Neufchâtel, a famous man.

A doctor of medicine, fifty years old, enjoying a good practice and a certain self-assurance, this colleague gave a bluntly disdainful laugh when he uncovered the leg, now gangrened as high as the knee. Bluntly declaring that it must be amputated, he went across to the pharmacist's, to sound off against the asses who could have reduced a poor man to such a state.

– Gimmicks from Paris, eh! Big ideas from the gents in the metropolis! It goes with strabismus and chloroform and lithotomy – a load of rubbish the government should put a stop to! But they just want to look cute, and they thrust their remedies at you quite regardless of the consequences. Oh, no; we're not that clever, not like them; we're not experts, dandified triflers, we are practitioners, healers; and we wouldn't dream of operating on anyone who was perfectly well. Straighten up a club-foot! How can you straighten up a club-foot? You might just as well try to flatten out a hunchback!

Homais was suffering as he listened to this sermon, and he hid his discomfort behind a courtier's smile, needing to appease Monsieur Canivet, whose prescriptions sometimes came as far as Yonville; so he didn't go to Bovary's defence, he didn't offer any comment, and, betraying his principles, he sacrificed his dignity to the more serious interests of his business.

In the village it was a great event, this thigh-amputation by Doctor Canivet. On the day itself, the inhabitants were up earlier than usual, and the main street, crowded though it was, seemed rather lugubrious, as though there were to be a public execution. At the grocer's they were discussing Hippolyte's illness; the shops did no trade, and Madame Tuvache, the mayor's wife, never left the window, in her eagerness to watch the surgeon arrive.

He came in his cabriolet, which he drove himself. But because the right-hand spring was sagging from years of carrying his plump bulk, this made the carriage lean over slightly as it went along, and on the other cushion, next to him, you could see a huge box, covered in supple red leather, with three brass locks that glittered magisterially.

Passing like a whirlwind through the archway of the Golden Lion, the doctor, in a very loud voice, ordered them to unharness his horse, then he went into the stable to see if she was eating her oats properly; for, whenever he called on a patient, he always looked first to his mare and his carriage. People even said of this: 'He's a character, is Monsieur Canivet!' And he was esteemed the more for this imperturbable aplomb. The universe could have fallen about his ears and he would not have failed in the smallest of his habits.

Homais made his appearance.

– I'm counting on you, said the doctor. Are we ready? Forward, march!

But the apothecary, with a great blush, confessed that he was too susceptible to attend such an operation.

– When you are only a spectator, he said, the imagination runs wild, you know. And my nervous system is peculiarly . . .

– Rubbish! Canivet interrupted, you look more like an apoplectic to me. And, indeed, that does not surprise me; seeing how you chemist fellows are forever stuck in your kitchens, it must damage your constitution in the end. Just look at me, now: every day, up at four o'clock, shave in cold water (never feel the cold), never wear flannel, never catch cold, my guts are fine! I eat what comes my way, this, that or the other, like a philosopher, take pot-luck. That's why I'm not a delicate thing like you, and it's all the same to me whether I carve up a Christian or the chicken on your table. I expect you'll say, just a habit . . . just a habit . . . !

Without any thought for Hippolyte, who was sweating with anguish between his sheets, these two characters now embarked on a conversation in which the apothecary compared the sang-froid of a surgeon to that of a general; and this analogy was pleasing to Canivet, who loquaciously expounded on the imperatives of his art. He regarded it as a sacred office, however much the officers of health might dishonour it. At last, returning to the patient, he examined the bandages supplied by Homais, the same ones that had appeared for the club-foot, and he asked for somebody to hold the limb for him. Word was sent for Lestiboudois, and Monsieur Canivet, his sleeves now rolled up, went through into the billiard-room, while the apothecary stayed with Artémise and the innkeeper, both of them paler than their aprons, ears pressed to the door.

Bovary, meanwhile, did not dare move from his house. He stayed downstairs, in the parlour, sat in the cold chimney-corner, his chin slumped on to his chest, his hands clasped, his eyes blank. What a blunder! he was thinking, what a failure! Though he had taken every precaution imaginable. Fate must have had something to do with it. Who cares? Well, if Hippolyte, later, were to die, he would be the one who had murdered him. What excuse would he give, on his rounds, when they began to question him? Perhaps, after all, he *had* just made a mistake somewhere? He wondered, he found nothing. Even the most famous surgeons made mistakes. That was what nobody ever believed! They would be laughing, worse than that, cursing. It would spread all the way to Forges! As far as Neufchâtel! As far as Rouen! Everywhere! Some of his colleagues might even write attacks on him. A controversy would follow, he'd have to reply in the newspapers. Hippolyte could even have him prosecuted. He saw himself dishonoured, ruined, lost! And his imagination, beset by a host of anxieties, was lurching about among them, just like an empty barrel carried out to sea and rolling on the swell.

Emma, sitting opposite, was watching him; she did not share his humiliation, she had her own to endure; that she had ever thought such a man could be worth anything, as if she had not already sufficiently observed his mediocrity at least twenty times.

Charles was pacing around the room. His boots creaked on the parquet floor.

– Sit down, she said, you're annoying me!

He sat down again.

How on earth had she done it? She who was so clever! How had she managed to botch it yet again? What stupid mania was it driving her like this into wrecking her existence by continual self-sacrifice? She remembered her cravings for luxury, the privations of her soul, the squalor of marriage, of housekeeping, her dreams falling in the mud like wounded swallows, everything she had wanted, everything she had denied herself, everything she could have had! And why? Why?

Across the silence that filled the village, a harrowing cry travelled through the air. Bovary turned pale, almost swooning. Her brow twitched into a frown, and she went on. It was for him, for this creature, for this man who understood nothing, who felt nothing! For there he sat, quite placidly, entirely unaware that the ridicule of his name would henceforth sully her as well as him. She had made an effort to love him, and she had repented tearfully after giving herself to another man.

– Well perhaps it was a *valgus* after all? abruptly declared Bovary, deep in his thoughts.

At the unexpected shock of this phrase dropping into her

mind just like a lead bullet on a silver dish, Emma raised her head with a shudder, to make out what he was saying; and they looked at each other in silence, almost startled by the sight, so far sundered were they in their thoughts. Charles was studying her with the vacant gaze of a drunkard, listening, motionless, to the last cries from the amputation which issued in a slow heavy wail, broken by jagged screeching, like the far-off bellow of some creature being slaughtered. Emma was biting her pale lips, and rolling a broken-off limb from the coral ornament between her fingers. She fixed on Charles the burning points of her eyes, like two arrows of fire ready to fly. Everything about him irritated her now, his face, his clothes, the things he didn't say, his whole person, his very existence. She repented, as of a crime, her past virtue, and whatever yet remained of that virtue was collapsing beneath the frenzied assault of her pride. She gloated over the malignant ironies of adultery triumphant. The memory of her lover came back to her with a dizzying pull: she cast her soul to him, drawn with new appetite to this image; and Charles seemed as remote from her life, as eternally absent, as impossible and annihilated, as if he were near death, and in his last agony before her eyes.

There came a noise of footsteps on the pavement. Charles looked up; and, through the lowered blinds, he could see, at the corner of the market, in full sunlight, Doctor Canivet, who was wiping his brow with a silk handkerchief. Homais, behind him, was carrying a large red box in his hand, and they were both making their way towards the pharmacy.

In sudden tenderness and discouragement, Charles turned towards his wife, saying:

– Kiss me now, my love.

– Leave me alone! she said, pink with anger.

– What is it? What is it? he kept saying, astounded. Do calm down, you're not quite yourself. You know how I love you! . . . Please! . . .

– Stop it! she cried out with a terrible look.

And, rushing from the parlour, Emma slammed the door so hard that the barometer jumped off the wall and smashed on the floor.

Charles slumped into his armchair, bewildered, wondering what was wrong with her, imagining some nervous ailment, weeping, and sensing vaguely circling round him something noxious and incomprehensible.

When Rodolphe arrived, that evening, in the garden, he found his mistress waiting for him at the foot of the steps, on the first stair. They embraced, and their rancour melted away like snow in the warmth of that kiss.

12

This was the new beginning of their love. Habitually, in the middle of the day, Emma would write to him on impulse; then, through the window, beckon to Justin, who, quickly untying his apron, flew off to La Huchette. Rodolphe would arrive; it was to tell him she was feeling bored, that her husband was odious and life was awful!

– And what can I do about that? he exclaimed one day, impatiently.

– Ah! If you wanted! . . .

She was sitting on the floor, between his knees, her hair unfastened, blankness in her eyes.

– What is it? said Rodolphe.

She gave a sigh.

– We could go away and live somewhere . . . together . . .

– You must be quite mad! he said with a laugh. How could we do it?

She came back to the idea; he pretended not to understand and changed the subject.

What he didn't understand was such a fuss about a thing as simple as love. She had a motive, a reason, and a kind of incentive for her affection.

This tenderness was, indeed, steadily nourished by the disgust she felt for her husband. The more she gave herself to the one, the more she loathed the other; never did Charles seem to her so unpleasant, to have such stubby fingers, such a dull mind, such common habits, as when they sat together after her

meetings with Rodolphe. Even as she was playing the wife
and the woman of virtue, she was kindled by the image of that
head with its black curls hanging over the sunburned brow,
that body so robust and still so elegant in form, that man
endowed with such experience in reason, with such fierceness
in desire. It was for him she shaped her nails with all the care
of an engraver; for him there was never enough lotion upon
her skin, never enough patchouli on her handkerchiefs. She
bedecked herself with bracelets, rings, necklaces. When he was
coming, she replenished the roses in her two great vases made
of blue glass, and arranged her room and her person just like a
courtesan awaiting a prince. The maid had to be endlessly
bleaching linen; and, all through the day, Félicité was cooped
up in the kitchen, where young Justin, who often kept her
company, watched her at work.

With his elbow on the long board she used for ironing, he
gazed avidly at these women's things spread around him:
damask petticoats, little lace shawls, collars, knickers with
draw-strings, voluminous around the hips and gathered at the
knee.

– What's that for? asked the young boy as he ran his fingers
over the crinoline or down the fasteners.

– You never seen anything, lad? Félicité answered, laughing;
as if your mistress, Madame Homais, don't wear the same sort.

– Oh, yes, of course! Madame Homais!

And then he added in a pensive tone:

– Is she a lady, like Madame?

But Félicité became impatient with having him hanging
around her all the time. She was six years older, and Théodore,
Monsieur Guillaumin's servant, had begun courting her.

– Be off with you! she said, moving her pot of starch. You'd
better go and pound the almonds; always snooping around the
women, you are; wait till there's beard on that chin, you bad
lad, before you start meddling.

– All right, don't you be cross, I'm going to go and *do her
boots* for you.

And he would quickly reach for Emma's boots on the shelf
over the fire, all crusted with mud – the mud of her assignations

– that crumbled to dust on his fingers, and he watched it rising slowly in a ray of sunlight.

– You're so fussy not to spoil them, aren't you! said the cook, who was not quite so meticulous when she cleaned them up herself, because Madame handed them on to her as soon as the fabric was past its best.

Emma had dozens of pairs in her wardrobe, and she went through them at a great rate, without Charles ever making the slightest comment.

So it was that he paid out three hundred francs for a wooden leg which she reckoned appropriate as a gift for Hippolyte. The socket was lined with cork, and it had spring-joints, a complicated device swathed in a black trouser-leg, with a polished boot on the end. But Hippolyte, not daring to use such a fine leg for everyday, begged Madame Bovary to procure him another more suitable. The doctor, naturally, met the cost of this purchase as well.

And so the ostler gradually took up his work again. He was to be seen as before, getting about the village, and whenever Charles caught the sound, in the distance, of that leg tapping along the pavement, he turned a corner rather quickly.

It was Monsieur Lheureux, the draper, who had taken on the order; this gave him an opportunity to pay several calls on Emma. He would chat to her about the latest deliveries from Paris, about dozens of feminine novelties, was most obliging in his manner, and he never asked for any money. Emma gave in to this easy way of satisfying her impulses. For instance, she wanted, as a present for Rodolphe, a rather fine riding-whip to be found in an umbrella-shop in Rouen. Monsieur Lheureux, the very next week, put it on the table for her.

But only the day after he called at the house with a bill for two hundred and seventy francs, not counting the centimes. Emma was greatly embarrassed: the drawers in the desk were empty; they owed Lestiboudois for more than a fortnight, two quarters' wages to the servant, a host of other things besides, and Bovary was waiting impatiently for a remittance from Monsieur Derozerays, who was in the habit of paying him, every year, round about Saint Peter's Day.

At first she managed to fend off Lheureux; in the end he lost patience: they were pressing him, his capital was tied up, and, if he didn't call some in, he would be forced to take from her the goods she had had.

– Oh! Take them! said Emma.

– I was joking, he replied. The only thing that worries me is the riding-whip. Of course! I'll ask Monsieur for it back.

– No! No! she said.

– Aha! I've got you! thought Lheureux.

And, sure of his little discovery, he went off reciting under his breath, with his habitual tiny wheezing noise:

– So be it! We shall see! We shall see!

She was wondering how to get off the hook, when in came the maid and put on the mantelpiece a small roll of blue paper, *from Monsieur Derozerays*. Emma pounced on it, opened it. Fifteen napoléons[21] were there. It was the account. She heard Charles on the stairs; she threw the gold to the back of his drawer and took the key.

Three days later. Lheureux reappeared.

– I want to suggest an arrangement to you, he said; if, instead of the amount agreed, you would care to take . . .

– Here you are! she said, putting fourteen napoléons in his hand.

The draper was amazed. Then, to mask his disappointment, he lavished apologies and offers of service which Emma flatly refused; then she stood for a moment fingering in her apron pocket the two five-franc pieces he had given her in change. She promised herself she would economize, in order to pay back later . . .

– Bah! she thought, he'll forget all about it.

As well as the riding-whip with the silver-gilt pommel, Rodolphe had had a seal with the motto *Amor nel cor*;[22] and then a scarf to use as a muffler, and most recently a cigar-case exactly like the Viscount's, the one Charles had picked up in the road and Emma now treasured. However, these gifts were a humiliation to him. Several he refused; she insisted, and Rodolphe finally yielded, finding her tyrannical and too importunate.

Besides, she did have the strangest ideas.

– When midnight chimes, she said, you must think of me!

And, if he confessed to having forgotten, there were extravagant reproaches, and they always ended with the eternal words:

– Do you love me?

– Yes, of course I love you!

– *Really* love me!

– Definitely!

– You've never loved anyone else?

– Did you think you were having a virgin? he burst out with
a laugh.

Emma was in tears, and he did his best to console her, embel-
lishing his vows with many a *double entendre*.

– Oh! It's because I love you! she went on, love you so much
I can't live without you, did you realize? Sometimes I'm longing
to see you again and the furies of love pull me apart. I say to
myself, 'Where is he? Talking to other women, perhaps? They're
smiling at him, he comes closer . . .' No! it's not like that, is it?
I am the only one, aren't I? Some are more beautiful; but me,
I'm a better lover! I'm your slave and your concubine! You're
my king, my idol! You are good! Beautiful! Intelligent! Strong!

He had heard such stuff so many times that her words meant
very little to him. Emma was just like any other mistress; and
the charm of novelty, falling down slowly like a dress, exposed
only the eternal monotony of passion, always the same forms
and the same language. He did not distinguish, this man of
such great expertise, the differences of sentiment beneath the
sameness of their expressions. Because he had heard such-like
phrases murmured to him from the lips of the licentious or the
venal, he hardly believed in hers; you must, he thought, beware
of turgid speeches masking commonplace passions; as though
the soul's abundance does not sometimes spill over in the most
decrepit metaphors, since no one can ever give the exact measure
of their needs, their ideas, their afflictions, and since human
speech is like a cracked cauldron on which we knock out tunes
for dancing-bears, when we wish to conjure pity from the stars.

But with that critical superiority vested in the man who, in
every relationship, holds back something of himself, Rodolphe

sensed that in this love there lay further pleasures to be exploited. He reckoned all delicacy irksome. He used her brutishly. He made of her a creature docile and corrupt. Hers was a sort of idiot attachment, full of admiration for him, of pleasure for herself; a beatific drowsiness; and her soul sank deep into this fuddle, drowning there, shrivelling up, like the Duke of Clarence in his butt of malmsey.

Simply from the effect of her amorous habits, Madame Bovary's appearance changed. There was insolence in her eyes, her speech was freer, she even had the audacity to parade with Monsieur Rodolphe, cigarette in mouth, *just to vex people*; in the end, those who still had doubts could doubt no longer when she was seen, one day, stepping down from the *Hirondelle*, squeezed into a tight waistcoat, looking like a man; and the elder Madame Bovary, who had come to take refuge with her son, after a frightful scene with her husband, was not the least scandalized among the respectable wives. Various other things displeased her: firstly Charles had not listened to her advice about the prohibition of novels; and *the tone of the house* upset her; she ventured certain remarks, and there was a quarrel, once in particular, over Félicité.

Madame Bovary senior, the evening before, as she went along the passage, had caught her with a man, a man with a brown fringe-beard, about forty years old, who, at the sound of her footsteps, had slipped quickly from the kitchen. Emma began to laugh when she was told; but the good lady was enraged, announcing that unless morals were to be a mockery, one ought to keep an eye on the servants.

– Just where do you come from? said her daughter-in-law, with such an impertinent look that Madame Bovary asked her if she were not perhaps defending her own case.

– Out of here! said the young woman jumping to her feet.

– Emma! Mamma! cried Charles to propitiate them.

But they had both gone off in exasperation. Emma kept stamping her foot, saying:

– Such vile manners! What a peasant!

He ran to his mother; she was quite unhinged, stammering out:

– Such an insolent girl! The giddy creature! And worse, I expect!

And she wanted to leave immediately, unless she were offered an apology. Charles went back to his wife and beseeched her to give way: he went on his knees; in the end, she said:

– All right! I'm going.

She held out her hand to her mother-in-law with the dignity of a marquise, as she said:

– I apologize, madame.

Once back up in her room, Emma threw herself down full length on her bed, and she lay there weeping like a child, her face buried in the pillows.

They had arranged, she and Rodolphe, that if ever anything out of the ordinary happened, she would fix a little piece of white paper to the shutter, and if, by any chance, he were in Yonville, he would go straight to the lane, behind the house. Emma gave the signal; she had been waiting three quarters of an hour when, suddenly, she noticed Rodolphe at the corner of the market-square. She was tempted to open the window, to call to him; but he had already disappeared. She slumped back in despair.

Soon, however, she thought she heard someone walking along the pavement. It was him, it must be; she came down the stairs, crossed the yard. There he was, outside. She ran into his arms.

– Do be careful, he said.

– Ah! If you only knew! she replied.

And she began to tell him about it, in a rush, incoherently, exaggerating the facts, making lots of things up, and so lavish with superfluous parentheses that he didn't understand a thing.

– Now, my poor angel, be brave, cheer up, be patient!

– But here I am suffering patiently for four years now! . . . A love like ours should be proclaimed to the face of heaven. They're torturing me! I cannot bear it any more! Save me!

She was clinging to Rodolphe. Her eyes, full of tears, sparkled like flames beneath the waves; her breast heaved fast; never had he felt such love for her; that was when he lost his head and he said to her:

– What's to be done? What do you want?

– Take me away! she cried. Carry me off! Oh! I beg you!

And she took his lips, as if to pluck there the unforeseen consent that was exhaled in his kiss.

– But . . . Rodolphe began.

– What is it?

– Your little girl?

She reflected a few moments, and replied:

– We'll take her with us, there's no alternative!

– What a woman! he said to himself, watching her go.

For she had slipped back into the garden. They were calling her.

The elder Madame Bovary, over the next few days, was much surprised by the transformation in her daughter-in-law. Emma's manner was more docile, and she even pushed deference to the point of asking her for a recipe for pickling gherkins.

Was this merely the better to dupe them both? Or, rather, did she want, out of a sort of voluptuous stoicism, to savour the bitterness of the things she was about to leave behind? But she was paying no attention to them, on the contrary; she lived as though lost in the anticipated relish of her approaching happiness. This was an eternal topic of conversation with Rodolphe. She would lean upon his shoulder, she would murmur:

– Just think, soon we'll be in the mail-coach! Does it make you wonder? Is it possible? To me, it seems the moment I feel the carriage moving, it'll be like going up in a balloon, just like launching off up to the clouds. Do you know, I'm counting the days? . . . Aren't you?

Never had Madame Bovary been so beautiful as she was now; she had that indefinable beauty which comes from joy, from enthusiasm, from success, the beauty which is simply a harmony between temperament and circumstances. Her cravings, her sorrows, her experience of pleasure and her still-fresh illusions had brought her gradually to readiness, like flowers that have manure, rain, wind and sun, and she was blossoming at last in the splendour of her being. Her eyelids seemed perfectly fashioned for those long ardent looks that drown the eye; while deep breathing dilated her fine nostrils and lifted the plump corners of her mouth, shadowed in the light with a faint black down. You would have said some artist skilled in corruption had arrayed about her neck the dropping coils of her hair; they twined in a great mass, neglectfully, betraying the accidents of adultery, that so dishevelled her every day. Her voice, these days, took on more mellow inflections, as did her figure; something subtle that ran straight through you breathed out even from the folds of her gown and from the curve of her foot. Charles, just as in the first days of his marriage, found her delicious and irresistible.

When he came home in the middle of the night, he did not dare to wake her. The porcelain night-light cast up on the ceiling circles of trembling brightness, and the drawn curtains on the little cradle made it look like a white tent spreading in the shadow, just by the bed. Charles looked at them. He thought he heard the soft breathing of his child. Now she was going to grow up: every month, quickly, would bring some progress; he could already see her coming home from school at the end of the day, all laughter, her cuffs stained with ink, and carrying her basket on her arm; she'd have to be sent to boarding-school, that would cost money; how would they manage? He thought it over. He might rent a small farm near by, one he could keep an eye on every morning, on the way to see his patients. He would hold on to the income, he would put it in the savings-bank; he would buy some shares in something or other, anything; anyway, the practice would grow; he was counting on that, for he wanted Berthe to be well brought up, to be talented, to learn the piano. She would be so pretty, later on, at fifteen, when, looking just like her mother, she would wear, like her, in the summer, one of those big straw hats! From a distance people would take them for two sisters. He pictured her to himself, working in the evening by their side, in the lamplight; she would be embroidering slippers for him; she would look after the house; she would fill every room with her charm and her gaiety. Eventually, they would think about settling her: find her some decent lad with solid prospects; he would make her happy; it would last for ever.

Emma was not asleep, she was pretending to be asleep; and,

while he was dozing off beside her, she was roused by other dreams.

Behind four galloping horses, she had been carried seven days into a new land, whence they would never return. On they go, on they go, close-embracing, wordlessly. Often, from a mountain-top, they suddenly glimpsed some splendid city of domes, bridges, ships, groves of lemon-trees and cathedrals of white marble, their elegant spires topped with the nests of storks. They moved at a walking pace, over the great flagstones, and on the ground there were bouquets of flowers, offered by women dressed in red bodices. You could hear bells, mules braying, with the murmur of guitars and the noise of fountains, whose drifting spray cooled piles of fruit, arranged in pyramids at the foot of pale statues, that smiled beneath dancing waters. And they came, one evening, to a fishing-village, where brown nets were drying in the wind, along the cliff by the huts. It was there they would settle down for all time: they would live in a low house with a flat roof, in the shade of a palm-tree, at the head of a gulf, on the edge of the sea. They would cruise in a gondola, they would swing in a hammock; and their existence would be easy and free like their silken garments, warm and starry as the soft nights they would contemplate. And yet, in the immensity of this future that she conjured for herself, nothing specific stood out: the days, each one magnificent, were as near alike as waves are; and the vision balanced on the infinite horizon, harmonious, blue-hazed, and bathed in sunlight. But the child began to cough in her cradle, or else Bovary snored more loudly, and Emma did not fall asleep until morning, when dawn was whitening the window-panes and young Justin was already in the square, opening the shutters on the pharmacy.

She had sent for Monsieur Lheureux and had said to him:

– I'm going to need a cloak, a big cloak, with a deep collar and a lining.

– Going away somewhere? he asked.

– No! But . . . anyway, I can depend on you, can't I? I'm in a hurry! He bowed.

– And I'll need, she went on, a trunk, not too heavy, a handy size.

– Yes, yes, I know, about three feet by one and a half, like they make them these days.

– And a travelling-bag.

– Obviously, thought Lheureux, there's ructions at the back of this.

– Here you are, said Madame Bovary, taking her watch from her belt, you have this: take the price out of it.

But the shopkeeper protested that there was no need for that; they knew each other; did he not trust her? What nonsense! However, she insisted that he take at least the chain, and Lheureux had already put it in his pocket and was going, when she called him back.

– You can leave everything at your shop. As for the cloak – she seemed to be thinking it over – don't bring that either; just give me the maker's address and tell him to keep it ready for me.

Next month it was, they were to run away. She would leave Yonville as if she were going shopping in Rouen. Rodolphe would have booked the seats, got the passports, and even written to Paris, to have the whole mail-coach as far as Marseilles, where they would buy an open carriage and, from there, travel straight through by the Genoa road. She would have seen to it that her luggage was sent to Lheureux, to be put directly on the *Hirondelle*, so that nobody would have any suspicions; and, in all of this, there was never any mention of her child. Rodolphe avoided the subject; perhaps she had forgotten about it.

He wanted to have another two weeks clear, to see to various arrangements; after one week, he said he needed two more, then he said he was ill; and he went off somewhere; the month of August passed by, and, after these delays, they resolved that it would irrevocably be on the 4th of September, a Monday.

At last the Saturday, the final Saturday, arrived. Rodolphe came in the evening, earlier than usual.

– Is everything ready? she asked him.

– Yes.

They walked round a flower-bed, and went to sit near the terrace, on top of the wall.

– You are sad, said Emma.

– No, why?

And yet he was looking at her peculiarly, quite tenderly.

– Is it because you're going away? she said, leaving behind the things you love, your life? I do understand . . . though, myself, I have nothing in the world! You are everything I have. And I'll be everything to you. I shall be your family, your country: I'll look after you, I'll love you.

– How sweet you are! he said, taking her in his arms.

– Am I? she said with a voluptuous laugh. Do you love me? Swear to it!

– Do I love you? Do I love you? But I adore you, my love!

The moon, quite round and coloured purple, was coming up from the earth, at the end of the meadow. Quickly it rose between the branches of the poplar-trees that screened it here and there, like a black curtain, in tatters. If appeared, immaculately white, brightening all the empty sky; and now, drifting easily, it cast upon the river a great stain, unfolding an infinity of stars, and that silveriness seemed to be coiling down into the far depths, like a serpent with no head, covered in luminous scales. It also looked like some kind of monstrous candelabra, dripping, all over, with diamond droplets, melting down. The tender night spread about them; pools of shadow were gathering amid the leaves. Emma, her eyes half closed, drank in, with sighings deep and slow, the cool wind off the river. There was not much to say, lost as they were in overwhelming reverie. Tenderness out of the past came to their hearts again, copiously, silently as the flowing river, with the softness of the perfume of white lilac, and it cast across their memory shadows more melancholy and more immense than those of the willows, motionless, spread full length upon the grass. Often some nocturnal creature, hedgehog or weasel, prowling about, disturbed the leaves, or they heard a ripe peach dropping from the espalier.

– What a lovely night! said Rodolphe.

– We shall have many more of them! replied Emma.

And, almost talking to herself:

– Yes, it will be good to travel . . . Why is my heart so sad, though? Is it fear of the unknown . . . the pull of old habits . . .

or else . . . ? No, it's too much happiness! Feeble thing that I am! Do you forgive me?

– There is still time! he cried. Think it over, you may regret it later.

– Never! she said impetuously.

And, drawing close to him:

– Anyway, what harm could come to me? There is no desert, no precipice, and no ocean that I wouldn't cross with you. The longer we live together, every day it'll be like clasping tighter, ever closer. There'll be no troubles, no cares, nothing in our way. We'll be alone, by ourselves, eternally . . . Say something, answer me.

At regular intervals he recited: Yes . . . Yes! She was running her fingers through his hair, and she kept saying in a baby voice, despite her big tears rolling out:

– Rodolphe! Rodolphe! Ah! Rodolphe, dear little Rodolphe!

Midnight rang out.

– Midnight! she said. There, it's tomorrow! One more day!

He stood to take his leave; and almost as if this gesture of his had been the signal for their flight, Emma said suddenly, with gaiety in her voice:

– You have the passports?

– Yes.

– You're not forgetting anything?

– No.

– Are you sure?

– Absolutely.

– You'll be waiting for me, won't you, at the Hôtel de Provence? . . . At noon?

He nodded.

– Until tomorrow! said Emma, with a final caress.

And she watched him as he went.

He did not look back. She ran after him, and, leaning out over the water's edge, from among the bushes:

– Until tomorrow, she cried.

He was already on the other side of the river and walking swiftly across the meadows.

After a few minutes, Rodolphe stopped; and, when he saw

her in her white dress bit by bit fading away into the dark like any ghost, it was now that the beating of his heart made him lean up against a tree, so as not to fall.

– What an imbecile I am! he said, swearing a monstrous oath. Never mind, she was a pretty mistress!

And, instantly, Emma the beautiful, with the many pleasures of her love, reappeared to him. At first, he felt some tenderness, then he turned against her.

– After all, he exclaimed gesticulating, I can't go into exile, with a child on my hands.

These things he said to himself, the better to harden his heart.

– And besides, the bother, the expense, oh! No, no, no, a thousand times! It would have been awfully stupid!

13

The moment he got back home, Rodolphe abruptly sat himself at his desk, under the stag's-head trophy hanging on the wall. But, once he had the pen in his hand, nothing came to him, and so, leaning on his elbows, he began to ponder. Emma seemed to be fading into a distant past, as if the resolution he had made had opened up between them, instantly, an immense void.

Trying to recapture something of her, he went looking in the cupboard, at the head of his bed, for an old Rheims biscuit-tin, where he usually stored his love-letters, and from it there emanated an odour of dusty dampness and withered roses. First he came across a pocket-handkerchief, covered in pale droplets. It was a handkerchief of hers, once when her nose had bled, out walking; he couldn't remember. Next to it, with all its corners crumpled, was Emma's miniature; her toilette he thought pretentious and her *simpering* look quite pitiful; from dwelling on this image and from calling up the memory of the original, Emma's features gradually blurred in his mind, as if the living and the painted faces, rubbing one against the other, were both being obliterated. Eventually, he read some of her letters; they were full of details connected with their journey, brief, practical and urgent, like business-letters. He wanted another look at the

longer ones, from the early days; to get them from the bottom
of the tin, Rodolphe took out the whole collection; and mechanically he began to hunt through this mound of papers and things,
turning up haphazard bunches of flowers, a garter, a black
mask, pins and locks of hair – what hair! Brown and blonde;
some, even, caught in the hinges of the tin, broke when he
opened it.

Playing with his souvenirs, he examined the handwriting and
the style of the letters, as diverse as their spelling. They were
tender or jovial, facetious, melancholy; there were some that
asked for love and some that asked for money. From a single
word, he conjured faces, from certain gestures, the sound of a
voice; sometimes, though, he could remember nothing.

Indeed, these women, crowding together into his thoughts,
hampered and diminished each other, as if worn down into a
single love, interchangeably. Taking a handful of mixed-up
letters, he entertained himself for several minutes by letting them
cascade from his right hand to his left. At last, bored and drowsy,
Rodolphe went to put the tin back in the cupboard, saying,

– What a load of nonsense!

Which quite summed up his opinion; for pleasures, like boys
in a school playground, had so trampled across his heart that
nothing green now sprouted there, and whatever passed that
way, more heedless than the children, left – unlike them – no
name carved upon the wall.

– Right, he said to himself, here we go!

He wrote:

*Be brave, Emma! Be brave! I do not want to blight your
life . . .*

– Anyway, that's quite true, thought Rodolphe; I'm acting in
her interest; I'm being straightforward.

*Have you thoroughly pondered your intention? Do you real-
ize to what an abyss I was dragging you, poor angel? No,
you don't, do you? You were going along in blind confidence,
believing in the future . . . Ah! Wretched things that we are,
senseless!*

Here Rodolphe paused to think up some good excuse.

– What if I told her that my money was gone? Ah! No, and

anyway that wouldn't put a stop to it. It would all start up again later. How can you make them listen to reason, women like that?

He thought for a moment, and added:

I shall not forget you, do believe me, and I shall always be deeply devoted to you; but, one day, sooner or later, this ardour (for such is the fate of things human) would have dwindled, no doubt! Weariness would have overtaken us, and who knows but that I might even have known the atrocious pain of witnessing your remorse and of sharing it myself, since I would have been its cause. The very idea of your suffering is a torture to me, Emma! Forget me! Why did I have to meet you? Why were you so beautiful? Is that my fault? Oh my God! No, no, blame only Fate!

– There's a word that always makes an impression, he said to himself.

Ah, if you had been one of those frivolous-hearted women that one meets, I could, from selfishness, have tried an experiment without any risk to you. But that delicious exaltation, which is both your charm and your torment, has prevented you from understanding, adorable woman that you are, the falseness of the position in which we should have found ourselves. Just like you, I did not think about any of this at first, and I was slumbering in the shade of an ideal happiness, just like someone under the poison-tree, without heeding the consequences.

– Perhaps she's going to think that I'm giving it up out of avarice . . . Well, never mind! It's just too bad, let's get it over with!

The world is cruel, Emma. Wherever we went, it would have pursued us. You would have been subjected to prying questions, calumny, disdain, perhaps even insult. You, insulted! And I who wanted to set you on a throne! I who carry the idea of you along with me as a talisman! For I am going into exile to punish myself for the harm I've done to you. I'm leaving. For where? I have no idea, I'm half mad! Farewell! Be ever kind! Cherish the memory of the wretched man who lost you. Teach your child my name, that she may say it over in her prayers.

The two candles were flickering. Rodolphe got up to close the window, and, when he had sat down again:

– Now, I think that's it. Oh, yes, just in case she comes to *flush me out* . . .

I shall be far away when you read these sad lines; for I wanted to make off as quickly as I could to escape the temptation of seeing you again. No weakening! I shall come back; and then, perhaps, we can reminisce together, prosaically, of our obsolete amours. Adieu!

And there was a final *adieu*, as two separate words, *À Dieu!*, which he thought in excellent taste.

– Now, how shall I sign it, he wondered. Yours devotedly . . . No. Your friend? . . . Yes, that's it. *Your friend.*

He reread his letter. It seemed fine to him.

– Poor little woman! he thought, softening a little. She'll think I'm made of stone; it really needs a few tears on it; but I don't have any tears, myself; it's not my fault.

Pouring some water into a glass, Rodolphe dipped in his finger and let a big drop fall off, making a pale smudge in the ink; then, looking for a seal, he came across *Amor nel cor*.

– Not very appropriate . . . oh well, who cares!

Whereupon, he smoked three big pipes and off he went to bed.

Next day, when he got up (it was nearly two o'clock), Rodolphe had them pick him a basket of apricots. He put the letter at the bottom, under some vine-leaves, and told Girard, his ploughman, to carry it carefully to Madame Bovary's house, This was how he used to communicate with her, sending fruit or game, according to the season.

– If she asks after me, he said, tell her I've gone away somewhere. The basket must be given directly to her, into her hands . . . Off you go, and take care!

Girard put on his best smock, knotted his handkerchief over the apricots, and, clumping along in his great iron-tipped clogs, he set off tranquilly down the road to Yonville.

Madame Bovary, when he reached her house, was in the kitchen with Félicité, sorting a bundle of washing on the table.

– There, said the ploughman, the master sends you this here.

She was seized with foreboding, and, searching her pocket for a coin, she fixed on the peasant a haggard look, and he gazed at her in astonishment, baffled that such a gift could so overwhelm anyone. At last he went off. Félicité was still there. She could bear no more; she rushed into the parlour as if to take the apricots, tipped out the basket, tore away the leaves, found the letter, opened it, and, just as if some great fire were raging at her back, Emma fled upstairs to her room, sickening with horror.

Charles was there, she realized; he spoke to her, she didn't hear, and she hurried on up the stairs, out of breath, aghast, befuddled, and still clutching that horrible piece of paper, that rattled in her hand like sheet-metal. On the second landing, she stopped outside the attic door, which was shut.

She wanted now to steady herself; she remembered the letter: it had to be read through, she didn't dare to. Anyway, where, how? They would see her.

– Ah! No, here, she thought, I'll be safe.

Emma pushed the door and went in.

The roof-slates were giving off an intense heat, it crushed her temples, stifling her; she dragged herself across to the roof-shutter, drew back the bolt, and dazzling sunlight flooded through.

Opposite, away across the roof-tops, open country spread as far as the eye could see. Down below, there beneath her, the village-square was empty; the paving-stones glittered, on the houses the weathercocks were still; at the corner of the street, from a lower floor, there came a sort of drowsy humming with strident modulations. It was Binet at his lathe.

She had leaned herself up against the window-frame and was reading the letter again, sneering with rage. But the more she fixed her attention on it, the more her thoughts were blurred. She could see him, she could hear him, she could hold him in her arms; and her heart's poundings, like a great hammer knocking inside her chest, came quick, quicker, in a broken rhythm. She cast her eyes around, waiting for the earth to open. Why not have done with it? Who was to stop her? She was free. And she edged forwards, she looked down at the pavement, saying to herself:

– Do it! Do it!

The ray of light coming up directly from below was tugging the weight of her body towards the abyss. It was just as if the swaying surface of the village-square flowed up into the walls and the floor tilted on its end, rather like a ship pitching about. She was standing right on the edge, almost hanging, swinging in empty space. The blue of the sky invaded her, air was circling in her skull, she had only to let go, to give in; and the snoring of the lathe went on and on, like a voice furiously calling to her.

– Wife! Wife! shouted Charles.

She stopped.

– Where are you? Come on!

The idea that she had just escaped death made her nearly swoon with terror; she closed her eyes, and she shuddered at the touch of a hand upon her sleeve: it was Félicité.

– Monsieur is waiting for you, madame; the soup is served.

And down she had to go! Down to sit at the table!

She tried to eat. The food choked her. So she unfolded her napkin as if to examine the darning and she really tried to become absorbed in this task, counting the threads in the linen. Suddenly, the memory of the letter came back to her. Had she lost it? Where could it be? But she felt such a weariness of spirit that she could not even invent an excuse for leaving the table. Besides, she had turned coward; she was afraid of Charles; he knew all about it, of course! Indeed, he did speak out peculiarly:

– It looks as if we won't be seeing Monsieur Rodolphe for a while.

– Who told you that? she said, with a shudder.

– Who told me? he replied, rather surprised by this abrupt tone of hers; it was Girard, I met him a minute ago just outside the Café Français. He's gone off on his travels, or he's just about to.

Out came her one sob.

– Why are you surprised? He goes off like that from time to time for a change, and, I must say, I don't blame him. If a man has money and he's a bachelor. In fact, he has a splendid time, does our friend. He's a real lad! Monsieur Langlois was telling me . . .

He stopped, discreetly, as the maid came in.

She put back in the basket all the apricots scattered about on the sideboard; Charles, unaware of his wife's blushes, had them brought over, took one and bit into it.

– Ah! Perfect, he said. Here you are, taste one.

And he held out the basket, which she gently pushed away.

– Just smell: how delicious! he said, passing it to and fro under her nose.

– I'm choking! she cried, jumping to her feet.

But, by an effort of will, this spasm passed over.

– It's nothing! she said, it's nothing! Just nerves! You sit down and eat.

For she was dreading his questioning her, fussing over her, never leaving her in peace.

Charles, not to vex her, had sat down, and he was spitting the stones from the apricots into his hand, then putting them on to his plate.

Suddenly, a blue tilbury crossed the square at a brisk trot. Emma shrieked out and fell stiff to the floor, on her back.

Rodolphe, after long thought, had decided to leave for Rouen. Now, since from La Huchette to Buchy there is only the road through Yonville, he had had to pass through the village, and Emma had recognized him in the gleam of the lanterns which flashed like lightning through the twilight.

The pharmacist, hearing the house in uproar, rushed over. The table, and the plates, had been overturned; the gravy, the meat, the knives, the salt-cellar and the oil and vinegar bottles, they were strewn about the room; Charles was calling for help; Berthe, in a fright, was crying; and Félicité, with trembling hands, was unlacing Madame, whose whole body was thrusting in convulsions.

– I'll run to my laboratory, said the apothecary, to get some aromatic vinegar.

As she opened her eyes, sniffing from the bottle:

– There you are, he said; this stuff will raise the dead.

– Speak to me, said Charles, speak to me! Come on! It's me, your Charles who loves you! Don't you recognize me? Look, here's your little girl, give her a hug!

The child held out her arms to clasp her mother's neck. But, turning her head aside, Emma said in a shaking voice:

– No, no . . . nobody!

She fainted once again. They carried her up to bed.

She was lying there stretched out, her mouth open, her eyelids sealed, her fingers straight, immobile, and paler than an image made of wax. From out of her eyes there came two streams of tears flowing slowly down on to the pillow.

Charles, standing upright, was at the back of the alcove, and the pharmacist, at his side, kept up that meditative silence appropriate to life's serious occasions.

– Don't you worry, he said touching his elbow, I think the paroxysm is over.

– Yes, she's resting a bit now! answered Charles, watching her as she slept. Poor woman! . . . Poor woman! . . . The same old trouble!

Then Homais asked how this accident had come about. Charles replied that it had come on suddenly when she was eating some apricots.

– Extraordinary! the pharmacist went on. But it is possible that the apricots caused the syncope! Some types are so sensitive to certain odours! And it would be a fine subject for study, you know, both the pathological aspect as well as the physiological. The priests have realized its importance, they've always employed aromatics in their ceremonies. It's done to dull the understanding and induce ecstasies, something actually quite easy with members of the weaker sex, who are more delicate than we. Some are quoted as fainting at the smell of burned horn, of fresh bread . . .

– Take care not to wake her! said Bovary in a low voice.

– And not only human beings, went on the apothecary, are subject to these anomalies, but animals too. You must, I'm sure, be aware of the singularly aphrodisiac effect produced by *Nepeta cataria*, popularly known as cat-mint, on the feline tribe; and, on the other hand, to quote an example which I vouch as authentic, Bridoux (he's an old schoolfriend of mine, currently set up in the Rue Malapu) has a dog that goes into convulsions as soon as you hold out a snuff-box to him. He often performs the experiment for an audience of friends, at his summer-house in the Bois Guillaume. Would you believe that a simple sternutatory could wreak such havoc on a quadruped organism? It's extremely peculiar, don't you agree?

– Yes, said Charles, not listening.

– It goes to show, the other went on, smiling with an air of benign fatuity, the numberless irregularities of the nervous system. With regard to your lady wife, she has always struck me, I do confess, as especially sensitive. And so, my good friend, I shall certainly not be recommending to you any of those so-called remedies which, under the guise of attacking the symptoms, attack the constitution. No, no otiose medications! Diet, that's the thing! Sedatives, emollients, sweeteners. Don't you think perhaps we ought to work on the imagination?

– In what way? How do you mean? said Bovary.

– Ah! That is the question. That is indeed the question: *c'est là la question!* as I read in the paper the other day.

But Emma, coming to, shouted:

– The letter? The letter?

They thought she might be delirious; by midnight she was: a cerebral fever had set in.

For forty-three days Charles did not leave her. He neglected his patients; he sat up every night, he was constantly taking her pulse, applying sinapisms, cold-water compresses. He sent Justin to Neufchâtel to look for ice; the ice melted on the way; he sent him back again. He called in Monsieur Canivet for a consultation; he had Doctor Larivière, his old professor, come over from Rouen; he was in despair. What alarmed him most was Emma's prostration; she didn't speak, didn't hear anything, hardly even seemed to suffer – as though her body and her soul were both in repose after their agitation.

By about the middle of October, she could sit up in her bed, with pillows behind her. Charles wept when he saw her eating her first piece of bread and jam. Her strength was coming back; she was up for a few hours in the afternoon, and one day when she was feeling better, he tried to take her, on his arm, for a walk around the garden. The gravel paths were disappearing under the dead leaves; step by step she went along, shuffling in her slippers, and, leaning her shoulder on Charles, she kept on smiling.

They reached the end of the garden, close to the terrace. She drew herself up, slowly, lifting her hand to shade her eyes: she gazed into the distance, far away; but on the horizon there were only big grass-fires, smoking on the hills.

– You'll tire yourself, my darling, said Bovary.

And, pushing her gently into the arbour:

– Just you sit down on this bench: you'll be fine.

– Oh! No, not there, not there! she said in a trembling voice.

She was taken dizzy, and, that evening, her illness set in again, a rather less distinct pattern this time, and with more complex symptoms. Sometimes she had pains in her heart, in her chest, her head, her limbs; there was vomiting and here Charles thought he saw the first signs of cancer.

And the poor fellow, on top of all this, was worried about money!

14

In the first place, he had no notion how he was to reimburse Monsieur Homais for all the medicaments supplied from his shop; and though, as a practitioner, he could have had them for nothing, nevertheless he was rather ashamed of this transaction. And the household expenses, now that the cook was in charge, were becoming horrendous; the bills came pouring in; the trades-men were grumbling; Monsieur Lheureux pestered him most of all. Indeed, at the height of Emma's illness, the latter, taking advantage of the situation to inflate his bill, had quickly delivered the cloak, the travelling-bag, two trunks instead of one, a quantity of other things as well. It was no good Charles saying he didn't want them, the draper retorted arrogantly that these items had been ordered from him and he wouldn't take them back; besides, it might vex Madame during her convales-cence; Monsieur ought to reconsider; in short, he was deter-mined to take him to court rather than give up his rights and take away his goods. Charles subsequently ordered them to be sent back to the shop; Félicité forgot; he had other things on his mind; it was overlooked; Monsieur Lheureux was relentless, and, alternately threatening and whining, he manoeuvred in such a way that Bovary ended up signing a bill due in six months' time. But hardly had he signed this bill than a bold idea came to him: it was to borrow a thousand francs from Lheureux. So, he asked, with an embarrassed air, if there were some way of getting the cash, adding that it would be for a year and at whatever rate he wanted. Lheureux ran off to his shop, brought back the money and made out another bill, whereby Bovary undertook to pay on demand, on the first of September next, the sum of one thousand and seventy francs; all of which, with the one hundred and eighty already stipulated, came to just twelve hundred and fifty. So, lending out at six per cent, together with a quarter commission, and the merchandise bringing him a good third, it ought, over twelve months, to give a profit of one hundred and thirty francs; and he was hoping that things would not stop there, that the bills could not be paid off, that they would be renewed, and that his little bit of money, nourished at the doctor's rather like in a nursing-home, would return to him, one day, considerably plumper, and stout enough to split the bag.

Indeed, everything of his was thriving. He'd been given the contract for supplying cider to the hospital at Neufchâtel; Monsieur Guillaumin had promised him some shares in the peat-works at Grumesnil, and he dreamed of setting up a new coach-service between Argueil and Rouen, which would soon, undoubtedly, ruin that old cart run by the Golden Lion, and, travelling faster, costing less, and carrying a bigger load, it would thus bring the entire Yonville trade into his hands.

Charles frequently wondered just how, by next year, he would be able to pay back so much money; and he hunted around, imagining various schemes, such as appealing to his father or selling something. But his father would turn a deaf ear, and he himself had nothing to sell. At this point he discovered such vexations that he quickly pushed to the back of his mind a topic so unpleasant to contemplate. He reproached himself with forgetting about Emma; just as if, with his every thought

belonging to this woman, it would have been swindling her out
of something not to have her perpetually in mind.

The winter was harsh. Madame's convalescence was slow.
When it was fine, they moved her in her armchair near to the
window, the one that looked on to the square, for she had now
taken a dislike to the garden, and the blinds on that side stayed
down the whole time. She wanted the horse to be sold; everything she had once loved she now disliked. Her thoughts seemed
confined to nursing herself. She stayed in her bed, eating little
snacks, rang for her maid to ask her about herb teas or simply
for a chat. Meanwhile, the snow on the market-roof filled the
room with a white light, unwavering; after, it was the rain
falling. And Emma awaited each day, with a kind of anxiety,
the unfailing circle of little events, though they scarcely concerned her. The most remarkable was, every evening, the arrival
of the *Hirondelle*. The innkeeper would be shouting and other
voices answering her, while Hippolyte's lantern, as he looked
out trunks on the roof, was like a star in the darkness. At noon,
Charles came back; later, he went out again; next she would
have some broth, and, around five o'clock, in the twilight, the
children coming home from school, scraping their clogs along
the pavement, used to rap their rulers on the shutter-hooks, one
after the other.

This was the time of day when Monsieur Bournisien came to
see her. He would ask after her health, bring her the news and
exhort her to religious thoughts in a cosy little chit-chat that
was really quite appealing. Just the sight of his soutane was a
comfort to her.

One day, at the climax of her illness, when she thought she
was dying, she had asked for communion; and, while they
were making her room ready for the sacrament, arranging her
bedside-table cluttered with medicine bottles as an altar, and
Félicité was scattering dahlia petals on the floor, Emma felt
some powerful thing sweeping over her, delivering her from
pain, from all perception, from all feeling. Her flesh lay down
its burden of thought, another life was beginning; to her it
seemed that her soul, rising towards God, would be annihilated
in His love, just like burning incense as it goes up in smoke.

Holy water was sprinkled on the sheets of her bed; the priest took the white wafer from the holy ciborium; and she was swooning with a celestial joy as she parted her lips to receive the body of the Saviour offered to her. The curtains over her alcove swelled out gently around her, rather like clouds, and the rays from the two candles burning on the bedside-table seemed to her eyes like dazzling haloes. She let her head drop back, fancying that she heard upon the air the music of the harps of seraphim, that she glimpsed in a sky of blue, upon a throne of gold, God the Father, resplendent and majestical, and with a sign He was sending to earth angels on wings of fire to carry her off in their arms.

This splendid vision endured in her memory as the most beautiful thing it was possible to dream; and even now she struggled to recapture the sensation, which somehow lingered on, though less intense yet just as delectable. Her soul, wearied by pride, was at last finding rest in Christian humility; and, savouring the pleasure of weakness, Emma contemplated within herself the destruction of her will, leaving thus wide an entrance for the irruption of His grace. So in place of happiness there did exist a higher felicity, a further love above all other loves, without intermission or ending, a love that would blossom eternally! She glimpsed, amid the illusions of her hope, a state of purity floating above the earth, mingling into the sky, where she aspired to be. She wanted to become a saint. She bought rosaries, she wore amulets; she yearned to have in her room, at the head of her bed, a reliquary set in emeralds, that she might kiss it every night.

The priest marvelled at these propensities, even though Emma's religion could, he recognized, in its fervour, end up close to heresy and even extravagance. But, not being very well versed in these matters, beyond a certain point, he wrote to Monsieur Boulard, bookseller to the archbishop, asking for *something decent for one of the fair sex with a good head on her shoulders*. The bookseller, as indifferently as if he were shipping kitchen hardware to negroes, threw together a parcel of everything recent in the way of pious literature. There were little question-and-answer manuals, dogmatic pamphlets in the style of de Maistre, and various novels in pink bindings and a sugary style, churned out by troubador seminarists or penitent bluestockings. There was *Pensez-y bien; l'Homme du monde aux pieds de Marie, par M. de —, décoré de plusieurs ordres; des Erreurs de Voltaire, à l'usage des jeunes gens,* etc.[23]

Madame Bovary was not yet clear-headed enough to be applying herself seriously to anything; indeed, she went at this reading in too great a hurry. She was irritated by the ritual ordinances; the arrogance of the polemical writings displeased her by their relentless carping at people she had never heard of; and the secular tales spiced with religion seemed written in such ignorance of the world that they imperceptibly diverted her from the verities she was expecting to have proved. She persisted, though, and, when the volume fell from her hands, she thought herself seized with the finest Catholic melancholy that ever an ethereal soul could conceive of.

As for the memory of Rodolphe, she had lodged it down in the very depths of her heart; and there he lay, more majestic and more serene than the anointed corpse of a king deep-entombed. A vapour seeped from out of this embalmed passion, permeating everything, scenting with tenderness the immaculate atmosphere in which she wished to dwell. Whenever she went to kneel at her Gothic prie-dieu, she called upon her Lord in the same sweet words she had once murmured to her lover, in the raptures of adultery. It was meant to arouse faith; but no delectation descended from on high; and she got to her feet, her limbs heavy, with the vague sense that it was just a great hoax. This quest was, she thought, all the more to her credit, and, in the pride of her godliness Emma compared herself with the great ladies of old, they whose glory she had dreamed of over a portrait of La Vallière, those who, so majestically trailing the bespangled flounces of their long gowns, had retreated into solitude, there to shed at the feet of Christ the tears of a heart wounded by the world.

Henceforth she dedicated herself to lavish works of charity. She sewed clothes for the poor; she sent firewood to women in child-bed; and Charles, coming home one day, found three tramps at the kitchen-table eating soup. She fetched home her little girl, whom her husband, during her illness, had sent to stay with the nurse. She wanted to teach her to read; Berthe could cry her fill, she showed no impatience. Her mind was fixed in resignation, in universal indulgence. Her language was habitually full of ideal expressions. She said to her child:

– Has your tummy-ache gone, my angel?

The elder Madame Bovary found no cause for criticism, except perhaps this maniacal knitting of vests for orphans, instead of mending her dusters. But, harassed as she was by domestic quarrels, the dear lady was happy to be in this quiet house, and she even stayed on until just after Easter, to escape the sarcasms of old Bovary who never forgot, on Good Fridays, to order a fat pork sausage.

Apart from the company of her mother-in-law, who steadied her a little by the rectitude of her opinions and her sober manner, Emma, nearly every day, had other visitors too. There was Madame Langlois, Madame Caron, Madame Dubreuil, Madame Tuvache, and, regularly from two until five, the excellent Madame Homais, who had never, personally, believed any of the tattle everyone was putting round about her neighbour. And the Homais children came to see her, along with Justin. He would go up to her room with them, and stand near the door, motionless, taciturn. Madame Bovary would quite often, unaware of him, sit down at her dressing-table. First she took out her comb, shaking her head with a quick gesture; and when he first saw it, that great mass of hair falling right down to her knees, the dark ringlets uncoiling, it was for him, poor boy, like a sudden initiation into something new and extraordinary, a splendour that set him trembling.

Emma, most likely, did not notice his dedicated silences or his timidities. She had no idea that love, vanished from her life, was pulsing there, by her side, beneath that coarse shirt, in that adolescent heart so open to the emanations of her beauty. Besides, she now enfolded everything in such indifference, her words were so tender and her looks so haughty, her moods so fleeting, that it was difficult to tell her egotism from her charity, her corruption from her virtue. One evening, for instance, she lost her temper with her maid, who was asking her if she could go out, stammering as she fumbled for an excuse; and abruptly, she said:

– Do you love him?

And, without waiting for an answer from Félicité, who was blushing, she added mournfully:

– Go on! Off with you! Enjoy yourself!

In the early spring, she had the whole garden turned upside-down, in spite of Bovary's objections; he was glad, even so, to see her at last taking an interest in something. She became ever more decisive as her health improved. First, she managed to evict Mère Rolet, the wet-nurse, who, during her convalescence, had taken to visiting the kitchen rather frequently along with her two babies and her lodger, who ate like a horse. Next she shook off the Homais family, turned away all the other visitors one after another and even frequented the church less assiduously, to the great approbation of the apothecary, who now remarked amiably:

– You were getting rather a taste for holy water!

Monsieur Bournisien, as usual, dropped in every day, on his way from catechism. He preferred to stay outside, taking the air *in the grove*; for so he called the arbour. This was the time Charles always came home. They were hot; sweet cider was brought out, and together they drank to Madame's complete recovery.

Binet would be there; just a bit further down the river, against the terrace wall, after crayfish. Bovary invited him to quench his thirst, and he was a great expert on the uncorking of stone bottles.

– The thing to do, he would say with his eye wandering contentedly around him even as far as the horizon, is to hold the bottle up straight on the table, like this, and, once the strings are cut, you have to push the cork very slowly, gently, gently, you see, just as they do with the seltzer-water in a restaurant.

But the cider, during his demonstration, often spurted out all over their faces, and the churchman, with a thick laugh, always made the same joke:

– The goodness smacks you in the eye!

He was a nice chap, obviously, and even, one day, he was not a bit shocked by the pharmacist, who advised Charles, for the amusement of Madame, to take her to the theatre in Rouen to see the famous tenor Lagardy. Homais, surprised by this silence, wanted to have his opinion, and the priest declared that he regarded music as less of a moral danger than literature.

But the pharmacist went to the defence of letters. The theatre, he claimed, helped to dislodge fixed ideas and, behind the mask of pleasure, taught virtue.

– *Castigat ridendo mores*,[24] Monsieur Bournisien! Just consider most of Voltaire's tragedies; they are ingeniously strewn with philosophical reflections which make them a veritable school for the people in morals and diplomacy.

– Now I, said Binet, once saw a play called *Le Gamin de Paris*, where you have this character . . . He really gives it to a little rich boy who had seduced a working-girl, who in the end . . .

– Certainly! continued Homais, there is bad literature just as there is bad pharmacy; but to condemn wholesale the most important of the fine arts strikes me as asinine, a barbarous idea, worthy of the infamous century that put Galileo in prison.

– I know very well, objected the priest, that there is good writing, good authors; even so, if only for the fact of persons of a different sex gathered in elegant surroundings, gilded with worldly pomp, and those heathen disguises, the grease-paint, the torch-light, the effeminate voices, in the end it begets a certain libertine mood and inspires unclean thoughts, impure longings. That at least is the opinion of all the Fathers. Ultimately, he added, adopting a tone of voice suddenly mystical, while he rolled a pinch of snuff on his thumb, if the Church has condemned theatrical shows, it's because she knows best; we must bow down to her decrees.

– Why, asked the apothecary, does she excommunicate actors? For, in the past, they used to take part openly in religious ceremonies. Oh, yes, they used to act, they performed in the middle of the chancel a kind of farce called a mystery, in which the laws of decency were often transgressed.

The ecclesiastic confined himself to venting a groan, and the pharmacist persisted:

– The Bible is just the same; there are . . . you know . . . some rather juicy . . . details, things . . . really . . . tasty.

And, seeing Monsieur Bournisien's gesture of irritation:

– Ah! You would agree that it isn't a book to put into the hands of any young person, and I should be vexed if Athalie . . .

– But it's the Protestants, and not us, shouted the other impatiently, who recommend the Bible!

– No matter! said Homais, I'm surprised, in this day and age, in this enlightened century, that anyone still persists in denouncing an intellectual relaxation which is inoffensive, morally sound and sometimes even hygienic, not so, doctor?

– Of course, answered the doctor nonchalantly, for either he had the same ideas, and wished to avoid offending anyone, or else he had no ideas at all.

The conversation seemed at an end, when the pharmacist saw fit to try a parting shot.

– Some I've known, priests I mean, who dress up in ordinary clothes to go and watch dancing-girls wiggling about!

– Come on! said the priest.

– Ah! Some I've known!

And, separating each syllable of the phrase, Homais repeated:

– Some-I-have-known.

– All right! They were in the wrong, said Bournisien, resigned to hearing the rest.

– By heck! It doesn't end there! proclaimed the apothecary.

– Monsieur! put in the churchman, with eyes so wild that the pharmacist was intimidated.

– I simply mean, he now replied in a less brutal tone, that tolerance is the surest way to draw hearts to the Church.

– How true! How true! the fellow conceded, sitting down on his chair again.

But he stayed only a few more minutes. As soon as he had gone, Monsieur Homais said to the doctor:

– Now that was what's called a rumpus! I really had him, you saw us, the whole way! . . . Anyhow, look here, you take Madame to the show, if only once in your life, to vex one of those old crows, by God! If anyone could fill in for me, I'd be coming with you myself. Hurry up! Lagardy's only giving the one performance; he's booked in England for a substantial fee. From what they tell me, he's a real lad! Rolling in money! Takes three mistresses and his chef around with him! Those great artists they burn the candle at both ends; they need a life of debauchery to excite the old imagination. But they die in the workhouse, because they don't have the sense, when they're young, to put a bit away. Well, enjoy dinner; see you soon!

This theatre idea germinated fast in Bovary's mind; for he mentioned it to his wife at once; she refused at first, pointing out the fatigue, the worry, the expense; but, extraordinarily, Charles insisted, so convinced was he that the excursion must be beneficial for her. He could see no obstacle; his mother had sent them three hundred francs which he had stopped counting on, the immediate debts were nothing enormous, and it was so long until he had to pay off old Lheureux's bills that there was no point in worrying. Indeed, imagining that she was only being tactful, Charles insisted the more; until in the end, after much coaxing, she made up her mind. And, next morning, at eight o'clock, they lurched off in the *Hirondelle*.

The apothecary, whom nothing kept in Yonville, though he was quite convinced that he must not budge from home, sighed as he saw them going.

– Safe journey! he called to them, lucky creatures that you are!

Then, turning to Emma, who was wearing a blue silk dress with four flounces:

– You look pretty as a picture! You'll be the *talk of the town* in Rouen.

The diligence set them down at the Hôtel de la Croix Rouge, on the Place Beauvoisine. It was one of those inns you always find on the outskirts of a country town, with large stables and small bedrooms, where you see hens in the middle of the yard pecking at the oats under the mud-caked cabriolets of the commercial travellers; – good old hostelries, with worm-eaten balconies that creak in the wind on a winter night, continually full of people, and racket and fodder, the black tables all sticky with coffee and whisky, the thick window-panes yellowed with flies, the damp napkins stained with cheap red wine; smelling of the countryside, like farmhands in their Sunday-best suits, with a café on the street and a vegetable garden at the back.

Charles, immediately, went off to buy the tickets. He got the stalls mixed up with the gallery, the pit with the boxes, asked for advice which he found incomprehensible, was sent from the box office to the manager, returned to the inn, and, several times, measured the whole length of the town, from the theatre to the boulevard.

Madame bought herself a hat, a pair of gloves, a bouquet. Monsieur worried dreadfully about missing the beginning; and, without even stopping to gulp down a plate of soup, they turned up at the theatre door, only to find it locked.

15

The crowd was lining up along the wall, fenced in symmetrically between the railings. On every street corner gigantic posters in baroque lettering recited: LUCIA DI LAMMERMOOR . . . [25] LAGARDY . . . OPERA . . ., etc. The sun was out; now it was hot; ringlets were running with sweat, handkerchiefs were fetched out for mopping red faces; and sometimes a warm breeze, blowing from off the river, gently stirred the fringes of the drill-cotton awnings hung from the doors of the taverns. A little lower down, though, there was freshness in a stream of ice-cold air that smelled of tallow, leather and oil. It emanated from the Rue des Charrettes, with all its big dark warehouses where barrels are rolled about.

For fear of looking ridiculous there, Emma fancied a stroll along the quay before they went in, and Bovary, prudently, kept the tickets in his hand, in a trouser-pocket, pressed to his stomach.

Her heart began to beat once she was in the foyer. She smiled quite obliviously, out of vanity, seeing the crowd rushing down the corridor to the right, as she was climbing the stairs, to the dress circle. She took a childish delight in pushing open the large upholstered doors with her finger; keenly she breathed down the dusty smell of the corridors, and, once she was sitting in her box, she arched her back with the insolence of a duchess.

The house was beginning to fill up, lorgnettes were being taken out of their cases, and the regulars, catching sight of each other, exchanged little greetings. They were there to seek some respite in the fine arts from the cares of business; but money was ever uppermost, and they were still talking about cotton, liquor or indigo. There you saw the old men's faces, expressionless and peaceful, with their white hair and their pale skin, looking like so many silver medals tarnished in fumes of lead. Stylish young men were strutting around the stalls, displaying, in the opening of the waistcoat, a cravat in pink or apple-green; and Madame Bovary was admiring them from above, leaning upon their gold-topped walking-canes with the smooth palms of yellow gloves.

But now the orchestra candles were lit; the chandelier was let down from the ceiling, spreading a flash of gaiety across the house from its sparkling crystals; the musicians came in one after another, and at first there was an immense racket of snorting double-basses, squeaking violins, blaring trombones, chirping flutes and flageolets. But three taps were heard from the stage; there began a rolling of drums, loud chords from the brass, and the curtain, rising, revealed a country landscape.

There was a crossways in a wood, with a fountain, on the left, shaded by an oak-tree. Peasants and lords, with plaids over their shoulders, were singing a hunting-song in chorus; there came a captain who invoked the Angel of Darkness by lifting both arms to heaven; another appeared; they left the stage, and the huntsmen resumed their song.

She found herself back in the books of her youth, deep in Walter Scott. She seemed to hear, through the mist, the sound of bagpipes, echoing across the moorland. Because her memories of the novel helped her to understand the libretto, she followed the plot phrase by phrase, while the thoughts that came to her were instantly scattered again by the blast of the music. She yielded to the rippling of the melodies and she felt herself trembling all over, as though the bows of the violins were being drawn across her nerves. Two eyes were not enough to take in the costumes, the scenery, the characters, the painted trees that shook when anyone walked past, and the velvet caps, the cloaks, the swords, that whole imaginary world pulsing to the music as though in the atmosphere of some other realm. But a young woman stepped forwards and threw a purse to a squire in green. There she stood alone, and now a flute was playing, like the murmur of a fountain or like the warbling of a bird. Lucia embarked gravely upon her cavatina in G major; she bewailed love's pangs, she cried aloud for wings. Emma, like her, was yearning to escape, to fly ecstatically aloft. Suddenly, Edgar Lagardy appeared.

He had that splendid pallor of the sort that bestows something of the majesty of antique marble upon the ardent races of the south. His powerful frame was tightly clad in a brown doublet; a small engraved dagger swung at his left thigh, and he rolled his eyes languorously, uncovering his white teeth. It was said that a Polish princess had fallen in love with him, listening to him sing, one evening on the beach at Biarritz, where he worked mending boats. She had thrown away everything for him. He had cast her off for other women, and his renown as a lover had infallibly enhanced his reputation as an artist. This artful performer even saw to it that some poetic phrase about the fascination of his person and the sensitivity of his soul was slipped into the playbills. A fine voice, imperturbable aplomb, more personality than intelligence and more affectation than true passion, all went towards the admirable power of this charlatan, a combination of the hairdresser and the toreador.

From his first scene, he cast a spell. He clasped Lucia in his arms, he left her, he returned, he seemed in despair: he bellowed in anger, he moaned elegies of infinite tenderness, and the notes poured from his bare throat, full of sobs and kisses. Emma leaned forwards to see him, sinking her fingernails into the velvet on her box. She crammed her heart with those lingering melodious lamentations accompanied on the double-bass, that were like the cries of the drowning in the tumult of a tempest. She recognized the exaltation and the anguish of which she had almost perished. The voice of the heroine seemed to be simply the echo of her own consciousness, and this enthralling illusion might almost have been contrived from the very stuff of her life.

But no earthly creature had loved her with a love such as this. He had not cried like Edgar, on their final evening in the moonlight, when they said, 'Until tomorrow, until tomorrow!' The house was ringing with cries of bravo; they did the whole finale over again; the lovers spoke of the flowers on their tomb, of vows, exile, Fate, hope, and, when they called their last adieu, Emma let out a sharp cry, that merged into the trembling of the final chords.

– But why, asked Bovary, is that lord set on tormenting her?

– No, no, she replied; that's her lover.

– But he's swearing vengeance on her family, whereas the other one, the one that was on just now, said, 'I love Lucia and I believe she loves me.' Anyway, he went off with her father, arm in arm. That is her father, isn't it, the ugly little one with the cock's feather in his hat?

In spite of Emma's explanations, once they reached the duet where Gilbert unveils his vile schemes to his master Ashton, Charles, seeing the false engagement-ring meant to trick Lucia, thought it was a love-token from Edgar. He confessed, anyway, that he didn't understand the story – because of the music, which almost drowned out the words.

– Does it matter? said Emma. Just be quiet!

– You know me, he said, leaning over her shoulder, what I'm like, I need to be in the know.

– Oh, do be quiet! she said impatiently.

Lucia came forward, half carried by her women, a wreath of orange-blossom in her hair, paler than her white satin gown. Emma was dreaming of her wedding-day; and she could see herself again, back in the corn-fields, on the little footpath, walking to the church. So why had she not, like that woman down there, resisted, entreated? Far from it, she had been delighted, oblivious of the abyss that lay not far ahead. If only, in the freshness of her beauty, before the blight of marriage and the disillusion of adultery, she could have founded her life upon some great and solid heart, then, with virtue, tenderness, sensuality and duty in harmony, never once would she have stooped from such high felicity. But such a happiness was, of course, the merest fraud, contrived to tease desire into despair. For now she knew the pettiness of the passions that art exaggerates. Struggling to turn her thoughts elsewhere, Emma resolved to see no more in this image of her sorrows than a supple fantasy apt to trick the eye, and she was even smiling to herself in scornful pity when, at the back of the stage, from under the velvet hangings, a man appeared in a cloak of black.

His big Spanish hat was cast aside in one gesture; and immediately both orchestra and singers embarked on the sextet. Edgar, sparkling with fury, eclipsed the others with his clear tenor; Ashton on a deeper note hurled homicidal provocations at him; Lucia uttered her shrill lament; Arthur modulated aside in the middle register, and the bass-baritone of the minister rang out like an organ, while the women's voices, repeating his words, sang in chorus, deliciously. They were standing in a row, gesticulating; anger, vengeance, jealousy, terror, pity and astonishment came forth together from their half-open mouths. The outraged lover brandished his naked sword: his lace ruff twitched up and down, to the heaving of his chest, and he went to the left and the right, striding out, jangling across the boards with the silver-gilt spurs on his soft boots, the kind that flare out at the ankles. There must be in him, she thought, a prodigious love, to be lavished upon the crowd in such great helpings. Her every mocking impulse vanished as the poetry of the role took possession of her, and, drawn to the man by the mirage of the character, she tried to imagine his life, that life of dazzling extraordinary splendour, the life that could have been hers, if only fate had willed it so. They would have met, they would have loved! With him, through all the kingdoms of Europe, she would have journeyed from capital to capital, sharing his weariness and his triumph, gathering the flowers thrown for him, embroidering his costumes herself; every evening, at the back of a box, behind the gold mesh screen, she would have savoured, ravenously, each effusion of the soul that was singing for her alone; from the stage, as he sang, he would be looking at her. A mad idea came to her: he was looking at her, she was sure of it. She yearned to fly into his arms, to find shelter in his strength, as if in love's highest incarnation, and to say to him, to cry aloud, 'Take me, take me away, away! For you, for you! All my longings and all my dreams!'

And the curtain came down.

The smell of gas mingled with stale breath; the waving of fans made the air even more stifling. Emma wanted to get out; people were crowding the corridors, and she sank back into her seat with suffocating palpitations. Charles, worrying that she was about to faint, rushed off to the buffet to fetch her a glass of barley-water.

He had real difficulty in getting back to his seat, his elbows were jogged at every step, because of the glass he was holding in both hands, and he even spilt three quarters of it over the shoulders of a Rouen lady in a short-sleeved gown, who, feeling the cold liquid trickle down her back, screeched like a peacock, as if she were being assassinated. Her husband, the owner of a textile-mill, was furious with the great oaf; and, while she was dabbing with a handkerchief at the stains on her splendid cherry-pink taffeta gown, he was muttering in a surly tone the words compensation, expense, reimbursement. At last, Charles reached his wife again, gasping for breath as he spoke to her:

– Good grief, I thought I'd never make it back! Absolutely packed, it is! . . .

He added:

– You'll never guess who I bumped into up there! Monsieur Léon!

– Léon?

– The man himself! He's on his way over to pay his respects to you.

And, as he spoke these words, the old clerk from Yonville came into the box.

He held out his hand with the casual air of a gentleman: and Madame Bovary, mechanically, offered hers, yielding no doubt to the fascination of a stronger will. She had not felt like this since that spring evening when the rain was falling on the green leaves, when they were saying their farewells, standing at the window. But, quickly, reminding herself what the situation required, she struggled to shake off this drowsiness of things past and she began to stammer out a few hasty phrases.

– Oh, good evening . . . What a nice surprise!

– Quiet! shouted a voice from the pit, for the third act was beginning.

– You're in Rouen now?

– Yes.

– And how long has it been?

– Out! Out! Out!

People were turning to look at them; they fell silent.

But, from that moment, she listened no more; and the chorus of wedding-guests, the scene between Ashton and his servant, the great duet in D major, it seemed to be happening at a distance, as if the instruments had become less sonorous and the characters more remote: she was remembering the card-games at the pharmacist's and the walk to the wet-nurse, the reading in the arbour, the quiet talks by the fireside, that poor love, so calm and so long, so discreet, so tender, and she had forgotten about it. Why was it coming back? What chain of events was bringing him into her life once again? He was standing behind her, his shoulder leaning against the partition; and, every so often, she felt herself shiver as his warm breath played upon her hair.

– Are you enjoying this? he said, leaning over her, so close that the tip of his moustache brushed across her cheek. She replied nonchalantly:

– Oh, goodness me, no! Not really.

He suggested they might leave the theatre, to go for an ice somewhere.

– Oh, not yet! Hold on! said Bovary. She has her hair down: something tragic coming up, I expect.

But the mad scene didn't interest Emma in the slightest, and she thought the heroine was overacting.

– She's too loud, she said, turning to Charles, who was all ears.

– Yes . . . I suppose so . . . just a little, he answered, torn between his own spontaneous pleasure and the respect he felt for his wife's opinions.

Léon said with a sigh:

– This heat . . .

– Unbearable! I do agree.

– Is it bothering you? asked Bovary.

– Yes, I'm stifling: time to go.

Delicately Monsieur Léon placed over her shoulders the long shawl made of lace, and they went all three to sit by the harbour, in the open, outside a café.

Their first topic was her illness, though Emma interrupted Charles now and again, for fear, she said, of boring Monsieur Léon; and the latter told them how he had come to spend two years in Rouen with a big law firm, so as to learn the ropes, very different in Normandy from things in Paris. He asked after Berthe, the Homais family, Mère Lefrançois; and, since they had, in her husband's presence, nothing more to say to each other, the conversation soon came to an end.

People coming from the theatre walked along the pavement, humming softly or yelling boisterously: 'Oh, sweet angel, my Lucia!' And Léon, to show off his passion for music, began to talk about opera. He had seen Tamburini, Rubini, Persiani, Grisi; and compared to them, Lagardy, for all his grandiosity, was nothing.

– Just the same, Charles broke in, sipping at his rum sorbet, they say he is quite superb in the last act; I do regret leaving before the end, just when I was beginning to enjoy myself.

– Anyway, said the clerk, he'll soon be giving another performance.

But Charles said they were going home again next morning.

– Unless, he added, turning to his wife, you would like to stay on alone, my pussy-cat?

And, changing his tactics at this unexpected opportunity which roused his hopes, the young man began to extol Lagardy in the final scene. It was something superb, sublime! Now Charles insisted.

– You can come back on Sunday. Now then. Make up your mind. Silly to say no if you feel it might do you even a tiny bit of good.

Meanwhile the tables, all around, were being cleared; a waiter came and stood discreetly near them; Charles, taking the hint, got out his purse; the clerk put a hand upon his arm, and even remembered to leave, extra, two silver coins, clinking them down on the marble.

– I'm really not very happy, mumbled Bovary, with you spending . . .

The other gave a lordly wave of great cordiality, and, picking up his hat:

– That's agreed, isn't it, tomorrow at six?

Charles announced once more that he couldn't be away any longer; but nothing prevented Emma . . .

– The thing is . . ., she murmured with an odd smile, I'm not really . . .

– Well, think it over, we'll see how it looks in the morning.

Then, to Léon, who was walking with them:

– And now that you're back in this part of the world, I do so hope that you'll call on us, now and again, for dinner.

The clerk declared that he most certainly would, especially as he needed to be in Yonville on some legal business. And they parted company by the Passage Saint-Herbland, just as half past eleven was striking from the cathedral.

Part Three

Monsieur Léon, as a law student, had been quite a visitor to the Paris dance-halls, where he had even done rather well with the girls, who thought he *looked distinguished*. He was a most sensible student: he wore his hair neither too long nor too short, didn't run through his term's allowance on the first of the month, and kept on good terms with his teachers. As regards dissipation, he had always abstained, as much from pusillanimity as from fastidiousness.

Often, when he stayed in his room reading, or when he sat of an evening under the lime-trees in the Luxembourg Gardens, he would let his law book fall to the ground, and the memory of Emma would come back to him. But gradually this feeling had begun to wane, and other cravings were now piled upon it, even though it endured; for Léon did not lose hope entirely, and there was in his mind a sort of vague promise floating somewhere in the future, like a golden apple hanging from some fabulous tree.

Now, seeing her again, after three years absence, his passion came back to life. He must, he thought, set his mind this time on having her. His timidity had been swept away by wild company, and he came back to the provinces full of scorn for all who had never walked the asphalt boulevard in patent-leather shoes. Faced with a Parisian lady dressed in lace, in the salon of some illustrious physician, a celebrity with medals and a carriage, the lowly clerk would, no doubt, have been trembling like a child; but here, in Rouen, on the quayside, with the wife of this paltry little doctor, he was quite confident of making a splendid impression. Aplomb depends on the time and the place: the language of the drawing-room is not the language of the attic, and rich women seem to have about them, to protect their virtue, all of their bank-notes, rather like a cuirass, in the lining of their corsets.

The evening before, after parting from Monsieur and Madame Bovary, Léon had followed them, at a distance, along the street; and having seen them stop at the Croix Rouge, he had turned about and spent the whole night meditating a plan.

Next day, at about five o'clock, he walked into the kitchen of the inn, his throat tightening, his cheeks pale, resolute in the fashion of the poltroon who stops at nothing.

– Monsieur is not in, a servant told him.

That seemed to augur well. Up he went.

She was not alarmed by his arrival; on the contrary, she apologized to him for having forgotten to tell him where they were staying.

– Oh, I guessed! said Léon.

He declared that he had been guided to her by chance, by an instinct. She began to smile, and immediately, to retrieve his blunder, Léon described how he had spent his morning searching for her at every single hotel in the town.

– So you decided to stay? he added.

– Yes, she said, and that was a mistake. No point in acquiring impossible tastes, when one has countless responsibilities . . .

– Oh, I can imagine . . .

– Oh, no! You, you're not a woman.

But men had their troubles, and the conversation set off with various philosophical reflections. Emma held forth on the miseries of earthly love and the eternal isolation that everlastingly entombs the heart.

Whether to make an impression, or whether in a naïve imitation of her melancholy, the young man declared that he had been prodigiously bored all the time he was a student. Legal formalities annoyed him, other professions attracted him, and his mother, in every letter, never stopped harassing him. So they went on, each explaining more and more of the reason for their sorrow, feeling, as they spoke, the excitement of these progressive mutual confidences. But often they stopped short of giving a full account of their thoughts, and tried to invent some phrase that could convey it anyway. She did not confess her passion for another man; he did not mention how he had forgotten her.

Perhaps he did not remember anything about his suppers eaten after the ball, with dancing-girls; and no doubt she did not recall any of those assignations, when she used to run across the morning fields, on the way to her lover's house. The sounds of the city scarcely reached them there; and the very room seemed small, the better to fasten them in alone together. Emma, in a cotton dressing-gown, was leaning her chignon against the old armchair; the yellow wallpaper was like a golden ground behind her; and her bare head was repeated in the glass, with the white parting down the middle, and the tips of her ears showing beneath the smoothly gathered hair.

– Forgive me, though, she said, it's not right. I'm boring you with my eternal troubles.

– No, not at all. Not at all.

– If you but knew, she went on, lifting her beautiful eyes to the ceiling, as a tear came, the dreams I've had.

– And I have too. How I've suffered! Many a time I would take off, plod along by the river, to addle my brain with the noise of the crowd, yet quite powerless to banish the obsession that was hounding me. On the boulevard, in a print-shop, there's an Italian engraving of one of the Muses. She's draped in a tunic and she's looking at the moon, with forget-me-nots in her unbound hair. There was something incessantly urging me to her; I've stood there for hours at a time.

Then, in a trembling voice:

– She looked rather like you.

Madame Bovary turned her face aside, to hide from him the irresistible smile she felt coming to her lips.

– Often, he went on, I used to write letters to you and tear them up.

She said nothing. He carried on.

– I used to imagine sometimes that an accident would bring you to me. I thought that I saw you at the corner of the street;

and I used to run along after any of the carriages that had a
shawl or a veil fluttering at the window like yours . . .

She seemed determined to let him speak without interruption.
Folding her arms and looking down, she was staring at the
rosettes on her slippers, and gently wriggling her toes, every so
often, inside the satin.

Eventually she gave a sigh:

– The most deplorable thing, surely, is to drag out a life as
useless as mine. If our miseries were only of use to some other
creature, there would be consolation in the thought of sacrifice!

He set off in praise of virtue, duty and silent immolation,
confessing to an extraordinary need for self-devotion which he
could never satisfy.

– I would very much like, she said, to be a Sister of Mercy.

– Alas, he replied, for men there are no sacred missions of
that sort, and nowhere can I see any vocation . . . unless perhaps
that of a doctor . . .

With a slight shrug of her shoulders, Emma interrupted him
to bemoan the illness that had nearly killed her; what a shame!
She would not have been suffering now. Léon instantly longed
for *the quiet of the grave*, and actually, one evening, he had made
his will, specifying that he was to be buried in that beautiful rug
with the velvet stripes, the one that she had given him; for that
was how they wanted it to have been, each of them now devising
for the other an ideal rearrangement of their past Language is
indeed a machine that continually amplifies the emotions.

But at this story of the rug, she asked:

– Why did you?

– Why?

He hesitated.

– Because I loved you so dearly!

And, congratulating himself on this bold move, Léon, from
the corner of his eye, watched her expression.

It was just like the sky, when a puff of wind sweeps away the
clouds. The burden of sadness that dimmed her blue eyes seemed
to be lifted; her whole face was shining.

He waited. At last she replied:

– I always suspected . . .

Now, they recounted the little events of that far-away time;
the pleasures and the pains, epitomized for them, just now, in
that single word. They remembered the arbour with the clematis,
the dresses that she wore, the furniture in her room, her entire
house.

– And our poor cactuses, where are they?

– Frost killed them off last winter.

– Oh, I did used to think of them, you know. Many's the time
I'd picture them, on a summer evening, with the sun beating on
the blinds, and a glimpse of your bare arms moving among the
plants.

– You poor thing! she said, holding out her hand to him.

Léon, deftly, pressed it to his lips. And, when he had taken a
deep breath:

– For me you were, in those days, some kind of fascinating
incomprehensible force. Once, for instance, I came to see you;
but you don't remember that, I suppose?

– I do, she said. Go on.

– You were downstairs, in the hall, ready to go out, on the
bottom-step; – you were even wearing a hat with little blue
flowers; and, without any invitation from you, quite in spite of
myself, I went along with you. Every moment, though, I was
more and more aware of my foolishness, and I kept near to you,
not quite daring to follow you, and not wanting to leave you.
When you went into a shop, I stood out in the street, I watched
you through the window undoing your gloves and counting the
change on the counter. You rang at Madame Tuvache's, they
let you in, and I stood there like an idiot at the great big door,
after it closed behind you.

Madame Bovary, as she listened, was astonished at being so
old; these things reappearing seemed to enlarge her existence;
they created a kind of sentimental infinity for her to visit in
her mind; and every so often, with her eyes half closed, she
murmured:

– Yes, that's right . . . that's right . . . that's right . . .

They heard it striking eight on all the different clocks of the
Beauvoisine quarter, which is full of boarding-schools, churches
and large deserted mansions. They had fallen silent; but they

felt, eyeing each other, a buzzing in their heads, as if something audible had emanated from their fixed mutual gaze. Now they were hand in hand; the past and the future, reminiscence and reverie, were now melting together in the sweetness of that ecstasy. Darkness was gathering along the walls, where, half lost in the shadows, there flared the crude colours of four prints representing four scenes from *La Tour de Nesle*,[1] with a text below in Spanish and French. Through the sash-window, they could see a scrap of dark sky between pointed roofs.

She got up to light a pair of candles on the chest of drawers, then she came to sit down again.

– Well . . ., said Léon.

– Well? she answered.

And he was wondering how to resume the interrupted conversation, when she said to him:

– How is it that nobody, until now, has ever uttered to me feelings such as these?

The clerk explained that the idealistic sort were difficult to understand. With him, it had been love at first sight; and it drove him to despair to think of the happiness they might have had if, by some stroke of luck, they had met sooner and been joined together indissolubly.

– It has occurred to me, she said.

– What a thought! murmured Léon.

And, delicately fondling the blue border of her long white sash, he added:

– So what is there to stop us from beginning again? . . .

– No, my friend, she said. I am too old . . . you are too young . . . forget about me. Other women will love you . . . you will love others.

– Not as I love you! he cried.

– You're such a child. Come on, let's be sensible. I mean it.

She demonstrated the impossibility of their love, and emphasized that they must stay, as they had been, within the innocent bounds of fraternal affection.

Was she serious in saying such things? Doubtless Emma herself had no real idea, being quite taken up with the charm of the seduction and the necessity of resisting it; and, gazing at the

young man, she gently repulsed the timid caresses that were
the most his shaking hands could manage.

– Sorry! he said, pulling back.

And Emma was gripped by a vague dread at this timidity,
more dangerous for her than Rodolphe's boldness, coming at
her with open arms. Never had any man seemed to her so
beautiful. There was an exquisite candour in his bearing. He
lowered his long fine curling eyelashes. His soft smooth cheek
was turning pink – she thought – with desire for her, and Emma
felt an invincible urge to press her lips upon it. Then, pretending
to peer up at the clock:

– Good heavens, it's so late! she said; we do chatter on.

He took her hint and picked up his hat.

– I'd quite forgotten about the theatre! And poor Bovary left
me here specially. Monsieur Lormeaux, from the Rue Grand-
Pont, was going to take me with his wife.

And that was the last chance, for she was leaving the very
next day.

– Yes.

– But I must see you again, he went on, I wanted to say
something . . .

– What?

– Something . . . important, serious. No, look, you're not
going, it's quite impossible! If you only knew . . . Listen . . .
Don't you see what I mean? Haven't you guessed?

– But you talk so well.

– You think it funny! That's enough. For pity's sake, let me
see you again . . . just once more . . .

– Well . . .

She stopped; and, as if she were changing her mind:

– Not here!

– Wherever you prefer.

– Would you . . .

She pretended to think, and, abruptly:

– Tomorrow, eleven o'clock, in the cathedral.

– I'll be there! he cried, seizing her hands, which she pulled
away.

And, now that they were both standing up, he behind her

and Emma with her head down, he reached out and kissed, lingeringly, the back of her neck.

– Oh, you're mad! You're quite mad! she said with a sharp ripple of laughter, as the kisses proliferated.

Leaning round over her shoulder, he seemed to be asking her eyes to say yes. They came down upon him, majestic and glacial.

Léon took three steps back, towards the door. He stood there on the threshold. In a trembling voice he whispered:

– Until tomorrow!

She gave a nod in reply, and disappeared quick as a bird into the next room.

Emma, that night, wrote the clerk an interminable letter in which she cancelled their rendezvous: it was over and done with, and they must never, for their own good, meet again. But, once the letter was sealed, and as she didn't know Léon's address, she was in great perplexity.

– I shall give it to him myself, she said; he'll be there.

Léon, next day, with his window open, out on his balcony, singing to himself, polished his own shoes, several times over. He put on white trousers, his best socks, a green coat, sprinkled on his handkerchief every perfume that he could find, and, after having his hair curled, he uncurled it, to give his hair a more natural elegance.

– Still too early! he thought, looking at the wig-maker's cuckoo-clock, which pointed to the hour of nine.

He read an old fashion magazine, went out, smoked a cigar, walked along three streets, thought it must be time and walked briskly towards the façade of Notre-Dame.

It was a lovely summer morning. The silverware was gleaming in the jewellers' shops, and the sunlight falling obliquely on the cathedral sparkled from the cracks in the grey stone; a flock of birds was circling in the blue sky, around the trefoiled bell-towers; the square, echoing with voices, was scented with flowers bordering the flagstones, roses, jasmine, pinks, narcissi and tuberoses, interspersed with moist green plants, catmint and chickweed; the fountain, in the centre, was gurgling, and, under big umbrellas, among pyramids of cantaloup melons, bare-headed flower-sellers were wrapping bunches of violets.

The young man took one. It was the first time he had bought flowers for a woman; and his chest, as he breathed in their scent, swelled with pride, as if the homage destined for her rebounded on him.

However, he was afraid of being noticed; he walked resolutely into the cathedral.

The verger was standing there, on the steps of the left-hand portal, beneath the Dancing Marianne,[2] plumes on his hat, rapier at his side, cane in his hand, more majestic than a cardinal and gleaming just like a ciborium.

He walked towards Léon, and, with that smile of sugary benevolence which ecclesiastics assume when addressing children:

– Monsieur, doubtless, is a visitor. Monsieur wishes to see the treasures of the church?

– No, he said.

And first he went around the near aisles. Then he went out to look around the square. Emma was not there. He went back inside as far as the choir.

The nave was mirrored in the brimming fonts, along with the lower part of the arches and a few pieces of window. But the images of the stained glass, obstructed by the marble rim, continued below, over the marble flagstones, like a patterned carpet. From without, daylight extended into the church in three great shafts, through the three open doors. Now and again, at the far end, a sacristan would pass by the altar with the oblique genuflexion of the devout man in a hurry. On the chandeliers the crystals were hanging motionless. In the choir, a silver lamp was burning; and, from the side chapels, from the dark corners of the church, there surged the occasional sigh, with the sound of a grill falling back, reverberating high up above in the vaulting.

Léon, deep in thought, was pacing along slowly by the walls. Never had life seemed so splendid. Soon she would be there, charming, agitated, keeping her eye on the people gazing after her – in her flounced dress, her gold lorgnon, her dainty little shoes, arrayed in the various refinements he had never tasted, in the poetry of adultery and the ineffable seductions of virtue relenting. The church was arranged about her; the vaulting was curving over to receive into its shadow the confession of her love; the windows were blazing to illuminate her face, and the incense would be burning that she might bear the appearance of an angel, in a perfumed cloud.

Yet still she did not come. He sat down on a chair and his eyes lighted on a blue stained-glass window with fishermen carrying baskets. He gazed at it for ages, attentively, and he counted the scales on the fish and the buttonholes in the doublets, while his thoughts went roaming in search of Emma.

The verger, standing back, was privately feeling most indignant towards this individual, who had the audacity to admire the cathedral unassisted. Such behaviour he regarded as quite monstrous, a species of theft, and little short of sacrilege.

A swish-swish of silk over the flagstones, the brim of a hat, a black headscarf . . . there she was! Léon stood up and ran to meet her.

Emma was pale. She was walking quickly.

– Read it! she said, holding out a piece of paper . . . Don't!

And she snatched her hand away, going over to the Lady Chapel, where, kneeling by a chair, she began a prayer.

The young man was irritated by this sanctimonious little whim; even so he felt a certain charm in seeing her, in the middle of an assignation, so engrossed in her devotions, like some marquess from Andalusia; but he soon grew bored, for she was still at it.

Emma was praying, or rather doing her best to pray, hoping that there would descend upon her from heaven some sudden resolve; and, to procure divine help, she feasted her eyes on the splendours of the tabernacle, she breathed down the scent from the large vases of white juliennes in full flower, and she harkened to the stillness of the church, which merely added to the tumult in her heart.

She stood up, and they were about to leave, when the verger hurried towards them, saying:

– Madame, doubtless, is a visitor. Madame wishes to see the treasures of the church?

– No! said the clerk.

– Why not? she said.

For her tottering virtue was clinging to the Virgin, the statues, the tombs, to anything and everything.

So, to go about it *in the proper order*, the verger led them back to the entrance near the square, and, pointing with his cane to a great circle of black paving-stones, without any inscription or carving:

– This, he said majestically, marks the circumference of the great bell of Amboise. It weighed forty thousand pounds. There was nothing to equal it in all of Europe. The workman who cast it died of joy . . .

– Enough, said Léon.

The old fellow set off again; and, when they got back to the Lady Chapel, he spread his arms in a comprehensive flourish, and prouder than a country landowner showing you his orchard:

– Under this simple stone lies Pierre de Brézé, Lord of Varenne and Brissac, Grand Marshal of Poitou and Governor of Normandy, killed at the Battle of Montlhéry on the 16th of July 1465.

Léon, biting his lip, tapped with his foot.

– And, on the right, this gentleman girded in steel, on a rearing horse, is his grandson Louis de Brézé, Lord of Breval and Montchauvet, Count of Maulevrier, Baron of Mauny, Chamberlain to the King, Knight of the Order and likewise Governor of Normandy, who died on the 23rd of July 1531, a Sunday, as the inscription records; and, below, that figure ready to descend into the tomb shows exactly the same person. Scarcely possible, you must agree, to imagine a more perfect representation of the void.

Madame Bovary took up her lorgnon. Léon, motionless, was watching her, now not even attempting a single word, a single gesture, so discouraged did he feel in the face of this double display of verbosity and indifference.

The eternal guide continued:

– Close by him, that woman on her knees weeping is his wife Diane de Poitiers, Countess of Brézé, Duchess of Valentinois, born in 1499, died in 1566; and, on the left, with a child in her arms, the Blessed Virgin. Now, turn this way: here are the

Amboise tombs. Both were cardinals and archbishops of Rouen. That one was a minister under King Louis XII. He was a great patron of the cathedral. In his will he bequeathed thirty thousand gold crowns to the poor.

And, without a pause, talking away, he pushed them into a chapel cluttered with balustrades, moved several of them aside, and revealed a sort of block that could well have been a crude statue.

– In former times, he said with a long groan, it adorned the tomb of Richard Coeur de Lion, King of England and Duke of Normandy. It was the Calvinists, monsieur, who reduced it to this state. They buried it, out of spite, in the ground, under the episcopal throne of his Grace. Look, here is the door that leads to his Grace's residence. Let us pass on to the Gargoyle Window.

But Léon quickly pulled a silver coin from his pocket and took Emma by the arm. The verger stood there quite dumbfounded, bewildered by this untimely munificence, when there were still so many things for the strangers to see. Accordingly, he called him back:

– Monsieur! The spire! The spire! . . .

– No thank you, said Léon.

– Monsieur is making a mistake! It will be four hundred and forty feet high, nine less than the great pyramid of Egypt. Made of cast iron, it's . . .

Léon fled; for it seemed to him that his love, which, for almost the last two hours, had been immobilized inside that church just like the stones, his love was now going to evaporate, to vanish, like smoke, up that sort of truncated tube, that elongated cage, that open chimney, raised aloft so grotesquely above the cathedral like the outlandish experiment of some eccentric iron-master.

– Where are we going? she said.

Without a word, he kept walking at a brisk pace, and Madame Bovary was already dipping her finger in the holy water, when they heard behind them a great panting sound, punctuated by the tapping of a stick. Léon turned round.

– Monsieur!

– What?

And he recognized the verger, clasping under his arm and steadying against his stomach about twenty stoutly bound volumes. They were works to do with the cathedral.

– Imbecile! muttered Léon, rushing from the church.

A lad was playing on the pavement.

– Go and find me a cab!

Quick as a shot, the boy went off along the Rue des Quatre-Vents; now they were alone together for a few minutes, face to face and rather embarrassed.

– Léon! . . . Really . . . I don't know if . . . if I should . . .!

She simpered. And, in a serious voice:

–It's most improper, don't you think?

– How exactly? replied the clerk. It's what people do in Paris!

And that phrase, like an irresistible argument, decided her.

However, the cab did not appear. Léon was afraid she might go back inside the church. At last the cab was there.

– At least go out by the north door! the verger shouted to them from the porch. To see the *Resurrection*, the *Last Judgement, Paradise, King David*, and the *Damned* in the fires of hell.

– Where to, monsieur? asked the coachman.

– Wherever you like! said Léon, pushing Emma into the carriage.

And the big machine began to move.

She went down the Rue Grand-Pont, crossed the Place des Arts, the Quai Napoléon, and the Pont Neuf, pulling up in front of the statue of Pierre Corneille.

– Keep going! said a voice from the inside.

The vehicle set off again, and, once she reached the Carrefour La Fayette, gathering speed on the hill, she drove at full gallop into the railway station.

– No, straight on! called the voice.

The cab came out through the gates, and soon, on the Drive, trotted gently along, between the tall elm-trees. The coachman wiped his brow, put his leather hat down between his knees and kept on beyond the side avenues, along by the water, near the meadow.

She went along the river bank, on the gravel tow-path, and some distance towards Oyssel, beyond the islands. She went down a little track and wandered along the sand. She rolled along very peacefully, with the unpolished straps cracking in the heat.

But suddenly, she dashed away across Quatremares, Sotteville, the Grande-Chaussée, the Rue d'Elbeuf, and stopped for the third time outside the Botanical Gardens.

– Just keep moving! shouted the voice in great fury.

And instantly, moving off again, she went through Saint-Sever, along the Quai des Curandiers, the Quai aux Meules, over the bridge again, across the Place du Champ-de-Mars and behind the hospital gardens, where the old men in black coats walk in the sunshine, along a terrace green with ivy. She went back up the Boulevard Bouvreuil, along the Boulevard Cauchoise, then up Mont-Riboudet as far as the Côte de Deville.

She turned back; and, with no plan or direction, at random, she wandered about. She was seen at Saint-Pol, at Lescure, at Mont Gargnan, at the Rouge-Mare, and the Place Gaillard-bois; Rue Maladrerie, Rue Dinanderie, outside Saint-Romain, Saint Vivien, Saint-Maclou, Saint Niçaise, – at the Customs House – at the Old Tower, the Three Pipes and at the Monumental Cemetery. Now and again, the coachman on his box cast a despairing glance at various taverns. He could not see what passion for locomotion drove this pair into never wanting to stop. He tried now and then, and immediately he heard exclamations of wrath coming from behind him. So now he lashed out harder at his two sweat-soaked nags, ignoring the pot-holes, scraping into this and that, heedless, demoralized, almost weeping with thirst, fatigue and affliction.

Down by the harbour, in among the wagons and the great barrels, and in the streets, on every corner, the bourgeois gaped in amazement at this extraordinary thing appearing in a provincial town, a carriage with its blinds shut, coming into view like this over and over again, as secret as the grave and shuddering along like a ship at sea.

Just once, around midday, on the open road, when the sun was beating down on the old silvered carriage-lamps, an unclad hand was pushed out from behind the little yellow linen curtains and threw away some scraps of paper, which scattered in the wind and settled a little way off, like white butterflies, on a field of red clover in flower.

Then, about six o'clock, the carriage stopped in a little back street in the Beauvoisine district, and a woman got out and walked away, her face veiled, without a backward glance.

2

Reaching the inn, Madame Bovary was surprised not to find the diligence. Hivert, after waiting fifty-three minutes for her, had finally set off.

There was nothing compelling her to leave; but she had given her word that she would be back that evening. Besides, Charles was waiting for her; and already in her heart she felt that feeble subservience which, for many women, is simultaneously the punishment and the expiation for their adultery.

Hurriedly she packed her trunk, paid the bill, hired a trap in the yard, and, by harassing the driver, urging him on, pestering him with asking what time it was and how many kilometres they had done, she managed to catch up with the *Hirondelle* as it reached the outskirts of Quincampoix.

Almost as soon as she sat in her corner, she closed her eyes and opened them again at the foot of the hill, where she recognized Félicité in the distance, keeping watch outside the blacksmith's. Hivert reined in his horses, and the cook, pulling herself up to the level of the window, said mysteriously:

– Madame, you must go to Monsieur Homais's at once. For something urgent.

The village was quite silent as usual. On every street corner, there were little heaps of pink stuff steaming in the air, for this was jam-making time, and everyone in Yonville prepared their supplies on the same day. But conspicuous outside the pharmacist's shop there was a much larger heap, one that excelled the others with the superiority of the laboratory over the mere kitchen, of public demand over private whim.

She went in. The big armchair was overturned, and even *Le Fanal de Rouen* lay on the floor, spread out between two pestles. She pushed open the inside door; and there, in the centre of the kitchen, among brown jars full of trimmed red currants, powdered sugar, sugar in lumps, scales on the table, pans on the fire, she saw the Homais family, large and small, with aprons up to their chins and forks held in their hands. Justin, standing there, hung his head, and the pharmacist was shouting:

– Who told you to go looking for it in the Capharnaum?

– What is it? What's the matter?

– The matter? said the apothecary. We are making jam: it's cooking away; but it was about to boil over because of the juice, so I shout for another pan. And this . . . feeble idle creature, went and took, from the nail where it hangs in my laboratory, the key to the Capharnaum!

This was the apothecary's name for a little room, under the roof, full of the implements and the merchandise of his profession. He often spent long hours up there on his own, labelling, decanting, packaging; and he regarded it as not just an ordinary store-room, but as a veritable sanctuary, from whence there emanated, under his hand, all sorts of pills, capsules, infusions, lotions and potions, which were to carry his name far and wide. No one else in the world ever set foot in there; and so great was his veneration for the place that he used to sweep it out himself. So, if the pharmacy, open to all comers, was the scene where he displayed his talents, the Capharnaum was the refuge where Homais, in a rapture of egotistical meditation, pursued his enthusiasms; therefore Justin's thoughtlessness struck him as a deed of monstrous irreverence; and, redder than the currants, he repeated:

– Yes, to the Capharnaum! The key that locks up the acids and the caustic alkalis! Fancy taking one of the special pans! A pan with a lid! One I might never have used! Everything has its place in the delicate operations of my art! For God's sake, though! Certain distinctions must be made, such as not employing for virtually domestic purposes things that are destined for pharmaceutical use. It's like someone carving a chicken with a scalpel, like a magistrate . . .

– Calm down now! Madame Homais was saying.

And Athalie, pulling at his coat, was saying:

– Daddy, daddy, daddy!

– No, leave me alone! the pharmacist was saying, leave me alone! Christmas! I swear I might just as well set up as a grocer! Go on, then! Desecrate the lot! Pulverize it! Let the leeches out! Set fire to the marshmallows! Pickle the gherkins in the big flagons! Tear up the bandages!

– You wanted to . . . said Emma.

– In a minute! Do you realize the risk you were taking? . . . Didn't you notice anything, on the left, on the third shelf? Speak up, reply, produce some sound!

– I d-d-don't know, stammered the young boy.

– Oh, you don't know! Well I do know! You saw a bottle, a blue one, sealed up with yellow wax, containing a white powder, one with *Danger* on it in my writing, do you know what was in it? Arsenic! And you were going to touch it! Going to get the pan that lives next to it!

– Next to it! shouted Madame Homais clasping her hands. Arsenic! You could have poisoned every one of us!

And the children started shrieking, as though down in their guts they had already felt the hideous pangs.

– Or poisoned a patient! the apothecary went on. Do you really want to have me up in court as a criminal? Watch me being dragged to the scaffold? Haven't you noticed how meticulous I am with the merchandise, even though I've been doing it for ages? I often give myself a fright, when I think of my responsibility! With the government persecuting us, and the absurd legislation which controls us like a veritable sword of Damocles hanging over our heads!

Emma had given up trying to ask what they wanted her for, and the pharmacist kept up a breathless flow of words:

– This is how you pay back our kindness! This is how you reward me for the truly paternal care I lavish on you! Now where would you be without me? What would you do? Who provides you with food, education, clothing, and the wherewithal to assume one of these days an honourable position in society! But you do have to sweat at the old oar, put your back into it, as they say. *Fabricando fit faber, age quod agis.*[3]

He was quoting Latin, such was his exasperation. He would have quoted Chinese and Icelandic, if he had known either of those languages; for now he was in one of those crises when the soul yields a blurred glimpse of all that it enfolds, like an ocean, tempest-torn, uncovering everything from the seaweed in the shallows to the sands of the abyss.

And he went on:

– I begin to repent exceedingly having taken you into my care! I should undoubtedly have done better to have left you there festering in the squalor and the filth where you were born. You'll never be any use, except for herding the beasts of the field! You have not the least aptitude for science! You hardly know how to stick a label on! And here you are, set up in my house, like a lord, leading a life of ease, just dawdling along!

But Emma, turning to Madame Homais, said:

– They asked me to come and . . .

– Dear goodness! the good lady broke in mournfully. I don't know what to say . . . It's bad news!

She was cut short. The apothecary was thundering:

– Empty it out! Clean it up! Take it back! Get a move on!

And, shaking Justin by the collar, he dislodged a book from his pocket.

The boy stooped down. Homais was quicker, and, picking up the volume, he contemplated it, his eyes bulging, his jaw sagging.

– *Conjugal . . . Love!* he said, carefully separating the two words. Very nice! Very pretty! With illustrations! This is too much!

Madame Homais came closer.

– No! Don't touch it!

The children wanted to see the pictures.

– Out of here! he said imperiously.

And out they went.

First he strode up and down the room, holding the volume open in his hand, rolling his eyes, choking, swollen, apoplectic. Then he came over to his pupil, and, face to face with his arms folded:

– So, you have all the vices have you, little wretch! . . . Be careful, the slope is smooth! . . . Has it not occurred to you that it could, this wicked book, fall into the hands of my children, and sow a seed in their minds, tarnish the purity of Athalie, corrupt Napoléon! He is already nearly a man. Are you quite sure, at least, that they haven't read it? Can you certify to me . . .

– Really now, monsieur, said Emma, you have something to tell me?

– Yes, indeed, madame . . . Your father-in-law is dead!

As a matter of fact, the aforementioned Bovary senior had passed away two days previously, without warning, from an attack of apoplexy, just after a dinner; and, in an excess of concern for Emma's feelings, Charles had begged Monsieur Homais to break the terrible news to her circumspectly.

The pharmacist had meditated every phrase, he had smoothed and polished it and made it flow; it was a masterpiece of deliberation and progression, of elegant style and tactfulness; but anger had obliterated rhetoric.

Emma, abandoning any hope of having the details, now left the pharmacy; for Monsieur Homais had resumed his vituperations. He was calming down, though, and, at that moment, he was grumbling away paternally, while fanning himself with his skull-cap.

– Not that I entirely disapprove of the work! The author was a doctor. It deals with certain scientific aspects which it's no bad thing for a man to know about, and, I'd venture to say, a man must know about. But not yet, not yet! At least wait until you're a man yourself and your character is formed.

At the sound of Emma's knock, Charles, who had been awaiting her return, came towards her with open arms and said with tears in his voice:

– Ah! My dear . . .

And gently he bent forward to give her a kiss. But at the touch of his lips, the memory of the other man was upon her, and she wiped her hand across her face with a shiver.

Yet she gave an answer:

– Yes, I know . . . I know . . .

He showed her the letter in which his mother narrated the incident, without any sentimental hypocrisy. Her sole regret was that her husband had not received the comforts of religion, having met his end in Doudeville, on the street, at the door of a café, after a patriotic dinner with his old army friends.

Emma gave the letter back; and, over the meal, out of politeness, she feigned reluctance. But since he insisted, she steadfastly set about eating, while Charles, opposite her, sat motionless, looking quite overwhelmed.

Every so often, lifting his head, he gave her a long look full of distress. Just once he sighed:

– I wish I could have seen him again!

She said nothing. Eventually, realizing something was expected:

– How old was he, your father?

– Fifty-eight.

– Oh.

And that was all.

A quarter of an hour later, he added:

– My poor mother . . . What will happen to her, after this?

She gestured her perplexity.

Seeing her so taciturn, Charles assumed she was distressed, and he made himself say nothing, to avoid aggravating the grief which he found so moving. Instead, taking hold of himself:

– Did you have a nice time yesterday? he asked.

– Yes.

Once the table-cloth was taken off, Bovary still sat in his chair, Emma likewise; and, as she gazed at his face, the monotony of that spectacle gradually banished the compassion from her heart. He seemed so feeble, a nullity, a creature pathetic in every way. How could she get rid of him? What an interminable evening! Something altogether deadening, like opium fumes, was taking hold of her.

They heard a tapping sound coming along the boards in the hall. It was Hippolyte bringing in Madame's luggage. To set it down, he painfully made a quarter circle with his peg-leg.

– It doesn't bother him one bit! she said to herself as she looked at the poor devil, his thick red hair dripping with sweat.

Bovary was searching for a centime at the bottom of his purse;

and, not appearing to grasp just what a humiliation it was for
him, the mere presence of this man standing there, personifying
a reproach to his incurable incompetence:

– Well, what a nice little bunch of flowers! he said, noticing
Léon's violets on the mantelpieces.

– Yes, she said casually; it's a bunch I bought just now ...
from a beggar-woman.

Charles picked up the violets, and he cooled his tear-swollen
eyes at them, delicately breathing in their scent. She took them
quickly from his hand, and went to put them in a glass of water.

Next morning, Madame Bovary senior arrived. She and her
son wept many a tear. Emma, under pretext of arrangements to
be made, disappeared.

The following day, there was the business of the mourning to
discuss. They went and sat, with their sewing-boxes, down by
the water, in the arbour.

Charles was thinking about his father, and he was surprised
to feel so much affection towards the man, for until now he had
believed that he loved him only very little. Madame Bovary
senior was thinking about her husband. The worst days of the
past now seemed appealing. Everything else was eclipsed by an
instinctive nostalgia for the ancient routine; and, every so often,
as she plied her needle, an enormous tear slid down her nose
and hung there for a moment, suspended. Emma was thinking
that it was hardly forty-eight hours ago they had been together,
secluded, delirious, and gazing so insatiably upon each other.
She tried to recapture the minutest details of that departed time.
But the presence of her mother-in-law and her husband thwarted
her. She wanted to hear nothing, wanted to see nothing, so as
not to interfere with this cherishing of her love that was fading
away, do what she might, beneath external sensations.

She was unstitching the lining of a dress, pieces of material
scattered around her; old Madame Bovary, without looking up,
was squeaking away with her scissors, and Charles, in his felt
slippers and the old brown overcoat which he used as a dressing-
gown, sat with his hands in his pockets and joined in the silence;
near by, Berthe, in a little white pinafore, was raking the gravel
path with her spade.

Suddenly, they saw coming through the gate Monsieur Lheureux, the draper.

He had called in to offer his services, *in view of the unhappy situation*. Emma replied that she thought she could manage without. The shopkeeper, however, was not defeated.

– I do beg your pardon, he said; I would like a few words in private.

Then, in an undertone:

– About that business . . . you know?

Charles turned crimson to the tips of his ears.

– Ah yes . . . of course . . .?

And, in his agitation, turning to his wife:

– Could you perhaps . . . darling?

She seemed to know what he meant, for she stood up, and Charles said to his mother:

– It's nothing, really! Probably something unimportant about the house.

He certainly didn't want her to know about the promissory note, for fear of what she would say.

As soon as they were alone, Monsieur Lheureux began, in fairly plain terms, to congratulate Emma on the inheritance, then began to talk inconsequentially about the espaliers, about the harvest, and about his own health, always only so-so, fair to middling. In actual fact, he was working harder than the devil himself, even though, whatever people said, he didn't even make enough to put butter on his bread.

Emma let him talk. She had been so prodigiously bored these last two days!

– And here you are back on your feet again? he went on. My goodness I've seen your husband in a pretty state! He's a good chap, even though we've had our problems, him and me.

She asked what problems, for Charles had hidden from her the dispute over her purchases.

– But you don't know? said Lheureux. It was about your little knick-knacks, the travelling-cases.

He had pulled his hat down over his eyes, and, with his hands behind his back, smiling and whistling, he was looking straight at her, in an insufferable way. Did he suspect something? She was left adrift among numerous anxieties. In the end, though, he said:

– We're reconciled now, and I was coming to suggest another arrangement to him.

This was to renew the promissory note signed by Bovary. The doctor, of course, would do as he thought best; he was not to worry himself, especially now that he was going to have a mass of problems.

– You know he'd be better handing it over to somebody else, to you, for instance; with a power of attorney, it'd be simple, and then you and I could do our little bit of business together . . .

She didn't understand. He stopped. And then, coming back to the point, Lheureux declared that Madame wouldn't be able to manage without having something from him. He would send her some black *barège*, twelve metres, enough to make a dress with.

– The one you're wearing is fine for the house. You need another one for visiting. I could see that, I could, as soon as I came through the door. I don't miss a thing!

He didn't send the material, he brought it himself. He came back for the measurements; kept coming back on various pretexts, striving constantly to make himself agreeable, useful, *enfeoffing* himself, as Homais would have said, and always slipping in a few words to Emma about the power of attorney. He didn't say anything about the promissory note. She gave it no thought; Charles had certainly said something to her about it, in the early days of her convalescence; but her mind had known such agitation that she didn't remember a thing. Besides, she avoided getting into any discussion about money; the elder Madame Bovary was surprised at this, and attributed the change in her disposition to the religious sentiments she had contracted during her illness.

But, as soon as she had gone, Emma promptly amazed Bovary with her practical good sense. Inquiries would have to be made, mortgages verified, and they would have to see if there was a case for an auction or a liquidation. She deployed technical terms, at random, made grand pronouncements about order, the future, foresight, and she continually exaggerated the difficulties of the probate; and eventually one day she showed him the draft of the general authorization to *manage and administer his affairs, negotiate loans, sign and endorse all bills, pay all monies, etcetera*. She had profited from her lessons with Lheureux.

Charles, naïvely, asked her where the document had come from.

– From Monsieur Guillaumin.

And, with the most perfect composure, she added:

– I'm not very happy with it. Notaries have such a bad name. Perhaps we ought to consult . . . Who do we know . . . There's no one!

– Unless Léon . . ., answered Charles, thoughtfully.

But it was very difficult to arrange everything by post. She offered to go to Rouen herself. He demured. She insisted. It was a ceremonious contest. Finally, she exclaimed in mock-defiance:

– No, I tell you, I'm going.

– You're so wonderful! he said, kissing her on the forehead.

The very next morning, she embarked for Rouen in the *Hirondelle* to consult Monsieur Léon; and she stayed for three days.

3

Three whole days of exquisite splendour, a veritable honeymoon.

They were in the Hôtel de Boulogne, down by the harbour. And there they lived, shutters closed, doors locked, with flowers spread over the carpet and iced drinks, brought up for them through the day.

In the evening, they took a little boat with an awning and went out to an island for their meal.

It was the hour of the day when you can hear, along the docks, the echo of the caulkers' mallets as they work on the ships' hulls. The tar-smoke was drifting away between the trees, and on the river you could see big drops of oil, clusters of it undulating in the purple sunset, like plates of Florentine bronze, floating about.

They made their way downstream in among vessels at their moorings, the long diagonal cables just grazing the top of their boat.

Imperceptibly the noise of the city was fading away, the rumbling of wagons, the tumult of voices, the barking of dogs from the decks of the boats. She undid her bonnet and they landed on their island.

They went to a room in a tavern with a low ceiling, and black nets hung over the door. They ate fried smolt, cherries and cream. They lay down on the grass; out of sight they embraced beneath the poplars; and they yearned to live perpetually, like Robinson Crusoes, in that little place, which seemed to them, in their beatific state, to be the most magnificent in the world. It was not the first time they had seen trees, blue sky, green grass, not the first time they had heard running water and the wind blowing through the leaves; but certainly they had never yet admired it all as though nature had only just come into existence, or only begun to be beautiful since the gratification of their desires.

At nightfall, they departed. The boat kept close to the islands. They lay in the stern, both of them hidden in shadow, without a word. The square-bladed oars were clanking on their iron pins; punctuating the silence like the beat of a metronome, while at their backs the trailing rope was rippling softly, perpetually, through the water.

By and by, the moon appeared; they managed a phrase or two, pronouncing it melancholy and full of poetry; she even began to sing:

Un soir, t'en souvient-il, nous voguions . . .[4]

Her weak melodious voice was lost upon the waters; and the wind carried away the trills he could hear gliding past like fluttering wings about his ears.

She was sitting opposite, leaning against the bulkhead, where the moon shone in through one of the open flaps. Her black dress, with its folds spreading out like a fan, made her look more slender and taller. She had her head back, her hands clasped, and her eyes turned to heaven. Sometimes the shadows of the willows quite concealed her, then she reappeared, fleetingly, like a vision, by the light of the moon.

Léon, on the floor, at her side, came across a scarlet ribbon.

The boatman examined it and said eventually:

– Yes! I think as it belongs to a party I took on the water the other day. Frisky crowd they were, gentlemen and ladies, with cakes, and champagne, and little trumpets, the whole works! One there was in particular, big handsome man with a little moustache, most amusing he was! And they kept saying: *Come on, tell us another . . . Adolphe . . . Dodolphe . . .* some such name.

She gave a shiver.

– What is it? said Léon drawing closer to her.

– Oh, nothing. Just the night air, I expect.

– And quite a one for the ladies, the old sailor added softly, by way of tribute to the stranger.

Spitting on his hands, he took up the oars again.

Time at last to say goodbye! It was a sad moment. He was to send his letters via Mère Rolet; and she gave him such precise instructions about double envelopes that he greatly admired her amatory ingenuity.

– So you can confirm that everything is all right? she said during the final kiss.

– Yes, of course!

– But why, he thought later, as he made his solitary way back along the streets, is she so set on this power of attorney?

4

Léon, very soon, adopted a rather superior tone with his friends, avoided their company, and completely neglected his work.

He would wait for her letters; he would read them again and again. He used to write to her. He used to picture her to himself, calling on all the powers of desire and memory. Far from diminishing with absence, the need to see her again was increasing, until one Saturday morning he slipped away from his office.

He reached the top of the hill, and when he looked down into the valley and saw the church-tower with its tin flag turning in the wind, he felt that delectable mixture of triumphant vanity and egotistical tenderness that surely comes over a millionaire when he returns to visit his native village.

He went prowling around her house. A light was shining in the kitchen. He watched for her shadow on the curtains. Nothing appeared. Nobody there.

Mère Lefrançois, when she saw him, exclaimed in great surprise, and she thought he was 'taller and thinner', while Artémise, on the other hand, thought he was 'plumper and not as pale'.

He had dinner in the little parlour, like in the old days, alone though, without the tax-collector; because Binet, *sick* of waiting for the *Hirondelle*, had irrevocably moved his meal-time back an hour earlier, and, nowadays, he dined at five o'clock sharp, still declaring more often than not that *the wretched clock was slow*.

But Léon was resolute; he went over and knocked on the doctor's door. Madame was up in her room, and it was a quarter of an hour before she came down. Monsieur was delighted to see him again; but he didn't budge all evening, nor the following day.

He saw her alone, in the evening, very late, at the end of the garden, in the lane; – in the lane, where once before she had met with the other one! There was a thunderstorm, and they talked under an umbrella as the lightning flashed.

Separation was becoming intolerable.

– I'd rather be dead! said Emma.

She was clinging to his arm, weeping the while.

– Goodbye! . . . Goodbye! . . . When shall I see you again?

They came back for one last kiss; and it was then that she gave him her promise to find, no matter how, some way of seeing each other, unconstrained, at least once a week. Emma was quite certain. Besides, she was full of hope. There was money coming to her.

Accordingly, she bought for her room a pair of yellow curtains with wide stripes, which Lheureux had extolled as a bargain;

she longed for a carpet, and Lheureux, insisting *it was a piece of cake*, politely undertook to provide her with one. She could no longer manage without his services. Twenty times a day she sent for him, and promptly he dropped whatever he was doing, without even a murmur. Nor could people understand why Mère Rolet had lunch every day at Emma's, and even visited her in private.

It was about this time, that is to say, near the beginning of the winter, that she seemed to be taken with a great passion for music.

One evening when Charles was listening to her, she began the same piece four times over, each time in a state of exasperation; meanwhile, not noticing any difference, he was exclaiming:

– Bravo! Lovely! Don't stop! Go on!

– No! It's dreadful! I've got rusty fingers.

Next day, he asked her to play something for him again.

– All right, if you want.

And Charles admitted that she had rather lost her touch. She got the staves mixed up, she floundered; and, stopping abruptly:

– It's no good! I ought to take some lessons; but . . .

She bit her lip and added:

– Twenty francs a time, it's too expensive!

– Yes, it is . . . just a bit . . ., said Charles, chuckling foolishly. Even so, I think you could do it for less; there are musicians without any big reputation who are often better than the famous ones.

– You find one, said Emma.

Next day, when he came in, he gave her a knowing look, and eventually he could contain it no longer:

– Sometimes you're so eager! I've been to Barfeuchères today. Well, Madame Liégeard assures me that her three daughters, who are at the convent school, are having lessons at two and a half francs a time, and with a well-known teacher!

She shrugged her shoulders, and didn't once open her piano again.

But, whenever she went near it (if Bovary happened to be there), she would sigh:

– Ah, my poor piano!

And when anyone came to see her, she infallibly announced that she had quite relinquished music and could not now take it up again, for important reasons. They were sympathetic. It was a shame! She who had such a great talent! They even mentioned it to Bovary. They were reproachful, and the pharmacist in particular:

– You are making a mistake! The natural faculties should never be left to lie fallow. Besides, dear friend, consider, by urging Madame to study, you are economizing on the future musical education of your child. Personally, I believe that mothers ought to educate their children themselves. It's one of Rousseau's ideas, still rather new perhaps, but it will triumph eventually, I'm quite sure, just like maternal breast-feeding and vaccinations.

So Charles returned to the question of the piano. Emma replied bitterly that it would be better to sell the thing. That old piano, so richly gratifying to her vanity, to see it go, it was like the indefinable suicide of a part of herself!

– If you like . . ., he said, now and then, just one lesson, that wouldn't be completely ruinous, would it?

– But lessons, she replied, are no use unless you keep them up.

And that was how she contrived to get her husband's permission to go into town, once a week, to see her lover. People even said, after just a month, that she had made considerable progress.

5

It was Thursday. She used to get up, and get dressed without a sound so as not to wake Charles, who would have reproached her for being ready too early. Then she would walk up and down, stop by the window, look out over the square. The early light was drifting between the pillars of the market-hall, and the pharmacist's house, with its shutters closed, was displaying to the pale dawn the great letters on his sign-boards.

When the clock was pointing to a quarter past seven, she

would go over to the Golden Lion, and Artémise, with a yawn, would let her in. For Madame the girl raked up the red embers buried under the ashes. Emma sat in the kitchen on her own. Now and again she went outside. Hivert would be harnessing the horses, taking his time, and listening the while to Mère Lefrançois, who, with her nightcapped head through a little window, was giving him instructions complicated enough to baffle any lesser man. Emma tapped her foot on the flagstones, in the yard.

Eventually, once he had drunk his soup, put on his woollen coat, lit his pipe and got his whip in his hand, he would install himself placidly up on the seat.

The *Hirondelle* would start off at a slow trot, and, for a couple of miles, stop here and there to pick up passengers, standing waiting, by the side of the road, at the farm-gate. People who had booked the day before kept everyone waiting; some would still be in their beds; Hivert called, shouted, cursed and he climbed down from his seat to go and hammer at the door. The wind came in through the little cracked windows of the carriage.

Gradually the four benches filled up, the coach was rolling along, rows of apple-trees drifted past; and the road, flanked by two long ditches full of yellow water, went on endlessly, converging at the far horizon.

Emma knew it from end to end; she knew that after a meadow there came a sign-post, an elm, a barn or a road-mender's hut; sometimes, to give herself a surprise, she would close her eyes. But she never lost an exact sense of the distance still to be covered.

At long last, the brick houses were more frequent, the wheels were rumbling along, the *Hirondelle* was gliding past gardens where you could see, through the fence, statues, a rockery, clipped yew-trees and a little swing. Now, in the twinkling of an eye, the town appeared.

Sloping down like an amphitheatre, submerged in the mist, it spread out beyond the bridges, chaotically. And the featureless curve of open country sloped away up until it touched the far pale blur of the skyline. Seen like this from above, the whole landscape had the stillness of a painting; ships at anchor were crowded together in one corner; the river curved smoothly around the foot of the green hills, and the islands, oblong in form, looked just like big black fish, motionless on the water. Factory chimneys were pushing out immense plumes of brown stuff that were swept away on the breeze. You could hear the rumbling from the ironworks and the clear sound of church-bells from spires that rose above the mist. The trees along the boulevards, quite leafless, looked like purple bushes in among the houses, and the roof-tops, all gleaming wet, were a great patchwork of mirrors, each piece at a different height. Sometimes a gust would blow the clouds towards Côte Sainte-Catherine, like sea-waves in the sky crashing silently against a cliff.

From that dense-packed humanity she inhaled something vertiginous, and it gorged her heart, as though the hundred and twenty thousand souls pulsing down there had discharged all together the fumes of the passions she imagined theirs. Her love unfurled across vast space, dilated to a chaos by the vague murmur rising from below. She rained it down again, on the squares, on the parks, on the streets, and the old Norman city seemed spread before her like some great metropolis, like Babylon unveiled for her. She leaned out of the carriage-window, on both hands, sniffing at the breeze; the three horses were galloping along, the stones were grinding into the mud, the coach was swaying about, and Hivert, from far away, was hailing the other carts on the road, while the bourgeois who had been spending the night in the Bois Guillaume were driving sedately down the hill, in their little family carriages.

They stopped at the city gate; Emma unbuckled her overshoes, changed her gloves, rearranged her shawl, and, twenty steps further on, she got down from the *Hirondelle*.

The town was just waking up. Apprentice boys, in their caps, were polishing the shop-fronts, and every so often women carrying baskets on their hips would let out a ringing cry, on the street corners. She walked along looking down, keeping close to the wall, and smiling with pleasure behind her black veil.

For fear of being seen, she did not ordinarily go by the quickest way. She scurried along dismal alley-ways, and she emerged in a sweat towards the far end of the Rue Nationale, near the fountain that stands there. This is the place for theatres, taverns and whores. Often a cart came along that way, carrying quivering stage-scenery. Waiters in aprons would be scattering sand over the paving-stones, in between the green shrubbery. There was a smell of absinthe, cigars and oysters.

She turned a corner; she recognized him by the curly hair pushing out from under his hat.

Léon would keep walking along the pavement. She would follow him all the way to the hotel; he went up, he opened the door, he went in . . . What embracings!

Now, after the kisses, the words came forth in a great rush. They told each other the week's little sorrows, the forebodings, the worries about their letters; but for the moment that was far away, and they looked into each other's eyes, laughing voluptuously over the amorous names they invented.

There was a great big mahogany bed in the shape of a boat. The curtains, made of red oriental stuff, hung from the ceiling, curving out rather too low over the wide bed-head; – and there was nothing in the world as lovely as her dark hair and her white skin set against that crimson colour when, in a gesture of modesty, she closed her bare arms, hiding her face in her hands.

The warm room, with its plain carpet, its frivolous decorations, its tranquil light, seemed quite perfect for the intimacies of passion. The arrow-headed curtain rods, the brass fittings, and the big balls on the fender would gleam suddenly, whenever the sun shone in. On the mantelpiece, between the candlesticks, there were two of those big pink shells that sound like the sea when you hold them to your ear.

How they loved that dear room, so delightful, despite its rather faded splendour. They always found the furniture set out the same way, and sometimes the hairpins she had left behind, the previous Thursday, underneath the clock. They had lunch by the fire, on a little table inlaid with rosewood. Emma would do the carving, putting morsels on his plate, seasoned with every sort of amorous badinage; and she laughed a splendid shameless laugh when the froth from the champagne ran down over the rings on her fingers. They were so completely lost in the possession of each other that they thought this was a house of their very own, where they would live for the rest of their lives, like perpetual young lovers. They used to say our room, our carpet, our chairs, she even said my slippers, a present from Léon, on an impulse of hers. They were pink satin slippers, edged with swansdown. When she sat on his knee, her leg, too short to reach the floor, would swing in the air; and the dainty shoe, which had no heel, would dangle from the toes of her bare foot.

He was savouring for the first time – and in the deed of love – the inexpressible delicacies of feminine elegance. Never had he met with such grace of language, such modesty of dress, such tableaux of drowsy maiden-innocence. He admired the exaltation of her soul and the lace on her skirts. Besides, was she not a *lady*, and a married woman! A real mistress?

By the variousness of her moods, successively mystical and joyful, talkative and taciturn, passionate and nonchalant, she roused a thousand desires in him, kindling instincts or memories. She was the lover in every novel, the heroine in every play, the vague *she* in every volume of poetry. On her shoulders he found the amber colours of *Odalisque au bain*; she had the long body of some feudal chatelaine; and she looked like the *pale woman of Barcelona*, but supremely she was the Angel.

Often, as he gazed at her, it seemed as if his soul, drawn out of him, surged like a wave about her head, ebbing swiftly away into the whiteness of her breast.

He would kneel on the floor, at her feet; and, with his elbows on her knees, he would gaze upon her with a smile, and a fretful look.

She leaned towards him and murmured, as though she were breathless with excitement:

– Don't move! Don't speak! Look at me! There's something so tender in your eyes, it does me good.

She used to call him child.

– Child, do you love me?

And she scarcely heard his answer, for the suddenness of his lips seeking her mouth.

On the clock there was a little bronze Cupid, smirking as he held out his arms under a shining garland. Often they laughed at him; but, when it was time to part, everything seemed serious.

Motionless they stood close, they kept saying:

– Next Thursday! . . . Next Thursday!

Suddenly she took his head in her hands, kissed him quickly on the forehead with a cry of 'Adieu!' and rushed away down the stairs.

She used to go to a hairdresser's in the Rue de la Comédie, to have her coiffure repaired. Night was falling; they lit the gas-lights in the shop.

She could hear the little theatre-bell calling the players for the performance; and across the way she caught sight of men with white faces and women in faded gowns, going in through the stage-door.

It was warm in that little low-ceilinged room, with the stove humming away among the wigs and the pomades. With the smell of the curling-tongs, and those plump hands working on her scalp, she would soon be feeling drowsy, and she dozed off in her dressing-gown. Often the young man doing her hair would offer her tickets for the masked ball.

Then off she went! She made her way back along the streets; she arrived at the Croix Rouge; she found her overshoes, which she had hidden under a bench that morning, and she squeezed into her place among the impatient passengers. Some of them got out at the foot of the hill. She had the carriage to herself.

At every bend, you could see more and more of the lights of the town, like a great luminous mist above the dim outline of the houses. Emma knelt on the cushions, and she let her eyes stray into the dazzle. She sobbed, she called to Léon, and sent him sweet words and kisses that were lost upon the breeze.

On the hill there was a poor old tramp wandering about with his stick, in among the carriages. A mass of rags covered his shoulders, and a squashed beaver-hat, bent down into the shape of a bowl, concealed his face; but, when he took it off, he exposed, instead of eyelids, two yawning bloodstained holes. The flesh was tattered into scarlet strips; and fluid was trickling out, congealing into green crusts that reached down to his nose, with black nostrils that kept sniffing convulsively. Whenever he spoke, he threw back his head with an idiot laugh; – then his blue eyes, rolling continuously, would graze the edges of the open sores, near both his temples.

He used to sing a little song as he followed the carriages:

> *Souvent la chaleur d'un beau jour*
> *Fait rêver fillette à l'amour.*[5]

And the rest was all about birds and sunshine and leaves of green.

Sometimes he appeared suddenly behind Emma, hatless. She pulled back with a cry. Hivert would be teasing him. He told him he ought to take a booth at the Saint-Romain fair, or asked him, with a laugh, how his sweetheart was keeping.

Several times, they were on the move, and his hat would be thrust in through the carriage-window, while he clung on tight with his other arm, on the footboard, between the splashing wheels. His voice, a feeble wail at first, became shrill. It trailed off into the darkness, like the muffled lamentation of some vague distress; and, above the jingling of the horses' bells, the murmur of the axles and the rumbling of the empty carriage, it had a far-away sound that Emma found overwhelming. It carried to the very bottom of her soul, like a vortex turning over the deep, and it swept her out across the expanses of a boundless melancholy. But Hivert, feeling the balance shift, would swipe briskly at the blind man with his whip. The lash would catch him on his sores, and he would fall off into the mud, bellowing.

And the passengers in the *Hirondelle* would eventually fall asleep, some open-mouthed, some with their chins sunk to their chests, leaning on neighbour's shoulder, or with one arm through a strap, swaying about to the rhythm of the moving carriage; and the light of the lamp swinging outside, above the rumps of the horses, filtering through the chocolate-coloured calico curtains, cast shadows of a bloody red over all those motionless passengers. Emma, crazed with sorrow, was shivering in her clothes, feeling her feet get colder and colder, sick at heart.

Charles, at home, was waiting for her; the *Hirondelle*

was always late on Thursdays: Madame was back at last! She scarcely kissed her little girl. Dinner wasn't ready, never mind! She forgave the cook. These days the girl seemed to get away with anything.

Often her husband, noticing her pallor, would ask her if she were feeling unwell.

– No, said Emma.

– But, he replied, you seem so strange this evening.

– It's nothing. Nothing.

Some days, almost as soon as she got home, she went off up to her room; and Justin, who just happened to be there, would move about with hardly a sound, more ingenious in her service than the finest chambermaid. He put out the matches, the candle, a book, arranged her camisole, turned back the sheets.

– Come on, she'd say. That'll do. Off you go!

For he was just standing there, his hands at his side and his eyes wide open, as though entangled in the endless web of his untimely reverie.

The next day was dreadful, and the following days felt even more intolerable because Emma was so eager to take hold of her happiness once again – a harsh concupiscence, inflamed by familiar images, which, on the seventh day, flowed forth copiously as soon as Léon caressed her. His own carnality was hidden away beneath displays of wonder and gratitude. Emma savoured this love of his with a fastidious concentration, prolonged it with every stratagem of tenderness, and fretted at the thought of it dwindling away.

She would often say to him, with a melancholy sweetness in her voice:

– You'll leave me, you will. You'll marry somebody. You'll be just like all the rest.

He asked:

– The rest?

– Why, men, of course.

And pushing him away with a weary gesture, she added:

– You are all despicable!

One day when they were talking philosophically about earthly disillusionment, she happened to say (to test his jealousy, or perhaps she was yielding to an overpowering need to unburden her heart) that she had once, before they met, loved somebody else, 'not as we are lovers', she added quickly, swearing on the life of her daughter that *nothing had happened*.

The young man believed her, but questioned her none the less to find out what he had been.

– He was a ship's captain, my dear.

This was to discourage further curiosity, and equally to set herself up very high, as the supposed object of fascination for a man who must have been naturally bellicose and well accustomed to admirers.

The clerk now felt the lowliness of his position; he coveted epaulettes, medals, titles. No doubt she enjoyed that sort of thing: he had guessed as much from her expensive tastes.

Actually Emma was keeping silent about many of her extravagancies, such as the desire for a blue tilbury, to take her to Rouen, drawn along by an English horse, and driven by a groom in top-boots. It was Justin who had inspired this caprice of hers, begging to be taken into her service as a valet; and, if this privation did not diminish the pleasure of arriving at her rendezvous, it certainly intensified the sourness of the journey home.

Often, when they were talking together about Paris, she would eventually murmur:

– What a life we could have there!

– But aren't we happy as we are now? the young man asked tenderly, stroking her hair.

– Yes, we are, she said. I must be mad. Kiss me!

With her husband she was more charming than ever, making him pistachio-cream and playing him waltzes after dinner. He accordingly considered himself the most fortunate of mortals, and Emma had an easy time, until one evening, suddenly:

– It is Mademoiselle Lempereur, isn't it, who gives you lessons?

– Yes.

– Well, I saw her just recently, at Madame Liégeard's. I mentioned your name; and she's never heard of you.

It was like a thunderclap. However, she replied in a natural voice:

– Oh, I suppose she must have forgotten who I am.

– But perhaps, said the doctor, there are several Mademoiselle Lempereurs in Rouen who are piano-teachers?

– It's possible.

Then, rapidly:

– I do have her receipts, though. Look.

And she went over to the writing-desk, rummaged through all the drawers, muddled the papers, and finally worked herself into such a state that Charles pleaded with her not to go to so much trouble for the sake of the wretched receipts.

– Oh, I shall find them, she said.

Indeed, on the following Friday, as Charles was pulling on one of his boots in the dark closet where his clothes were kept, he felt a sheet of paper down between the leather and his sock. He picked it up and read: 'Received, for three months' lessons, and various items supplied, the sum of sixty-five francs. Félicité Lempereur, Teacher of Music.'

– How the devil did this get into my boots?

– Obviously, she said, it must have fallen out of the old box of papers up on the shelf.

From that moment on, her existence was little more than a tissue of lies, in which she swathed her love, as if behind a veil, to hide it from view.

It was a necessity, an obsession, a pleasure, to the extent that, if she said she had walked yesterday along the right-hand side of the street, it actually meant she had walked along the left-hand side.

One morning when she had just set off, as usual rather lightly clad, it suddenly began to snow; and, as Charles was looking out of the window at the weather, he noticed Monsieur Bournisien in the Tuvache dog-cart setting out for Rouen. So he went out and presented the cleric with a thick shawl to be given to Madame as soon as he arrived at the Croix Rouge. When he reached the inn, Bournisien asked after the wife of the doctor from Yonville. The landlady replied that she was very rarely to be seen on those premises. So, that evening, greeting Madame Bovary in the *Hirondelle*, the cleric told her of his dilemma, without appearing to attach any importance to it; for he began to sing the praises of a new preacher who was working wonders at the cathedral, all the ladies flocking to hear him.

No matter that he had not asked for any sort of explanation, next time other people might be less discreet. Consequently, she decided it would be better always to alight at the Croix Rouge, so that the decent folk from her village who saw her on the stairs would suspect nothing.

One day, though, Monsieur Lheureux met her coming out of the Hôtel de Boulogne on Léon's arm; and she was worried, imagining he would gossip. He was not that stupid.

But three days later, he came to her room, shut the door and said:

– I do rather need some money.

She announced that she could not give him any. Lheureux grumbled away and reminded her of his kindnesses.

Of the two bills signed by Charles, Emma had so far paid off only one. As to the second, the draper, at her entreaty, had agreed to replace it with two others, which had actually been renewed at a very long date. He took from his pocket a list of goods not paid for, namely: the curtains, the carpet, the material for the chair-covers, several dresses and various items of toiletry, to a total value of about two thousand francs.

She hung her head; he went on:

– Well, if you haven't any cash, you do have *property*.

And he mentioned a broken-down cottage situated in Barneville, near Aumale, which didn't bring in very much. It had originally been part of a small farm sold off by Monsieur Bovary senior, and Lheureux knew every detail, down to its acreage, and the names of the neighbours.

– If I were you, he said, I'd sell it off, settle up and you'd still have some money over.

She argued that it would be difficult to find a purchaser; he said he had hopes of finding one; but she asked how she could go about selling it.

– What about your power of attorney? he said.

This phrase came to her like a breath of fresh air.

– Leave the bill with me, said Emma.

– Oh, it's not worth the bother! replied Lheureux.

He came back the following week, and vaunted how, after immense efforts, he had finally discovered a certain Langlois who, for years now, had had his eye on the property, though without naming his price.

– Never mind the price! she exclaimed.

On the contrary, they ought to wait, and sound the fellow out. The whole business was worth making a journey for, and, since she couldn't do it, he offered to make the trip himself and to see to things with Langlois. On his return, he announced that the purchaser was offering four thousand francs.

Emma looked delighted at this news.

– Frankly, he added, it's a good price.

Half the amount was paid to her immediately, and, when she was about to settle her account, the draper said:

– It grieves me, upon my word it does, to see you handing over all at once a sum as *considerable* as that.

She gazed at the bank-notes; and, dreaming of the unlimited number of rendezvous which these two thousand francs represented, she stammered:

– What! What do you mean?

– Well! he laughed genially, we put whatever we like on receipts, don't we? I do know some of the finer points of housekeeping!

And he looked at her steadily, holding up two long documents and letting them slide down between his fingers. Finally, opening his pocket-book, he laid on the table the four bills payable to order, each for one thousand francs.

– You just sign these for me, and keep the lot.

She exclaimed in surprise, quite scandalized.

– But if I'm giving you the surplus, retorted Monsieur Lheureux impudently, I'm doing you a service, aren't I?

And, picking up a pen, he wrote across the bottom of the account: 'Received from Madame Bovary, four thousand francs.'

– What is there to worry about, since in six months' time you'll be drawing the balance on that shack of yours, and I'm making the last bill payable after that?

Emma was rather confused by these calculations, and there

was a ringing in her ears as if gold coins, bursting from their bags, were clinking around her feet. Finally Lheureux explained that a friend of his, Vinçart, a banker in Rouen, would discount these four bills, and he himself would hand over to Madame the balance from the actual debt.

But instead of two thousand francs, he only brought eighteen hundred, for friend Vinçart (as was *only fair*) had deducted two hundred, for commission and discount.

He casually asked for a receipt.

– You understand . . . in business . . . sometimes . . . And with the date, please, with the date.

A panorama of attainable fantasies now unfolded before Emma's eyes. She was prudent enough to put aside three thousand francs, which paid off the first three bills, when they fell due, but the fourth one, unluckily, was delivered to the house on a Thursday, and Charles, most perturbed, was impatiently awaiting his wife's return to have her explanation.

If she had not told him anything about this bill, it was simply to spare him little domestic worries; she sat on his knee, caressed him, cooed at him, and recited a long list of indispensable items bought on credit.

– Really, you must admit, considering the number of things, it's not that expensive.

Charles, at his wits' end, soon had recourse to the eternal Lheureux, who gave his word that he would smooth things over, if Monsieur would sign two bills, one for seven hundred francs, payable in three months' time. To do this, he wrote a pathetic letter to his mother. Instead of writing back, she came in person; and, when Emma wanted to know if he had got anything out of her, he answered:

– Yes. But she's asking to see the account.

Next day, at first light, Emma ran over to Monsieur Lheureux's and asked him to make out a new bill, for not more than one thousand francs; had she shown the bill for four thousand, she would have had to say that she had paid off two thirds of it, and reveal, consequently, the sale of the house, a transaction seen through by the merchant, and something that only ever came to light much later.

Despite the very low price of each article, the elder Madame Bovary inevitably found the expenses preposterous.

– Couldn't you have managed without a carpet? Why have new covers for the armchairs? In my day, people had only the one armchair in their house, for the old folks; anyway, that's how it was in my mother's house, and she was a respectable woman, I can tell you. Not everybody can be rich! Any amount of cash will trickle away through your fingers a penny at a time. I should be blushing pink if I pampered myself like you! And mind you, I'm an old woman, I need my comforts . . . The very idea! Frills and flounces! What! Linings made of silk! At two francs! When you can have cotton jaconet for ten sous, or even eight, that does perfectly well.

Emma, sitting back on the sofa, was reacting as calmly as possible:

– Enough, madame, that's enough.

The other woman continued lecturing her, predicting they would end up in the workhouse. Of course it was Bovary's fault. Thank goodness he had promised to cancel that power of attorney . . .

– What?

– He gave me his word, said the good woman.

Emma opened the window, called Charles over, and the poor boy had to confess to the promise extracted from him by his mother.

Emma went out of the room, and quickly came back in again, majestically handing her a large sheet of paper.

– Thank you very much, said the old woman.

And she threw the document into the fire.

Emma began to laugh, a loud strident continuous laugh: she was having a nervous attack.

– Oh, my God! shouted Charles. It's just as much your fault! Coming here, making a scene with her!

His mother, with a shrug of her shoulders, declared *it was just a big act*.

But Charles, rebelling for the first time in his life, took his wife's side, so that old Madame Bovary said she was going. She left next day, and, on the doorstep, as he was trying to keep her, she said:

– No! You love her more than you love me, and quite right too, that's just as it should be. Anyway, so be it. You'll see . . . Take care. I shall not be back here again, making a scene with her, as you call it.

Even so, Charles was left feeling greatly mortified in front of Emma, and she did not disguise how bitterly she still felt about his lack of trust; much pleading was required before she would consent to renew her power of attorney, and he even went along with her to Monsieur Guillaumin's to have a second one made out, exactly the same.

– I do understand, said the notary; a man of science can't be worrying himself about life's little practicalities.

And Charles was soothed by this unctuous remark, which gave his feebleness the flattering appearance of a lofty preoccupation.

What exuberance, the following Thursday, at the hotel, in their room, with Léon! She laughed, she cried, she sang, she danced, she sent down for ices, she wanted to smoke cigarettes; he thought her extravagant, but adorable, superb.

He had no idea what reaction of her entire being it was, driving her ever harder to throw herself into the pleasures of the flesh. She was becoming irritable, greedy and voluptuous; and she walked the streets with him, unabashed, oblivious, she said, of compromising herself. Sometimes, though, Emma shuddered at the sudden thought of meeting Rodolphe; for even though they had parted for ever, she still felt that she was not completely free of him.

One night, she didn't appear back in Yonville. Charles lost his head, and little Berthe, who wouldn't go to bed without her mummy, was sobbing her heart out. Justin had set off aimlessly down the road. Monsieur Homais had closed the pharmacy.

Finally, at eleven o'clock, almost out of his mind, Charles harnessed the trap, jumped in, lashed his horse and reached the Croix Rouge at about two in the morning. Not there. He thought the clerk might have seen her; but where did he live? Charles, fortunately, remembered the address of his employer. He ran straight there.

Day was just breaking. He noticed a brass plate above a door;

he knocked. Someone, from inside, shouted an answer to his question, along with lavish abuse of people who come waking everybody up in the night.

The house where the clerk lived had neither a bell, nor a knocker, nor a porter. Charles hammered at the shutters with his fists. A policeman happened to be passing; he took fright and walked away.

– Fool that I am, he told himself; of course, she must have stayed for dinner with Monsieur Lormeaux.

The Lormeaux family had left Rouen.

– She's stayed to look after Madame Dubreuil. Madame Dubreuil had been dead for six months! . . . So where is she?

An idea came to him. In a café he asked for a directory; and he quickly looked up Mademoiselle Lempereur, who lived at No. 74 Rue de la Renelle-des-Maroquiniers.

Just as he was turning into that street, Emma herself appeared at the far end; it was not exactly an embrace, rather he threw himself upon her, shouting:

– What kept you last night?

– I've been ill.

– What was it? . . . Where? . . . How? . . .

She passed a hand across her forehead, and said:

– At Mademoiselle Lempereur's.

– I knew it! I was on my way there.

– Oh, it's not worth it, said Emma. She went out a few minutes ago; but, in future, you are not to take it so to heart. I feel tied down, you see, if I know that the slightest delay is going to upset you like this.

It was a way of giving herself permission to be entirely heedless in her escapades. And she made the most of it, repeatedly. Whenever she was taken with the idea of seeing Léon, off she went on any sort of pretext, and, as he would not be expecting her that day, she used to seek him out at his office.

It was a great delight the first few times; but soon he no longer hid the truth, that is to say: his employer was grumbling about these distractions.

– Oh, him! Come on, she said.

And he sneaked away.

She wanted him to dress in black and grow a little beard, so as to look like the portraits of Louis XIII. She wanted to see his lodgings, found them shabby; he blushed, she took no notice, advised him to buy some curtains like hers, and when he protested at the expense:

– Ah, you hold on to your little pennies, don't you? she said with a laugh.

Léon had to tell her, each time, all his doings since their last meeting. She demanded verses, verses written for her, a *love poem* in her honour; he could never manage to find the rhyme for the second verse, and in the end he copied out a sonnet from a keepsake.

This was not so much from vanity but from a simple desire to please her. He didn't question her ideas; he accepted her tastes; he became her mistress rather than she becoming his. She spoke tender words mingled with kisses that carried his soul away. Where could she have learned such corruption, almost intangible, so profoundly had it been dissembled?

6

On the journeys he made to see her, Léon had often dined at the pharmacist's house, and he felt obliged, in all politeness, to invite him back in turn.

– A pleasure! had been Homais's reply; anyway, the fact is I need to splash out a bit, I'm vegetating here. We'll go to the theatres, the restaurants, we'll have a time of it!

– Oh, my dear, murmured Madame Homais tenderly, aghast at the vague perils to which he was about to expose himself.

– Well! What! Don't you think I'm ruining my health fast enough here, living amid the continual emanations of the pharmacy? There now, see how women are: jealous of science, and protesting whenever a man takes his innocent little pleasures. Never mind, you can count on me; one of these days, I'll turn up in Rouen and we'll paint the place red.

The apothecary, hitherto, would certainly have refrained from any such expression; but these days he was cultivating a sprightly Parisian style which he thought in the best taste; and, just like Madame Bovary, his neighbour, he eagerly interrogated the clerk about life in the capital, even using slang so as to dazzle ... the bourgeois, saying *roost, digs, dandy, dandiest, Cock Street*, and *I'll hook it*, instead of: I'm going.

And so, one Thursday, Emma was surprised to meet, in the kitchen of the Golden Lion, Monsieur Homais in travelling costume, that is to say, wrapped in an old cloak never seen on him before, carrying a bag in one hand, and, in the other hand, the foot-warmer from his shop. He had not confided his plans to anyone, for fear of alarming the public by his absence.

No doubt he was excited at the idea of revisiting the scenes of his youth, for he never stopped talking all the way to Rouen; the instant they arrived, he leaped out of the carriage and set off in search of Léon; and the clerk's struggles were in vain, Monsieur Homais dragged him off to the big Café de Normandie, which he entered majestically without taking off his hat, thinking it most provincial to uncover in a public place.

Emma waited three quarters of an hour for Léon. In the end, she rushed to his office, and, lost in various conjectures, accusing him of indifference and reproaching herself for her weakness, she spent the afternoon with her nose glued to the window.

At two o'clock the men were still sitting at the café-table together. The main room was emptying; the stove-pipe, in the shape of a palm-tree, unfurled its gilded cluster across the white ceiling; and next to them, outside the window, in full sunlight, a little fountain was gurgling into its marble basin where, in among the watercress and the asparagus, three sluggish lobsters were spread out, next to the quails, arranged in a pile, on their sides.

Homais was enjoying himself. Though he was befuddled more by the luxury of the place than by the rich food, the bottle of Pomard, even so, was stimulating his faculties rather, and, when the *omelette au rhum* appeared, he began to expound theories about women which were most immoral. What he found seductive above all else was *chic*. He adored an elegant toilette in a richly furnished room, and, when it came to physical attributes, he had no aversion to a *nice little morsel*.

Léon was watching the clock in despair. The apothecary carried on drinking, eating, talking.

– You must be rather deprived in Rouen, he said suddenly. Anyway your true-love lives near at hand.

And, as the other man blushed:

– Come on, be honest! Do you deny that in Yonville . . .

The young man stammered something.

– At Madame Bovary's, you are courting . . .?

– Courting who?

– The maid!

He was quite serious; but, vanity prevailing over prudence, Léon, in spite of himself, protested. Besides, he only liked dark women.

– I quite approve, said the pharmacist; they have more temperament.

And, leaning forward to whisper in his friend's ear, he specified the symptoms which reveal if a woman has temperament. He even launched into an ethnographic digression: German woman are vaporous, French women are libertine, Italian women are passionate.

– And what about negresses? asked the clerk.

– An artistic taste, said Homais. Waiter! Two coffees!

– Shall we go? said Léon finally, losing patience.

– *Jawohl.*

But, before they left, he wanted to see the proprietor, and he paid him various compliments.

In order to escape, the young man declared that he had some business to see to.

– Oh, I'll come with you! said Homais.

And, as he walked along the street with him, he was talking all about his wife, his children, and their future, and his pharmacy, telling him what a sorry state it had been in, and to what perfection he had raised it up.

Once they reached the Hôtel de Boulogne, Léon broke away from him, ran off upstairs, and found his mistress in turmoil.

At the mention of the pharmacist, she lost her temper. However, he had a fund of excuses; it wasn't his fault, didn't she know what Homais was like? How could she believe that he

preferred that man's company? But she turned away; he held on
to her; and, sinking to his knees, he put his arms around her
waist, in a languorous pose that proclaimed his beseeching
desire.

She was standing there, her great flaming eyes resting upon
him with a look that was solemn and almost terrifying. They
were eclipsed by tears, her swollen eyelids fell shut, she yielded
her hand, and Léon was raising it to his lips when a servant
appeared, to inform Monsieur that he was required below.

– Are you coming back? she said.

– Yes.

– But when?

– Immediately.

– It was a *spoof*, said the pharmacist when he saw Léon. I
thought I would interrupt your visit because it seemed to be
irksome to you. Let's go to Bridoux's for a glass of *garus*.

Léon swore that he had to go back to his office. The apothecary made jokes about legal screed.

– Leave your Cujas and Bartole alone for a bit, damn it!
What's to stop you? Be a good chap! Let's go to Bridoux's;
you'll be able to see his dog. It's quite fascinating!

And as the clerk was still insisting:

– I'll come along too. I can read the paper while I'm waiting
for you, or I can be leafing through the Penal Code.

Léon, bewildered by Emma's anger, by Homais's chatter and
perhaps by the bulk of his lunch, could not make a decision,
apparently fascinated by the pharmacist, who kept saying:

– Let's go to Bridoux's! It's only round the corner, on the Rue
Malapu.

And so, out of cowardice, out of stupidity, from that unname-
able feeling which urges us to the most antipathetic actions, he
let himself be led to Bridoux's; and they found him in his little
yard, supervising three waiters who were gasping for breath as
they turned the big wheel on a machine for making seltzer-water.
Homais gave them some advice; he embraced Bridoux; they
drank the *garus*. Twenty times Léon tried to get away; but the
other man took him by the arm, saying:

– In a minute! I'm coming. We'll go along to *Le Fanal de*

Rouen, and see the people there. I'll introduce you to Thomassin.

However, he managed to escape and he ran all the way to the hotel. Emma was no longer there.

She had only just left, in exasperation. For now she detested him. It felt like an outrage, his breaking of the promise he had made to her, and she searched around after other reasons for breaking with him: he was incapable of heroism, feeble, banal, softer than a woman, as well as being miserly and pusillanimous.

Calming down, she eventually realized that she had probably slandered him. But the denigration of those we love always detaches us from them in some degree. Never touch your idols: the gilding will stick to your fingers.

They reached the stage of talking more often about things of no consequence to their love; and, in the letters that Emma sent to him, there was a great deal about flowers, verses, the moon and the stars, naïve devices of a depleted passion, attempting to rejuvenate itself from external sources. She repeatedly promised to herself, from their next meeting, an intense happiness; then she realized that she was feeling nothing remarkable. This disappointment soon gave way to new hopes, and Emma came back to him more inflamed, more voracious. Her undressing was brutal, tearing at the delicate laces on her corset, which rustled down over her hips like a slithering snake. She tiptoed over on bare feet to check once again that the door was locked, and in one motion she shed all her clothes; – pale and silent and serious, she fell upon him, shivering.

And yet, on that brow covered in cold drops, on those murmuring lips, in those wild eyes, and in the clasping of those arms, there was something excessive, something empty and lugubrious, which Léon felt sliding, imperceptibly, between them, as if to push them asunder.

He did not dare to question her; but, seeing her so experienced, she must, he told himself, have been through every ordeal of suffering and of pleasure. What had once charmed him, he now found rather frightening. Besides, he was rebelling against the grip, tightening every day, of her personality. He begrudged Emma this perpetual triumph. He even tried to stop himself from loving her; but, at the sound of her boots creaking, he would feel helpless, like a drunkard at the smell of strong liquor.

She made every effort, it is true, to lavish on him various little attentions, from exquisite meals all the way to coquettishness of dress and smouldering glances. From Yonville she brought roses in her breast, and threw them over him; she showed her concern for his health, gave him advice in matters of conduct; and, to strengthen her hold on him, hoping perhaps that heaven would intervene, around his neck she hung a medallion with an image of the Virgin. She made inquiries, like a virtuous mother, about his companions. She said to him:

– You are not to see them, you are not to go out, you must not think about anyone else; you are to love me!

She would have liked to be able to keep a constant eye upon him, and it occurred to her to have him followed in the streets. Near the hotel, there was always a kind of tramp who accosted people and he would have been . . . But her pride forbade it.

– Well, so what! If he is deceiving me, what does it matter! I really don't care!

One day when they had parted early, and she was making her way back on her own along the boulevard, she noticed the walls of her convent; and she sat down on a bench in the shade of the elms. How peaceful it had been in those days! How she used to long for the ineffable sentiment of love which she endeavoured to conjure up from the books she was reading.

The early months of her marriage, horse-riding in the forest, the Viscount waltzing with her, and Lagardy singing, it passed before her eyes again . . . And Léon suddenly appeared to her just as far away as the others.

– And yet I love him! she told herself.

No matter! She was not happy, had never been so. Where did it come from, this feeling of deprivation, this instantaneous decay of the things in which she put her trust? . . . But, if there were somewhere a strong and beautiful creature, a valiant nature full of passion and delicacy in equal measure, the heart of a poet in the figure of an angel, a lyre with strings of steel, sounding to the skies elegiac epithalamia, why should she not, fortuitously, find such a one? What an impossibility! Nothing, anyway, was worth that great quest; it was all lies! Every smile concealed the yawn of boredom, every joy a malediction, every satisfaction brought its nausea, and even the most perfect kisses only leave upon the lips a fantastical craving for the supreme pleasure.

A noisy metallic wheezing lingered on the air and four strokes were heard from the convent clock. Four o'clock! And she felt as though she had been there, on that bench, for an eternity. For an infinity of passion can be contained in one minute, like a crowd in a small space.

This was how Emma lived, quite immersed in her passions, and worrying herself about money no more than would a duchess.

But one day, a sickly looking man, rubicund and bald, came to the house, announcing that he had been sent by Monsieur Vinçart of Rouen. He took out the pins that fastened up the side-pocket of his long green overcoat, stuck them in his sleeve and politely handed over a document.

It was a bill for seven hundred francs, with her signature, which Lheureux, despite his reassurances, had passed on to Vinçart.

She sent her maid to see Lheureux. He couldn't come.

Then the stranger, who had remained standing, throwing right and left curious glances obscured by his bushy blond eyebrows, asked innocently:

– What answer shall I give to Monsieur Vinçart?

– Well, said Emma, tell him . . . that I haven't any . . . Not until next week . . . He'll have to wait . . . yes, next week.

And the fellow left without a word.

But, next day, at noon, she received a writ; and the sight of the stamped document, variously adorned with the words MAÎTRE HARENG, BAILIFF AT BUCHY in large letters, frightened her so greatly that she hurried over to the draper's.

She found him in his shop, tying up a parcel.

– Madame! he said, I am at your service.

Lheureux nevertheless carried on with what he was doing, assisted by a young girl of about thirteen, slightly hunchbacked, who worked for him in both the shop and in the kitchen.

Clattering across the floorboards in his clogs, he went up the stairs in front of Madame, and showed her into a little office, where on a large pinewood desk stood a number of ledgers, secured behind a padlocked iron bar. Against the wall, under some calico remnants, you could just see a safe, but one of such dimensions that it must have contained other things besides bills and money. Monsieur Lheureux made small loans on security, and this was where he kept Madame Bovary's gold chain, along with the ear-rings of poor old Père Tellier, who, forced eventually to sell up, had bought an ailing grocery business in Quincampoix, where he was dying of a catarrh, with a face yellower than the candles in his shop.

Lheureux sat down in his large wicker armchair and said:

– What's the news?

– Look.

And she handed him the sheet of paper.

– Well, what am I supposed to do about it?

She grew angry, reminding him of his promise not to circulate her bills; he acknowledged it.

– But my hand was being forced, there was a knife at my throat.

– And what's going to happen now? she said.

– Oh, very simple: a court order, and then the bailiffs . . . *Kaput!*

Emma restrained herself from hitting him. Calmly she asked if there were any way of pacifying Monsieur Vinçart.

– Oh, really! Pacify Vinçart? You've no idea what he's like. More ferocious than an Arab.

Anyway Monsieur Lheureux would have to do something.

– Listen here! It seems to me that so far I've been pretty good to you.

And, opening one of his ledgers:

– Here you are!

Running his finger up the page:

– Let me see . . . let me see . . . 3rd of August, two hundred francs . . . on 17th of June, one hundred and fifty . . . 23rd of March, forty-six . . . In April . . .

And he stopped short, as if he were afraid of committing some blunder:

– And that's without mentioning the bills signed by Monsieur,

one for seven hundred francs, another for three hundred! As for
your little instalments and the interest, there's no end to it, it's
a mess. I want no more to do with it!

She wept, she even called him 'my dear Monsieur Lheureux'.
But he kept on blaming that rascal Vinçart. Besides, he didn't
have a penny, nobody was paying up these days, they were
eating the shirt off his back, a poor shopkeeper like him couldn't
be advancing money.

Emma said nothing; and Monsieur Lheureux, who was nibbling at the end of a pen, was doubtless worried by her silence.

– Unless, one of these days, I have something coming in . . . I
could . . .

– Anyway, she said, as soon as the Barneville arrears . . .

– What? . . .

– And, when he heard that Langlois had not yet paid up, he
seemed much surprised. Now, in a honeyed voice:

– And what terms shall we say . . .?

– Oh, whatever you like!

At this he closed his eyes to ponder the matter, wrote down a
few figures, and, declaring that he would have great problems,
that the whole thing was irksome and he was bleeding himself
white, he made out four bills for two hundred and fifty francs
each, to fall due at intervals of one month.

– Provided Vinçart is willing to listen to me! Otherwise, it's
settled, I don't drag my feet, and I deal fair and square.

He nonchalantly showed her several new pieces of merchandise, but none of it, in his opinion, worthy of Madame.

– When I look at this dress at seven sous a metre, and guaranteed colour-fast! They all swallow it, though. Of course you
don't let on what it really is, as you can imagine. (By this display
of his rascality towards others he was hoping to convince her
thoroughly of his probity.)

He called her back, to show her three ells of lace he had
recently picked up *at a sale*.

– Lovely, isn't it? said Lheureux; lots of people have it these
days, for the backs of armchairs, it's the fashion.

And, more deftly than a conjuror, he wrapped the lace in blue
paper and put it into Emma's hands.

– But how much is it going . . .?

– Oh, some other time! he answered as he turned away.

That same evening, she prompted Bovary to write to his mother and ask her to send them the whole residue of the inheritance. The mother-in-law replied that there was nothing more; the estate had now been wound up, and all that was left, apart from Barneville, was an income of about six hundred francs a year, which she would send to them promptly.

Madame sent out accounts to two or three clients, and, when it was a success, she soon made extensive use of this method. She was always careful to add a post-script: 'Don't mention this to my husband, you know how proud he is . . . Do forgive me . . . Your obedient servant . . .' There were a few complaints; she intercepted them.

To make some money, she began selling off her old gloves, her old hats, any old junk; and she bargained rapaciously – her peasant blood having given her a taste for making a profit. On her trips to town, she would pick up bits of things, which Monsieur Lheureux, if nobody else, would certainly take from her. She bought ostrich feathers, Chinese porcelain and wooden caskets; she borrowed from Félicité, from Madame Lefrançois, from the landlady at the Croix Rouge, from everyone, from anyone. With the money that eventually came to her from Barneville, she paid off two bills; the other fifteen hundred francs trickled away. She renewed the bills, and so it went on!

Now and again, it's true, she did try to reckon up; but she uncovered such a preposterous state of affairs that she could not believe her own figures. She started the calculations again, soon got in a muddle, gave it up as a bad job and thought no more about it.

The house was a gloomy place, nowadays. Tradesmen were to be seen leaving with fury on their faces. There were handkerchiefs lying about on the stoves; and little Berthe, to the great horror of Madame Homais, had holes in her stockings. If Charles, timidly, ventured to say anything, she retorted brutally that it wasn't her fault.

Why these outbursts? He explained it by her old nervous ailment; and, reproaching himself with having treated her infirmities as defects, he accused himself of selfishness, longed to run and take her in his arms.

– Oh, no, he said to himself. It'd vex her.

And he held back.

After dinner, he used to walk around the garden on his own; he would take little Berthe on his knee, and, opening his medical journal, he tried to teach her to read. Before very long, the child, who was never given any lessons, would be staring at him with her big sad eyes and begin to cry. So he comforted her; he went to fill the watering-can for her to make rivers across the gravel, or broke branches off the privet for her to plant trees in the flower-beds, which made little difference to the garden, covered in weeds; they owed Lestiboudois so many days' wages!

– Better call nanny, my little one, said Charles. You know mummy doesn't like to be disturbed.

Autumn was coming and the leaves were already falling – just as it was two years ago, when she had been ill! When would it be over! . . . And he walked on, with his hands behind his back.

Madame was up in her room. Nobody went in to her. She stayed there all day long, sluggish, half naked, and, every so often, burning oriental pastilles which she had bought in Rouen, from a shop run by an Algerian. To avoid having that man lying asleep up against her body every night, she managed, after many a grimace, to banish him up to the second floor; and she used to read until dawn, bizarre books, full of orgiastic set-pieces and bloodthirsty adventures. Terror-stricken, she screamed. Charles would rush in.

– Oh, do go away! she'd say.

Or, at other times, when she felt the fierce heat of that intimate flame which adultery had kindled in her, breathless and shaking with desire she would open her window, breathe down the cold air, spread upon the wind the abundance of her hair, and, gazing up at the stars, dream of princely lovers. She was thinking of him, of Léon. At that moment she would have given everything for a single one of those rendezvous which brought her contentment.

Those were her gala days. She wanted them to be splendid!

And, when he couldn't pay for everything himself, she liberally
made up the difference, which happened almost every time. He
tried to convince her that they would be just as comfortable
somewhere else, in some more modest hotel; but she raised
objections.

One day, she took from her bag six little silver spoons (they
had been a wedding-present from Père Rouault), and she asked
him to take them for her, at once, to the pawn-shop; and
Léon obeyed, though he disliked the business. He was afraid of
compromising himself.

Then, upon reflection, he decided that his mistress was beginning to behave strangely, and perhaps people were right in
wanting to disentangle him from her.

In fact, somebody had sent a long anonymous letter to his
mother, warning her that he was *ruining himself with a married
woman*; and the good lady, immediately detecting the spectre
that haunts every family, in other words, the vague pernicious
creature, the siren, the fantastical monster that lives down in
the fathomless places of love, wrote to Maître Dubocage, his
employer, who acted splendidly in the affair. He kept Léon for
three quarters of an hour, trying to open his eyes, to keep him
from the abyss. An intrigue of this sort would harm his chances
of setting up later on. He pleaded with him to break it off and,
if he would not make the sacrifice in his own interest, then do it
at least for him, for Dubocage!

In the end Léon had sworn not to see Emma again; and he
was reproaching himself for not having kept his word, considering the vexations and the remarks that this woman could still
bring down upon him, not to mention the pleasantries that came
from his colleagues, gathered around the stove, in the morning.
Besides, he was about to be made senior clerk: it was time to be
serious. So he gave up the flute, exalted sentiment, the imagination. For every bourgeois, in the heat of youth, if only for a day,
for a minute, has believed himself capable of immense passions,
of heroic enterprises. The most mediocre libertine has dreamed
of oriental princesses; every notary carries about inside him the
debris of a poet.

These days he was bored when Emma, suddenly, wept upon

his breast; and his heart like people who can only tolerate a certain dose of music, was sluggishly indifferent to the tumult of a love whose refinements he no longer appreciated.

They knew each other too well for any of those astonishments which multiply a hundredfold the joys of possession. Emma was rediscovering in adultery the platitudes of marriage.

But how could she get rid of him? Humiliated though she might feel at such ignominious satisfaction, she still clung to them from habit or depravity; and, every day, she craved for him more and more, spoiling any pleasure by demanding too much from it. She blamed Léon for her disappointment, as though he had betrayed her; and she even longed for some catastrophe that would bring about their separation, since she didn't have the courage to make a decision.

None the less she continued to write love-letters to him, by virtue of the following notion: a woman should always write to her lover.

But, as she was writing, she beheld a different man, a phantom put together from her most ardent memories, her favourite books, her most powerful longings; and by the end he became so real, so tangible, that her heart was racing with the wonder of it, though she was unable to imagine him distinctly, for he faded, like a god, into the abundance of his attributes. He lived in the big blue country where silken rope-ladders swing from the balconies, scented by flowers and lit by the moon. She felt him so near, he was coming and he was about to carry her away quite utterly with a kiss. But she fell quite flat again, broken; for these shadowy ecstasies wearied her more than any wild debauchery.

She now experienced an incessant and universal lassitude. Many a time, Emma received writs, pieces of official paper that she barely gave a glance. She would have liked to stop living, or to be sleeping continuously.

On the day of the mid-Lent carnival, she did not return to Yonville; in the evening she went to a masked ball. She wore velvet breeches and red stockings, a gentleman's wig, and a paper lantern over one ear. She jumped about all night to the furious sound of trombones; people made a circle around her;

and in the morning she found herself on the steps of the theatre among five or six maskers, dressed as dockers and sailors, friends of Léon's, who were talking about finding some supper.

The neighbouring cafés were full. Down by the harbour they spotted a very inferior restaurant where the proprietor showed them to a small room up on the fourth floor.

The men were whispering in a corner, no doubt deliberating the bill. They comprised one clerk, two medics, and a shop-assistant: what companions for her! As for the women, Emma soon realized, from their voices, that they must be, nearly all of them, of the lowest sort. Now she felt frightened, pushed her chair back from the table and lowered her eyes.

The others began to eat. She ate nothing; her face was on fire, her eyes were itching and her skin was as cold as ice. In her head she could feel the ballroom-floor, still bouncing up and down from the rhythmic pulsation of a thousand dancing feet. The smell of the punch along with the cigar smoke made her dizzy. She fainted; they carried her over to the window.

Day was beginning to break, and a great patch of red was spreading across the pale sky, over the Côte Sainte-Catherine. The blue-grey river was shivering in the wind; there was no one on the bridges; the street-lamps were going out.

Nevertheless she revived and happened to think of Berthe, who was asleep somewhere over there, in the maid's room. But a cart loaded with long steel bars went past, making a deafening clatter of metal echo back from the walls of the houses.

She left them abruptly, got rid of her costume, told Léon he must go home, and at last she was alone in the Hôtel de Boulogne. It was quite unbearable, beginning with herself. She wanted to fly away like a bird and become young again, some-where, far away, under a wide immaculate sky.

She went out, she crossed the boulevard, the Place Cauchoise and the suburbs, until she came to a wide open street over-looking some gardens. She was walking quickly, the fresh air calming her: and gradually the crowd of faces, the masks, the quadrilles, the chandeliers, the supper, those women, dis-appeared like a mist in the wind. Back at the Croix Rouge, she threw herself on to her bed, in the little room on the second floor, with the pictures of *La Tour de Nesle*. At four o'clock in the afternoon, Hivert woke her up.

When she got home, Félicité showed her a grey sheet of paper from behind the clock. She read:

By virtue of the order consequent upon the judgment . . .

What judgment? The previous day, in fact, they had delivered another document which she had not seen; consequently she was astounded by the words:

By Order of the King, in the name of the law, to Madame Bovary . . .

Skipping several lines, she read:

Within twenty-four hours, without fail . . . What? *To pay the sum of eight thousand francs.* And further down the page: *She will be constrained thereto by every form of law, and notably by the seizure of her furniture and effects.*

What was to be done? In twenty-four hours it was; tomorrow! Lheureux, she thought, was no doubt trying to frighten her again; for suddenly she realized what he was up to, the purpose behind his kindnesses. What reassured her, was precisely the absurdity of the sum in question.

However, by repeatedly buying things on credit, borrowing, signing bills and renewing them, while they augmented every time they expired, she had managed to create for the esteemed Lheureux a capital sum, which he was awaiting impatiently to employ in his speculations.

She walked into his shop with a casual air:

– Do you know what's happening to me? It must be a joke!

– No.

– What do you mean?

He turned to her slowly, folded his arms and said:

– Did you think, my little lady, that I was going to be your supplier and your banker until the very end of time, just for the love of God? I do have to recover my outgoings, you must admit!

She protested at the amount of the debt.

– That's too bad! The court has recognized it! Judgment has been given! You've been notified! Anyway, it's not me, it's Vinçart.

– Couldn't you . . .

– Nothing whatsoever!

– Well . . . all the same . . . we can talk it over.

And she began to manoeuvre; she hadn't realized . . . it was such a shock . . .

– Whose fault is that, eh? said Lheureux with an ironic bow. While I'm slaving away here just like a nigger, you're gadding about!

– Not a sermon!

– It never does any harm, he replied.

She lost her nerve, she pleaded with him; and she even put her pretty hand, her slender white hand, on the draper's knee.

– Now you leave me alone. Anyone would think you wanted to seduce me!

– You are a wretch! she cried.

– Such a little hothead! he said with a laugh.

– I shall tell people about you. I'll tell my husband that . . .

– Well, I shall show him a thing or two, that husband of yours!

And from his safe Lheureux took out the receipt for eighteen hundred francs, which she had given him at the time of the Vinçart transaction.

– Do you really think, he added, that he won't see through your little robbery, the poor dear man.

She crumpled, just as if she'd been hit on the head with a club. He was pacing up and down between the window and the desk, saying over and over again:

– I'll show it to him, I will . . . I'll show it to him, I will . . .

He came up to her, and, in a gentle voice:

– It's not very pleasant, I know that; but after all it never did kill anyone, did it, and, since it is the only way left for you to pay me back my money . . .

– But where will I find it? said Emma wringing her hands.

– Bah! What about those good friends of yours?

And he looked at her with a glance so perspicacious and so terrible that it made her innards flutter.

– I promise you, she said, I'll sign any . . .

– I've had about enough of your signatures.

– I can still sell . . .

– Come on! he said, with a shrug of the shoulders. You've nothing left.

And he shouted down the judas-hole that opened into the shop:

– Annette! Don't forget the three remnants of number fourteen.

The servant appeared; Emma understood, and asked how much money would be needed to stop the proceedings.

– It's too late!

– But if I were to bring you several thousand francs, a quarter of the total, a third, nearly all?

– No, it's pointless!

He pushed her gently towards the stairs.

– I implore you, Monsieur Lheureux, a few more days!

She was sobbing.

– Oh, look! A few tears!

– You drive me to despair!

– I really don't give a damn! he said as he shut the door.

                                   7

She was stoical, next day, when Maître Hareng, the bailiff, with two witnesses, arrived at the house to make out the inventory for the seizure.

They began in Bovary's consulting-room and they didn't list the phrenological head, which was deemed to be one of the *instruments of his profession*; but in the kitchen they counted the plates, the pots, the chairs, the candlesticks, and, in her bedroom, the ornaments on the little shelf. They examined her dresses, the linen, the dressing-room; and her existence, down to its most intimate secrets, was exposed, like a cadaver at an autopsy, to the eyes of those three men.

Maître Hareng, buttoned up in a thin black coat, with a white cravat and extremely tight boot-straps, kept saying every so often:

– With your permission, madame? With your permission?

Frequently he exclaimed:

– Charming! . . . Very pretty!

Then he would begin writing again, dipping his pen in the ink-horn he was holding in his left hand.

When they had finished with the rooms, they went up to the attic.

There she kept a desk, in which Rodolphe's letters were locked away. It had to be opened.

– Ahah! A correspondence! said Maître Hareng with a discreet smile. Allow me please! I must make sure the box contains nothing else.

And he tilted the papers, gently, as if to dislodge any gold coins. She felt indignant, to see that coarse hand, the pink flabby fingers just like slugs, touching those pages which had set her heart beating.

At last they went away! Félicité came back into the house. Emma had sent her to watch out for Bovary and keep him away; and they hurriedly installed the bailiff's man up in the attic, where he promised to stay.

Charles, that evening, looked troubled. Emma watched him in great anxiety, imagining accusations in every line on his face. When her eyes strayed over the Chinese screens around the fireplace, the big curtains, the armchairs, the things that had assuaged the bitterness of her life, she was seized with remorse, or rather an immense regret which, far from obliterating her passion, served to inflame it. Charles was placidly poking the fire, with his feet on the fender.

On one occasion the bailiff's man, probably bored up in his hiding place, made a slight noise.

– Is there somebody walking around up there? said Charles.

– No, she said, there's a window been left open and it's tapping in the breeze.

Next day, a Sunday, she set off for Rouen, to call on those bankers whose names she had heard of. They had gone into the country or were away on their travels. She was undeterred; and those she managed to see, she asked for money, declaring that she must have some, that she would pay it back. Some of them laughed in her face; all refused her.

At two o'clock, she hurried over to Léon's, knocked on his door. There was no answer. He eventually appeared.

– What brings you here?

– Am I disturbing you?

– Not really . . . but . . .

And he confessed that his landlord didn't like people having 'women' there.

– I must talk to you.

So he got his key down. She stopped him.

– No, not here. In our room.

And so they went to their room, at the Hôtel de Boulogne.

She drank a big glass of water when they arrived. She was very pale. She said to him:

– Léon, you are going to do something for me.

And, grasping both his hands tight in hers, she shook him as she said:

– Listen, I need eight thousand francs!

– You must be mad!

– Not yet!

And, telling him about the seizure, she explained her predicament; Charles knew nothing at all about it, her mother-in-law detested her, Père Rouault couldn't help; but he, Léon, was going to set to work to find this indispensable sum . . .

– How am I supposed to . . .?

– What a weakling you are! she cried.

He said stupidly:

– You're panicking. Perhaps a few thousand francs would keep your chap quiet.

All the more reason for trying to do something; it must be possible to get hold of three thousand francs. Besides, Léon could offer security instead of her.

– Go on! You must! Hurry up! I shall love you famously!

He went off, came back after an hour with a solemn face, and said:

– I've been to see three people . . . it's useless!

They sat there facing each other, on either side of the fireplace, motionless, without a word. Emma shrugged her shoulders, and tapped her foot. He heard her muttering:

– If it were me I'd soon get it.

– From where?

– From your office!

And she gazed at him.

An infernal audacity radiated from her burning eyes, the eyelids slowly closing in a message lascivious and inviting; and now the young man felt himself weakening beneath the calm determination of this woman who was inciting him to crime. He felt afraid, and to avoid any explanations, he clapped his hand to his forehead, crying:

– Morel is supposed to be back this evening. He won't refuse me (this was a friend of his, the son of a rich merchant), and I'll try to bring it to you tomorrow, he added.

Emma did not appear to greet this idea as joyfully as he had expected. Did she suspect a lie? He continued with a blush:

– However, if you don't see me by three o'clock, don't wait for me, my dear. Now I must be going, excuse me. Goodbye!

He took her hand, but it felt limp and cold. Emma's powers of feeling were exhausted.

The clock struck four; and she rose to return to Yonville, like an automaton, obeying the stimulus of habit.

It was a fine day; one of those hard bright March days, when the sun is shining in a clear pale sky. In their Sunday best, the people of Rouen were strolling contentedly. She reached the square in front of the cathedral. They were coming out of vespers; the crowd was flowing through the three doors like a river through the three arches of a bridge, and, there in the midst, as steady as a rock, stood the beadle.

She remembered that day when, in great anxiety and hopefulness, she had entered in beneath that huge vault which spread above her less capacious than her love; and she walked on, weeping behind her veil, distracted, swaying on her feet, almost fainting.

– Clear the way! came a shout from behind a courtyard gate as it swung open.

She stopped to make way for a black horse, prancing between the shafts of a tilbury driven by a gentleman in a sable coat.

Who could it be? She knew him . . . The carriage sped away and disappeared.

But it was him, the Viscount! She turned her head: the street was empty. And she felt so crushed, so saddened, that she leaned up against a wall to keep herself on her feet.

She thought she had been mistaken. Anyway, it was just a blur. Everything, within and without, was forsaking her. She was bewildered, sinking helplessly into a great gulf; and it was almost a joy to her, when she arrived at the Croix Rouge, to see the good Monsieur Homais, who was watching over the loading on to the *Hirondelle* of a large box full of pharmaceutical supplies. In his hand, wrapped in a handkerchief, he had six *cheminots* for his wife.

Madame Homais was very fond of these solid little turban-shaped loaves, eaten in Lent with salted butter: last remnant of Gothic foodstuffs, going back perhaps to the age of the Crusades, on which the robust Normans had gorged themselves in those days, fancying they saw upon the table, in the yellow torchlight, between the flagons of mulled wine and the gigantic sides of pork, Saracens' heads ready to be devoured. The apothecary's wife used to munch them like her ancestors, heroically, in spite of the dreadful state of her teeth; so, whenever Monsieur Homais made the journey into town, he never failed to bring some back for her, always getting them from the best shop, in the Rue Massacre.

– Delighted to see you! he said, offering his hand to help Emma up into the *Hirondelle*.

He put the *cheminots* up on the rack, and sat there bare-headed, with his arms folded, in an attitude pensive and napoleonic.

But when the Blind Man, as usual, appeared at the foot of the hill, he exclaimed:

– I cannot understand why it is that the authorities still tolerate such scandalous activities. Those wretched people ought to be locked away and made to do some work! Progress, upon my word, goes at a snail's pace! We are wallowing in the worst barbarism!

The Blind Man held out his hat, and it flapped at the carriage-window, like a piece of the upholstery hanging off.

– There, said the pharmacist, is a scrofulous affection!

And, even though he knew the poor devil, he pretended to be seeing him for the first time, muttered the words *cornea, opaque cornea, sclerotic, facies*, and asked him in a paternal tone:

– How long, my friend, have you had this terrible affliction? Instead of getting drunk in the tavern, you would do better to follow a diet.

He recommended good wine, good beer, good roast meat. The Blind Man carried on with his song; he seemed almost an idiot. Finally, Monsieur Homais opened his purse.

– Here you are, here's a penny, I want some change; and don't forget my advice, it'll do you good.

Hivert ventured to express certain doubts as to its efficacy. But the apothecary guaranteed that he would cure the man himself, with an antiphlogiston ointment of his own creation, and he gave his address:

– Monsieur Homais, just near the market, you ask anyone.

– Well, after all that, said Hivert, you'd better *give us a performance*.

The Blind Man squatted down, and, with his head back, rolling his greenish eyes, and sticking out his tongue, he rubbed his hands on his belly as he let out a kind of muffled howl, like a ravenous dog. Emma, in disgust, flung at him, over her shoulder, a five-franc piece. That was all she had left. It seemed splendid to throw it away like this.

The carriage was moving again, when suddenly Monsieur Homais leaned out of the window and shouted:

– No farinaceous or dairy products! Wear wool next to the skin and expose the affected parts to the smoke from juniper berries.

The spectacle of familiar objects passing by in steady sequence gradually turned Emma's thoughts away from her present troubles. An intolerable fatigue overwhelmed her, and she arrived home in a stupor, demoralized, almost asleep.

– Whatever will be, will be, she said to herself.

Who knows? At any moment, something extraordinary might happen. Lheureux might even drop dead.

She awoke, at nine o'clock in the morning, to the sound of voices down in the square. There was a crowd gathered in the market to read a large notice pasted up on one of the pillars, and she saw Justin, who was standing up on a stone and tearing it down. But, just at that moment, the village policeman took hold of him by the collar. Monsieur Homais came out from the pharmacy, and Mère Lefrançois, in the middle of the crowd, looked as if she were holding forth.

– Madame! Madame! shouted Félicité, running in. It's abominable!

And the poor girl, most upset, handed her the sheet of yellow paper she had just torn down from the door. In a single glance, Emma read that her furniture was to be sold off.

Now they gazed at each other in silence. The two women, the servant and the mistress, had no secrets from each other. At last Félicité sighed:

– If I were you, madame, I'd go to see Maître Guillaumin.

– Would you? . . .

And this question meant:

– You know the lawyer's house, through his servant. Has the master ever spoken of me?

– Yes, you should go.

She got dressed, putting on her black gown and the bonnet with the jade beads; and, to avoid being seen (there was still a crowd of people on the square), she left the village by the path along the river-bank.

Quite out of breath, she reached the notary's front gate; the sky was dull and it was snowing a little.

At the sound of the bell, Théodore, in a red waistcoat, appeared on the doorstep; he came to open the gate for her in an almost familiar manner, as though for an acquaintance, and he showed her into the dining-room.

A large porcelain stove was humming away, near a cactus plant that quite filled the alcove, and, in black wooden frames, against the oak-pattern wallpaper, there hung Steuben's *Esmeralda*,[6] and Schopin's *Potiphar*. The table laid ready, a pair of silver warming-dishes, the door-knobs made of crystal, the parquet floor and the furniture, all gleaming with a meticulous

English cleanliness; the window-panes were decorated, at each corner, with coloured glass.

– Here is the kind of dining-room, thought Emma, that I should have.

In came the notary, his left arm clutching his palm-leaf dressing-gown close to his body, his other hand meanwhile hastily raising and lowering his maroon velvet skull-cap, perched pretentiously over to the right, just where three strands of blond hair, collected together at the occiput, encircled his bald skull.

After he had offered her a chair, he sat down to eat his breakfast, with many apologies for his impoliteness.

– Monsieur, she said, I would like to ask you . . .

– Yes, madame? I am listening.

She began to explain her position.

Maître Guillaumin already knew, being secretly in league with the draper, from whom he always obtained the capital for the mortgage loans he was required to undertake.

Thus it was that he knew (and rather better than she did) the long story of those bills, minute at first, endorsed in various names, payable at long intervals and continually being renewed, until the day when the merchant, gathering his writs together, had delegated his friend Vinçart to take the necessary proceedings in his own name, not wishing to be thought a shark by his fellow citizens.

Interspersed in her story were recriminations against Lheureux, recriminations that the notary responded to now and again with some insignificant remark. Eating his cutlet and drinking his tea, he tucked his chin into his sky-blue cravat, fastened with a pair of diamond pins linked together on a little gold chain; and he smiled a peculiar smile, a sugary ambiguous smile. Noticing that her feet were damp:

– Bring yourself a bit closer to the stove . . . put your feet up there . . . against the porcelain.

She was afraid of getting dirt on it. The notary retorted gallantly:

– Pretty things can do no harm.

Now she tried to play on him, and, rousing her own feelings, she started to tell him about her household difficulties, her personal troubles, her needs. He quite understood: an elegant woman! And, without a pause in his eating, he had turned right round to face her, so close that his knee brushed against her boot, the sole curving as it steamed in contact with the stove.

But, when she asked him for five thousand francs, he pursed his lips, and declared he was very sorry he had not had the management of her affairs earlier, for there were hundreds of very easy ways, even for a lady, of putting money to work. They could have invested it, say in the Grumesnil peat-bogs or the building-land around Le Havre, with excellent profits at almost no risk; and he worked her into a devouring rage at the thought of the fantastic sums she would certainly have made.

– How is it, he went on, that you never came to me?

– I don't really know.

– Why was it, mmm? . . . Did I frighten you so very much! Indeed, I am the one who ought to complain! We scarcely know one another! However, I'm a great devotee of yours; you do realize that, I hope.

He put out his hand, took hers, covered it in greedy kisses, held it on his knee; and he played with her fingers very delicately, coaxing her on with many an elegant phrase.

His feeble voice was murmuring softly, like a flowing stream; behind the gleaming spectacles a spark flashed out from his eye, and his fingers were working their way up Emma's sleeve, so as to stroke the softness of her arm. On her cheek she felt the touch of his panting breath. This man was plaguing her horribly.

She sprang to her feet and said to him:

– Monsieur, I am waiting!

– What for? said the notary, suddenly turning extremely pale.

– The money.

– But . . .

Yielding to the surge of an overpowering desire:

– All right, yes! . . .

He crawled on his knees towards her, without any regard for his dressing-gown.

– Stay, for pity's sake! I love you!

He seized her round the waist.

– This is detestable, she said, now give me the . . .

– Ahah! said Maître Guillaumin, in a voice both angry and
cajoling. Afterwards!

A flood of pink rose into her face. She pulled away with a
terrible look, shouting:

– You are taking insolent advantage of my distress, monsieur.
I may be in a pitiful state, but I am not up for sale!

And out she went.

The notary stood there in great astonishment, his eyes fixed
upon his splendid embroidered slippers. They were a love-gift.
The sight of them eventually consoled him. Besides, he imagined
an adventure of that sort would have taken him too far.

– What a wretch! What a swine! What vileness! she said to
herself, as she fled, trembling, beneath the aspen-trees along
the road. The disappointment of her failure strengthened the
indignation of her outraged modesty; it felt as though Provi-
dence were relentlessly pursuing her, and, fortifying herself with
pride, never had she felt such self-esteem nor such disdain for
the rest of the world. A spirit of belligerence enthralled her. She
wanted to do battle with men, spit in their faces, crush them
all; and she strode rapidly onward, pale, trembling, enraged,
hunting with tear-filled eyes over the empty horizon, and quite
rejoicing in the hatred that was choking her.

When she saw her own house a numbness came over her.
She couldn't move; but she had to; besides, where else could
she go?

Félicité was waiting for her at the door.

– Well?

– No! said Emma.

And, for a quarter of an hour, the two women both went
through the different people in Yonville who might be disposed
to help her. But, every time Félicité mentioned a name, Emma
replied:

– Do you think so? They wouldn't do it!

– And Monsieur will be here soon.

– I know . . . You'd better go.

She had tried everything. There was now nothing more to be
done; and, when Charles appeared, she was going to say to him:

– Keep off. This carpet under your feet is no longer ours. Not a chair, not a pin, not a feather in your own house, and it's me, I'm the one who has ruined you, poor man!

Then there would be a great sob, and he would weep copiously, and eventually, once over the shock, he would forgive.

– Yes, she muttered as she ground her teeth, he will forgive me, the man I could never pardon for just knowing me even if he had a million . . . Never! Never!

This idea of Bovary's superiority was exasperating to her. Whether or not she confessed, be it now, or be it in a little while, or tomorrow, he would none the less learn of the catastrophe; so, she must await that horrible scene and take the burden of his magnanimity. There came an impulse to pay another call on Lheureux: what would be the point? To write to her father; it was too late; and now perhaps she was repenting her refusal to yield to that man, when she heard a horse trotting along the back lane. It was him, he was opening the gate, he was as white as a sheet. Leaping down the stairs, she ran off across the square; and the mayor's wife, who was standing in front of the church talking to Lestiboudois, saw her going into the tax-collector's house.

She hurried over to tell Madame Caron. The two women went up to the attic; and, concealed behind the linen spread across the drying racks, they conveniently stationed themselves where they could see right inside Binet's house.

He was alone, up in his attic, busy making a wooden replica of one of those indescribable ivories, composed of crescents and spheres one inside the other, the whole thing erect like an obelisk and entirely useless; he was working on the very last piece, he was nearly there! In the chiaroscuro of the workshop, the golden dust was streaming off the lathe, like the plume of sparks at the hoof of a galloping horse; the two wheels were turning, buzzing; Binet was smiling, chin down, nostrils dilated, apparently lost in that state of complete happiness which belongs no doubt only to mediocre pursuits, those that amuse the intelligence with facile difficulties, and appease it with an achievement that quite dulls the imagination.

– Ah, there she is! said Madame Tuvache.

But it was scarcely possible, because of the lathe, to hear what she was saying.

Eventually, the ladies thought they identified the word *francs*, and Mère Tuvache whispered very softly:

– She's pleading with him, for more time to pay her taxes.

– That's the way it looks! said the other.

They saw her walking up and down, examining the serviette rings along the walls, the candlesticks, the banister-knobs, while Binet was stroking his beard with satisfaction.

– Has she come to order something from him? said Madame Tuvache.

– But he doesn't sell any of it answered her neighbour.

The tax-collector seemed to be listening, with a wide stare, as if he were baffled. She was still speaking, tenderly, imploringly. She moved closer; her breast was heaving; they were silent now.

– Is she making advances to him? said Madame Tuvache.

Binet had turned very red. She took his hands.

– Well, this is too much!

And she was no doubt proposing some abomination; because the tax-collector – he was a brave man for all that, he had fought at Bautzen and at Lutzen, had gone through the French campaign, and even been *mentioned in dispatches* – suddenly, as if he had seen a snake, leaped backwards, shouting:

– Madame! What is your meaning? . . .

– Those women ought to be whipped! said Madame Tuvache.

– Where has she gone? said Madame Caron.

For she had disappeared as those words were spoken; seeing her hurry along the main road and turn right as if heading for the cemetery, the two women were lost in speculation.

– Mère Rolet, she said as she reached the nurse's house, I'm choking! . . . Unlace me.

She fell on to the bed; she was sobbing. Mère Rolet covered her with a petticoat and stood close by her. When she made no reply, the woman moved away, took her wheel and began spinning flax.

– Oh, stop it! she murmured, thinking she could hear Binet's lathe.

– What's the matter with her? the nurse was wondering. Why has she come here?

She had rushed over, pursued by a sort of panic that thrust her out of her own home.

Lying there on her back, motionless, eyes fixed in a stare, she could only vaguely recognize the objects around her, even though she fastened her attention on them with an idiot stubbornness. She gazed at the cracks in the plaster, a couple of sticks smouldering on the fire, and a big spider up above her head, walking along the cleft in the beam. At last she collected her thoughts. She remembered . . . one day, with Léon . . . that was so far away! . . . The sun glittering on the river and the clematis scenting the air. And now, swept along by things past as though by a foaming torrent, she soon found herself recollecting the events of the previous day.

– What time is it? she asked.

Mère Rolet stepped outside, held the fingers of her right hand up towards the brightest part of the sky, and came in slowly, saying:

– It's three o'clock, nearly.

– Ah, thank you!

He was going to come. She was sure! He would have found some money. But perhaps he would go to the house, not realizing she was here; and she told the nurse to run and fetch him.

– Hurry up!

– My dear lady, I'm going, I'm going!

She felt surprised, at that moment, that she hadn't thought of him in the first place; yesterday, he had given his word, he wouldn't forsake her; and she already saw herself in Lheureux's office, laying the three banknotes on his desk. She would have to invent a story to explain everything to Bovary. What should she say?

Meanwhile, the nurse was a very long time returning. But, since there was no clock in the cottage, Emma feared that she might perhaps be exaggerating the length of time. She began taking little walks around the garden, one step at a time; she went along the path by the hedge, and hurried back again, hoping the woman had come home by a different route. Finally, weary of waiting, assailed by suspicions that she thrust away, forgetting whether she had been there a century or a minute, she sat in a corner, closed her eyes and stopped her ears. The gate creaked: she jumped up. Before she could utter a word, Mère Rolet had said to her:

– There's nobody there!

– What?

– Nobody! And Monsieur is crying. Calling your name. People are looking for you.

Emma did not respond. She was panting, rolling her eyes, and the peasant woman, frightened by the look on her face, drew back instinctively, thinking she was mad. Suddenly she clapped her hand to her forehead and gave a shout, for the memory of Rodolphe, like a great flash of lightning on a dark night, had entered her mind. He was so good, so sensitive, so generous! And anyway, if he hesitated to do her this service, she could soon bring him to it, by her merest glance recalling their old love. So she set off towards La Huchette, quite unaware that she was now about to rush into what had so recently infuriated her, oblivious from first to last of her prostitution.

8

As she walked along she was asking herself: 'What am I going to say? Where shall I begin?' And as she continued, she recognized the bushes, the trees, the gorse up on the hill, the château away over yonder. She rediscovered the original sensations of her love, and her poor stifled heart was blossoming with tenderness. A warm breeze was blowing in her face; the snow was melting, falling drop by drop from the young buds on to the grass below.

She went, as she had done before, through the little door into the park, and reached the courtyard, with the double row of bushy lime-trees. Their long branches were whispering as they swayed about. The dogs in their kennels began to bark, and the din echoed all around without bringing anyone out of the house.

She climbed the wide straight staircase, with its wooden

balusters, leading to the dusty stone-flagged corridor with rows of doors, like in a monastery or an inn. His room was at the very far end, on the left. When she put her hand on the latch, her strength suddenly deserted her. She was afraid he might not be there, almost wished it so, and yet it was her only hope, her last chance of salvation. She collected herself for a moment, and, fortifying her resolve from the sense of present necessity, she went in.

He was by the fire, both his feet on the fender, smoking a pipe.

– Well, well! It's you! he said, standing abruptly.

– Yes, it's me! . . . Rodolphe, I need to ask your advice.

And in spite of all her efforts, she found it impossible to open her mouth.[7]

– You haven't changed, you're as charming as ever you were.

– Hah! she answered bitterly. These have been sad charms, my friend, since the day you spurned them.

He embarked upon an explanation of his conduct, offering vague excuses, for want of any better story.

She let herself be taken in by his words, even more by his voice and his physical presence; until she pretended to believe, did perhaps believe, in the pretext for their rupture; it was a secret which involved the honour and even the life of a third person.

– No matter, she said, looking at him sadly. I have suffered a great deal.

He replied philosophically:

– Such is life!

– And has the world, asked Emma, at least been kind to you since we parted?

– Oh, not kind . . . not unkind.

– Perhaps it would have been better if we had stayed together.

– Yes . . . perhaps.

– Do you think so? she said, coming closer.

And she sighed.

– Oh, Rodolphe! If you only knew! . . . How I loved you!

And this was when she took his hand, and for some time they stayed with their fingers entwined – just like the first day, at the show. Out of stubborn pride, he struggled against his feelings. But, settling her head upon his breast, she said:

– How did you expect me to live without you? You never lose a taste for happiness! I was in despair. I thought I was going to die. I shall tell you all about it, and you'll see. And you . . . you stayed away from me!

Indeed, for the last three years, he had carefully avoided her, as a result of that natural cowardice so characteristic of the stronger sex; and Emma was keeping up the pretty little movements of her head, more caressing than an amorous tabby-cat.

– You have other women, don't you? I can understand it, you know. I forgive them. You must have seduced them, just like you seduced me. You're a man. You have everything it takes to make yourself admired. But we'll begin again, won't we? Look, I'm laughing, I'm happy . . . say something!

And she was ravishing to behold, with the tear-drop trembling in her eye, like the moisture a passing storm might leave in the cup of a blue flower.

He drew her on to his lap, and with the back of his hand he caressed the smoothness of her hair, which, in the early twilight, flashed like a golden arrow, from the last rays of the sun. She bent her head; he kissed her eyelids, very delicately, tentatively, with his lips.

– But you've been crying! he said. Why have you?

She burst into tears. Rodolphe believed it was the overflowing of her love; because she gave no answer, he took her silence as the last token of her modesty, and he exclaimed:

– Ah, forgive me! You're the only woman I want. I've been an imbecile and a scoundrel! I love you, I shall always love you! . . . What's the matter? Tell me.

He went down on his knees.

– Well . . . I'm ruined, Rodolphe. And you're going to lend me three thousand francs!

– But I . . . I'm . . . he said, as he slowly rose to his feet, and his face took on a serious expression.

– You know, she went on quickly, that my husband placed his entire fortune in the hands of a notary; well, he absconded. We've borrowed money; patients haven't been paying us. Any-

way, the sale of the estate isn't finished; that'll come in eventually. But today, for want of three thousand francs, they're going
to seize our goods; and that means now, this very moment; so,
counting on your friendship, I came here.

– Ah! thought Rodolphe, turning suddenly very pale. That's
what she came for!

He said calmly:

– I haven't got it, dear lady.

He was not lying. If he had had it he would have given it to
her, without a doubt, even though such splendid gestures are
generally disagreeable: financial demands, of all the rough winds
that blow upon our love, being quite the coldest and the most
biting.

For a few moments she just stood looking at him.

– You haven't got it!

And she repeated several times:

– Haven't got it! . . . I should have spared myself this mortification. You never loved me! You're no better than the rest of
them!

She was betraying, undoing herself.

Rodolphe interrupted her, declaring that he himself happened
to be hard up.

– Oh, I am sorry for you, said Emma. Tremendously sorry . . .

And her eyes came to rest on a damascened rifle gleaming in
its display case.

– But anybody who is so very poor doesn't have silver on his
rifle-butt! Doesn't buy a clock inlaid with tortoiseshell! she
continued, pointing to his Boulle timepiece; or silver-plated
whistles for their whips – she touched them – or trinkets for their
watch-chain! Oh, he wants for nothing! With a liqueur-stand in
his bedroom; you do love yourself, you live well, you have a
château, farms and woods; you ride to hounds, you go to Paris
. . . Even these, she shouted as she picked up his cuff-links from
the mantelpiece, even the least little bit of this frippery! You can
turn it into money! Oh, I don't want them! You keep them!

And she threw the cuff-links across the room, so hard that
the gold chain snapped when they hit the wall.

– And I would have given you everything, sold everything,

worked with my own hands, begged on the streets, for a smile, for a glance, just to hear you say 'thank you'. And you sit so calmly in your armchair, as if you hadn't already caused me enough suffering. But for meeting you, do you realize, I could have lived a happy life. What made you do it? Was it for a bet? You loved me, though, you said so . . . Just now you did . . . Better to have driven me from your door! My hands are warm from your kisses, and here's the place, on the carpet, where you went down on your knees to swear your eternal love to me. You made me believe you; for two years you led me on, through a dream so magnificent and so exquisite! . . . Hah! The journey we planned, do you remember? That letter of yours! It broke my heart! . . . And, when I go to him, the one who is rich and happy and free, to plead for the help that almost anyone would give, beseeching and offering him my tenderness, he spurns me, because it would cost him three thousand francs!

– I haven't got it! replied Rodolphe, in the perfectly calm tone one uses to shield suppressed anger.

She walked out. The walls were shaking, the ceiling was crushing her; and she went back down the long avenue, stumbling in the piles of old leaves that were being demolished by the wind. She finally reached the boundary ditch and the gate; she tore her fingernails on the latch, she was in such a hurry to open it. A hundred steps further on, out of breath, almost falling over, she stopped. Turning her head, she looked once more upon the impassive château, with the park, the garden, the three courtyards, and the windows in rows along the façade.

She stood there bewildered, quite oblivious, but for the sound of the blood pounding along her arteries, which she thought she could hear seeping out of her, like a trumpet-call echoing everywhere. The earth beneath her feet was undulating gently, and the furrows looked like enormous brown waves, pounding the beach. Everything in her head, all her reminiscences, all her ideas, poured out at once, in a single spasm, like a thousand fireworks exploding. She saw her father, Lheureux in his office, their room in town, a different landscape. Terrified, she felt the touch of madness, and managed to take hold of herself again, in some confusion, even so; because she had no memory of the cause of her terrible condition, that is to say the problem of money. She was suffering purely for love, and in remembering him she felt her soul slip from her, just as injured men, in their agony, feel life seeping away, through their bleeding wounds.

In a darkening sky, crows were on the wing.

All of a sudden, it looked as if fiery red globules were bursting in the air, like bullets that explode on impact, spinning, spinning, and melting away on the snow, among the branches. In the centre of each one, Rodolphe's face appeared. They began to multiply, they clustered together, they penetrated her; everything disappeared. She recognized the light from the houses in the distance, shining through the mist.

Now her situation, like an abyss, came back to her. She was panting, her chest almost bursting. And in a rapture of heroism which was almost joyful, she ran down the hill, crossed the plank-bridge, along the footpath, down the alley, over the market-square, and arrived in front of the pharmacist's shop.

There was nobody there. She was about to go in; but, at the sound of the shop-bell, somebody might come; and, slipping through the side-gate, holding her breath, feeling her way along the wall, she got as far as the kitchen door, where a candle stood burning on the stove. Justin, in his shirt-sleeves, was carrying out a plate.

– They're having dinner. I'll wait.

He returned. She tapped on the window. He came out.

– The key! The one for upstairs where he keeps . . .

– What?

And he gazed at her, astonished at the paleness of her face, vivid white against the blackness of the night. She looked extraordinarily beautiful, majestical as any ghost; not understanding what she wanted, he had a premonition of something terrible.

But she spoke again, in an urgent whisper, soft and melting:

– I want it! Give it to me.

Through the thin partition wall, they could hear the forks clinking on the plates in the dining-room.

She said she needed to kill the rats that were keeping her awake.

– I'd have to let the master know.

– No! Wait!

In a casual tone:

– Oh, it's not worth the bother, I'll tell him later. Come on, light my way.

She went along the corridor that led to the door of the laboratory. Hanging on the wall there was a key labelled *Capharnaum*.

– Justin! shouted the apothecary, tired of waiting.

– Upstairs!

And he followed her.

The key turned in the lock, and she went straight to the third shelf, her memory serving her well, she got the blue jar, pulled out the cork, stuck her hand inside, and, taking a fistful of white powder, she put it straight into her mouth.

– Stop! he cried, jumping on her.

– Quiet! Somebody might come up.

He was in despair, wanting to call for help.

– Not one word about this! The blame would fall upon your master.

And she went home, suddenly appeased, almost serene, her task accomplished.

When Charles got in, appalled at the news of the seizure, Emma had just gone out. He shouted, he wept, he fainted, but she didn't come back. Where could she be? He sent Félicité over to Homais's, to Monsieur Tuvache's, to Lheureux's, to the Golden Lion, everywhere; and, in the intervals of his distress, he saw his reputation destroyed, their money gone, Berthe's future in ruins. For what reason? . . . Not one word of explanation! He waited until six in the evening. Finally, unable to bear it any longer, and, thinking she might have set off for Rouen, he went along the main road, a mile or two, met nobody, waited a while and came back home again.

She was there.

– What was it? . . . Why? Tell me! . . .

She sat down at her writing-table and penned a letter, sealed it carefully, adding the date and the time. In a solemn tone she said:

– Read this tomorrow; until then, please, don't ask me any questions! Not a single one!

– But . . .

– Leave me alone!

And she lay down full length upon her bed.

An acrid taste in her mouth woke her up. She saw Charles and closed her eyes again.

She was observing herself with a certain curiosity, to see if she felt any pain. No, nothing yet. She could hear the clock ticking, the noise of the fire, and Charles, standing there by her bed, breathing.

– Oh . . . death is really nothing very much! she thought; I'm going to fall asleep, and it'll all be over!

She drank a mouthful of water and turned to face the wall.

That awful taste of ink was still there.

– I'm thirsty! . . . Oh I'm so thirsty! she sighed.

– What is the matter? said Charles, handing her a glass.

– Nothing! . . . Open the window . . . I'm stifling!

And she felt such a sudden nausea that she scarcely had time to pull her handkerchief from under her pillow.

– Take it away! Throw it out! she said quickly.

He asked her questions; she didn't answer. She was keeping still, afraid that the slightest agitation would make her vomit. Even so, she could feel an icy chill mounting from her feet up towards her heart.

– Ah, this is how it begins! she murmured.

– What did you say?

She was rolling her head from side to side, very gently, in great anguish, and continually opening her jaws, as if she had something very heavy sitting on her tongue. At eight o'clock, the vomiting reappeared.

Charles noticed that in the bottom of the bowl there was a kind of white sediment, clinging to the porcelain surface.

– That is extraordinary! Most unusual! he kept saying.

But she said in a loud voice:

– No, you're mistaken.

And then, delicately, almost caressing her, he passed his hand across her stomach. She screamed. He leaped back in alarm.

Now she began to groan, feebly at first. A great shudder ran through her shoulders, and she turned whiter than the sheet she was clutching with her rigid fingers. The irregular pulse was now almost imperceptible.

Drops of sweat were trickling down her face, which was turning blue and looked as though it had been coated in the fumes from some metallic compound. Her teeth were chattering, her bulging eyes stared vaguely around the room, and to every question she replied with merely a shake of the head; she even smiled two or three times. Little by little, her groans became louder. A stifled scream escaped her lips; she said she was feeling better and would be getting up soon. But she was seized by convulsions; she cried out:

– Oh, my God, it's horrible!

He fell to his knees by her bed.

– Tell me! What have you eaten? Say something, for heaven's sake!

And he looked at her with a tenderness in his eyes that she had never seen before.

– All right, over there . . . there! she said haltingly.

He leaped over to the writing-table, broke the seal and read aloud: *Let nobody be blamed* . . . He stopped, rubbed his eyes, and read it over again.

– What? Help! Help me!

And all he could do was to repeat the word: 'Poisoned! Poisoned!' Félicité ran to tell Homais, who shouted the word across the square; Madame Lefrançois heard it in the Golden Lion; several people rose from their beds to tell it to their neighbours, and all that night the village was wide awake.

Demented, mumbling, near to collapse, Charles was wandering about the room. He bumped into the furniture, tore at his hair, and the pharmacist had never believed that there could be such an appalling spectacle.

He returned home to write to Monsieur Canivet and to Doctor Larivière. He lost his head; he went through at least fifteen drafts. Hippolyte set off for Neufchâtel, and Justin spurred Bovary's horse so hard that he had to leave him somewhere on the hill at Bois Guillaume, lamed and nearly ready for the knacker's yard.

Charles tried to leaf through his medical dictionary; he couldn't focus, the lines were dancing about.

– Don't panic! said the apothecary. It is simply a question of administering some powerful antidote. What poison was it?

Charles showed him the letter. It was arsenic.

– Right, said Homais, we have to do an analysis.

For he knew that in all cases of poisoning you have to do an analysis; and Charles, who didn't understand, said:

– Do it! Do it! Save her . . .

Returning to her side, he sank down on to the carpet, and he lay there with his head against the edge of her bed, weeping.

– Don't cry! she said. Soon, I shan't torment you ever again!

– Why did you do it? Who made you?

She replied:

– It had to be, my dear.

– Were you not happy? Is it my fault? But I've done everything I could.

– Yes . . . you have . . . you were good, you were.

And she ran her fingers through his hair, slowly. The pleasure of that sensation intensified his sadness; he felt his very substance crumbling away in despair at the idea that he must lose her now, when, for once, she was professing such a love as she had never shown to him before; and he couldn't think, he didn't know what to do, didn't dare, for the urgent need to make an immediate decision overwhelmed him entirely.

She had done, she thought to herself, with all the treachery, the vileness and the endless cravings that tormented her. She felt no hatred now, for anyone; shadowy confusion was settling on her mind, and among all the sounds of this world Emma could hear nothing but the faltering lamentation of her poor heart, soft and indistinct, like the final echoing note of a distant symphony.

– Bring me my little girl, she said, raising herself on to her elbow.

– The pain isn't getting any worse, is it? asked Charles.

– No!

The child was carried in on her nurse's arm, wearing a long nightgown with her bare feet sticking out, lost in thought and still almost asleep. She gazed in wonder at the disordered room, closing her eyes, dazzled by the candles burning on the table. They probably reminded her of New Year's Day or Easter, when, woken up early just like this by candlelight, she used to get into her mother's bed to be given her presents, for she began to say:

– Where is it, mummy?

And when nobody said a word:

– But I can't see my little stocking!

Felicité was holding her over the bed, while the child kept looking towards the fireplace.

– Has nurse taken it? she asked.

And, at this word, which brought back the memory of her adulteries and her calamities, Madame Bovary turned her head away, as if at the sharp taste of a different and a stronger poison seeping up into her mouth. Berthe, meanwhile, stayed sitting on the bed.

– Oh, what big eyes you have, mummy! How pale you look! You're all sweaty!

Her mother was looking at her.

– I'm frightened, said the little girl, pulling back.

Emma took her hand to kiss it; the child was struggling.

– That's enough! Take her out! cried Charles, who was sobbing in the alcove.

Then the symptoms left off for a moment; and, with every little word, with every calmer breath, he found new hope. At last, when Canivet appeared, he threw himself into his arms and wept.

– Ah! Here you are! Thank you! So kind of you! Actually, things are going better. Look at her . . .

His colleague was certainly not of the same opinion, and, not being a man, as he himself put it, *to beat about the bush*, he prescribed an emetic, in order to evacuate the stomach completely.

Soon she was vomiting blood. Her lips were drawn tighter. Her limbs were rigid, her body covered in brown patches, and her pulse raced away beneath your fingers, like a taut thread, like a harp-string just before it breaks.

Now she started screaming, horribly. She cursed the poison,

vilified it, begged it to hurry, and with her stiffened arms pushed away everything that Charles, his agony greater than hers, tried to make her drink. He was standing there, with his handkerchief to his lips, choking, weeping, and racked by the sobbing that shook him from head to foot; Félicité was running here and there around the room; Homais, motionless, was sighing deeply, and Monsieur Canivet, though preserving his aplomb, was nevertheless beginning to feel uneasy.

– Damnation! . . . After all . . . she has been purged, and, as soon as the cause ceases . . .

– The effect should cease, said Homais; it's obvious.

– Save her! exclaimed Bovary.

Accordingly, without listening to the pharmacist, who was venturing the further hypothesis that perhaps it was a salutary paroxysm, Canivet was about to administer an antidote, when they heard the crack of a whip; the windows rattled, and a post-chaise drawn by three horses in full harness up to their ears in mud came round the corner of the market-hall in a single bound. It was Doctor Larivière.

The descent of a god would have caused no greater commotion. Bovary raised his hands, Canivet stopped short, and Homais took off his skull-cap long before the doctor appeared.

He belonged to the great school of surgery that sprang up around Bichat, to that generation, now extinct, of philosopher–practitioners who, cherishing their art with fanatical passion, exercised it with exaltation and sagacity. Everyone in his hospital used to tremble when Larivière lost his temper, and such was his students' veneration for him that they endeavoured, as soon as they were set up in practice, to imitate him as closely as possible; thus you saw them, in the local towns, wearing the same long merino overcoat and the loose black jacket, with the unbuttoned cuffs half covering his plump hands, such beautiful hands, and never gloved, as though in even greater readiness to plunge into wretchedness. Disdaining medals, titles and academic honours, hospitable, generous, a father to the poor, a man who practised virtue without believing in it, he might almost have passed for a saint had not the keenness of his intellect made him feared like a demon. His gaze, slicing cleaner than his scalpel, went right down into your soul and dissected the lies swathed in discretion and pretence. And so he went about his business, full of the majestic affability that comes of the consciousness of great talent, of wealth and forty irreproachable years of hard work.

He frowned as soon as he came through the door, when he saw the cadaverous face of Emma, lying on her back, with her mouth open. Apparently listening to Canivet, he rubbed at his nose with his forefinger and kept saying:

– That's fine, that's fine.

But he gave a slow shrug of the shoulders. Bovary noticed: they looked at one another; and this man, so accustomed to the sight of pain, could not hold back the tear that fell on to the lace front of his shirt.

He called Canivet into the next room. Charles followed him.

– She's very ill isn't she? Couldn't we try mustard plasters? Something or other! Do think of a way! You who have saved so many lives.

Charles had both his arms around him, and he was gazing wildly, beseechingly at him, virtually swooning upon his chest.

– Come on, my poor boy, be brave. There is nothing more I can do. And Doctor Larivière turned away.

– Are you going?

– I shall be back.

He went out as if to give an order to the coachman, followed by Canivet, who was equally anxious not to have Emma die on his hands.

The pharmacist joined them out on the square. He was incapable, temperamentally, of keeping away from famous men. Accordingly he begged Monsieur Larivière to do him the signal honour of taking breakfast at his table.

Quickly he sent across to the Golden Lion for some pigeons, to the butcher's for every cutlet in his shop, to Tuvache for some cream, to Lestiboudois for some eggs, and the apothecary himself helped with the preparations, while Madame Homais, pulling at the strings on her bodice, said:

– You must excuse us, monsieur; in this wretched place, unless we have a day's notice . . .

– The wine-glasses!!! whispered Homais.

– Now at least if we lived in town we could fall back on stuffed trotters.

– Be quiet! . . . Do come and sit down, doctor!

He thought fit, after a few mouthfuls, to supply certain details of the catastrophe:

– First of all we had a desiccation of the pharynx, then intolerable pains in the epigastrium, super-purgation, coma.

– How did she poison herself?

– I have no idea, doctor, nor do I know where she was able to procure that arsenious acid.

Justin, who was just bringing in a pile of plates, began to tremble.

– What's the matter? said the pharmacist.

And the young man, at these words, dropped everything on to the floor, with a great crash.

– Imbecile! shouted Homais. Clumsy! Bungling! Wretch! Blockhead!

Suddenly, taking hold of himself:

– I wanted to perform an analysis, doctor, and *primo*, I delicately introduced a tube . . .

– You'd have done better, said the surgeon, to have introduced your fingers into her throat.

His colleague was silent, having just received in private a severe reprimand on the subject of his emetic, such that the estimable Canivet, so arrogant and verbose on the day of the operation on the club-foot, was now very unassuming; he was smiling without pause, in a display of approbation.

Homais was blossoming proudly as he played host, and the woeful thought of Bovary somehow contributed to his pleasure, because of the gratifying contrast. And he found the presence of the doctor enthralling. He paraded his erudition, alluding carelessly to cantharides, the upas-tree, the manchineel, the viper.

– I've even read that various people have suffered toxic effects, doctor, have been virtually struck down by black puddings subject to excessive fumigation! Anyway, it was in a very fine report, composed by one of our leading pharmacists, one of our masters, the illustrious Cadet de Gassicourt!

Madame Homais reappeared, carrying one of those unpredictable contraptions that you heat up with a spirit-lamp; for
Homais liked to make his coffee at the table, having previously
roasted and ground and blended it himself.

– *Saccharum*, doctor? he said, passing the sugar.

He had his children brought downstairs, eager to hear the
surgeon's opinion of their constitution.

Eventually, Monsieur Larivière was about to leave when
Madame Homais asked him for a consultation concerning her
husband. He was thickening his blood by always falling asleep
in the evening after dinner.

– Oh! It's certainly not his blood that's thickening.

And, smiling to himself at this unremarked piece of wordplay, the doctor opened the door. But the pharmacy was swarming with people; and he had great difficulty getting away from
Monsieur Tuvache, who feared that his spouse's lungs would
become inflamed because of her habit of spitting into the cinders;
from Monsieur Binet, who sometimes had strange cravings for
food; and from Madame Caron, who had pins and needles;
from Lheureux, who had vertigo; from Lestiboudois, who had
rheumatism; from Madame Lefrançois, who had heartburn. At
last the three horses rushed him away, and it was generally
agreed that he had not been at all obliging.

Public attention was distracted by the appearance of Monsieur Bournisien, making his way through the market-hall with
the holy oil.

Homais, out of loyalty to his principles, compared priests to
carrion crows lured by the smell of death; to him the sight of a
clergyman was personally offensive, because the cassock was a
reminder of the shroud, and he abhorred the one partly from
fear of the other.

Nevertheless, not shrinking from what he called *his mission*,
he returned to Bovary's house in the company of Canivet, whom
Monsieur Larivière, before he left, had strongly urged to remain;
and, but for his wife's objections, he would have taken his two
sons along with him, so as to accustom them to scenes of distress,
that it might be instructive for them, an example, a solemn
picture to be remembered hereafter.

The bedroom, when they went in, was full of a mournful solemnity. On the work-table, covered with a white cloth, there were five or six little balls of cotton-wool on a silver dish, next to a large crucifix, between a pair of lighted candles. Emma, her chin down upon her breast, had her eyes opened abnormally wide; and her poor hands were wandering over the sheets, with the hideous and tender gestures of the dying when they apparently struggle to put on the shroud for themselves. Pale as a statue, his eyes as red as burning coals, Charles was standing at the foot of the bed, without weeping, facing her, while the priest, on one knee, was murmuring in a low voice.

Slowly she turned her head, and joy seemed to come to her the moment she saw the purple stole, doubtless rediscovering, in this instant of singular calm, the forgotten delights of her first mystical raptures, along with a dawning vision of eternal blessedness.

The priest arose and took the crucifix; now she stretched forth her neck like one in thirst, and, pressing her lips to the body of the Man-God, she laid upon him with all her ebbing strength the greatest loving kiss she had ever given. He recited the *Misere-atur* and the *Indulgentiam*, dipped his right thumb in the oil, and began the unctions: first upon the eyes, which had so coveted worldly splendours; then upon the nostrils, so greedy for warm breezes and amorous perfumes; then upon the mouth, which had uttered lying words, which had groaned with pride and cried out in lustfulness; then upon the hands, which had found delight in sensual touches; and finally upon the soles of the feet, so swift ere now in running towards the satisfaction of her desires, but now would walk no more.

The *curé* wiped his fingers, threw the bits of oily cotton-wool into the fire, and came over to sit by the dying woman, telling her that now she must join her sufferings to those of Jesus Christ and yield herself up to divine mercy.

Finishing his exhortations, he tried to put into her hand a consecrated candle, symbol of the celestial glories that were very soon to surround her. Emma, too weak, could not clasp her fingers, and the candle, but for Monsieur Bournisien, would have fallen to the floor.

However, she was not quite so pale now, and on her face there was an expression of serenity, as though the sacrament had cured her.

The priest of course remarked the fact; he even explained to Bovary that the Lord, sometimes, prolonged a person's life when he deemed it useful for their salvation; and Charles remembered the day when, equally close to death, she had received communion.

Perhaps, he thought, there was no need to despair.

Indeed, she looked around the room, slowly, like someone waking from a dream; in a clear voice, she asked for her mirror, and her eyes lingered there a good while, until great tears began to flow down her cheeks. She turned her head away with a sigh and fell back upon the pillow.

Now her chest began to heave rapidly. Her tongue was sticking right out of her mouth; her eyes, rolling about, were turning pale, just like the globe of a lamp as it expires, as if she were already dead, but for the ghastly jolting of her ribs, shaken by the furious breathing, as if her soul were jerking to break free. Félicité knelt before the crucifix, and even the pharmacist was crouching slightly, while Monsieur Canivet was gazing vaguely down into the square. Bournisien had resumed his prayers, his face bowed over the edge of the bed, with his long black cassock trailing out behind him across the floor. Charles was on the other side, kneeling down, his arms reaching out to Emma. He had taken hold of her hands, and he was gripping them, trembling at every beat of her heart, like a man inside a falling house. As the death-rattle grew louder, the cleric hastened his prayers; the words mingled with Bovary's stifled sobbing, and at times everything seemed to disappear into the dull murmur of the Latin syllables, tolling out like the passing bell.

Suddenly, they heard the sound of heavy clogs on the pavement below, with the tapping of a stick; and a voice rang out, a raucous voice, singing:

Souvent la chaleur d'un beau jour,
Fait rêver fillette à l'amour.

Emma roused herself, like a cadaver being galvanized, her hair unfastened, her eyes fixed wide open.

> *Pour amasser diligemment*
> *Les épis que la faux moissonne,*
> *Ma Nanette va s'inclinant*
> *Vers le sillon qui nous les donne.*[8]

– The Blind Man! she cried out.

And Emma began to laugh, an atrocious, frantic, desperate laugh, at the imagined sight of the beggar's hideous face, stationed in the eternal darkness like a monster.

> *Il souffla bien fort ce jour-là,*
> *Et le jupon court s'envola!*[9]

A convulsion threw her down upon the mattress. They all drew near. Her life had ended.

9

After any death there always comes a kind of stupefaction, so difficult is it to take in this advent of nothingness and resign ourselves to believing in it. But, when he saw that the body wasn't moving, Charles threw himself upon her, shouting:

– Goodbye!

Homais and Canivet dragged him from the room.

– Calm down!

– Yes, he said struggling, I'll be sensible, I won't do anything. But leave me alone! I want to see her! She is my wife!

And he wept.

– Weep away, said the pharmacist, let nature take its course, you'll feel much better!

Weaker than a child, Charles let himself be led downstairs, into the parlour, and Monsieur Homais soon went off back home.

On the square he was accosted by the Blind Man, who, having

dragged himself all the way to Yonville in the hope of getting the anti-phlogiston ointment, was asking everyone he met where the pharmacist lived.

– Goodness me! As if I didn't have enough things to be seeing to! It's just too bad; come back another day.

And he made a hasty exit, into the pharmacy.

He had two letters to write, a sedative to make up for Bovary, a story to concoct so as to explain the poisoning and an article to put together for *Le Fanal*, not to mention the people waiting to ask him questions; and, once the whole village had heard his account of how she had mistaken arsenic for sugar when she was making a vanilla custard, Homais, yet again, went back to see Bovary.

He found him on his own (Monsieur Canivet had just left), sitting in an armchair, by the window, staring idiot-like at the tiles on the parlour floor.

– You really ought to decide now, said the pharmacist, what time you want the ceremony.

– Why? What ceremony?

In a stammering frightened voice:

– No, I don't think so. No. I want to keep her.

Homais, to hide his embarrassment, took a jug off the shelf and began watering the geraniums.

– Oh, thanks, said Charles, you are kind.

And he faltered, smothered under the profusion of memories released by the pharmacist's actions.

To distract him, Homais ventured a few horticultural re-marks; plants needed humidity. Charles bowed his head in sign of agreement.

– Anyway the nice weather will soon be back again.

– Aahh, said Bovary.

The apothecary, running out of ideas, began to open very gently the little curtains over the window.

– Look, there's Monsieur Tuvache going past.

Charles repeated like a machine:

– Monsieur Tuvache going past.

Homais did not dare mention funeral arrangements again; it was the priest who eventually persuaded him to it.

He shut himself away in his consulting-room, picked up a pen, and, after sobbing a while, he wrote:

I wish her to be buried in her wedding-dress, with white shoes and a crown of flowers. Her hair is to be arranged loosely about her shoulders: three coffins, one of oak, one of mahogany, one of lead. Let no one speak to me and I shall manage. Cover everything over with a large piece of green velvet. Such is my wish. Let it be done.

These gentlemen were greatly astonished at Bovary's romantic ideas, and the pharmacist hurried in to say to him:

– This velvet looks to me rather a superfetation. Besides, the expense . . .

– Is that any business of yours? shouted Charles. Don't interfere! You don't love her, so just clear off!

The priest took him by the arm and walked him round the garden. He discoursed upon the vanity of the things of this world. God was very great, very good; we must submit to his decrees without a murmur, nay, we must thank Him.

Charles exploded into blasphemy.

– I hate that God of yours!

– The spirit of revolt is still upon you, sighed the priest.

Bovary made off. He was striding along by the wall, near the espalier, and he was grinding his teeth, sending curses to heaven from his eyes; but not a single leaf did stir.

A fine rain was falling. Charles, with his chest bare, finally began to shiver; he went indoors and sat in the kitchen.

At six o'clock, there was a clanging noise out on the square: it was the *Hirondelle* coming in; and he stood there with his forehead pressed to the window-pane, watching the passengers step out one after the other. Félicité laid out a mattress for him in the parlour; he toppled on to it and fell asleep.

For all his philosophy, Monsieur Homais respected the dead. And so, bearing no grudge against poor Charles, he came back again that evening to sit by the body, carrying three great tomes, and a pocket-book, intending to write notes.

Monsieur Bournisien was there, and two tall candles were

burning at the head of the bed, which had been pulled out from the alcove.

The apothecary, uneasy in any silence, promptly expressed his regrets over the unfortunate young woman; and the priest replied that there was now nothing but to pray for her.

– All the same, Homais went on, it must be one thing or the other; either she died in a state of grace (as the Church puts it), in which case she has no need of our prayers; or else she perished impenitent (that is, I believe, the ecclesiastical expression), and therefore . . .

Bournisien interrupted, asserting brusquely that it was none the less necessary to pray.

– But, argued the pharmacist, since God knows our needs, what can be the use of prayer?

– What! cried the priest. Prayer! I take it that you are not a Christian?

– Excuse me! said Homais. I admire Christianity. First because it abolished slavery, and introduced a morality . . .

– That is hardly the point! All the texts . . .

– Ahah! The texts! You read some history; we all know they were falsified by the Jesuits.

Charles came in, and, walking across to the bed, he slowly drew back the curtains.

Emma had her head resting on her right shoulder. The corner of her mouth, set open, looked rather like a black hole in the lower part of her face; her thumbs were curved across the palms of her hands; a sort of white powder besprinkled her eyelashes; and her eyes were beginning to blur under a pale film of mucus that was like a soft web, just as if spiders had been at work upon them. The sheet curved across smoothly from her breasts to her knees, making another peak at the tips of her toes; and to Charles it seemed as if an infinite mass, an enormous weight, lay pressing upon her.

The church-clock struck two. They could hear the prodigious murmur of the river flowing in the darkness, at the foot of the terrace. Monsieur Bournisien, now and again, blew his nose loudly, and Homais's pen was scratching across the paper.

– Come along, my dear friend he said. Off you go now, the
sight is an agony to you!

Once Charles had left, the pharmacist and the *curé* resumed
their altercation.

– Read Voltaire! said the one; read Holbach, read the *Ency-
clopédie*.

– Read *Les Lettres de quelques juifs portugais*! said the other;
read *La Raison du christianisme*,[10] by Nicolas, an ex-magistrate.

They were excited, they were red-faced, they were both talking at once, heedlessly; Bournisien was shocked at such audacity;
Homais was astonished at such stupidity; and they were near to
trading insults, when Charles, suddenly, reappeared. He was
fascinated. He kept on coming back up the stairs.

He settled himself just opposite, the better to see her, and he
lost himself in contemplation of her face, lost so deep that his
pain was eased.

He remembered stories about catalepsy, the miracles of magnetism; and he told himself that by wishing it with all his might,
he could perhaps bring her back to life. On one occasion he
even leaned over her, and he cried in a low voice:

– Emma! Emma!

His breath, coming with such force, set the candle-flames
dancing across the wall.

At daybreak, the elder Madame Bovary arrived; Charles,
when he embraced her, burst into tears once again. She attempted, as had the pharmacist, to offer a few remarks on the
subject of the funeral expenses. He became so angry that she fell
silent, and he even instructed her to go into town immediately to
buy what they needed.

Charles spent the entire afternoon alone; Berthe had been
taken over to Madame Homais; Félicité was upstairs, in the
bedroom, with Mère Lefrançois.

In the evening, visitors called. He would stand up, shake their
hands without a word, then they sat down along with the others,
in a big half-circle around the fireplace. With heads bowed and
legs crossed, they sat there swinging one foot, heaving a great
sigh every so often; and everyone was immeasurably bored; yet
nobody wanted to be the first to go.

Homais, when he came back at nine o'clock (he seemed to have been perpetually crossing the square for the last two days), was laden with a supply of camphor, benzoin resin and aromatic herbs. He also brought a jar full of chlorine water to purify the air. Just at that moment, the maid, Madame Lefrançois and Mère Bovary were busy about Emma, finishing dressing her; and they drew over her the long stiff veil, which covered her all the way down to her satin slippers.

Félicité was sobbing:

– Oh, my poor mistress! My poor mistress!

– Just look at her, said the innkeeper with a sigh, so pretty as she is still! You'd almost swear she'll be back on her feet again in a minute.

They bent over the bed, to arrange the wreath of flowers in her hair.

They had to lift her head slightly, and a black liquid streamed out, like vomit, from between her lips.

– Oh! Good Lord! The dress, look out! cried Madame Lefrançois. Well, give us a hand, then! she said to the pharmacist. Are you afraid by any chance?

– Afraid, me? he answered with a shrug of the shoulders. Ever so likely! I saw a thing or two at the hospital, I did, when I was studying pharmacy! We used to make punch in the dissecting-room! The void holds no terrors for a philosopher; and, as I have often said, I intend to bequeath my body to a hospital, that it may subsequently benefit Science.

When he arrived, the *curé* asked after Monsieur; and, when the apothecary told him, he remarked:

– The blow, you understand, is still too recent.

Homais congratulated him on not being exposed like other men to the risk of losing a beloved companion; whence followed an argument about the celibacy of priests.

– You see, said the pharmacist, it isn't natural for a man to do without a woman! There have been crimes . . .

– Good grief! cried the cleric. How do you expect anyone who is married, for instance, to keep the secrets of the confessional?

Homais attacked confession; Bournisien defended it; he dwelt upon the acts of restitution to which it gave rise. He quoted various anecdotes of thieves who had suddenly turned to honest ways. Soldiers, when they approached the confessional, had felt the scales fall from their eyes. In Fribourg there was a minister . . .

His companion was asleep. Finding it rather stifling in the oppressive atmosphere of the bedroom, he opened the window, and this woke the pharmacist.

– Have a pinch of snuff! he said to him. Go on, it clears the head.

There was a continuous barking in the distance, somewhere or other.

– Can you hear a dog howling? said the pharmacist.

– They do say that they can smell death, replied the clergyman. It's like bees: they fly away from the hive when anyone dies.

Homais did not contest these superstitions, he had gone back to sleep.

Monsieur Bournisien, the more robust of the two men, continued for some time the silent movement of his lips; imperceptibly, he let his chin fall, let go his big black book and began to snore.

They sat facing each other, their stomachs bulging, their cheeks swollen, their mouths set in a scowl, coming together after such strife in the same simple human weakness; and they kept quite as still as the corpse itself, which seemed to be asleep.

Charles came in without waking them. It was the last time. He was going to say goodbye to her.

The aromatic herbs were still smoking, and the swirling blue vapours blended into the mist that was coming in through the window. There were a few stars, and the night air was mild.

The wax from the candles was falling in great drops on to the bedclothes. Charles looked at them, until his eyes were aching from the brightness of their yellow flame.

Ripples were washing over the satin dress, as pale as moonlight. Emma was disappearing into its whiteness; and to him it was just as if, flowing out of herself, she were passing darkly into the things around her, into the silence, into the night, into the passing breeze and the damp smell rising from the earth.

He had a sudden vision of her in the garden at Tostes, on the bench, by the thorn-hedge, or else on the streets of Rouen, at the door of their house, in the yard at Les Bertaux. He could still hear the laughter of the little boys dancing for joy beneath the apple-trees; the room was full of the perfume of her hair, and her dress was rippling in his arms with a crackle of sparks. The same dress, it was, the one she had on now!

He spent a long time like this, remembering his lost happiness, her movements, her gestures, the sound of her voice. After every misery, there came another, and yet another, relentlessly, like the waves of a flood-tide.

He felt a terrible curiosity: slowly, with fingertips, his heart trembling, he lifted her veil. But he gave out a cry of horror that woke the other two men. They hauled him downstairs, to the parlour.

Félicité came to say that he wanted some of her hair.

– Cut some off! said the apothecary.

She didn't dare, and so, he stepped forward himself, with the scissors in his hand. He was trembling so violently that he stabbed several little holes in the skin around her temples. In the end, steeling himself to do it, Homais chopped two or three times at random, leaving patches of white in that beautiful black hair.

The pharmacist and the *curé* immersed themselves once again in their occupations, each of them falling asleep every so often, each accusing the other of doing so every time they awoke yet again. Monsieur Bournisien sprinkled the room with holy water and Homais poured a little chlorine over the floor.

Félicité had thoughtfully left out for them, on the chest of drawers, a bottle of brandy, some cheese and a large brioche. And the apothecary, quite worn out, sighed, at about four in the morning:

– My goodness, I could manage a little sustenance!

The clergyman needed no persuading; he went off to say mass, came back again; they ate and they chinked glasses, chuckling quietly the while, without knowing why, stirred by that peculiar hilarity that comes over us after periods of grief; and, at the last glass, the priest said to the pharmacist, as he clapped him on the shoulder:

– You and me, we'll see eye to eye, in the end!

Downstairs, in the hall, they met the undertaker's men arriving.

Charles, for the next two hours, had to endure the torture of the noise of the hammer banging away on the planks. And they brought her down in her oak coffin, which they boxed up in the other two; but because the outer one was too large, they had to stuff the empty spaces with the wool from a mattress. Eventually, when the three lids had been planed off, nailed down and sealed up, they put it outside by the door; the house was thrown open, and the people of Yonville began to flock in.

Père Rouault arrived. He fainted in the square when he saw the black cloth.

10

He had not had the pharmacist's letter until thirty-six hours after the event; and, out of consideration for his feelings, Monsieur Homais had phrased it in such a way that it was impossible to know what to make of it.

When he first read it, the old fellow fell over just as if he had been struck by apoplexy. Then he grasped that she wasn't dead. But she might be. Finally, he had put on his smock, taken his hat, fixed a spur to his boot, and set off at full tilt; and, all the way there, Père Rouault, as he gasped for breath, was consumed with anguish. At one point, he even had to get off his horse. He couldn't see, he was hearing voices, he thought he was going mad.

It was daybreak. He saw three black hens roosting in a tree; he shuddered, terrified at the omen. He made a promise to the Blessed Virgin that he would give three chasubles for the church, and go barefoot from the cemetery at Les Bertaux all the way to the chapel at Vassonville.

He rode into Maromme, yelling for the inn-people, burst the stable-door open with his shoulder, leaped on a sack of oats, poured a bottle of sweet cider into the manger, and raced off on his nag, sparks flying from her hoofs.

He told himself that they would surely save her; the doctors would of course find some remedy. He remembered all the miraculous cures that he had heard of.

She appeared to him, dead. There she was, at his feet, on her back, in the middle of the road. He reined in, and the hallucination disappeared.

At Quincampoix, to keep up his courage, he drank three cups of coffee one after another.

He thought they might have written the wrong name by mistake. He looked for the letter in his pocket, felt it there, but dared not open it.

He even began to wonder if it were all perhaps a *hoax*, somebody having their revenge, a drunkard's little prank; and, besides, if she were dead, wouldn't you be able to tell? Not at all! There was nothing unusual about the countryside: the sky was blue, the trees were swaying about, a flock of sheep went past. He caught sight of the village; they saw him come galloping along bent over his saddle, lashing at his horse, its girth dripping blood.

Once he came to, he fell weeping into Bovary's arms.

– My daughter! Emma! My child! Tell me how it . . .?

And the other man replied, sobbing:

– I don't know! I don't know! There is a curse!

The apothecary separated them.

– These horrible details are futile. I will inform Monsieur. Here come the people now. Dignified! For goodness' sake! Philosophical!

The poor chap wanted to look brave, and he kept saying:

– Yes . . . steady!

– All right, shouted the old man, I'll manage it, by God and his thunder I shall. I'm a going with her to the end.

The bell was tolling. Everything was ready. It was time to move off.

And, sitting in a choir-stall, side by side, they watched the three choristers passing continually backwards and forwards, chanting the words. The serpent sounded raucously. Monsieur Bournisien, in full apparel, was singing in a shrill voice; he bowed before the tabernacle, raised his hands, spread wide his arms. Lestiboudois moved about the church with his verger's staff of whalebone; near the lectern, the coffin stood between four rows of candles. Charles had an urge to go and put them out.

Even so, he did try to kindle a feeling of devotion, to ascend in the hope of an after-life in which he would see her again. He pretended she had gone on a journey, far away, long ago. But, when he thought of her inside that thing, thought that it was all over, that they were going to take her away and put her in the earth, he was filled with rage, fierce and black and hopeless. At certain moments he thought he felt nothing, and he savoured this respite from his sufferings, even as he reproached himself for being despicable.

Coming across the flagstones they heard the tap-tap-tap of a stick with an iron tip. It came from the back of the church, and stopped short in the aisle. A man in a coarse brown jacket knelt down painfully. It was Hippolyte, the ostler from the Golden Lion. He had on his best new leg.

One of the choristers came round the nave to take the collection, and the coppers, one after the other, clinked on to the silver plate.

– Do hurry up! I can't bear it! cried Bovary, as he angrily tossed him a five-franc piece.

The churchman thanked him with a ceremonious bow.

The singing, the kneeling down, the standing up, it was endless! He remembered how, once, in the early days, they had been to mass together, sitting over on the other side, on the right, by the wall. The bell began to toll again. There was a great scraping of chairs. The bearers slid their three staves under the coffin, and they left the church.

At that moment Justin appeared at the door of the pharmacy. He stepped abruptly back again, pale, quivering.

People were standing at the windows to watch the cortège passing. Charles, at the front, held himself straight. He was putting on a brave front and nodded a greeting to the people who appeared from side-streets and doorways to join the crowd of mourners.

The six men, three at each side, went along at a slow pace,

panting slightly. The priests, the choristers and the two choir-boys recited the *De Profundis*; and their voices carried way across the fields, rising and falling in surging waves. From time to time they would disappear along the winding path; but the great tall silver cross still rose into view amid the trees.

The women were following, clad in black cloaks with the hoods down; in their hands they carried tall candles burning, and Charles felt himself swooning at this continual repetition of prayers and torches, at the stupefying smell of candles and cassocks. A fresh breeze was blowing, the rye and the flax had green shoots, tiny drops of dew were trembling on the thorn-hedge at the roadside. Joyful sounds filled the air: the distant clatter of a cart rolling along over the pot-holes, a cock crowing again and again, a foal galloping away beneath the apple-trees. The clear sky was flecked with pink clouds; there was a soft blue haze of flowering iris in the cottage gardens; Charles recognized them as he went past. He was remembering mornings just like this, when, after visiting one of his patients, he used to set off home to her.

The black cloth, strewn with white tear-drops, would billow up every so often and uncover the coffin. The bearers were weary, walking more slowly, and the coffin went lurching along, like a little ship bobbing on the waves.

They arrived.

The men kept on to the far end, to the place where a grave had been dug in the turf.

They stood around; and, as the priest was speaking, the red earth, piled up along the sides, went trickling down at the corners, a silent cascade.

Once the four ropes were ready, the coffin was pushed into position over them. He beheld its descent. It kept on descending.

At last they heard a thud; the ropes were drawn up with a creak. Bournisien took the spade from Lestiboudois; while sprinkling water with his right hand, he vigorously cast a big spadeful with his left; and the coffin, as the stones hit the wood, made that terrible noise that sounds almost like the lingering echo of eternity.

The clergyman passed the sprinkler to his neighbour. It was Monsieur Homais. He shook it gravely, and handed it to Charles, who sank down to his knees, throwing in great handfuls of earth as he cried, 'Goodbye!' He sent her kisses; he crawled to the grave's edge, wanting to be swallowed up with her.

They led him away; and it wasn't long before he calmed down, perhaps feeling, like everyone else, a vague satisfaction that it was over and done with.

Père Rouault, on the way back, started placidly smoking his pipe; a thing that Homais, in his heart, considered to be in rather bad taste. He also noticed that Monsieur Binet had refrained from attending, that Tuvache 'had disappeared' after the mass, and that Théodore, the notary's man, was wearing a blue coat, 'as if they couldn't get him a black one, since it is the custom, damn it all!' And so as to impart his observations, he went around from one group to another. Everyone was deploring Emma's death, and particularly Lheureux, who had made a special effort to come to the funeral.

– The poor little lady! What an awful thing for her husband.

The apothecary followed with:

– But for me, do you realize, he would have been driven to lay fatal hands upon his own person.

– Such a good woman! To think that I saw her in my shop only last Thursday.

– I have not had a moment, said Homais, to prepare a few words I might have cast upon her grave.

When they got back, Charles went to change, and Père Rouault put on his blue smock again. It was a new one, and because he had wiped his eyes on the sleeves so many times, along the way, the dye had stained his face; and the tears had left long tracks through the dirt on his cheeks.

Madame Bovary senior was with them. All three sat there in silence. Eventually the old man gave a sigh.

– Do you remember, my friend, the time I came to Tostes, when you had just lost your first wife. I did give you comfort that day! I knew what to say; but this time . . .

Then, with a great long groan that came from the very depths of his chest:

– I've got nobody left now, you see. I've seen my wife go . . .
my son after . . . and now my daughter, today!

He wanted to be off back to Les Bertaux right away, saying
how he couldn't spend the night in that house. He even refused
to see his grand-daughter.

– No! It would be too big a grief. Any rate, you give her a
good kiss! Goodbye, you're a grand chap! And I never shall
forget this, he said slapping his hand on his thigh. Don't you
worry! You'll still get your turkey.

But, when he reached the top of the hill, he turned to look
back, just as he had turned once before on the Saint-Victor road,
the day he left her. All of the windows in the village were on fire
with the rays of the evening sun, as it set over the meadows. He
put his hand half over his eyes; and on the horizon he could see
the churchyard walls with the trees here and there, tufts of black
among the white stones, then he went on his way again, at a
slow trot, for his horse was half lame.

Charles and his mother, for all their weariness, sat up late
that evening, talking together. They talked about the old days
and about the future. She would come and live in Yonville, she
would keep house for him, never again would they be apart.
She was tactful and understanding, rejoicing inwardly at winning back an affection that had eluded her for so many years. It
struck midnight. The village, as usual, was silent, and Charles,
lying awake, was still thinking of her.

Rodolphe, who had been wandering the woods all day, by
way of distraction, was sleeping peacefully in his château; and
Léon, far away, was asleep.

There was one other who, at that hour, was not sleeping.

On the grave, among the pine-trees, a boy knelt weeping,
and his poor heart, cracked with sorrow, was shaking in the
darkness, under the burden of an immense regret, softer than
the moon and fathomless as night. The gate suddenly gave a
squeak. It was Lestiboudois; he'd come to fetch the spade he'd
left behind. He recognized Justin scaling the wall, and now he
knew the name of the malefactor who had been stealing his
potatoes.

11

Charles, next day, had the little girl back again. She asked for her mummy. They told her she had gone away, would bring some toys back for her. Berthe mentioned her again several times; but, eventually, gave her no further thought. The gaiety of the child was a torment for Bovary, and he had to endure the intolerable condolences of the pharmacist.

Difficulties over money soon began again, with Monsieur Lheureux once more inciting his friend Vinçart, and Charles binding himself on exorbitant terms; for he would never consent to sell off even the least little item that had belonged to *her*. His mother was annoyed with him. His anger was louder than hers. He had changed completely. She left the house.

Now everyone began to *help themselves*. Mademoiselle Lempereur sent a bill for six months' lessons, though Emma had never had a single one (in spite of that receipt she had shown to Bovary): it was an arrangement between the two women; the lending library demanded three years' subscription; Mère Rolet was claiming for the delivery of about twenty letters; and, when Charles asked for some explanation, she did have the discretion to reply:

– Oh, I don't know! It was for her bits of business.

As each debt was paid off, Charles thought that it must be the last. And another one would turn up, endlessly.

He wrote to patients asking for fees now long outstanding. They showed him the letters sent by his wife. He had to apologize.

Félicité took to wearing Madame's dresses; not every one, for some of them he had kept back, and he used to go to her dressing-room to gaze at them, with the door locked; she was almost the same build, and often, when he saw her from behind, Charles was caught in an illusion, and cried out:

– Oh, don't go! Stay there!

But at Whitsun, she ran away from Yonville, carried off by Théodore, stealing everything left in the wardrobe.

It was around this time that the widowed Madame Dupuis

had the honour to inform him of 'the marriage of Monsieur
Léon Dupuis, her son, a notary in Yvetot, to Mademoiselle
Léocadie Lebœuf, from Bondeville'. Charles, in his letter of
congratulation, included the sentence: 'How very happy my
poor wife would have been.'

One day when he was wandering aimlessly around the house,
he was up in the attic and his slippered foot trod on a
crumpled-up piece of paper. He unfolded it and he read: 'Be
brave, Emma! Be brave! I do not want to blight your life!' It
was Rodolphe's letter, fallen down in between the boxes, and
hidden there, until just now when the draught from the window
had blown it towards the door. And Charles stood there open-
mouthed, exactly where, long ago, paler than he, Emma, in
despair, had wished for death. He came across a little *R* at the
bottom of the second page. What did it mean? He remembered
Rodolphe's little attentions, his sudden disappearance and the
awkwardness in his manner when they had met since then, two
or three times. But the respectful tone of the letter misled him.

– Perhaps they loved one another platonically, he said to
himself.

Indeed, Charles was not one of those men who like to get to
the bottom of things: he shied away from the evidence, and his
faltering jealousy was lost in the immensity of his sadness.

Everyone, he thought, had adored her. Every man, of course,
had wanted her. It made her seem even more beautiful; and it
engendered in him a harsh perpetual desire, inflaming his
despair, a desire that had no limits because it could never now
be realized.

To please her, as though she were still alive, he adopted her
predilections, her ideas; he bought patent-leather boots, he took
to wearing white cravats. He waxed his moustache, he signed
bills just as she had done. She was corrupting him from beyond
the grave.

He was forced to sell the silverware, piece by piece, then he
sold all the furniture in the parlour. All the rooms were stripped
bare; but the bedroom, her room, had been kept just as it used
to be. After dinner, Charles used to make his way up there. He
would push the round table over to the fire, and draw up *her*

armchair. He would sit facing it. A candle was burning in one of the gilded candlesticks. Berthe, at his side, was colouring in prints.

He suffered, poor man, at seeing her so badly dressed, with no laces in her boots and her blouses ripped from the arm to the waist, because the housekeeper hardly bothered with such little details. But she was so sweet, so charming, and her little head dipped so gracefully, tumbling her lovely blonde hair over her pink cheeks, that it gave him an endless delight, a pleasure alloyed with bitterness like those inferior wines that taste of resin. He used to repair her toys, make her puppets from cardboard, or sew up her dolls when their seams burst open. If his eye chanced upon the work-basket, a stray ribbon or even a pin left in a crack in the table, he fell into a dream, and he looked so very sad, that she became as sad as he.

Nowadays nobody came to see them; for Justin had run away to Rouen, where he became a grocer's boy, and the apothecary's children visited the little girl less and less often, because Monsieur Homais, in view of the difference in their social positions, did not care to continue the intimacy.

The Blind Man, whom his ointment had failed to cure, had gone back to the hill at Bois Guillaume, where he told travellers the story of the pharmacist's fruitless efforts, until Homais, whenever he went to town, used to hide behind the curtains of the *Hirondelle*, to avoid meeting him. He detested him; and, in the interests of his reputation, eager to get rid of him at all costs, he quietly trained his guns upon him in a campaign which revealed the depth of his intelligence and the malevolence of his vanity. For six consecutive months, you could read in *Le Fanal de Rouen* little paragraphs of the following kind:

Every traveller who makes his way towards the fertile plains of Picardy will no doubt have remarked, on the hill at Bois Guillaume, a wretched creature afflicted with a horrible facial sore. He importunes and he persecutes you, and levies a veritable tax on all who pass that way. Are we still stuck in the gruesome days of the Middle Ages, when vagabonds were permitted to expose upon the public streets the leprosy and the scrofula they had brought back from the Crusades?

Or else:

In spite of the laws against vagrancy, the approaches to our large towns continue to be infested by gangs of paupers. There are those who have been seen to wander unaccompanied, and they are, perhaps, among the more dangerous. What can our magistrates be thinking of?

Homais invented anecdotes:

Yesterday, in the Bois Guillaume, a skittish horse . . . and there followed the story of an accident caused by the presence of the Blind Man.

He managed it so well that the man was incarcerated. But he was released. He took up where he had left off, and so did Homais. It was a battle. He was the victor; for his enemy was condemned to perpetual confinement in an asylum.

This success emboldened him; and from that day on there was not a dog run over, not a barn burned down or a wife beaten anywhere in the parish but he immediately conveyed it to the public, guided always by a love of progress and a hatred of priests. He drew comparisons between the primary schools and those of the Christian Brothers, to the detriment of the latter; he alluded to the Saint Bartholomew's Day massacre in connection with a grant of a hundred francs given to the Church; he denounced abuses, he fulminated. That was his phrase. Scheming Homais: he was getting dangerous.

Yet he felt stifled within the narrow limits of journalism, and soon he was yearning for a book, for authorship! Accordingly, he composed a *Statistique générale du canton d'Yonville, suivie d'observations climatologiques,*[11] and statistics led him on to philosophy. He became preoccupied with the major issues: the social problem, the moralization of the poorer classes, pisciculture, the manufacture of rubber, railways and so on. He even felt embarrassed at being a bourgeois. He affected *the artistic style*, he took up smoking. He bought a pair of *chic* Pompadour statuettes, to adorn his parlour.

He did not give up his pharmacy; on the contrary! He kept up with the latest discoveries. He followed the great chocolate craze. He was the first to introduce *cho-ca* and *revalentia* into Seine-Inférieure. He had a passionate enthusiasm for

Pulvermacher hydroelectric body-chains; he wore one of them himself; and, at night, when he took off his flannel vest, Madame Homais lay there bedazzled by the golden spiral wound around his body, and she felt a redoubling of her ardour for this man who was garrotted like a Scythian and splendid as a magus.

He had wonderful ideas for Emma's tomb. First he proposed a broken column with drapery, then a pyramid, then a temple of Vesta, a sort of rotunda . . . or else a *mass of ruins*. And in all his plans, Homais never relinquished the weeping willow, which he regarded as the indispensable symbol of grief.

Charles and he went together to Rouen, to look at tomb-stones, in a mason's yard – accompanied by a painter, one Vaufrylard, a friend of Bridoux's, who was endlessly making puns. Finally, after looking at about a hundred drawings, ordering an estimate and making another trip to Rouen, Charles decided on a mausoleum which was to display on its two main walls a 'spirit holding an extinguished torch'.

As for the inscription, Homais thought nothing finer than: *Sta viator*, and he could get no further. He racked his brains; he kept saying *Sta viator*. At last he hit upon *amabilem conjugem calcas!*,[12] which was adopted.

It was peculiar, that Bovary, though he thought continually of Emma, began to forget her face; and he was in despair as he felt the image slipping from his memory no matter what he did to keep hold of it. Every night, he dreamed about her; always it was the same dream: he came nearer; but when he went to embrace her, she turned to putrid flesh in his arms.

For a whole week he was seen going into church in the evenings. Monsieur Bournisien even paid him two or three visits, but gave up. Indeed, according to Homais, the old chap was swinging towards intolerance and fanaticism; he railed against the spirit of the age, and never failed, every fortnight, in his sermon, to recount the last hours of Voltaire, who died devouring his own excrement, as everyone knows.

In spite of his frugal way of life, Bovary was far from being able to pay off his old debts. Lheureux refused to renew any of the bills. Distraint was imminent. At that point he had recourse to his mother, who agreed, in a letter full of recriminations against Emma, to let him take out a mortgage on her property; and she demanded, in return for her sacrifice, a shawl that had survived the ravages of Félicité. Charles refused to give it to her. They quarrelled.

She made the first overtures in reconciliation, offering to take the little girl, who would be a help to her in her house. Charles agreed to this. But, at the moment of parting, his courage quite failed him. This time, the break was irrevocable and complete.

As his other affections vanished, he began to cling ever tighter to the love of his daughter. Even so, she was a worry to him; sometimes she had a cough, and there were red patches on her cheeks.

In the house across the square, flourishing merrily, was the pharmacist's family, and everything seemed to further his contentment. Napoléon helped him in the laboratory, Athalie was embroidering him a skull-cap, Irma used to cut out the little circles of paper to cover the jam-pots, and Franklin could recite the multiplication table in a single breath. He was the happiest of fathers, the most fortunate of men.

Not quite! A secret ambition irked him; Homais wanted the medal of the Legion of Honour. His claims were not insubstantial:

Firstly, at the time of the cholera epidemic, having distinguished myself by a boundless devotion to duty; secondly, having published, at my own expense, various works of public utility, such as . . . (and he referred to his pamphlet entitled *Du cidre, de sa fabrication et de ses effets*; further, his observations on the woolly aphid, as sent to the Academy; his volume of statistics, and even his pharmaceutical thesis); without mentioning that I am a member of several learned societies (he belonged to one).

– Anyway, he cried out, doing a pirouette, it would look most distinctive when I'm on fire-duty!

And now Homais inclined towards the powers that be. He secretly rendered the Prefect great services in the elections. He sold himself in fact, he prostituted himself. He even addressed a petition to the sovereign imploring him to *do justice*; he called him *our good king* and compared him to Henry IV.

And every morning, the apothecary would fall upon the newspaper to look for his nomination; it was never there. Finally, in exasperation, he had laid out in his garden a lawn in the shape of the star of honour, with two little strips of grass running from the top to look like the ribbon. He used to stroll around it, arms folded, meditating on the ineptitude of governments and the ingratitude of men.

Out of respect, or out of a sort of sensuality that made him wish to linger in his investigations, Charles had not yet opened up the secret compartment in the rosewood desk that Emma had generally used. One day, at last, he sat down, turned the key and pushed the spring. All the letters from Léon were in there. No doubt about it, this time! He devoured them right down to the last line, rummaged about in every corner, in every piece of furniture, in every drawer, along the walls, sobbing and roaring, out of his mind. He discovered a box, smashed it open with a kick. Staring him straight in the face was the portrait of Rodolphe, in among a toppling pile of love-letters.

People wondered at this state of dejection. He never went out, had no visitors, even refused to go and see his patients. It was said *he'd shut himself away with the bottle*.

Sometimes, though, the curious would hoist themselves up on to the garden hedge, and observe in amazement a wild man with a long beard, dressed in shabby clothes, weeping out loud as he went along.

On summer evenings, he would take his little daughter along to the cemetery. They used to come back at nightfall, when the only light to be seen on the square was in Binet's attic window.

But his voluptuous sorrow was incomplete, for he had no one there to share it with him; and he used to visit Mère Lefrançois so that he could talk about *her*. But the innkeeper was only half listening, for she had troubles of her own, now that Monsieur Lheureux had set up the *Favorites du commerce*, and Hivert, who enjoyed a great reputation for his commissioned purchases, was insisting on an increase in his wages, and threatening to go and work for the Competition.

One day when Charles had gone to the market at Argueil to sell his horse – his last resource – he met Rodolphe.

They went pale when they saw each other. Rodolphe, who had only ever sent his card after the funeral, at first muttered some apology, then he grew bolder and even had the aplomb (it was a very hot day, in the month of August) to invite Charles into the tavern for a bottle of beer.

With his elbows on the table, he sat opposite, chewing at his cigar as he talked, and Charles went into a dream as he looked at the face she had loved. He felt as if he was seeing something of her. It was miraculous. He so wanted to have been this other man.

Rodolphe went on talking about farming, cattle and manure, blocking up with banal phrases every little crevice that might have let some allusion leak through. Charles was not listening; Rodolphe noticed, and he was aware of the memories that were visibly moving across the other man's face. It was slowly turning a deep red, the nostrils were quivering, the lips were trembling; there was even a moment when Charles, brimming with a sombre fury, fixed his eyes on Rodolphe, who, in some terror, stopped talking. But before long the same look of dismal lassitude returned.

– I don't hold it against you, he said.

Rodolphe sat there in silence. And Charles, his head in his hands, went on in a blank voice with the resigned intonations of infinite sorrow:

– No, I don't hold it against you any more!

He even added a grand phrase, the only one he had ever uttered:

– Fate is to blame!

Rodolphe, who had controlled this particular fate, thought the man rather soft-hearted for someone in his position, comical even, and slightly despicable.

The next day, Charles went to sit on the bench, in the arbour. The sunlight was coming through the trellis; the vine-leaves threw their shadows over the gravel, jasmine perfumed the air, the sky was blue, cantharides beetles were droning round the flowering lilies, and Charles was choking like an adolescent from the vague amorous yearnings that swelled up in his aching heart.

At seven o'clock, little Berthe, who had not seen him that afternoon, came to fetch him in for dinner.

He had his head back against the wall, his eyes closed, his mouth open, and in his hand was a tress of long black hair.

– Come on, daddy! she said.

And, thinking that he was only playing, she gave him a gentle push. He fell to the ground. He was dead.

Thirty-six hours later, at the apothecary's request, Monsieur Canivet arrived. He opened him up and found nothing.

Once everything had been sold, there were just twelve francs and seventy-five centimes left over, which was enough to pay for Mademoiselle Bovary's journey to her grandmother's house. The good lady died that same year; because Père Rouault was paralysed, it was an aunt who took her in. She is poor and she sends the girl to earn her living in a cotton-mill.

Since Bovary's death, three different doctors have worked in Yonville without success, such has been the force of Monsieur Homais's immediate onslaught. He is doing infernally well; the authorities handle him carefully and public opinion is on his side.

He has just received the Legion of Honour.

illusion / delusion
of grandeur, passion
bliss
- opera in Rouen

*
AL
- Words of the day *
- Flogbert }
- Grandier }

* Is happiness found ~~through~~
by living through the
eyes of others, or on
one's own terms

Emma is educated in a
convent school.

→ Have to be able to spend money before
offering affection. Buy cradle for
daughter. (can't afford it, can't be affectionate)

- child is kind of an afterthought.
→ operation is Emma's idea

Hippolyte - stable boy
"club foot" (operation attempt at fame)
- gangrene; worse, may die.

shoes:
Priest † Homeis   Emma wears ex-
- faith   - Rous   pensive ~~black~~
+ don't trust either black boots,
                    peasants wear
                    wooden ~~boots~~
                    shoes.

eyes wider - Marianne Dashwood ✓
              eyes showing

Provincial Life = constant in itself. (don't change
- Emma came and went.

Notes

Part One

1. *one of those hats of the Composite order*: The Composite Order is a precise architectural term. It designates one of the five kinds of classical column. To the original three Greek orders of Ionic, Doric and Corinthian, the Romans added the Composite and the Tuscan. The Composite was a mixture of Ionic and Corinthian.

2. *the Polish chapska*: Originally Polish headgear, worn by French lancers in the nineteenth century.

3. *hurled out one word: Charbovari*: The class's wild reaction to the word *Charbovari* makes more sense once we realize that they are implicitly giving Charles's name a further twist, miming the sound *Charbovari* as a *charivari*. They are enacting a spontaneous collective pun. Originally, the *charivari* was a serenade of rough music made by a crowd of villagers banging on kettles and pans under the windows of a newly-wed couple. It was used especially to deride an incongruous marriage. Perhaps this is an ominous anticipation of Charles's fate as a husband. However, by the middle of the nineteenth century *charivari* described the anarchic ritual mockery of an unpopular person. *Le Charivari* was also the name of a satirical magazine published in Paris during the early nineteenth century. It was the favourite reading of Flaubert's boyhood, and when he was twelve years old, in 1833, there appeared within its pages a cartoon of a grotesque composite hat which may be the distant model for the one worn by Charles Bovary.

Critics have often pointed to the peculiar recurrence in Flaubert's writings of various forms of the surname *Bovary*. In addition to Charles Bovary, he creates characters called Bouvard, Bouvigny and Bouvignard. And there was a hotel-keeper in Cairo, where Flaubert stayed in 1850, called Bouvaret.

4. *like Quos ego*: A reference to the first book of Virgil's *Aeneid*. The

god Neptune speaks to calm the angry waves of a storm. In this context it seems intended as an aptly schoolboyish mock-epic reference to a Latin set text.

5. *Anacharsis*: The *Voyage du Jeune Anacharsis en Grèce* (1788) by the antiquarian writer Abbé Barthélemy (1716–95). It describes, in popular style, the culture of classical Greece, as seen by a young Scythian visitor.

6. *the Eau de Robec*: A tributary of the Seine that flows through the poorest quarter of Rouen. But the real point is that the reference assumes in the reader an intimate local knowledge of Normandy. Such small touches cumulatively encode the writing as being deliberately provincial, non-metropolitan.

7. *enthused over Béranger*: Jean-Pierre Béranger (1780–1857) was the popular and mildly subversive French national poet of the early nineteenth century. Flaubert put 'admiration for Béranger' at the top of his list of the things he instantly disliked in other people.

8. *The Officer of Health, riding along*: Charles is often referred to, flatteringly, as a doctor by the other characters. But he is in fact qualified only as an Officer of Health. This is an important nuance of professional status. Throughout the nineteenth century Officers of Health were decidedly inferior creatures, glorified medical orderlies who were permitted to practise medicine only within their department. They were not supposed to perform major surgical operations except under the supervision of a doctor. The post had been created in 1803, among Napoleon's reforms, in the hope of bringing medical services to the poorer regions of France. It was finally abolished in 1892, after many years of pressure from doctors.

9. *Emma, however, yearned to be married at midnight, by torchlight*: A local custom, not an eccentricity.

10. *She had read Paul et Virginie*: A novel by Bernardin de Saint-Pierre, published in 1788. It was a romance set on a tropical island, telling an idyllic story of childhood and of adolescent love, followed by separation and the untimely death of the heroine. Flaubert especially admired the scene of Virginie's death.

11. *the story of Mademoiselle de la Vallière*: Mademoiselle de la Vallière was the mistress of King Louis XIV (1638–1715).

12. *the Lectures of the Abbé Frayssinous*: Lectures on theology and religion, part of the revival of Christianity that came with the Restoration of the French monarchy in 1815. Frayssinous's lectures were first published in 1825.

13. *passages from the Génie du christianisme*: Le Génie du christianisme was an aesthetic and moral vindication of Christianity by

the royalist writer François-René Vicomte de Chateaubriand (1768–1848), published in 1802. Flaubert greatly admired Chateaubriand as a stylist.

14. *Agnès Sorel, La Belle Ferronière, and Clémence Isaure*: Agnès Sorel was the mistress of King Charles VII (1403–61); La Belle Ferronière was the mistress of King François I (1494–1547); and Clémence Isaure was a legendary woman of the fourteenth century, associated with the poetry of the troubadours.

15. *Saint Louis under his oak-tree . . . Saint Bartholomew's something or other*: King Louis IX (1215–70) supposedly sat beneath an oak-tree to give judgment; Pierre Terrail, Seigneur de Bayard (1473–1524), was a sixteenth-century French soldier who died heroically in battle; King Louis XI (1423–83) was notably astute and unscrupulous in retaining power; and the notorious massacre of Saint Bartholomew's Day (1572), when thousands of French Protestants were slaughtered.

16. *she drifted with the meanderings of Lamartine*: Alphonse Lamartine (1790–1869) was an immensely popular romantic lyric poet, on the model of Byron. Flaubert regarded him as ludicrously facile. Emma quotes from Lamartine to Léon.

17. *little breadcrumb pellets*: Breadcrumbs were used to erase charcoal lines.

18. *She called Djali*: Emma's greyhound is named after the goat owned by Esmeralda, the gypsy dancer, in Victor Hugo's *Notre-Dame de Paris*.

19. *the ladies had not put their gloves inside their glasses*: Provincial women of Emma's social class did not customarily drink wine at dinner parties. They would signify their intention to abstain by putting their gloves inside their wineglasses. Emma is impressed by the sophistication of those who are not intending to abstain.

20. *singing 'La Marjolaine'*: A folksong which opens:

> *Qui est-ce qui passe ici si tard*
> *Compagnons de la Marjolaine?*

21. *Eugène Sue*: Eugène Sue (1804–57) was the author, in the early 1840s, of an immensely popular series of sensational novels about Parisian low life.

Part Two

1. *Yonville-l'Abbaye*: According to Flaubert, Yonville-l'Abbaye was 'a place which doesn't exist' (letter of 4 June 1857); but it was put together from the details of several different places which did. The name *Yonville* is based on the Rue de la Croix d'Yonville in Rouen. The general location points to the Normandy village of Forges-les-Eaux, where Flaubert had stayed in 1848. The details of the streets and buildings follow those of the village of Ry, where Eugène Delamare had lived. Certain features of the surrounding country are derived from the landscape around Forges.

2. *the final years of the reign of Charles X*: Charles X (1757–1836) was king from 1824 until 1830.

3. *a Gallic cockerel, resting one foot on the Charter*: The Charter was the emblem of France's restored constitutional monarchy. It was originally granted by Louis XVIII in 1814, and a revised version was accepted by King Louis-Philippe after the revolution of 1830.

4. *a patriotic tournament for Poland or the flood victims in Lyon*: There had been a nationalist insurrection in Warsaw in 1830, and all through the period of the July Monarchy (1830–48) there were fund-raising events organized in France to help Polish refugees.

   The river Rhône flooded catastrophically in the winter of 1840. The allusion to Lyons (on the river Rhône) implicitly dates the action.

5. *he had at home a lathe*: In the *Dictionary of Received Ideas*, under *lathe*, we find: 'essential to have one in the attic, if you live in the country, for rainy days'.

6. *Béranger! I'm one for the creed of the Savoyard Curate*: Homais is referring to the section of Rousseau's *Emile* (1762), which expounds the superiority of natural religion.

7. *you were singing 'L'Ange gardien'*: A popular sentimental romance by Pauline Duchambre (1778–1858), who wrote verses for keepsake albums.

8. *L'Echo des feuilletons . . . various periodicals, among them Le Fanal de Rouen*: *L'Echo des feuilletons* is *The Literary Echo*. The *feuilleton* was the literary section of a newspaper, usually featuring serialized novels.

   From Flaubert's letters we learn that Homais was to have been correspondent for the real *Journal de Rouen*. But their editor demanded that the name be altered, and Flaubert, not wanting to break the rhythm of his phrases, changed *Journal* into *Fanal* ('Beacon'). In the early manuscripts Homais has a massive hoard of old newspapers in a cupboard.

9. *the law of 19th Ventôse, Year XI, Article I*: In the Republican Calendar (introduced in 1793 and abolished in 1806) this designates 3 March 1803. Homais's reference is historically accurate.

10. *Athalie*: A reference to the heroine of Racine's final play, *Athalie* (1691).

11. *'Le Dieu des bonnes gens'*: The title of an anti-clerical poem by Béranger.

12. *'La Guerre des dieux'*: The title of a blasphemous poem published in 1799 by the libertine poet Evariste-Désiré de Forges, Vicomte de Parny (1753–1814).

13. *a Mathieu Laensberg*: A farmer's almanac first published in Liège by Mathieu Laensberg in the seventeenth century. It ceased publication in the 1850s.

14. *would have recalled Sachette in Notre-Dame de Paris*: An allusion to the novel *Notre-Dame de Paris* (1832) by Victor Hugo. But there seems to be a calculated inaccuracy: the mother in *Notre-Dame de Paris* is in fact called Paquette. Emma's extravagant display of affection for her daughter is an attitude which Flaubert satirized in his *Dictionary of Received Ideas*. Under *children* we find the entry: 'affect a lyrical tenderness for them, in public'.

15. *Monsieur Rodolphe Boulanger de la Huchette is here*: The name Rodolphe would have been familiar to contemporary readers of popular fiction. There is a Rodolphe in Eugène Sue's *Les Mystères de Paris* (1842–3). He is a mysterious prince in disguise who haunts the Paris underworld, punishing the wicked and rewarding the virtuous. There is also a Rodolphe in Henry Murger's *Scènes de la vie de Bohème* (1848).

16. *She looked up at him, her eyes full of admiration*: This sentence was deleted by Flaubert from the definitive 1873 edition of the text.

17. *Du cidre … ce sujet*: Cider: Its Manufacture and Operation; Together with Some Original Remarks Thereupon.

18. *He sent to Rouen for Dr Duval's treatise*: Vincent Duval's *Traité pratique du pied-bot* (1839). After Flaubert's father had failed to cure a club-foot, it was successfully treated by Duval.

19. *Ambroise Paré*: Ambroise Paré (1517–90) devoted his life to the improvement of surgery.

20. *Duputryen*: Flaubert's father had been anatomy demonstrator for the surgeon Duputryen (1777–1835).

21. *Fifteen napoléons*: The napoléon was a gold coin worth twenty francs, introduced in 1812. It carried the effigy of Napoleon.

22. *a seal with the motto Amor nel cor*: An Italian phrase meaning

'love in my heart'. Louise Colet had given Flaubert a love-token with this motto on it.

23. *Pensez-y bien . . . des jeunes gens*: These works translate as: *Think on This; The Man of the World at the Feet of Mary, by the highly distinguished Monsieur de —; On the Errors of Voltaire, for the Use of Young Persons.*

24. *Castigat ridendo mores*: 'It corrects morals by laughter', the motto of a seventeenth-century French harlequin.

25. *Lucia di Lammermoor*: An opera in three acts by Donizetti, based on Walter Scott's novel *The Bride of Lammermoor* (1819). The opera was first produced in Naples in 1835. Flaubert had seen it when he was in Constantinople.

Part Three

1. *four scenes from La Tour de Nesle*: A historical melodrama, first performed in 1832, written by Alexandre Dumas (1802–70). *La Tour de Nesle*, set in early fourteenth-century Paris, deals with adulterous female desire. It tells the story of the debaucheries of the three daughters-in-law of King Philippe IV. Lithographs of scenes from the play were published in 1840.

2. *the Dancing Marianne*: The popular name for a stone carving on the cathedral in Rouen which shows Salomé dancing before Herod.

3. *Fabricando fit faber, age quod agis*: Homais's motto means 'Practice makes perfect, whatever you do'.

4. *Un soir, t'en souvient-il, nous voguions*: 'One night, do you remember, we were sailing'. A line from Lamartine's poem 'Le Lac', published in his *Méditations poétiques* (1820). The poet is reminiscing to himself as he sails in his boat.

5. *Souvent la chaleur d'un beau jour . . . à l'amour*: These are lines from a poem by Restif de la Bretonne (1734–1806). They come from his *L'Année des dames nationales* (1794). Eleanor Marx translates as follows:

> *Maids in the warmth of a summer day,*
> *Dream of love, and of love always . . .*

6. *Steuben's Esmeralda*: A print of a painting based on a scene from Hugo's novel *Notre-Dame de Paris*.

7. *she found it impossible to open her mouth*: At this point Flaubert deleted from his manuscript a short passage describing Rodolphe's feelings at seeing Emma again. Originally it read:

And in spite of all her efforts, she found it impossible to open her mouth.

Rodolphe was gazing at her as though her absence had metamorphosed her into a different woman – and he felt himself assailed by a sudden desire; – the situation inflaming his appetite with a new voluptuousness, in which old pleasures would be recaptured.

But human respect restrained him – and in a tone of feigned gallantry he said: – You haven't changed, you're as charming as ever you were.

8. *Souvent la chaleur d'un beau jour . . . les donne:*

> *Maids in the warmth of a summer day,*
> *Dream of love, and of love always . . .*
>
> *Where the sickle blades have been*
> *Nanette gathering ears of corn,*
> *Passes bending down my queen*
> *To the earth where they were born.*

9. *Il souffla bien fort ce jour-là . . . s'envola:*

> *The wind is strong this summer day,*
> *Her petticoat has flown away!*

10. *Les Lettres de quelques juifs portugais . . . La Raison du christianisme: Letters from Portuguese Jews; The Meaning of Christianity.*

11. *Statistique générale du canton d'Yonville, suivie d'observations climatologiques: General Statistics of the Canton of Yonville, Followed by Climatological Observations.*

12. *Sta viator . . . amabilem conjugem calcas:* 'Traveller, halt: a worthy wife lies buried here'.

PENGUIN CLASSICS

THE LETTERS OF ABELARD AND HELOISE

'God knows I never sought anything in you except yourself. I wanted simply you, nothing of yours'

The story of the doomed relationship between Abelard and Heloise is one of the world's most celebrated and tragic love affairs. It is told through the letters of Peter Abelard, a French philosopher and one of the greatest logicians of the twelfth century, and his gifted pupil Heloise. Through their impassioned writings unfolds the story of a romance, from its reckless, ecstatic beginnings through to public scandal, an enforced marriage and its devastating consequences. These eloquent and intimate letters express a vast range of emotions from adoration and devotion to reproach, indignation and grief, and offer a timeless and moving analysis of love.

This is a revised edition of Betty Radice's acclaimed translation, in which Michael Clanchy, the biographer of Abelard, provides new notes and introductory guidance through recent scholarship concerning the authenticity of these letters. This volume comprises Abelard's remarkable autobiography and the subsequent correspondence between Heloise and Abelard, including his spiritual advice to her and her nuns, together with the letters of Peter the Venerable concerning them.

Translated by Betty Radice
Edited with an introduction and notes by Michael Clanchy

PENGUIN CLASSICS

THE LAIS OF MARIE DE FRANCE

'Anyone who does not hear the song of the nightingale knows none of the joys of this world'

Marie de France (fl. late twelfth century) is the earliest known French woman poet and her *lais* – stories in verse based on Breton tales of chivalry and romance – are among the finest of the genre. Recounting the trials and tribulations of lovers, the *lais* inhabit a powerfully realized world where very real human protagonists act out their lives against fairy-tale elements of magical beings, potions and beasts. Throughout, Marie de France takes a subtle and complex view of courtly love, whether telling the story of the knight who betrays his fairy mistress, or describing the noblewoman who embroiders her sad tale on a shroud for a nightingale killed by a jealous and suspicious husband.

Glyn S. Burgess and Keith Busby's prose translation is accompanied by an introduction that examines authorship and the central themes of the *lais*. This edition also includes a bibliography, notes, an index of proper names and three *lais* in the Old French original: Lanval, Laüstic and Chevrefoil.

Translated with an introduction by Glyn S. Burgess and Keith Busby

PENGUIN CLASSICS

THE COUNT OF MONTE CRISTO
ALEXANDRE DUMAS

'On what slender threads do life and fortune hang'

Thrown in prison for a crime he has not committed, Edmond Dantes is confined to the grim fortress of If. There he learns of a great hoard of treasure hidden on the Isle of Monte Cristo and he becomes determined not only to escape, but also to unearth the treasure and use it to plot the destruction of the three men responsible for his incarceration. Dumas's epic tale of suffering and retribution, inspired by a real-life case of wrongful imprisonment, was a huge popular success when it was first serialized in the 1840s.

Robin Buss's lively English translation is complete and unabridged, and remains faithful to the style of Dumas's original. This edition includes an introduction, explanatory notes and suggestions for further reading.

'Robin Buss broke new ground with a fresh version of *Monte Cristo* for Penguin' *Oxford Guide to Literature in English Translation*

Translated with an introduction by Robin Buss

PENGUIN CLASSICS

SENTIMENTAL EDUCATION GUSTAVE FLAUBERT

'He loved her without reservation, without hope, unconditionally'

Frederic Moreau is a law student returning home to Normandy from
Paris when he first notices Madame Arnoux, a slender, dark woman
several years older than himself. It is the beginning of an infatuation that
will last a lifetime. He befriends her husband, an influential businessman,
and their paths cross and re-cross over the years. Through financial
upheaval, political turmoil and countless affairs, Madame Arnoux
remains the constant, unattainable love of Moreau's life. Flaubert
described his sweeping story of a young man's passions, ambitions and
amours as 'the moral history of the men of my generation'. Based on his
own youthful passion for an older woman, *Sentimental Education* blends
love story, historical authenticity and satire to create one of the greatest
French novels of the nineteenth century.

Geoffrey Wall's fresh revision of Robert Baldick's original translation is
accompanied by an insightful new introduction discussing the personal
and historical influences on Flaubert's writing. This edition also contains
a new chronology, further reading and explanatory notes.

Translated with an introduction by Robert Baldick
Revised and edited by Geoffrey Wall

THE STORY OF PENGUIN CLASSICS

Before 1946 ...'Classics' are mainly the domain of academics and students, without readable editions for everyone else. This all changes when a little-known classicist, E. V. Rieu, presents Penguin founder Allen Lane with the translation of Homer's *Odyssey* that he has been working on and reading to his wife Nelly in his spare time.

1946 *The Odyssey* becomes the first Penguin Classic published, and promptly sells three million copies. Suddenly, classic books are no longer for the privileged few.

1950s Rieu, now series editor, turns to professional writers for the best modern, readable translations, including Dorothy L. Sayers's *Inferno* and Robert Graves's *The Twelve Caesars*, which revives the salacious original.

1960s The Classics are given the distinctive black jackets that have remained a constant throughout the series's various looks. Rieu retires in 1964, hailing the Penguin Classics list as 'the greatest educative force of the 20th century'.

1970s A new generation of translators arrives to swell the Penguin Classics ranks, and the list grows to encompass more philosophy, religion, science, history and politics.

1980s The Penguin American Library joins the Classics stable, with titles such as *The Last of the Mohicans* safeguarded. Penguin Classics now offers the most comprehensive library of world literature available.

1990s The launch of Penguin Audiobooks brings the classics to a listening audience for the first time, and in 1999 the launch of the Penguin Classics website takes them online to a larger global readership than ever before.

The 21st Century Penguin Classics are rejacketed for the first time in nearly twenty years. This world famous series now consists of more than 1300 titles, making the widest range of the best books ever written available to millions – and constantly redefining the meaning of what makes a 'classic'.

The Odyssey continues ...

The best books ever written

PENGUIN (🐧) CLASSICS

SINCE 1946

Find out more at www.penguinclassics.com